ISTORIA BOOKS

– *good stories, well-told* –

presents

SLOANE HALL

A novel by

Libby Sternberg

Get on the Istoria Books mailing list!
Subscribers learn of special limited-time-only discounts. Sign up at the website where you can also view other Istoria Books titles: www.IstoriaBooks.com

Copyright Libby Sternberg 2013
Originally published by Five Star/Cengage 2010

ISBN-13: 978-0615858555
ISBN-10: 0615858554

Publication date: September 2013

www.IstoriaBooks.com

Books written by Libby Sternberg are available through the author's official website: **www.LibbySternberg.com**

ACKNOWLEDGEMENTS

Sloane Hall is a work of fiction set against the backdrop of a momentous time in film history. As fiction, it stretches some facts to suit the story. In doing so, I hope not to have offended any film buffs or historians. I hope, too, that fans of Charlotte Bronte's *Jane Eyre* are able to lose themselves in this story, which is inspired by that classic romance.

Although I used numerous sources for background material when writing this book, several were exceptionally helpful. Scott Eyman's book *The Speed of Sound* was a treasure trove. The American Film Institute's collection of interviews, *The Great Moviemakers of Hollywood's Golden Age*, was also very useful, as was Scott Berg's Pulitzer-prize-winning biography of Samuel Goldwyn. Each of these books sent me scurrying to the internet and other sources and experts for more information, often just for details that I hope give this tale verisimilitude. These experts included my daughter, Hannah E. Sternberg, a fine writer in her own right and a student of film.

I am extremely grateful to Roz Greenberg for taking a chance on this unusual, genre-bending book and first publishing it in hardcover, and to Jerri Corgiat Gallagher, its editor, whose deft touch and masterful insights helped me see characters and scenes anew.

Finally, I'm enormously thankful to the Bronte experts at the Bronte Blog and at the *Bronte Studies* journal, who took the time to read my novel and pen some of the most thoughtful and erudite reviews I've ever received. With their permission, I include their reviews at the back of the book.

As always, I want to thank my family for their continued support of and belief in my writing, especially my husband, Matthew, to whom I dedicate this book with all my love.

Chapter One

Summer 1929

SILENT AS A TOMB and thick with heat, the place felt like a steambath. We'd had to delay the shoot a good quarter hour while the director figured out how to keep vapor from rising off the leading man's pomaded hair.

"Come here, boy," he'd called to me. A tall confident man with dark wavy hair that fell over his brow, the director was always looking for small ways to show he was in charge. "Give me your comb." But I'd not had one, and when he'd borrowed one from another crew member, he'd made a joke of me, setting the whole set to laughing as he told the actor to use my glasses as a mirror.

It had made my teeth grind. I might wear spectacles, but I was strong-muscled and built to fight. I could have taken him down with a few blows. I'd resisted.

Now the morning's work was coming to a merciful close. A final line and exit by the now-dry-haired actor would put an end to our misery.

"I'm going to find her! Yes, I'm going to find my Elizabeth!" His eyes wide as saucers, his rouged mouth over-enunciating every word so that the microphone hidden in the flowers on the table picked up each syllable, he stared into Leo's camera, clasped his hands together in what I guess was supposed to be glorious anticipation, mugged one last time something that looked like either boundless joy or cramped digestion, and exited through a phony door behind him.

The door closed.

One second, two, three, four, five, six….

"Cut!" the director yelled and everyone exhaled. The

director, along with the rest of the cast and crew, looked up at the glass-walled booth nearly thirty feet above the stage in the corner of the room. Finally, a small man came to the window and nodded his approval, a god bestowing blessings. The sound was all right.

The door to a wooden camera booth flew open, letting out a stink of sweat as Leo Bartenstein stepped out of the seven-foot box. His hair drenched, his face slick, Leo looked so pale I thought he'd pass out. The director called a break, and I grabbed Leo's arm, leading him toward the door.

"Leo, like I told you, I need a place to stay—"

But he wasn't listening, dammit. "Did you see that, boy?" he whispered, shrugging his shoulder toward the director. "Cutting the scene so long after the actor leaves? *After!* He'll probably edit it that way, too, the *dumkopf*. He should cut while the actor is still moving. Why do you think they call 'em *moving* pictures, for crissake? Where'd they get this fellow?"

Leo and I both knew where they'd got him—Broadway or some other New York stage. Now that pictures had sound, the studios needed directors who could work with actors who had to talk. Only problem was these directors didn't know shit about cameras and pictures. In live theater, the curtain might close on a scene after an actor left the stage, but in pictures, the curtain—the camera, in this case—should come down while people were still in motion.

This was one of the many lessons Leo had passed along to me when he'd hired me six months ago.

I was good with mechanical things and had arrived in Los Angeles with nothing but my name, a rucksack, and a letter of recommendation that didn't get me far. But Leo had taken pity on me and hired me to load film cartridges and do other odd jobs. It was lowly work, fumbling around in a lightproof sack to load the reels so that no light exposed the film's emulsified side, but I was glad of the money and wanted to learn as much as I could to keep working. Leo had been a cameraman for all the greats, working with Harold Lloyd, King Vidor, and names I didn't recognize even now. But with sound, he was relegated to an airless booth and an immovable camera.

We watched some of the stars go by, laughing and talking with each other, on their way to the commissary. They were the aristocrats. We were the plebeians. I had a salami sandwich in a bag in a corner of the studio.

The director passed by, not even nodding a hello, deep in conversation with the leading man.

"Doesn't know an iris shot from his asshole," Leo sneered when the man was out of hearing.

He was one of the "idiots," according to Leo, the hundreds who descended on this town to make money while film rattled out of silents into sound.

"Leo," I tried again, my frustration growing. But still he ignored me, continuing his lecture.

"Their day of judgment is coming. Woe unto them," he said, regaining his equilibrium and returning to his favorite topic, a running denunciation of all that was wrong with those who worked in the motion picture business, especially now that it had gone to sound. We walked off the soundstage into the light, blinking our eyes as California's scouring sun exploded away the silence of the stage.

I patted my pocket for a cigarette. That would calm me. Finding none, I looked to Leo who was already handing me one of his. He lit both and took a drag as we leaned against the wall, getting away from the stale air and artificial light of the claustrophobic stage. Funny how such a big room with so many lights can make you feel closed in and dark.

"Leo, I was wondering...." But he was off in his own world, oblivious to the needs of mine.

"The high and mighty, how they do fall," Leo said. He rubbed his eyes and rolled his shoulders, pushing out the strain of bending behind the camera.

We were working on a real sound picture, not the mongrels that some studios released after the success of the Warners' Jazz Singer two years ago. Some of those had been shot as silents with sound added for a scene here and there—a bell ringing, a hammer tapping, a band playing. No, this was a pure-bred sound picture with all the problems such projects involved—microphones hidden every which way on the set and cameras that had to be hushed like little children.

"Leo, about a place to stay. You give it any more thought?"

I'd been in a fight that morning with Clyde, one of the other boys rooming at Jake's Coach Service and Tip Top Garage. The little shit had left a wrench out and I'd tripped over it. Then the runt wouldn't pick up the tool when I told him to. They never heeded, the little rats. So I'd made him heed. I'd punched him. Thirty seconds into the fight and I'd not seen him as Clyde anymore but Brice Clement from the Canfield Home for Wayward Boys, as evil incarnate, as something the world was better rid of. I'd been an avenging angel in the City of the Queen of Angels. Stay out of my way. I was doing God's work.

Jake, the owner of the garage and rooming house, hadn't seen it that way. He'd told me I didn't fit in, and suggested I find another place to live.

"Say, are there any rooms at your place open?" I prodded.

Leo acted as if I hadn't spoken at all.

"The high and mighty—smote against a stone like a serpent." Leo talked Biblical but it had no relation to Bible stories I'd learned.

We ambled forward through the studio's outdoor sets, the façade of a city street here, the remnants of a battlefield in the distance. They weren't used so much any more, except for establishing shots. Everything took place on the airtight, noiseless sound stage.

He looked into that distance, taking a puff of his smoke, warming to his sermon. "I care not whether Clara Bow sounds like a Brooklyn fishwife or Vilma Banky speaks Hungarian. They can labor like the rest of us, humbling themselves to do an honest day's work, paid an honest wage for the sweat of their brow, not a fortune they've not earned nor justly deserve.

As far as I'm concerned, they've reaped what they've sown — you build your life on fooling people and you get fooled, too."

His last words resonated off the pretend storefront of an old Western town. My stomach growled. Sweat trickled down my brow. Irritation rippled up my throat.

"Leo, about a place to live…"

No luck. He didn't even look at me, going on and on about the way things used to be.

I tried to be patient with him. After all, he'd taken a chance on me. The moving picture business was where I'd wanted to be ever since I'd sneaked into the projection booth in an Austin theatre at the age of eight. The projectionist had taken pity on me and let me help out. I was hypnotized by those flickering images beyond the glass. There was life. There was happiness. I wanted some of it.

By the time the break was over, I was crazy with hunger, tired, and mad about Leo's inattention to my pressing problem. As we walked back into the darkness, Leo continued his lecture, now intent on teaching me why the director of this film was an artless boob:

"They all think it's the stars and starlets that make the magic," he said, coughing as he moved from camera to set. "But it's not them at all. And it's not the director, neither"

He glanced at the door to make sure our own director hadn't returned. "Some with their riding crops and kingly attitude — yea, verily, they too shall pass. It's the cameraman. Johnny. The cin-e-ma-tog-ra-pher. He's the real king."

He gestured to the set. "What see you here? A bedroom, with a hundred different images making their imprint on the emulsion of your brain. But a camera — she only sees some of it, and only for some of the time. Yes, she can get to it all eventually. Or she can hint at it all. But she only has that frame, like a horse with blinders on, to take it in, one sweet flash at a time."

He walked to the vanity on the set and pointed to the objects there. "The director, he pronounces: 'take an establishing shot' so folks get the sense they're in the bedroom.

But I choose what to focus on."

He held up a silver-plated hand mirror. "This?"

Replacing the mirror, he lifted a small bible. "Or this?" He put it down as the door opened, and more crew and actors tumbled into our cave.

"That shot," he said, whispering now that others gathered to work, "will tell you all you need to know about who lives in this room. You don't need no words after that. No *el-oh-cue-shun*. No *dye-uh-log-ue*. When the star comes to the camera, you already know who she is. Because I told you first!"

I stopped myself from pointing out that Leo didn't get the chance to use his camera to tell anybody anything anymore. With sound, his was a stationary piece of equipment, and his job was merely to be its sentry through the shoot.

He went back to his booth—the box that housed cameraman and camera so the microphones on set wouldn't pick up the machine's whir. Stepping into it took the wind out of his rhetorical sails. If he was so powerful in this land of foolery, why was he imprisoned so? These thoughts were bitter for me to swallow. He must have choked on them. There were three such vertical coffins around the stage, completely rooted to their respective spots—two for medium shots and one for close-ups. Cameras stopped speaking when movies talked, Leo had said many times.

ca

During the afternoon shoot, all I could think of was how high blown and stupid his stories were, how Leo talked big, but was nothing but a small cog in this wheel, and how I'd give him a piece of my mind as soon as the director shut us down for the day.

And so it was that I became lower than one of the "idiots." At the end of the day, Leo and the director roared and bellowed. I'd loaded the film in the wrong way, blind side out. An afternoon's shooting was lost and not because the sound had gone bad. They'd never have vented their rage on the sound man as they did on me.

Leo had no choice but to fire me on the spot. Now I was

jobless as well as homeless.

"I tried to get you to pay attention!" I yelled at Leo. "I tried to tell you I had a problem that needed solving fast!"

He didn't rise to the bait, didn't point out that I was the one who'd not paid attention, in the way that counted. He just looked at me, quiet.

"That was a stupid shit thing to do, boy," he said, his eyes narrowed and his voice sad.

"Yeah." His lack of ire doused the flame of mine. No use crowing about how good I was with mechanical things when my actions just made a liar out of me on that score. This was progress at least, my anger sputtering out so quick.

"You got some other work you can do?" he asked. I knew one of the reasons Leo had a soft spot for me was because he'd been an orphan and spent some time in a home himself.

I shrugged.

He rummaged in his pocket, pulling out a smudged scrap of paper with penciled handwriting on it. A phone number. A name. Sloane Hall. Marta Escobar.

"They're looking for a driver," he said quickly, handing me the paper. "And they'll throw in room and board." Putting his arm around my shoulder, he escorted me beyond the door into the warm afternoon. He pointed to the northwest. "Off Mulholland. They're new houses. Outpost Estates. Sloane Hall's at the very top."

Like ice in my face—he'd had this information the whole time I'd been pleading for leads on places to stay. But he hadn't handed it over because it would have meant leaving the studio work. Now that I had to go, he gave it up easy.

"Sloane Hall?" I swallowed.

"Yeah, Pauline Sloane. Shooting her first talkie soon. Maybe you saw her in 'Dangerous Night'? She's no Lillian, but she's not bad."

The name was familiar, but I didn't know her pictures. At twenty-one, I was catching up on the world.

He dug again into his pockets and pulled out a dollar, which he pressed on me. "You'll be back. Nobody remembers a thing in this town anymore, good or bad."

"Yeah, I know," I said, "as well as you do." I regretted my bitter tone as soon as the words left my mouth. Leo was a kind soul. He didn't need to be reminded that Hollywood was fast forgetting what men like him had brought to film.

There was only one king on the sets now, and Leo was wrong in saying it was the cinematographer. It was the sound technician. Even in my short stint in the studio as a cartridge loader, I'd seen directors sweat gallons waiting to hear the sound man declare the morning's shoot usable.

The sound man—who didn't know shit about Buster Keaton's prank set-ups or D.W.'s continuity or King Vidor's rejiggering of perspective—he was the Top Man now. Everyone waited on his word like the Israelites at the foot of the mountain.

"I'm sorry," I mumbled. "I didn't mean…"

He patted me on the shoulder. "I know. Take care of yourself, kid. Come see me. You'll be back."

ଔ

I made my way back to Jake's to get my things. Maybe Jake would let me stay just one more night, and I could apply at Sloane Hall in the morning. A chauffeuring job? Shit. I'd thought I could learn from Leo, maybe make it to cameraman like him. Another new start. I was tired of them already.

With every mile toward Jake's, the anger grew. Mostly anger at myself. I was a good worker and could handle things. Why'd I screw up? A hundred reasons came to mind, none of them related to how my fingers groped for the film in the lightproof bag, nimbly opening cartridges and loading the precious celluloid into canisters ready to mount on cameras.

It's a good thing none of the boys was around when I got back, or I'd probably have picked a fight with all of them. Jake was there, leaning into the engine of some dusty old Ford. When he heard me come in, his grease-stained face appeared from under the hood. One look in his eyes told me I'd not find shelter there that night.

"I'll get my things packed up," I said and turned to go.

But Jake stepped forward to block me, grabbing a rag to wipe his hands clean. Upstairs, I heard the muffled sound of the radio. Rudy Vallee's nasal voice cut through the walls as he crooned about how "You'll do it someday, so why not now…"

"You stay put. I'll get your things," Jake said. He didn't want me riling things up anymore, I guess. He walked to the stairs that led to the rooms above the garage. While I waited for him, I cursed Clyde. But I couldn't muster any true righteous anger, so as soon as the cursing was done, the silence of despair swamped me. Nothing to do but stare at the wall with its rusty nails hung with tools and gloves and belts, their ordinariness reminding me just how un-ordinary I was. The music grated, making things worse. Somewhere people were listening and happy. A sour taste crawled up my throat. I gritted my teeth.

The clip-clop of Jake's feet on the wooden steps broke my trance. He walked over fast and handed me a duffle bag and was about to hand me change, but I pushed his fist away. Leo's dollar was enough humiliation.

Without a word, I left, breathing in the warmed air of a summer evening. I didn't look back. Rev. Milqueton had taught me that. *There's no point in dwelling in the past, John*, he'd say. *Now's the time to move beyond your transgressions. You've paid for them.*

Where to go — to a flophouse or alley? Maybe this Sloane Hall tonight, right now.

I headed past closed shops and dusty roads lined with swaying palm trees. The city still had the feel of the frontier to it, still had the sense that it could be reclaimed by wild men or wild nature. That's what I'd liked about the film work, too, how it made things new.

When I'd first arrived in Los Angeles, the city had revived me. A big, fat, messy town, a city to get lost in. I'd had the feeling that no matter what you'd done before you got there, someone else probably had done it too. Now I wasn't sure.

I heard a raucous syncopated piano cadence waft from

behind closed doors and smelled liquor on the breath of speakeasies. I walked from Sixth to Wilshire, crowded with cars on a Saturday night, crowded enough for me to hitch a ride with a talkative salesman north past Sunset to the corner of Hollywood Boulevard and Highland Avenue. I passed a drug store and heard more music—a radio tuned to dance songs—and if I'd heard someone laughing I think I would have picked a fight with him.

There's no point in dwelling in the past.

Poor old Milqueton, burdened with a name that surely made him the object of tomfoolery in his youth. I sometimes wondered if that's what drove him to the church, seeking some kind of solace that family can't offer when bullies are beating at the doors of your soul.

When I'd left Canfield, I hadn't intended to dwell in the past at all. No where near anything that could remind me of it. I'd hopped trains from Texas to California with only a buck fifty in my pocket and landed on Jake Tinsdale's door with its sign in the window: ROOMS FOR RENT.

The light would fade soon. Stopping, I pulled my duffel bag in front of me to scrounge for the paper Leo had handed me. Sloane Hall. An all-night walk up the hill. Maybe I'd try something else.

I was tired. Not just bone tired. Tired of trying. Why should I be banished when I paid my rent, and Clyde and those boys just pretended to work, hardly earning their keep? I noticed. Damn, damn, *damn!* Injustice has a way of always surprising you with its fresh sting. You're never immune.

Whom shall I send? Here am I, send me. I heard Milqueton intoning those words from Isaiah.

Well, sir, every time I answer that call to right a wrong, I end up in trouble.

Pride is a sin, Milqueton was also fond of saying. *And sin only brings misfortune.*

Heaving the bag higher on my back, I bent forward and trudged north one block, turning westward onto Franklin, eventually coming upon new streets lined with eucalyptus and sycamore trees, their fresh sweet scents blocking out the dust and grease of the city below.

Before long, I found Outpost Drive and was surrounded by wealthy houses with red-tiled roofs and stucco walls. "Outpost Estates — Hillside Homes of Happiness," a sign at the bottom of the hill read, with a phone number in black letters for prospective buyers to call for appointments.

The air was warm as wool. Sweat beaded on my brow as I climbed the hill.

It was taking too long, and I was too tired. I looked back. Railroad tracks were on a flat stretch. I could head there, maybe hop something going north this time. Maybe California wasn't paradise after all, and thinking I could do well in film was a fool's dream.

I came upon a small field of twisted vines, curling in fantastic shapes in the blue shadows. Their tortured limbs looked dry and spent. Sad, too, like they were waiting for someone to put them out of misery. Just beyond these, cut into Mulholland Drive, was a private road so overgrown with trees and bushes that a passer-by would easily miss it in an automobile. Another sign was stuck back in the woods next to an open gate. Sloane H ll, it read in iron letters, the "a" missing.

I shifted my bag up and walked. The driveway was steeper than the road and curved sharply twice before leveling out. I took my time.

Darkness beat me to the house, a strange building set atop a hill that overlooked the city below. It loomed over the surrounding area like a huge gravestone, in fact, and I almost turned back. Weak light cut the dark from a room on the building's south end.

Unlike the other homes I'd passed, this one was not open like a hacienda. It was heavy, sprawling left and right beyond a central three-story tower, with gables cut into its roof and a thick-posted veranda along the front of the house creating an ominous air of death and shadow. Although its walls were stucco and its roof terra cotta tile, these touches looked as if they'd been added on as an afterthought to make a manor home look Californian, as if the owner had gazed at the architect's plans and said, "That's all well and good, but make it fit in." But it didn't fit in.

To my right was a spacious garage, separated from the house by a gravel-covered yard in the midst of which sat a silent fountain, its statue of an urn-carrying woman lonely in the dusk.

I considered for a long time whether to approach. Fatigue sent a cold shiver up my spine, but I shrugged it away. Pauline Sloane must be wealthy. They had a few cars. I'd settle for that work and mind my own business. If they'd have me, I'd give it a month or two, trying again at the studios, hoping they'd forget.

Slinging the bag behind me, I walked toward the lit rooms at the end of the house.

Chapter Two

THROUGHOUT MY STAY at Sloane Hall, I drove up that path a hundred times. Each time I felt a sigh forced out of me when I saw that hulking house glinting at the top of the hill. With its massive weight poised on the crest, it always looked like it could topple into the valley with a strong wind. I felt the need to rush to stop the impending disaster. Or maybe I really felt like running away from it before it pulled me down, too.

A fool or a coward — that's how it made me feel.

The night I arrived, however, hunger and fatigue won out over fear. I'd spent the long walk up the hill mulling the sequence of events of that day, like looking at the individual frames of a piece of film. Viewed in such isolation, it seemed to me my trouble had begun with the distracting fight with Clyde. If I'd just let that go ... why, I might not need new lodging, nor even a new job.

Ever since my days at Canfield, I was fighting a losing battle to learn to turn the other cheek. I could have paid Clyde as much mind as a barking dog or yowling cat. But I didn't. No man nor boy would do me wrong again without comeuppance. I struggled every day to keep that demon inside.

I sighed and looked at Sloane Hall. No point in being scared off by shadows. After knocking hard on the lit kitchen door, I almost gave up and walked away, but a thick-waisted woman eventually opened the door, squinting at my face.

This was Marta Escobar, the woman Leo had told me to see. She had dark skin and hair and wore a black dress and heavy shoes. After I introduced myself and told her Leo Bartenstein at the studio said they had an opening, she looked me up and down. She took her time, too, drying her hands on a cotton dishtowel, the light of the kitchen silhouetting her against the door, spilling onto the steps and walkway on the far side of the home like honey spreading from an overturned jar. In that dark, lonely place it felt like the only light in the world, and we the only remaining inhabitants after some unseen catastrophe.

"Can you drive?" she asked at last.

"Yes, ma'am."

"And you fix the cars, too?"

"Yes."

"Let me show you the cars." Throwing the towel onto her shoulder, she led me to the garage and recited the names of the models as she'd memorized them. A Packard Speedster. A serviceable Ford Model A in Niagara Blue. A stylish Nash with its twin ignition system — I couldn't wait to touch it. And an empty bay for a "new one." Marta didn't know what kind.

Beyond mentioning Leo, I had no need to offer other recommendations, even though I was prepared to hand her the dog-eared letter from Rev. Milqueton attesting to my skills and good nature. Leo was a good man, she informed me, very good to Miss Sloane. This I took to mean that he'd captured her good side in some silent I'd not yet seen.

"There is the driving and the fixing," she told me, hands on her hips. "And other odd jobs around the house." She peered at me in the shadows by the door of the garage. "Are you interested?"

She seemed eager to solve the problem of having no driver, and willing to believe I was a bit of good luck dropped into her busy hands.

Marta's lack of questions at first made me suspicious about the kind of job I'd be signing up for — I was sure there was a catch — but those feelings were pushed aside when I saw the chauffeur's quarters above the garage. Immediately my bad luck turned to gold.

This was a palace. Not just one tiny bedroom I had to share with other boys, like at Jake's. Not a dormitory room where I'd learned to block out the sounds of snoring and crying lost souls, like at the Home. For the first time in my life,

I'd have my own private apartment. It was the rooms that first tempted me. Other temptations would follow soon enough.

Up a long flight of stairs, there was a parlor, more like a hall than a real room. It held a small wooden table and two chairs. Beyond this was a bedroom just big enough for an iron-post bed, a chest of drawers and even a three-shelf bookcase. Off of this room was the greatest of luxuries — my own private bath, with a battered clawfoot tub under a high narrow window. Yes, I thought of these things as mine as soon as I saw them. Why had Leo been reluctant to tell me of this job?

All its comforts bought off any nagging sense of unease drifting over from the big house itself. Comfort does that. Steals your good sense faster than drink. Don't expect the Devil to offer you a sack full of silver when he wants your soul. A warm cup of coffee on a cold night will do the trick every time.

೮ಪ

After I slept in that bed, I thought I'd gone to heaven. So it seemed appropriate that my first job at Sloane Hall was chauffeuring Marta to Sunday Mass, all the way back into the city to St. Vibiana's, a big cathedral on 2nd Street. I'd passed the heavy-looking church with its awkward bell tower capped by a cupola on my wanderings around the city. Was curious to see its insides, but I never went in. I'm not much for the Roman way. Marta told me to wait for her. Before she got out, I 'fessed up about my past, figuring maybe it was another reason Leo hadn't been so forthcoming about the job. He hadn't wanted to foist an ex-prisoner on a friendly acquaintance. But after I told Marta why I had been incarcerated, she just nodded and frowned, saying nothing.

While she went inside her church and prayed for sinners like me, I rubbed down the Packard with a cheesecloth, making it gleam in the screaming sunshine. Maybe that kind of work is its own prayer. I like to think so.

On the way back to Sloane, she criticized my driving, telling me to slow down a block away from a traffic light and sucking in her breath fast when I passed a slow-paced flivver trying to climb a hill. From the corner of my eye, I could see her clutching the door handle like she was ready to jump out at the first sign of trouble. By the time we arrived back at the estate, I was convinced I hadn't passed my first test of employment. I'd gotten one good night's sleep out of it, so I figured I shouldn't complain. But she surprised me as I slowed near the kitchen.

"I am so glad you are here to do the driving, *Señor* Doyle." She smiled at me while she removed her black lace scarf. "I have had to learn to do it, and I cannot stand to drive. Too dangerous." She shivered and grinned at me before exiting. "Sunday dinner is at two in the kitchen," she said through the open window.

Already the smell of something good spread over the lonely yard. All right. Maybe California wasn't paradise, but this hill was coming pretty close. That fight with Clyde was beginning to look like a nudge toward destiny, and I wondered if it was wrong to thank God for setting up a brawl if it led to something as sweet as this.

I changed my shirt an hour later to get ready for my first big meal. I was wondering when I'd see the mistress of the house—the actress Pauline Sloane—and what she'd look like. By now, my disappointments and my rage were farther than memory, replaced by pity for Jake, Clyde, and the other boys, and a bit of youthful nostalgia for my friend of yesterday, Leo.

With a hopeful heart—something like a gift to me since I wasn't prone to optimism any longer—I walked to the kitchen on the rear of the house. When I entered the large bright room, Marta was setting out plates on a long table covered in blue-checked oilcloth. This room *was* Sunday. A vague warm memory passed quickly by—my mother by the stove, smiling at me, telling me she was fixing pot roast. Like all my memories of her, it stung my eyes, and I blinked fast.

Marta nodded her head at me and then toward a short woman who tasted something at the stove. She was the kind of girl the boys at Jake's would whistle at—soft seduction in every curve. There was a sharpness to her, too, though, that sent out the signal she was only a certain kind of man's gal. I wasn't him. Her dark hair was pulled back so tight in a bun it had an edge of meanness to it. She wore a gray uniform and white apron, and when she moved I swear her body sent the message loud and clear that she wasn't meant for uniforms.

"This is Julia Nons, our cook," Marta explained. Julia did not acknowledge the introduction, so I said nothing and sat down at the table where Marta pointed to a place across from her. When Julia put the food out a few seconds later, she sat next to me and stared at her plate while Marta murmured a blessing.

"Julia is French," Marta said, and I took this to mean that the girl didn't speak much English. But this was proven wrong a few minutes into the meal—one of the best I'd ever had in my young life so far—when Julia asked Marta a series of questions in a low quiet voice.

"When did she say she'd be back?"

"I told you I don't know, Julia."

"Is he with her?"

"No."

"How do you know?"

"He telephoned yesterday. And the day before."

"Does he know where she is?"

"No. He is worried. Just like us."

After silently eating her soup, she tried again.

"Will he come here to wait for her?"

"I don't know!" Marta's voice rose. Her eyes widened and watered. "I pray every night for her. I have thought even of contacting the police!"

My curiosity was getting the best of me, but I tried to mask it with helpfulness. "Is she a worker here, too? I could drive into town and ask around."

Julia laughed, nearly spitting out her soup, while Marta frowned at her before turning a pleasant face to me. "We are talking about Miss Sloane. She was supposed to be back last Wednesday, but she is delayed."

The blush of the fool warmed me. I hadn't figured they'd

be talking about their employer in such familiar terms. I didn't ask any more questions. Marta, however, misinterpreted my silence as anxiety about my job.

"Don't worry, John. Miss Sloane is a very fair employer. She will talk to you when she returns and tell you more about the job."

But Miss Sloane didn't show up that day or the next or even within the week. I forgot about her for the most part, drifting into a happy routine—free from ambition or regret for the time being—driving Marta and Julia to the market on Broadway and on other errands, and getting each automobile into top-notch shape. They'd been ignored for some time, so I had plenty to occupy myself with, and when I had time to spare I made myself useful around the estate doing small repairs and generally being available to Marta, who was as motherly and warm as Julia was distant and aloof. In fact, I think Julia preferred the company of Pilot, the estate's golden retriever, to that of any of her fellow employees.

It didn't bother me. I enjoyed silence, and took a strange satisfaction in the fact that I was the only worker on the estate who didn't even try to engage Julia in conversation. The three of us were the only live-ins. Gardeners, pool keeper, and repairmen came when called or on some schedule I was not privy to.

In this sunny island cut off from the world, I added to my dream of great success as surely as the architect had added to this house. I would improve myself, be a good worker with a fine reputation, impress my boss and be taken into her confidence, return to the studios ready to grab opportunity wherever it might fall, and eventually be no man's slave. It was a hard dream to cherish for a boy like me, but I was not so cynical that I could repress the natural inclinations of youth.

It was a separate world up there on that hill, a world where I didn't need to worry about fitting in, where I didn't need to fear my own inclination to fight or run. In those first weeks, my life was a veritable Eden. Nothing but peace and comfort. You don't know—you can't know— the paradise of simple comforts unless you've suffered their loss. I could breathe easy again, and I was close enough to a time when breathing easy had been a rarity that I realized its value. I felt as young as my years.

Thursdays and Sunday afternoons were my own, Marta had explained to me, and I used them to take walks and read at first, and then to visit Leo back on the set.

He was glad to see me looking happy and well-fed and told me so when I went to see him my second week at Sloane Hall.

"You met her yet?" he asked as he began his break.

"Nope. Nobody's seen her. Marta's fit to be tied."

"She's scheduled to make her first talkie, you know. She'll be skittish as a horse about to run the Derby. Be careful, John, when she shows up." He rubbed his chin and grabbed my arm. "Here, let me show you something…"

He led me to his beat-up old Ford—the fact that he had a car had impressed me mightily when he'd first hired me—and pulled out a camera, something different from what I'd seen him use on the set.

"They ain't using these no more. They would have thrown it out, the bastards. Wheat with the chaff!"

It was an old camera, one used in the silents, he explained, and as he cranked it, it made a soft, regular clicking sound, a mechanical lullaby that reminded me of the humming pistons of a well-running motor. With this kind of manual control, a director like Harold Lloyd had been able to shoot scenes that slowed the action. With this camera, nuance was possible. When Leo saw me smile, he smiled, too. "It's sweet, ain't it? You don't hear that anymore. Just them mouthing off now." He shrugged back toward the soundstage building we'd left.

As I looked it over, his voice grew soft and distant. "You ever hear of a movie called Sunrise?" He didn't wait for an answer. "Around the same time The Jazz Singer comes out, Fox releases it. Most beautiful thing you ever seen. Directed by a Kraut—Murnau. Some said it was the best film ever could be made. And it was made with this camera. This thing." He made it sound like I was handling a sacred icon. I gave it back to him for fear of breaking it. But this little re-exposure to Hollywood movie-making had me hankering to return to its charms.

"When you think I could try again here?" I asked.

Leo laughed. "It's only a few weeks, boy. Give it some time. Besides, you don't seem unhappy with your job."

"I'm not. But this is where I want to be." I spread my arms toward the warehouse-like studio buildings.

"I'll let you know when the time is ripe." He looked up, as if remembering something. "Say, if Miss Sloane has any parties, I know some good piano players. Out of work organists, really. No need for them in the theaters much now."

"Sure, Leo, I'll let you know." I was glad to be asked for a favor, even if I wasn't sure I'd be able to grant it.

We talked for a few more minutes. Or rather, he talked, the same old lessons and lectures. I half-listened, now eager to get back to Sloane Hall where at least there was an empty room and a good book waiting for me.

"Well, you take care, boy. Don't forget. Watch out around Miss Sloane."

03

By my third week at Sloane Hall, I'd been through my small supply of books twice over. I used them to improve myself, to widen my vocabulary, to broaden my horizons. When I took one with me on a walk, it was with a notebook and pencil that I used to write down words I didn't recognize or whose meaning I wasn't quite sure of. Later, when I returned home to my apartment above the garage, I'd look them up in a battered dictionary.

I knew enough about the world to appreciate the value of a well-spoken man, and the doors that would open for him.

Filling a sack with food and a book, notebook, paper, and pencil, I'd take off down the road (a different one each time) and explore my surroundings. Sometimes, I'd stop and draw a landscape or a plant, looking it up later in one of the books from the estate's library. When Marta saw my interests, she'd retrieve books for me. In a short span of time I began to feel like a different person, like the person I was meant to be before my stepfather's death. No, before even that. Before my own father, whom I'd hardly known, before he had passed away and my mother had become ... lost.

In this refreshed frame of mind, I decided one Thursday afternoon to set out on a dirt road just north of the house, one that led away from the fields and into more barren land. I'd traveled nearly five miles by my reckoning and just made my way to the crest of a hill when I saw a tiny ball of fur in the middle of the road, trying to scamper to the side with no success.

Pushing my hat back on my head, I bent forward to help the poor creature. It was a baby rabbit with a leg cramped tight against its body, and it wouldn't last long. Not in this land with sun and wind and other creatures aiming to hurt it. I felt the need to do something, if only to prove I wasn't one of those creatures that would do it harm. I took my hat off to scoop it up and into the brush where it could at least rest peacefully before death surely claimed it. Before I had a chance to touch its downy back and soothe its fright, I was put into a fright myself.

Heehaw, heehaw! A motor car horn split the air, as out of place in that barren region as a snow-draped Christmas tree. I jumped back, just in time to save myself from being run over by a spitting new Dusenburg J, its long nose jutting down the road like a ramrod.

"What the..." Jesus! My head twitched as I saw the large wheels crush the animal into the earth. Damn that driver! Damn him to hell!

My gaze turned up to the vehicle, careening into a ditch while its driver cursed with a vocabulary I thought only my fellow reform school inmates had mastered.

My hands clenched into fists again. I marched toward the car, ready to give that driver more than just a piece of my mind. Out here on this sun-baked road, I could pound that rascal's head into the ground, and no one would know but me and God. And I was sure, at that moment, He was on my side.

But that feeling faded as I took long strides toward the car and... damn. Damn if the driver wasn't beautiful. Soft and pretty like the small thing she'd destroyed. I'm not different than most men. A girl like that, she touches you.

A porcelain doll. That's what she was. A translucent face, too pale for California's savage sun, and eyes as piercing as old Milqueton's but blue instead of brown. Blue ice. Or blue flame, I suppose, depending on your perspective. Now they burned with anger, and her small, rosebud of a mouth pursed in annoyance. Her hair was blonde—white blonde, like blinding sun— in one of those new short, wavy styles all the girls were favoring, and she wore a long-sleeved dress— something yellow and silky that gave the impression she had nothing on underneath. I was beaten back by all that, by the softness and the beauty.

But only for a moment.

You see, if she had been gentle and maidenly, I would have stayed cowed, and perhaps never would have dared say anything. Soft things, no matter how seductive, are deceptive.

But, because she was thoughtless and gruff, I responded by instinct, as I'd always done to the harsh word or gesture, with a desire to meet her blow for blow, to show her I was made of tough stock and could take harsh treatment like any man.

"Look what you've done, ma'am!" I cried, my hands on my hips.

She didn't reply at first but stared at her hands on the wheel with her head tilted to one side, thoughts locked inside. She turned the engine on and tried to race out of the ditch. The wheels, two of which were barely touching earth, gained no traction, and she went nowhere. Over and over, she gunned the motor and let the wheels spin furious dust into the air without moving forward. At last, the engine coughed out its despair, but she still did not look my way.

"Stop it!" I shouted. "You'll ruin the engine!" It was bad

enough she crushed that rabbit. She wouldn't kill this magnificent piece of machinery, too.

Her face drained of everything, and she looked at me as if I had ruined the engine myself.

"All right then, *you* get it out of this damned canyon," she said in a dark, velvety voice. Opening the door, she jumped onto the road, but the car was leaning at an angle that made the distance from running board to ground farther than she'd counted on. Her knees buckled for an instant and she herself would have fallen had I not stretched out my hand to catch her arm.

Here was Eve herself. Soft skin, even though she herself was thin and bony, and sweet scent. Touching her made me want to touch her more, especially her hair, and maybe a stroke against that doll-face cheek.

Despite my help, her ankle turned, and I had to steady her with both my hands, while she latched onto my arms with her slender fingers. It was then that she looked me in the eyes and laughed. Here was the apple. That laugh. A silvery sound that rippled into the empty space like birds trilling in the distance, jangling my nerves some place deep in my gut.

I smelled gin on her breath. Gin had been my mother's drink.

"Dear boy, you look like you've seen a ghost."

I didn't say anything but looked down at her foot.

She let go of my hand and bent to rub her twisted right ankle. None too gingerly, she put her weight on the offending extremity, only to cry out with a whimper and pull it up. Pain was replaced by quick laughter. "Seems you're nothing but trouble. You run me off the road and then twist my ankle."

I'd done no such thing! I opened my mouth to say as much, but she shushed me before I could utter a word. "Calm down. I'm only joking."

"I can go get help," I offered. At least the walk would get me away from her.

"You *are* the help for now. Come on." She draped her arm around my shoulder. "I'll get back in the car. You drive."

After she slid into the passenger seat, I threw my rucksack in after her but didn't get in myself. Instead, I stood outside the vehicle with my hands in my pockets.

"She won't start now. You've flooded the engine. We need to wait awhile."

Squinting into the sun, she pulled a wide-brimmed straw hat from the back and tied it on her head with a white scarf.

"Damn it. What a bother! Do you have a cigarette?"

"No, ma'am." I stared at her straight on. If she'd meant to shock me by requesting a smoke, she'd have to do more. My mother had smoked on occasion, a bad habit she'd acquired with her other bad habits.

"For god's sake, don't call me 'ma'am.' Makes me feel ancient. I'm only twenty-six." As if to prove to herself she was still youthful, she opened a tiny handbag and looked at herself in a gold-rimmed compact, puckering her lips to smooth the rosy paint there, and brushing back a stray lock of hair. Grimacing, she snapped the mirror shut. "How old are you?"

"Twenty-one, ma'am." I ran my hand along the edge of the open window. It was a fine new automobile.

She sighed. "Eleanor. It's Eleanor Brickman." Another laugh, this one mischievous. What's your name?"

"John Doyle," I said. "I'd like to take a look at the engine, if that's all right." Might as well use the incident to advantage. When would I get to see a car like this one ever again?

"Go right ahead. Maybe you can unflood it or something. A cigarette—did you have one?"

"No, I don't."

I moved to the front of the vehicle and unlatched the bonnet. The sickly sweet smell of gasoline hit me immediately, confirming my diagnosis. The Duesenberg's trademark green enameled engine looked as if it had hardly been used. From the shiny look of the caps and belts, it was clear this was a recent purchase, not often driven. After I'd had my fill of touching and admiring the workmanship of the engine, I turned my attention to the rest of the car. No wheels were bent nor axles twisted. Once it was on the road, it should run fine.

To get it out of the ditch would mean pushing it onto more level land. Luckily, we were pointed downhill. If I could get the car rolling, then run to jump in the driver's seat, it should be a smooth ride. My pulse raced. I'd like to drive this car.

"Well?" Eleanor called out. "Has the flood receded, John Doyle?"

"I guess we could try it now. But I'll have to give it a push. Can you slip it out of gear? Once it gets going, I'll jump in."

She complied, and the car lurched just a hair. Heaving with all my might, I shoved at the automobile. Nothing happened.

"Is the brake off?" I asked.

"Do you think I'm an idiot? Of course the brake is off!" She scooted back to the driver's side and turned on the engine. This time, it caught. Before I could protest, she was pushing on the gas pedal, with the same result as before. Lots of noise and dust. No action.

"Don't!"

She disregarded me. With a wince of pain, she shifted the car into reverse, and I had to jump out of the way as she backed it up an inch or two, then switched back to first gear. Still no movement forward. She rocked the automobile back and forth that way, paying no heed to my calls to stop, so I could shove again. She made enough progress with this technique, however, to persuade me it was working. When she shifted into first for the fifth time, I quickly moved behind the car and gave it a mighty heave.

Whether it was from my push or the rocking, the car finally broke free, the wheels found purchase on the rocky ground, and it started to speed away.

"Thanks," she cried over the hum of the motor, wagging her hand in the air in my direction.

"Hey! My things!"

I ran after her, but she didn't hear, continuing down the road as serenely as a queen. The momentum of the slope and the fine-running engine would have outdone me, too, if it weren't for the fact that a railroad crossing loomed ahead, and an old steam locomotive was lumbering into view. Huffing and puffing, I stopped with my hands on my knees, waiting for her to pause as the train went by.

But she kept going. In fact, a mere ten yards from the track, she seemed to speed up. She was going to try to beat the train, a fatal error in that long car.

"Goddammit!" I shouted.

The roar of the train drowned out my voice. I ran again, hollering her name, calling for her to brake. At this point I cared more about that beautiful car than I did about her well-being. It was foolish and stupid to risk ruining it.

"Eleanor! Miss Brickman!" Even I could barely hear myself yell. But something convinced her she wasn't going to win that game, and with a screech, the car finally halted, sliding to the right at the fierceness of the stop, just a hair's breadth away from the rushing train.

As it clacked by, I caught up and jumped in.

"What were you doing? You have my things." I was screaming at her, and only partly because of the noise of the train.

I expected her to laugh again, to raise her eyebrows and say, "A close one, wasn't it?" I expected it because she irritated me, and that would have irritated me most of all, to have her make light of a near-catastrophe. Instead, she turned a shaken face to me, one as haunted as the ghost she'd claimed I'd seen. Her eyes swam with tears, and her mouth hung slightly ajar, while her brows were creased from some inner pain. I couldn't tell if she was frightened by her brush with danger or sad she'd missed a chance at...something. Something that sent a chill of despair through me. I'd seen that look before.

"I'm sorry." Her voice was gentle now, the kind of voice that should have sent me away. "Get in. I'll drop you somewhere."

"Why don't you let me drive? Your ankle..." I pointed to her swollen foot.

Pulling up the hand brake, she slid back to the passenger

side.

"Where you headed?" she asked in a faraway voice while we waited for the train to pass.

"Nowhere in particular. It's my day off. I was just walking."

"Where do you work?"

"Sloane Hall. I'm the chauffeur and mechanic."

The laugh returned, a specter of itself. "Good! That's where I'm headed."

"You know Miss Sloane?" Just my luck to have annoyed one of the great Miss Sloane's friends.

"Hmm…as well as one knows anybody, I suppose."

"Then you should know that Miss Sloane is not at home."

Her eyebrows arched up. "It doesn't matter," she said.

We sat in silence while the remaining cars streamed past. From my vantage point, I could see the outlines of hoboes inside the freight cars. How glad I was to be done with that kind of wandering. I looked forward to lying on my bed that night with a good book after a good meal.

Slipping the car into gear after releasing the brake, I crossed the tracks as soon as the caboose had passed. Eleanor leaned her head back on the seat.

"God, I need a cigarette. Smoked my last one an hour ago."

"You've been driving all that time?"

"No. Most of the time I was thinking. Sitting in a theater and thinking."

I looked over at her, trying to place her in some occupation or home. Nothing fit. Her features and wealth indicated a high social station, but her habits and language indicated another. For a moment, the fleeting thought that she might be a working woman crossed my mind. But she wasn't quite hard enough for that type. I knew, from speakeasies my mother frequented, what those were like. She didn't have that kind of used-up look. My best guess was she wanted to use her friendship with Miss Sloane to get into the pictures.

We didn't speak for the rest of the drive back to Sloane

Hall, and by the time I pulled up to the front of the estate, she was asleep. Since she claimed to know the estate's owner, I figured I'd tell Marta, then head to my little apartment.

Before I could make my way to the kitchen in back of the house, Marta ran outside, excitedly waving a handkerchief in front of her face, as if she were crying. Bounding after her was Pilot, his tail wagging and his tongue lolling out.

"The *Señorita*! You have brought her home. Thank goodness. I was so worried."

My mouth hanging open like the idiot I felt like, I stood and watched as Marta gently roused Eleanor. Except she didn't call her Eleanor. She called her "*Señorita* Sloane."

"Oh, Marta, don't make a fuss. I just fell asleep."

"You were supposed to be home weeks ago. *Señor* Morgan calls every day, twice a day, sometimes three times a day, for you. He said he would hire a detective if you didn't come home."

Julia appeared at my shoulder, standing straight and prim in her gray uniform with its sheer white apron. Forced by my curiosity, I spoke to her.

"She told me her name was Eleanor Brickman."

Julia smirked. She had won our silent battle. "That was her real name."

I should have guessed. Dammit to hell.

Marta clucked over Miss Sloane as she limped up the steps to the house. Just as she reached the door, Miss Sloane turned and stared at me.

"Put the car away, John. And in an hour, come into the house. I want to talk with you."

I did as I was told, but I wasn't happy about it. Already she'd lied to me.

Chapter Three

AS IT TURNED OUT, she didn't see me in an hour, even though I showed up at the big house early. I was still angry, but I'd managed to talk myself out of the worst of it. If I wanted to keep myself from getting fired in my first interview with my employer, I had to let it go. I wouldn't be suckered into a fight like I had been at Jake's or angered into messing up like I had been at the studio.

But that didn't mean I didn't get mad every time I thought of it. She had nearly run me over. She had nearly ruined a great piece of craftsmanship by racing a train. She'd not told me who she was when she'd found out who I was. It didn't say good things about her as a boss, and I was already thinking the same glum thoughts that had occupied me at Jake's, that had followed me from Texas, about not fitting in, about it not being fair. The sunshine of promise had turned into the twilight of uncertainty. This was the dividing line.

Marta and Julia were both in the kitchen when I arrived for my "appointment" with Miss Sloane. Julia was whipping something in a big copper bowl, seeming to take an unnatural pleasure in beating it to a pulp. A malicious smile played at her lips, and I knew part of her happiness came from seeing my confusion over learning my passenger had been the mistress of the house. Aw, to hell with her. I straightened my collar.

"John," Marta said when she saw me, "go back and make the fountain go. Here, I'll show you." She led the way back outside again and around to the water, pointing to the nozzle and pump that would start the contraption. A few twists and yanks later, I was damp, and the fountain's raucous burble cut the air, disturbing the glass-smooth water and the peace as well.

Because my shirt and trouser cuffs were now wet, I had to retreat to my room once again to change. Miss Sloane felt like an intruder to me, upsetting the harmony of my household. I remembered what Leo had told me — to be careful around her. And now I expected her to fire me, just as I'd been fired from the studio, for my lack of care.

A few minutes later, I was back in the kitchen where Marta was going over menus, a pencil lost in her thick black hair, her eyes focused on a list before her.

"Julia, what did you serve when the Schulbergs were here three months ago?" she asked. "I didn't make a note."

"*Poulet a la Nicoise* — chicken with artichokes and anchovies. Asparagus. Crème brulee," Julia said without looking at her.

Marta wrote it down, then looked up at me, confused.

"Miss Sloane said I should talk to her," I reminded her.

"She is resting, *pobrecita*. She is so tired." Marta made another notation on her list. "I will send for you when she is ready."

The phone buzzed, and Marta plucked the receiver from the wall in the middle of the first ring.

"Sloane residence." At the sound of the caller's voice, her lips came together in a tight line. "*Si, Señor.*" And then she spoke in Spanish. Sprinkled throughout her speech, I could hear Miss Sloane's name, but the rest was lost to me.

With nothing to keep me there, I left the kitchen and headed back to my apartment over the garage, not able to plan for anything except waiting to be beckoned to my employer's presence. I gritted my teeth and reminded myself this was a small price for what I had. When I arrived in my room, I flung myself on my bed. I folded my arms behind my head and stared at the ceiling, waiting.

I saw her face as she drove off without me, smiling at her joke at my expense. My lips tightened. When she'd driven the car toward the tracks, I'd assumed she was trying to outrun the train. Maybe she'd been trying to do the opposite and deliberately smash the beautiful Duesenberg's gleaming nose into the side of the powerful steam engine.

I bristled. She was young, beautiful, and wealthy. She had no claim to the kinds of feelings that drove a soul to that variety of desperation. Pauline Sloane would not best me at misery. I'd had a lifetime's share.

Years after the "accident" that had landed me at Canfield, I still wondered what life would have been like had things turned out differently. I wondered if this was why I couldn't fit in—my stay at Canfield and what had led to it. I couldn't shake the feeling that when people looked at me, whether they knew my history or not, they'd see right through to the core and know I was a murderer. Is that what she had seen? Is that why it was all right for her to mock and tease me?

I'd only been ten years old, young enough that judges and do-gooders could see in me a potential for a good life.

My mother was dead; she'd been beaten and locked in a dark room where she'd screamed with terror. When the screaming stopped, I'd thought she'd finally gone to sleep. I hadn't known that she had passed by then, that her last breath had been ripped out of her. An artery bursting in her neck, they told me later. Scared to death.

He went to the door with a shovel in his hand. A shovel. How could I not try to stop him? I knew what he intended to do with it. He'd broken her arm once, nearly broken mine, too. So I couldn't let him go after her when she'd finally quieted down.

I ran after him and grabbed it.

"Damn you, kid," he said, barely moving his mouth as if I wasn't worth the effort. That made me angrier still, that he didn't think I was worth fighting. Angry enough to do what I'd never been able to do in the past. He was taller and more agile. He was stronger. I'd found that out the hard way the first time he'd come after me. But for once in my life my own fury vanquished my fear, teaching me a valuable (and dangerous) lesson. Rage conquers all. It conquers fear, weakness, an unbalanced fight. Righteous rage is the weapon of the angels. I was filled with it. So much so, I don't even think I saw him. He was a blur, a gray ghost even before I sent him to hell.

It happened slow, then fast, then slow again. All mixed up, like someone had fooled with the camera speed, like that hazy sleep I'd been knocked into the first time he hit me. I think I yelled, a rebel yell, something inhuman and loud. I think I shouted "No!" and held onto the shovel with all my might.

His mouth was open—was it a smile, was he thinking I couldn't do it, was he laughing at me—when I smashed his head the first time, so hard the reverberations stung my hands.

Before he'd had a chance to react, I'd slammed the shovel on his head a second time, and this time I felt victory—I'd caved in something. He crumpled, his eyes glazed. And I didn't stop then, even when he was down. I slammed his head again and again when he fell to the floor. God, it felt good. Even when I remember it, I get a shiver, it felt so right. His face was unrecognizable by the time I'd finished with him. I'd cried because it felt so good.

When I remembered that night, I closed my eyes.

I was lucky to get sent to Canfield and not to the state prison after what I'd done. I'd meant to kill him. I'd wanted his blood. I'd enjoyed killing him.

I was saved from myself by a well-meaning sheriff who'd lived nearby and had known my stepdaddy's history. He testified that my mother had cried out all night, and I'd saved her from the monster, even though I couldn't save her from her own weak constitution. But we both had known I'd killed him after he'd represented no threat to my mother, quiet and still and no longer in fear, in the other room.

In a strange way, it's just as well that Canfield was a hall of horrors when I went there, with thin gruel for dinner and lukewarm tea for breakfast, regular beatings by Brice Clement and his crew, hard labor in the hot sun, and capricious punishments that made us all savages. I needed something hard and cruel to sear the cruelty out of my heart. By the time old Milqueton arrived, I was ready to be rehabilitated.

"*Mademoiselle* will see you now." Julia stood in my doorway with a grin on her face, her frizzy auburn hair taut against her head, pulled into a vicious bun at the nape of her neck.

"What?" I sat up, orienting myself to the room. Soft blues and muted yellows lit it as evening crept in. I must have fallen asleep. My mouth was dry.

"*Mademoiselle*," she repeated slowly as if I were a dolt, "she is ready to talk to you."

Mademoiselle. Señorita. No one called her ma'am or miss or even Pauline, let alone Eleanor. I had to let it go. Turn the other cheek.

When I stood, Julia looked me up and down with such critical eyes that I thought I'd ripped my pants or had a stain on my shirt.

"What's the matter?"

"You should dress. *Mademoiselle* likes people to dress."

I was about to comment on the fact that I wasn't buck naked or anything, when her meaning penetrated. Dress up. Dress for dinner. But I had no really fancy clothes, no dinner jackets or expensive suits.

"All right. Give me a minute."

"When you're ready, Marta will take you to her." Julia left as silently as she'd arrived.

Quickly, I pawed through my dresser drawer and found a clean shirt. I paired that with my best pants, light gray flannels that I'd worn for special occasions at the Home. Just a few days ago, I'd bought myself a new set of navy blue suspenders, so I snapped those into place as well. The only jacket I owned was an old overcoat for harsh weather. Knowing that would make me look more ridiculous than polite, I left it behind. After cleaning my spectacles and washing up, I headed for the house which now blazed with light, the front windows stretching their yellow rectangles onto the gravel and gardens. If anything, all that light made the house appear even lonelier amidst the huge black void of the hill.

In the kitchen, Marta stood alone and gave me the same kind of hard-edged gaze that Julia had used just moments before. From her tight-muscled face, I could tell that I wasn't passing muster.

"Don't you have a tie?" She pointed to my open collar.

"Uh, no." I fumbled to fasten the top button on my shirt.

"Wait here." She left, to return a few moments later with a blue-and-green striped tie which she helped me put on. While she fussed over me, I noticed the table was set for supper and something was on the stove—chicken. My favorite. Lordy, it smelled good. My dinner would have to wait, though, while I met with my employer.

"This will have to do," Marta said, standing back. "Come with me."

Except for the kitchen, I'd never seen the rest of the house before and was confused by the maze of hallways, each of the passing rooms furnished in incomprehensible wealth and deep in shadow. Despite the home's attempt at a sunny Spanish feel, the décor was dark and oppressive.

We finally reached a long rectangle of a room facing the back of the house. Its walls, dark umber, drank the light from the fire licking at the hearth at the far end of the room. On either side of a stone chimney, windows burdened with yards of dark velvet opened to a view of mountains stabbing a bruised night sky. Below, I could see water shift from black to white and back again in the weak rays of an early moon. The swimming pool.

Above the mantelpiece, a portrait dominated the room and drew my eyes away from everything else. It was a painting of a woman. Standing, dressed in a gossamer white gown more appropriate for the turn of the century than modern times, she appeared to be my employer. The eyes were the same, the set of the mouth, even the slender fingers. But the hair was golden brown, not blonde, piled on top of her head in a bun, a fashionable style in years gone by. She stared down at us all, a fairy queen living in a distant world. I assumed it was Miss Sloane in costume for some historical epic I'd not seen.

"Mister Doyle is here, *Señorita*," Marta said.

It was then that I noticed my employer. She was lounging on a sofa in front of the roaring fire, her ankle propped on a satin pillow.

"Have him come in. And I'd like another drink, Marta."

Without turning to me, she added, "Would you like something, Mister Doyle?"

"No, thank you." I walked into the room while Marta disappeared and eventually stood near the warm fire so that I could see her. The yellow silk dress of the afternoon's adventure was replaced by a pinkish robe in an Oriental design. Tied at the waist, it fell open so far that I could see the curves of her breasts. I looked down.

"For God's sake, don't stand there like a butler. Sit down." She waved one hand while sipping crystal clear liquid from a sharply-angled cocktail glass. Something with gin in it. I smelled it even across the room.

I sat in a chair across from her and put my hands on my knees, wondering if my hair was slicked down enough or sticking up in a cowlick like some hick who just rolled off the train.

I was prepared to listen to a lecture—even a tirade—about my role in her accident. I'd prepared myself for silence, for acceptance of unjustified wrath. But as I sat there, watching her drink, her eyes not focused on any one thing, it occurred to me that she might just want a report on her vehicles. Quickly, I made a mental list of the repairs I'd performed.

"So, I understand I've hired you." She looked me up and down, squinting at the tie, a sign I took as disapproval.

"If you say so, ma'am."

"Stop calling me ma'am! Didn't we go over that already?" Her voice echoed in the large room.

"Yes, Miss Sloane."

"Call me Pauline. And why wouldn't I 'say so' about

hiring you? Is there something I should know?" she snapped at me.

There was no time to answer. Marta returned, carrying a tray upon which rested a tall, narrow pitcher filled with more clear liquid. She silently filled Miss Sloane's glass, before setting the tray on a low table in front of us.

"Do you want anything else, *Señorita* Sloane?" Marta stood with her hands clasped in front of her, not looking at me but staring at Miss Sloane with the same concerned look of a mother for her child.

"No. Thank you, Marta." Her voice was still sharp.

After Marta left, I looked defiantly at Miss Sloane, *Señorita* Sloane, whoever she was. Let her be angry with me, but Marta was a good soul who deserved gentleness.

"Earlier you told me to call you Eleanor," I said. And immediately regretted it. I'd told myself to let it go. Why couldn't I let anything go, goddammit.

"Does that bother you?" She seemed amused, not angry.

"It's confusing."

"Then call me Eleanor. Or Ellie. Only people who know me well call me that." Her voice had slurred. "Really, really well." She sipped her drink, and apparently her spirits lifted, pulling that perfect face into a grin. Here was real light. When she smiled, she looked … like a spirit, something unearthly.

"You really should have one. Martinis."

"I don't drink."

"What *do* you do, Mister John Doyle?"

I started to offer my speech on the state of the estate's automobiles when she cut me off.

"That's not what I meant. I mean, who are you? Where are you from?" She leaned back, her arm draped over the top of the sofa, her robe pulling apart even farther. I felt my face warm and looked away again. I wanted to leave. I was hungry and tired. And tired of being played with. It had been too good to be true, of course. I should have known as soon as Marta had shown me my quarters.

"Most recent, Canfield Home for Wayward Boys." Let the

axe fall and be done with it.

"Well, well. No wonder you look so worldly wise. You were there a long time?" She lowered her head and smiled up at me, as if she were posing for a picture.

"Eleven years. I stayed on to help out past my time."

"Past your time. Exactly what were you serving time for?" She seemed pleased, not disturbed, by my background.

"I accidentally killed a man."

"Accidentally?" She pushed herself up and laughed, again that silver rainfall of sound, and it wasn't clear if she was mocking me or mocking life itself. "I suspect a judge thought otherwise if you ended up at a 'Home for Wayward Boys.'"

"Yes'm." I shifted in my chair. No matter how many times I thought of it, it didn't get easier over time. Admitting to killing my stepfather was a failure on my part—a failure to take care of him in other ways, to get my mother away safe and free. "Involuntary manslaughter they called it."

"You don't like to talk about it." She poured herself another drink, spilling some on the tray. She touched the spilled liquid with her finger and then sucked it clean. "All right. Just tell me this: was it a beast of a man who'd done something horribly wrong, a tyrant, a villain, a con man, or a cheat?"

"All of those and then some."

"Then you're welcome in my house, John Doyle. In fact, maybe we'll raise your pay."

I looked up at her to see the reflection of the flames dancing in her blue irises, her cheeks flushed, her lips a lively pink. Was she teasing me again?

"Canfield must have been good to you if you stayed on." Her voice was steady and direct. No jabs there.

"It was rough at first. But got better with time. After Reverend Milqueton took over from Mister Clement."

"Clement, Clement. I seem to remember reading something about that. A scandal of some sort. Yes, Brice Clement, a terror to troubled boys." She recited it as it had appeared in newspaper headlines at the time.

It had been a huge scandal, one that had attracted reporters from miles away with their flashing cameras and small notebooks. Brice Clement had been a cruel man who'd beat us all, used food money for gambling and whores, and made us sleep in filth and degradation. My friend Pete Salerno hadn't survived him, not with a broken back that kept him bedridden. Pneumonia might have been the final blow, but the first one had been struck by Clement.

"Well, let's talk about happier things. Your family. I like to get to know my employees."

"My parents are dead."

"Oh. So sorry," she said casually. She was distracted by pain as she put weight on her bandaged foot. She flinched. "Then we have something else in common. So are mine. Two orphaned souls."

She hoisted herself to her feet, keeping the sore one raised in the air an inch above the carpet. I went to help her. "I'm told you like to read and draw," she said.

"In my spare time. I sketch a little."

"I'm an artist myself. In a different way, of course. I paint with my body on a silver screen. I'd like to see your drawings some time."

Leaning on my arm, she made her way to the fire. Struggling to maintain her balance, her hand gripped my wrist and her fingers felt frail and light, like a cat's paw. The scent of alcohol mingled with her perfume.

"Despite all that sun, it does get chilly here at night." At the fire, she held her hands to the warmth, still leaning against me.

"You're not wearing very warm clothes," I said a little testily. It was impossible not to see beyond the wide edging of her robe, to her naked flesh beneath. I did not avert my gaze this time but studied the outline of her breasts instead. If she wanted to flaunt it, I would oblige her.

She seemed surprised at my remark and quickly looked up at me, a grin widening on her face. "Does that bother you, too?" She drew her robe tighter, suppressing a laugh.

I wanted to leave but couldn't go until she dismissed me. It was a test of wills. She wanted to afflict me with bother. I ignored her question and looked up at the portrait.

Following my gaze, she released her laugh, a hearty ripple this time.

"That's my mother." She reached out and opened a lacquered box on the mantel, pulling out a long cigarette. "Be a dear and light this for me, will you?"

After finding matches, I did so. "She was quite a beauty," she said, blowing smoke up toward her mother's likeness. "Charmed everyone. Ask Marta. She worked for Mummy, as my nanny."

"Did Julia work for her, too?"

A look of irritation flickered across her face. "No. Julia's someone I picked up because ... she's a damned good cook. Someone I know suggested her."

When I said nothing, she continued. "I was born in San Francisco. My father was a shipping king. Owned a fleet of them. That's how Mummy and Daddy died. On a tour of the South Seas. Sunk in a typhoon."

She said it so matter-of-factly that it was hard to believe she'd wept a single tear for their passing. Just as I was forming this opinion of her cold heart, however, she reshaped it.

"That was a dark day," she murmured, so quiet it was hard to hear her. "The first of many. One would think, after so much darkness, one could expect a flicker of light..." She stared up at her mother's portrait, tears glistening in her eyes, looking as if she wanted her mother to comfort her or, perhaps, to tell her she was sorry.

She turned to me, her tone and face changing to something brighter. "But you know a thing or two about dark days, don't you? Living at Canfield under Brice Clement?"

"Were you very young when they died?" I asked.

"Yes." She shook her head. "No. Old enough to know better."

"Better than what?"

She turned to me, her head tilted to one side, and she let her lips push up into a smile, the same kind, I imagined, she turned on for the cameras when the direction called for joy. It held no joy. She didn't answer.

"How long have you dreamed of being a chauffeur?"

A cynical question that deserved no answer.

"Go ahead and be coy. You'll leave like all the rest. You'll get a screen test or find someone who can get you in to see Jack or Louie or Irving..." Her voice rose and filled the room as I reddened. No, I hadn't thought of screen tests. My interest was behind the camera, not in front of it. But she'd struck close enough to truth to make me sweat.

To keep myself from saying something I'd regret, I turned and stared at the fire. "I don't know what your other experiences have been," I said, "but you'll find I am responsible. I worked with Leo Bartenstein before—maybe Marta told you. And he found me very reliable." I left out the one moment of unreliability that had sunk me.

"Leo Bartenstein, the cameraman?"

"That's him. Done a lot in silents. But you'd know that."

"I hate that word." Her voice was low and soft, so warm it felt like velvet to hear, just the kind of voice they liked nowadays. The higher-pitched ones came off thin and squeaky. "They aren't silent to us. They are bursting with sound! Sets being constructed right next to your stage. Orchestra playing to feed the mood. And the director—always there, always coaching you, nudging you.... *You go to the window, you hear something, you're afraid, you see a face—could it be him? Yes, yes...you see him!* All the time you're performing, he's leading you through it, his voice becoming the voice in your head."

She took another sip of her drink. "And now with sound, my God, The silence that descends when the microphones are turned on. No one speaks but you. No one. It's like no one exists outside that silent stage, and you have to beg people to pay attention, so they can save you." She shivered, then laughed artificially. "You'll save me, won't you, John? Do you mind fetching me another drink?"

Being the servant, I did as I was told, pouring another martini and handing it to her. "I heard you've not made a talking picture yet," I said, remembering Leo's counsel.

She glowered at me. "We've all had to do new screen tests, John, for sound. I read a nursery rhyme in mine. And I've been on the set of a talking picture. Wretched afternoon it was. But I'm sure you know all this, being apprenticed to Mr. Bartenstein? How did that turn out?"

Again, I reddened. She might not know that story, but she'd find out soon enough, and her suspicions would be confirmed: that I was a climber, waiting for my chance.

So what? I might be ambitious, but she was drunk, and I don't like drunks. I knew, from my experience with my mother, that they are unpredictable. Sweet one moment, angry the next, unreliable always. And ultimately, sick. At least Marta would have to clean up after this one. Not me. I wasn't going to hang around to hear her crying about how bad she had it because she had to speak into a microphone while the world waited in awe to hear her. I moved away a step, changing the subject.

"Let me tell you about the automobiles," I said. "The Packard needs some transmission work … "

"My god, you smell good. Like soap." She leaned closer to me."Nothing else but soap. I could breathe you in all day." Closing her eyes, she swayed. I grabbed her arm to steady her.

"The transmission work," I continued, holding her arm while she stared at me, "might need a more skilled mechanic. I'll do what I can, but … "

"Do you think I'm pretty?" she asked, and scraped a long nail lightly along my cheek.

"I can recommend a mechanic …"

"That doesn't sound like a yes." She rested her hand on my arm to hold herself steady.

Damn it. If she wanted truth, she'd get it. "In an artificial way," I announced and lifted her hand from my arm to the mantle.

She barked out a laugh. "Well, now we know you're not a sycophant. So refreshing." She finished her drink and rested her hand again on my arm. "Why am I artificially pretty, John, and not a real beauty like my mother?" She waved a hand up to the painting.

I looked up at the portrait as well. "Your hair is ..."

"Dyed?"

"Isn't it?" I snapped.

She nodded like a child. "And I wear make-up."

"That too." I studied her face. Under the rouge and lip paint, the carefully-drawn eyebrows and the powder, was a perfectly-proportioned face with small nose and delicate lips, high cheekbones, and large eyes. Penetrating eyes. Her fingers dug into my arm. I swallowed.

"Here, let me help you." I pulled her hand in the crook of my arm and escorted her to the sofa. As we walked, I smelled her perfume. Something like lemons or oranges. She leaned heavily on me and hopped, stopping once after accidentally shifting her weight to the injured foot. She didn't cry out, but she sucked in her breath at the pain. A tear fell from her eye.

"Isn't that silly?" she said, sniffling. "It's just a sprain. Nothing to cry over."

I was hot. I wanted to leave. I'd ... I'd go tonight. I'd pack up and leave a note for Marta, and I'd find another job.

At the sofa, I placed the pillow again under her ankle.

"Maybe you could tell Marta to bring me some ice?" She looked up at me, and her eyes were still watery. "For my foot, that is." She leaned forward and rubbed it. "Just a sprain. It'll be fine in the morning. Nothing to worry about."

Nothing to worry about, Johnny. It's just a bruise. He didn't mean it. Get me some ice; that's a good boy.

She looked up at me. Her mood shifted, and she was the mistress of the estate again. "You really should get some new clothes, some evening clothes. We have some marvelous parties here. I might want you to come to one."

"This is about the best I have, Miss Sloane."

"Ellie. I told you already to call me Ellie."

I said nothing.

"I'll have Marta take your measurements, John. She'll ring up Devlin's, a tailor in the city that Robbie uses. They'll make you something." Her eyebrows flew upwards as if she'd just thought of something. "And don't worry. It's on me. A little bonus for pulling me out of that ditch this afternoon."

"Yes, ma'am."

She glared at me. I couldn't bring myself to call her Ellie.

"Say it." She closed her eyes waiting. I thought of how she'd looked at her mother's portrait. Did she long for a kind voice speaking her given name?

"Ellie."

She let out a close-mouthed sigh, as if I'd given her good news when she'd been expecting bad.

"That's all, John."

"Thank you." I stepped away, then paused. "Ellie." I hissed it, angrily.

Making my way out of the room as fast as possible, I nearly collided with Julia who was polishing silver just around the corner at a sideboard in a hallway. Her eyes met mine with a thousand mocking phrases. No longer hungry, I looked away and headed for the solace of my own bed.

Chapter Four

MISS PAULINE SLOANE was "a bit skittish," as Leo had predicted, but hell if I would let it get to me. That's what I told myself that evening when I left her presence, all hot and ready to quit.

As Leo would say, "The high and mighty, how they do fall." She could be on the brink of a fall herself as she approached her first talkie. I shouldn't be so harsh with judgment.

Besides, a decent paycheck, good food, a roof over my head — those were things I wouldn't let her take away from me, boss or not. I'd be a good worker. I could stay out of her way. I didn't even live in the same building, for crissake. I had the cars. I had Marta and even Julia as company. I had my books and sketchpad. I had my friend, Leo, who I could count on to fill me in on Pauline Sloane's troubles. And most of all, I had my history. It was a shield against all intruders.

During the next few days, I did not see Ellie, or Pauline, or whatever she was called. She was going to hold a party, Marta informed me, something to "let everyone know she is back." The household seemed to speed up. It wasn't a comfortable feeling.

First of all, there was more noise. Not just the eternal gurgle of that fountain, but music, sometimes late into the night. She must have owned a large collection of recordings because I heard every popular tune that had come across Jake's radio the month I had stayed there — I Want to Be Bad, Heigh-Ho, and jazz hits by Negro orchestras. These kept me awake some nights, and I had to work real hard to get myself into a place where the narcotic of sleep would overtake me at last.

Sometimes her voice cut through the clear air, calling

Marta or laughing or talking on the telephone. And there was now the daily sound of glass being thrown into the trash. She was always drinking. Empty bottles filled the garbage bin every day, and I swore I could smell it on the air even in the kitchen, along with the odor of her strong cigarettes.

Marta and Julia used my services more, averaging a ride into the city at least once a day, to buy food, supplies, or pick up special orders. And to pick up crates of mail from the post office which Marta had let languish until Miss Sloane's return.

"The fans." Marta smiled at me as I lugged the heavy box to the car. "They love her. They write to her every day."

Because of this, I was busier than ever, often poring over maps of the area, so that I didn't need to ask for directions, and doing more with cars, either washing them, or making sure they had gas, or fixing a broken gasket or wire. When I wasn't busy with those chores, I helped out around the estate doing odd jobs — everything from tightening a leaky pipe in the kitchen to getting an extra generator going in the field house near the vineyard.

I liked that job. It took me out into a quiet place again, like Sloane Hall had been before she'd returned.

The vineyard was not a working farm, but merely part of the property when Miss Sloane purchased it. While Marta hired workers to tend it, this was more an act of charity than a money-making operation. Or maybe it was merely art on display for the pleasure of its owner. Miss Sloane, Marta told me, liked to look at the vines. She found them soothing.

Marta told me these things when she took my measurements in an awkward session the day after my meeting with Miss Sloane. I had wanted to forgo the task, thinking that it was the result of drunken generosity, which, in my experience, lasted no longer than the fog from the alcohol. So I had been surprised when Marta, after breakfast that day, had told me to step over to the cupboard where she pulled out a measuring tape and pad and pencil. While Julia laughed quietly, Marta stretched the tape from shoulder to wrist, waist to ankle, and more.

"I will telephone these in today." Marta stood upright and rolled up her tape.

"I really don't want to make extra work for you," I said.

"It is not extra work. It is something Miss Sloane wants." Marta smiled at me, easing my discomfort. "She is a generous lady."

Whatever she was, I was thinking about her too much. The more I tried not to, the more she wandered into my mind. I found myself mentally practicing the things I should have said when I'd met her, when I'd found out who she was, when she'd questioned me again and mocked me. I saw myself laughing back at her and saying "I knew who you were all along. Did you think you fooled me? I fooled you!"

I still couldn't seem to master letting things go. Yet that lesson was as easy as breathing when nothing was bothering me. I'd heard it, agreed with it, intended to live it when Rev. Milqueton took over Canfield and told me it was his job to take away my excuses. When he first had come into our lives there, I'd learned to stay out of trouble by staying out of the way. But my heart had been a mess of mischief, nothing good, just waiting for someone to light the fuse attached to my dark thoughts. He'd made sure I knew I couldn't escape his gaze or his expectations. When I was brought into his office for poor performance in class, he'd looked through my records, stared at me in silence, and then closed my file with such a clap that I'd jumped in my seat.

"My job is to make sure you leave this here when you go." His bony finger had jammed at the file. "Your past doesn't make you special in any way. My job is to take away all your excuses, so you can begin to save yourself and live again. And if you choose to sin instead, it will be a conscious choice, not one predicated on the excuses in this file."

First time I'd met him, I'd thought he was a joke of a man, who'd be just as bad as Brice Clement, or worse. He'd proven me wrong. He taught me the value of a man who means what he says.

So when thoughts of Miss Sloane started to tempt me to

retaliate, I thought back to Milqueton's words, as if they'd set me right just by their repetition. *If you choose to sin instead, it will be a conscious choice.* I would not sin again. I wouldn't give her the satisfaction.

About a week after my visit with Miss Sloane, I returned to my rooms late in the day and fixed a leaking faucet. Tired, I was thinking of rest, of reading in the evening and of writing a letter. In two days' time, I'd have another afternoon off, and I decided to finish the walk that was aborted when I'd met Miss Sloane. My dreaming was interrupted by Julia, who knocked at the door of my rooms even though it was open.

"Devlin's just delivered these," she said, handing me a box. "They said the rest would be ready next Friday."

Like a child at Christmas, I ripped the paper away.

It wasn't what I'd expected. Instead of a new suit, a gray chauffeur's uniform with a double row of shiny buttons down its front lay neatly folded in the box.

I didn't realize until that moment of disappointment that somehow in the back of my mind I had hoped for a gift, had looked forward to it, had even built up a specific desire — for clothes I could use after this job was over. So much for avoiding sin.

I hid my disappointment from Julia, who stood and watched while I pulled the uniform from the box. This is your place, John Doyle, I thought to myself.

Shaking my head, I fingered the heavy cloth. It was good material, not cheap, a wool of some kind.

"Very nice," I said for Julia's benefit.

"Miss Sloane says you only need to wear the uniform when you drive the Duesenberg," Julia said.

Was she smirking? It didn't matter. Wearing the dandified chauffeur's uniform was a small price to pay to drive that grand automobile.

"You are needed at the house," Julia added.

I put the uniform back in its box. "What for?"

"Marta will show you."

She didn't wait for me, so I headed to the kitchen where

Marta instructed me to look at a busted drain pipe near the sun room. After retrieving the tool kit, I made fast work of the task, standing on a ladder outside the house while I maneuvered two pieces of pipe back into place. Dinner time neared, and I was hungry. The scent of Julia's cooking drifted up to my perch.

While I worked, I couldn't help but overhear the mistress of the house on the phone. She was angry, actually hanging up on her caller at one point, then impulsively picking it up and asking to be put through again. Her frustration gave me pleasure.

"If you come home, I promise I'll be a good girl. I need you. You know I start filming soon ...."

Another pause.

"There's one tonight. Uh-huh." Then something I couldn't make out. Just the tone — regret, desperation. And then: "All right. But you promise — no later than next week! I'm having a party. I'll need you *here*."

After the repair was done, I headed back to the garage where I planned to spend the time before dinner polishing the Duesenberg. I'd looked forward to this task all day, even putting it off to the afternoon because of the sense of ease it offered.

I was barely into the job when she silently appeared.

"Have the car ready at eight, John," she said.

"Yes, ma'am," I replied, and she didn't correct me and ask me to call her "Eleanor." I remembered her voice on the phone. *I'll need you here.* She needed something, someone, and that made me wary. Brice had been at his cruelest when he couldn't have something he wanted. Leo's warning to be careful came to mind as well.

"I'm going to the Trocadero and then to the Goldwyns' party." She shoved her hands into the pockets of her wide sailor-style trousers and watched me polish the Duesenberg.

"You'll want this car then, I assume?"

"Yes."

From the depths of one pocket, she pulled a cigarette and

asked me to light it. She enjoyed having someone do that for her. My goal was to make it in Hollywood somehow, some way. Lighting a star's cigarette was as good a way as any. After retrieving a match from a nearby cabinet, I walked to the edge of the bay.

"Fire and gasoline don't mix," I said, waiting for her to follow me. She did, with an amused smile on her face, as if I were fussy. I tensed. I was a fool to think I had the upper hand with her.

When I held the flame to the end of her smoke, her hand was not steady, trembling bad enough to make her blush. After the cigarette was lit, she swiftly waved her hand in the air, as if to banish the memory of her shakes.

"You don't like me," she said and blew smoke at me to emphasize her point.

That's right, I wanted to spit. Only a bitch of a boss would ask that question. Either I lied and swallowed my bile, or I told the truth and risked my job.

I said nothing. Instead I retrieved my cloth and resumed polishing the car.

"You think I have it easy, and yet I feel sorry for myself." She leaned against the car so that I had to go around her. Her stomach was flat under the oversized trousers, and the silky top she wore was almost transparent. I continued staring at the car once I was past her. So this is why the first chauffeur left, I thought. You couldn't win this game.

"Did you hear me?" she asked, her arm arching down to tap ash from the smoke.

"Yes."

"Then why don't you answer?"

"I'm not sure what to say."

"Say the truth. That's one of the things I liked about you when I first met you. Nobody talks the truth out here. Nobody even remembers what it sounds like."

Without looking at her, I kept polishing. I hadn't given her the whole truth, though. I hadn't shared my ambitions. But she knew those already, didn't she?

"I don't know you well enough to form an opinion," I said evenly.

She inhaled a puff of smoke again, and it was clear she didn't care about my response. She just wanted to go on with her excuses for self-pity. "You know, everybody out here started poor. Even Goldwyn himself. My god, you should hear the stories about him. Walked hundreds of miles to get a boat to America. Jack Warner, too — poor as dirt and worked his way up. They all moved up in the world."

I stopped and stared at her. "But not you."

She shook her head. "No, not me. I moved down. And I keep wondering when I'll stop." Her eyes were wide and — bleary, unfocused.

"I sometimes wish I knew how to live like that, like all the ones who started poor. If I knew ... well, then, I wouldn't have to work so hard to keep all this." She swept her hand around toward the house. "And I do work hard, John. You know that, don't you?"

"Yes," I said, hoping she'd go away. She might work hard, but at what? Fooling people. What kind of work was that?

But she felt she hadn't made her case.

"Let me put it to you this way." She smashed the cigarette out under her foot and turned to me, putting her hands on my shoulders. Light as feathers. "Let's say I did this...."

She leaned forward and kissed me. It was so sudden I didn't have a chance to pull back, and once her lips were on mine, I didn't want to. She was warm and soft and sweet. Her breath carried the perfume of wine, and any man would want her. My hands found her waist and held fast. My body responded.

A bird chirped. Or the dog barked. Something. Something to break the mood. I found myself. Not with her. It would cost me my job. Was that what she wanted to teach me — how easy it was to lose your place in life? With both hands, I pushed her away. I wanted to slap her. But I held myself back. Thank god, I held myself back.

"Hey—I was supposed to do that!" She pouted with real irritation.

"So I'd know what it felt like to move down in the world like you?" I said with disgust.

I wiped my mouth with the back of my hand, which seemed to anger her even more. She shoved her hands in her pockets, where her balled fists made her knuckles protrude. "What I was going to say... was that if you enjoyed that, and it was taken away, you'd hurt. But if you'd never enjoyed it— kissing me that is—then you wouldn't miss it. Oh, hell, maybe you're not that kind of guy. What a waste!"

She squared her shoulders and walked off toward the house. But I wasn't about to let her think I was some queer just because I wouldn't let her use me as a toy.

"I'm not a fairy," I called after her. And for good measure, I spat out her name. "Eleanor."

Over her shoulder, without looking at me, she said, "Don't worry, *Mister Doyle*. Your *honor* is safe with me."

Hell. This was a fine way to impress someone with connections in Hollywood. Why couldn't I have just kissed her and be done with it? My god—pride even got in the way of the natural pull of man toward woman. I went back to my task, and if I had continued to polish the car like I did that afternoon, nothing would have been left of its finish within a week. Lucky for it, Marta called me to the kitchen for an early supper, so I put my things away and washed up, determined to forget about this latest incident. It's a good job, I reminded myself. Take the money, live the life, forget about the rest. Find out how often "Eleanor" is away.

In the kitchen, a little while later, I had my chance.

"Miss Sloane—how often is she here?" I asked, trying to sound casual.

Marta passed me a steaming bowl of soup. She shrugged. "She has only had this house two years. She has been here most of that time."

"She never takes a holiday?"

"No."

My heart sank.

"This is good," Marta said to Julia, looking at the soup and then at me. "The *Señorita* sent her to cooking school. She did very well."

Julia's mouth pursed into a sour grin. To my surprise, she spoke, and it didn't escape my notice that she changed the subject. I wondered how many of us at the estate had something in our pasts we'd rather not talk about.

"Don't forget to give me the menu for the party," Julia said to Marta. "I have made my suggestions a day ago ,and still you have not told me what she wishes me to make."

"She has not made up her mind. When she does, I will tell you," Marta said. The housekeeper then turned her attention and good spirits to me, asking me how the automobiles were running, whether I was warm enough at night in my quarters, and finally, if I wanted to borrow any more books from the Sloane library. "The *Señorita* said to make sure you know you are free to borrow whatever you like."

After that afternoon's encounter with her, I couldn't imagine her having a kind thought about me. Her offer didn't ease my mind. If anything, it made me angrier. Baiting and teasing one moment, benevolent the next. She was a tyrant, just like all people with wealth and power.

Not all people, a small voice inside reminded me. Not like Milqueton. Not like Jake. Jake, after all, had not been cruel. Hold fast, I told myself. Hold fast to these memories, not the others.

"What is the matter, John? You look feverish." Marta sipped at her coffee while she gazed at me, a motherly frown creasing her forehead.

"Nothing. Just warm."

After dinner, I went back to my rooms, washed up and changed. The uniform was scratchy and heavy, and I looked like a toy soldier in it. I was almost embarrassed to walk outside, afraid Julia would laugh at me.

To hell with her, too, I thought as I straightened my cap. This is my job, and I'll do what it takes to keep it. Things could be worse. Unlike Miss Sloane, I was rising in the world, not falling. I could take the inconveniences along the way.

At the appointed hour, I pulled the Duesenberg out of the garage and drove it around the cackling fountain to the front door where I waited. And waited and waited. Marta came out after I'd been standing by the car for a half hour to tell me that "Miss Sloane is almost ready."

As I waited, I perspired in unusual twilight heat. If she didn't appear soon, I'd have to retreat to my rooms and wash up again.

At last, a good forty-five minutes after eight, she appeared. She was dressed all in white, a long shiny dress with a deep neckline. Her arms were hidden in a draping wrap of soft, chestnut-colored fur. Her make-up and hair were perfect. Neat waves of platinum shining in the light from the windows, alabaster skin and long smoldering eyelashes, deep red lips—she looked like she would break if handled too roughly. She didn't glance at me, but focused instead on the steps, her bag, the hem of her dress.

As I held the door for her, I wondered who she was tonight. Was she the woman who'd told Marta I could use the library? Or was she the tease who'd baited me in the garage that afternoon?

"Do you know where it is?" she asked after I got behind the wheel.

"Yes, ma'am." I adjusted the mirror and saw her frowning at me.

She drummed her fingers on the seat next to her. "You know I don't like that, yet you use it all the same." Her voice sounded like a child's, hurt and cross.

Women are so easily hurt. My mother would weep if her favorite dress was stained. Or when a rose from a suitor died.

"Eleanor."

Her head came up, and she stared at me in the mirror. Although I scoured her face for signs of mockery, I found none.

"I know it seems silly," she said, "but I so rarely get to

hear my given name. It will be our little secret, all right? You call me Eleanor. And I'll call you John."

I didn't point out that she had that privilege without my permission. She was already tipsy. Even from the front seat, I could smell the gin. And by the time we got to the Trocadero, she'd sipped from a flask several times, making no effort to hide it. At least she didn't lie to herself.

When I held the door for her to exit, she smiled at me. "I shouldn't be longer than two hours. Just meeting someone. In fact, I offered him a ride to the party. Don't go far!"

Not wanting to be absent when she came out of the restaurant, I didn't go anywhere. I sat in the car, hat and gloves by my side on the passenger seat, cursing myself for not bringing something to occupy the time. A book or a sketchpad would have done. Like the nature I observed on my occasional walks, this place was a study in wildness all its own. Sparkling women and well-dressed men entered and left the restaurant, followed by laughter and music, by the smell of sizzling steaks in the air.

I got out and leaned against the car to catch some air, and another chauffeur stepped out of his car as well, a black V-16 Cadillac. "You can get a sandwich in the kitchen," he said, lighting a cigarette. "They won't charge you, either, if you're in your uniform."

"Thanks." I didn't want to leave the car or risk not being there when Miss Sloane, Eleanor, returned.

"Roland Maguire's my name," he said, holding out his hand to shake. He was friendly-looking, with dark hair combed straight back. Lucky for him, he was also big, because his navy blue uniform would have made a smaller boy look girly—blousy riding pants and tall black boots. At least I didn't have to wear something like that. My uniform had straight-legged trousers.

"I drive for Irving Thalberg," he said.

"Pauline Sloane," I offered, and he nodded when I said her name.

He smoked in silence for a while, then spoke again.

"Hubert was Miss Sloane's chauffeur before you. Hubert Towle."

Yes, I wanted to know about him, what happened to him, but I didn't want to ask. I'd get the story from Leo next time I saw him.

After a few more puffs on his smoke, Roland continued, but his offerings were slim. "He went East I think."

"Another job?" I asked, trying to sound nonchalant.

"Not that I know of."

"Family." I said it as if I knew it to be true.

"Nope. Just wanted to get as far away as he could." Roland pulled a flask from his pocket and offered me some, but I shook my head. After he'd taken his own drink and put it in his pocket, he looked at me from the corner of his eye. "You meet Morgan yet?"

"No." I didn't even know who Morgan was, but I guessed he was the man Julia had asked about and Marta had spoken with on the telephone. The man Eleanor needed here.

"Morgan doesn't like chauffeurs much." He said it as a warning, and I took it as such, putting it together with Leo's cautions.

For the rest of our wait, Roland and I talked amiably. He was from a small town in Washington State and had gotten out as soon as he could, looking for warmer and more prosperous times. Although he'd hoped to get into acting, he'd had to supplement his meager earnings as an extra with "real work." When the position as Thalberg's chauffeur had come open, he'd landed the job, pretending he knew how to drive.

"I taught myself on his driveway." He laughed. "And told him something was wrong with the danged motor when I stripped the gears learning!"

Because he was so talkative, there was little chance for me to share my own story. I only told him I'd come here from Texas, and both my parents were dead, but had gotten out little beyond that before the door to the restaurant opened and four people exited. My employer was among them, on the arm of a tall, self-confident man.

When she saw me, she waved and called out. "We're all piling into Irving's car, John. Just follow us to the Goldwyns."

The man at her elbow whispered something to her, and she laughed, and I couldn't help but think that it was a joke at my expense. Shoving the hat on my head, I got back into the Duesenberg and started the engine too quickly. It screeched and fell silent, and I had to try again. Meanwhile, Roland was on the road with his full car. Miss Sloane, Eleanor, was in the seat by the window. As they drove by, she waved again and threw me a kiss. I cursed and started the engine successfully.

I didn't bother to keep up with Roland, whose driving skills still needed work, in my opinion. He raced and then slowed down, took curves too widely, and nearly ran an old Buick off the road.

There was no hurry. I knew once we got to the Goldwyn house there would be more waiting, and, besides, the ride calmed me, carrying my anger out the window with the passing breeze, with the sense I was leaving bad things behind as long as I stayed in motion.

I didn't make it to the grand house on Camino Palmero in time to see her go in, but I did see Roland talking to other drivers by the garage where they admired the Goldwyns' magnificent Rolls-Royce, parked by a more workaday blue Packard. While taking off his jacket, Roland motioned me over and introduced me. Like me, he was sweating—large dark stains decorated his shirt under the heavy coat.

The other drivers were a mixed lot, some rough boys and some, like Roland, who were waiting for their chance to leap to the silver screen themselves. It was an instructive evening. The other boys looked up to Roland, whose boss evoked awe-struck tones when his name was mentioned. Whether that was because of Roland's own nature, or his boss's stature, was unclear to me. Someone mentioned Victor Fleming, a director who'd started out in this town doing just what we were doing, driving stars around.

There was no risk of boredom here. The bustling kitchen help served us ham sandwiches and pie, and we played cards in a corner of the drive hidden by the cars. From inside the house, music and shouts of laughter were so loud that we sometimes had to strain to be heard amongst ourselves. Some of the other boys told stories of whoring and drinking. Some talked about their employers. I held my tongue. Now that I'd been forewarned about Morgan, whoever he was, I intended to walk straight and narrow down the path of responsibility.

Hours later, people drifted from the party, and the boys snapped to attention, rushing to don jackets and caps and fetch cars, an army called to duty. One by one, they drove off into the black night, Roland among them. Soon, there were only a couple of us left.

And. eventually, only me.

There is something about the loneliness of night, the empty sound a stone makes when it's accidentally kicked down a drive drenched in moonlight. There's something about it that takes each grievance of the day and writes it large across the sky to scream and taunt you, to cry out for action. As I waited in that empty moonlight, a wrong word would have sent me into a fighting crouch. Where was she?

Some of the guests drove their own cars, so while the drive was still filled with a few roadsters and Packards and even a Peerless, I was the only chauffeur in sight. I didn't have a watch, but I figured it must be approaching dawn. I settled into the car to wait. Pushing my cap back on my head, I slumped in the front seat and closed my eyes.

In a few minutes—or was it an hour—I heard a noise. A ripple of her laughter cutting the night as birds' songs cut the morning. It was unique yet familiar, and, in my hazy half-awake state, I thought of my mother and her laugh when she'd come home from a spree, of that light-hearted, no-trouble-in-the-world laugh that filled me with both sorrow and relief—relief that she'd found something joyful, and sorrow that she'd found it in something artificial and unworthy. She was her most lovable and her most hateful during those times—sweet and funny and vulnerable, she always made me smile. But the key—and even now I swallow hard thinking of it—the key to her joy sickened both her and me. And after awhile I couldn't separate the happiness from the sadness that would follow. So you see, she ruined happiness for me, making it a question and not an answer, or a question whose answer was sometimes light, but more often dark, and always unknown, always something to fear.

Sitting up straight, I prepared to turn on the engine, as I focused my vision on Eleanor coming out of the door.

Spilling out of the door was more accurate. My lips pressed tight, I looked at her careen down the steps, as a man—a different one from the one she'd met before—tried to steer her. But he was just as intoxicated as she was and weaved dangerously from side to side. I was about to get out to help her when their feet landed safely on the path together, both of them laughing uproariously at their stupid drunken dance.

Her fur slipped off her shoulders, and he caught her in a vise-like grip by holding tight onto the sleeves against her body. He pushed her against a car, and I distinctly heard her say "No!" in a high, tight voice. My blood rose. I saw him ignore her protestations and bow his head down close to hers. He was forcing himself on her.

With a rush, leaving the door hanging open, I left the car and ran toward the man. I pulled at his shoulder and yelled for her to make a dash to the car. Here was the action I'd craved earlier—vengeance, retribution, justice.

"Get off her," I said in a stern voice, the voice of Rev. Milqueton when things went bad, and my fists tingled with anticipation at my side. I wanted to beat him. Twice her weight and nearly a foot taller. What kind of a man ...

She didn't run for the car. She stayed where she was, bent over, unable to catch her breath as the laughs broke over her like waves.

"John, John, what the hell are you doing?" she managed to sputter, while the man, who had looked ready to strike me as quickly as I was ready to hit him, relaxed and laughed as well. He pulled a cigarette from a pocket and lit it while

Eleanor regained her composure. "You weren't trying to rescue me, were you? Ohmygod, you were! How precious! You sweet boy!" Her gloved hand stroked my cheek, but I pulled my head away.

Johnny, my sweet boy, what would I do without you to protect me?

I turned on my heel and went back to the car where I sat fuming, warm in the summer air in the damned uniform, hot from humiliation. As I yanked my collar open, I heard her laughing and talking with the man and then the click of her heels on the walkway and the tap of her finger on the passenger window. Acting startled, as if I hadn't known she had been approaching, I snapped to attention, got out of the car and went around to open her door to the back seat.

After we were both inside, she lit a cigarette and waved her fingers good-bye to the man who'd attacked her.

"That was Howard Hughes you were saving me from."

I said nothing.

"What are you waiting for?" she asked.

"Are we giving him a lift?"

"God, no! He has some new one-of-a-kind sports car. I'm surprised you didn't notice it."

Pressing the accelerator pedal, I peeled away, making her jolt back in her seat.

"Damn!" she cried. "Watch it!"

I drove east on Franklin and north up Outpost Drive, now gray in mysterious shadows, the expensive homes silent and scolding.

"When I need someone to help me out in a pinch, I'll let you know," she said coldly.

I made no reply. The road was clear. We'd be home in twenty minutes or so. I was looking forward to sleep.

She let out an irritated groan. "So you're giving me the cold shoulder, are you? Let me remind you who's the employer around here."

I touched my hat as if in salute. "Yes, ma'am!"

"Hah!" She blew smoke out so forcefully I felt her breath

on my neck. "You're jealous."

My hands gripped the steering wheel, and I clenched my teeth.

"You *are* jealous," she continued softly, maliciously. "You couldn't have me, so you didn't want anyone else to. That's the truth, John. You're good at truth."

I slammed on the brakes causing her to roll forward.

"What's gotten into you?"

"An animal crossing the road, *ma'am*. That's all." I breathed deeply, flexed my stiff fingers, and stared into the rear-view mirror at her wide, frightened eyes. "I was just trying to protect you. Perhaps I should have asked permission first."

Now she was the silent one, and we took off up the hill, both of us lost in our mute recriminations.

When I pulled the car up to the front door of Sloane Hall, the kitchen light was on, and I saw Marta's shadow. She'd waited up like a mother for her daughter.

Although still irritated, I was eager to get to bed and to sleep, tired after a full day and a long evening, and in need of some time alone to reason out what bothered me, what tangled up everything around her.

When I opened the car door, though, she didn't immediately exit. After a last long puff, she threw her cigarette onto the gravel then swiveled around in the seat to crush it with her foot. Her shapely leg stretched out beyond her dress, her dimpled knee showing, the tops of her stockings and a lace garter glowing in the milky moonlight. Her ankle was completely healed by now. No swelling marred its perfect angles. As she stood, she gripped my arm for balance, and, by the time her body was fully erect, she was so close to me that her eyelashes could have brushed my cheek if she'd blinked.

But she didn't blink. She lifted her head and stared straight into my eyes. Deeply, slowly, she whispered, "Thanks for trying to save me, John," and squeezed my other arm with her free hand.

Something shifted inside me like the gears on that

magnificent automobile when it clicked into second. Her body's heat was a magnet, and I was too tired now to resist any urges of mine or hers. Eleanor. She'd asked to be called Eleanor. She wanted to be touched. She wanted to be kissed. I took off my hat and bent to her …

And as I was about to kiss her, I saw the right corner of her mouth twitch up.

She was laughing at me again! Straightening, I replaced my hat and removed her hand from my arm.

"You're drunk, Eleanor, and you need to sleep it off," I said, as if she were my equal. "Go to bed."

She laughed again. This was all part of the joke, as if she'd planned it to end this way.

"G'night, John, you silly boy." She walked away toward the steps, teetering a little as her heel sank unevenly into the gravel. When I didn't go to help her, she stopped and beckoned me with a wave. In two steps, I had her elbow and guided her to the firmer surface. Walking up three steps until she was even with me, she turned and bestowed on me the kiss I would not steal. It was quick and wet and smelled like brandy and smoke and her and it lasted as long as she wanted it to. I did not pull away.

"There," she said when she was finished, "now you know what you'd be missing if I never kissed you again. Now you know what it's like to be me." The laugh was still in her voice as she went into the house, leaving me standing below on the gravel path.

Chapter Five

SHADOWS OF LEAVES danced across the paned grid of my window as late morning sunlight streamed into my room. I lay on my back, arms behind my head.

At Canfield, bars on the windows had tempered any pleasure at a view like this in the still early moments before morning prayer. The bars had been an unnecessary addition, put in place by Brice one year after a twelve-year-old in on a burglary charge escaped. Anyone who was really interested in leaving Canfield only had to pry up some rotting boards. The bars were merely a show, something Brice Clement could let the authorities see, something that said he'd fixed a problem.

No, the real bars at Canfield weren't the hard steel that stretched across windows, or the wire fence that would cut you to the quick if you decided to force your way through. The real bars were the town and the acres of land beyond it.

Canfield sat on the edge of a town of the same name, a small place with few residents, its well-being dependent on the reform school. The most successful businesses were those that sold food and supplies to the Home.

You ran away from the Home, and everybody in town would know. They knew their neighbor's business as well as their own. I often thought the residents of Canfield were imprisoned as much as we were. They had no body of anonymous souls surrounding them, nothing to run to or turn to for distraction or comfort, nothing to make them feel bigger or smaller than they actually were. They were alone, as alone as we were in our prison. Small towns, I decided in my stay at Canfield, are a special kind of hell.

I awoke with a dry ache in my throat and head. For those few moments I didn't stir, trying to ground myself as fragments of the day before came back to me. As each memory of Eleanor's changeable behavior returned, a gloom settled over me that weighted me to the bed. She was like the rest, like Brice, like my stepfather! I had to leave. It was becoming a whispered order in the back of my mind, as constant and easy to ignore as the fountain's eternal rush. I couldn't work for someone like that, who would mete out pleasure or pain at whim. No wonder Leo had been reluctant to recommend this place for me.

And yet, I knew I wouldn't leave. Another prison.

I got out of bed, heaved a breath, and washed the sleep from my face. As I came out of the bathroom, towel in hand, I heard a soft knock at my door.

"*Señor* Doyle, are you up?"

It was Marta. I threw on some clothes and went to greet her. She was carrying a heavy tray with coffee and toast on it.

"When you have the late nights, I fix breakfast for you since you miss it at the big house," she explained, putting the tray on my little table. She waited on me, pouring coffee into a cup, stirring in cream the way she knew I liked it.

"You're sure you're not ill?" she asked, handing the cup to me. "You looked so flushed last night."

"No, I'm fine." I drank the strong brew and let it rouse me to life. "What time is it?"

"Nearly eleven. I will need to go to the market this afternoon, sometime before three."

"I can be ready sooner."

"Well, maybe around one would be better."

"Will my services be needed elsewhere?" I took a bite of toast not because I was hungry, but because I knew Marta expected me to eat.

"She will go out this evening again. I will let you know where and when."

I forced myself to smile.

"I can be ready at a moment's notice."

She patted my hand. "You are a good boy."

After she left, I bathed and shaved. And then my routine began. I gave Marta a ride to the market, I fixed a loose gasket in the Nash, I washed some shirts, and most of all, I waited. Now my time was divided between when I was working for Eleanor and when I was *waiting* to work for her. During those times, I devised schemes, ways in which I'd cleverly get information on who was looking for camera help at the studios, or what directors were most respected, or what cameramen, like Leo, knew the ropes.

Marta didn't tell me until supper what the evening duties would be.

"She will need you to drive her to the Warners' house at nine. But she says she will not need you to stay."

The full meaning of this became clear when I dropped her off at the party that evening. She was dressed in a yellow gown, something like satin. It floated around her ankles and wrists and outlined her body so that nothing was hidden.

Before going into the house, she leaned down and whispered into the open passenger window: "Don't bother coming back. If no one offers to take me home, I'm through anyway." Then she threw me a wink that was as staged as her haughty walk up the steps to the door, her back straight, her shoulders proud, walking as if to a trial, not a celebration.

This was the "hard work" she talked about, looking good, making men lust for her, just so they'd put her on a screen for others to want and like her, too. All to keep what she'd known before, all to support the life she couldn't give up.

You would have thought it'd be an easy night for me, knowing I didn't have to wait for her. Didn't have to fret about what games she'd play at night's end when gin tickled her cruel side to life. But like Marta, I waited up that night all the same, listening as I lay on my bed for the sound of a car on the gravel. Listening and watching the moonglow paint my room in shadows.

Dawn was just a few hours away when I heard her child-like giggle and rambling thanks to the man who'd seen her to the door, followed by a whispered conversation and quick pause as she let him kiss her before going in. I know because I arched up to spy on her, my face so close to the window I could smell the sill's paint.

In the next few days, I heard that giggle often, and it became a marker of time, just as a rooster crowing marked the dawn.

No use dwelling on the past, Milqueton had told me. *No use dwelling on anything that causes trouble.* I threw myself into my routine with more vigor, doing everything at double time—my work, my walks, my drawing, and writing a letter or two to the Reverend and others back at the Home who might share some concern about my fate. And I even got a chance to go in to the studio to see Leo, catching him at the end of an early day's shoot, hacking so hard he could barely talk to me.

"You should get that checked," I said, pointing to his balled up handkerchief.

He shook his head. "Already have."

"What they say?" I asked, but I could tell from the way he didn't look at me that I didn't really want to know.

"They got this machine, see, and they're telling me if I come in regular they'll use it on my lungs and clean 'em all up. I think I'll try it, Johnny. What have I got to lose? He laughed, which quickly deteriorated into a cough that went on too long for anything but grim determination when he was through.

"You sure it's okay—this machine?" I knew Leo didn't like newfangled things. He still clung to the idea, as many in Hollywood had for the past few years, that sound would be a passing fancy or that at least silents would continue to be popular along with the new talking pictures. Not a single trade publication had listed sound as one of the past year's biggest innovations, he'd told me once, as if it proved his faith.

"Something to do with x-rays," he said as we walked to his car. "I'm willing to give it a shot if it offers me a chance. But if it don't—that's the way it is. When you get to my age, you get awfully tired of people leaving, Johnny. You begin to miss 'em before they go. I spend a lot of time missing folks who ain't even gone yet."

We'd arrived at his car, and, now that I knew how ill he was, I didn't want to delay him with questions about work or complaints about Pauline Sloane. But he guessed the reason for my visit.

"Nothing opening up just yet for a boy like you," he said, "but maybe in a few months. I hear Paramount's shooting something big soon. And Goldwyn always has some crazy idea up his sleeve. He's a shrewd one, keeping the Banky mess in the can until he had something better to release. And I'll be talking to Walter Lundin—he's Harold Lloyd's cinematographer, been with him from the dawn of creation— next week, so I'll see if he knows of anything...." He peered at me, half-amused, half-worried. "Is it that bad up there?" He shrugged toward the general direction of the hills.

"Not too bad. You were right about Miss Sloane, though. She sure is nervous."

Leo chuckled. "They all are. Watch out for that agent of hers, Morgan. I hear he's trying to get her schedule moved up so she'll release before Garbo."

Garbo's first talkie would be in production soon.

"How's he gonna do that?" Pauline Sloane might be a star, but Garbo outshone them all.

Leo shook his head. "Offer 'em the sun and the moon. Or the star herself."

I could guess what he meant. I'd heard of auditions where a studio chief wanted more from an actress than a screen test. My stomach turned.

"You keep an eye on yourself up there," Leo continued. "Don't be falling into no she-traps."

"Is that what happened to the last fellow?" I asked.

"The last fellow..." He stood, trying to remember. "Could have been her. More likely Morgan that chased him away."

And that was all of our conversation, unsatisfying and sad, one more worry to add to my growing pile. As I left him, I felt a burden of guilt settle on my shoulders. I was always asking him about work, and I'd not once mentioned to Eleanor that Leo had some friends who could play piano at parties.

附

Lucky for me, Miss Sloane's big party was approaching,

and there was plenty to do. No time for moping. The entire house was in a stew getting ready for it. Extra workers showed up during the day to trim bushes and clean the pool. Several young ladies came in one afternoon for a training session with Julia and Marta on serving the guests. How Julia preened and strutted for that poor crew, humiliating them with a glance, a sharp word, a cruel laugh. I liked the looks of one or two of them, too. Sweet girls with freckled faces and long hair.

My other new clothes arrived as well, and, this time, I was not disappointed.

Inside several boxes, wrapped in tissue and tied with ribbon, were four new shirts, neatly sewn and pressed, a new gray pinstripe suit, and a black evening suit, the kind I believed they called a tuxedo. I tried them on and felt important. These duds would help me in this town. It would have taken me months to afford them on my own.

Remembering the lessons about gratitude Reverend Milqueton had taught us, I penned a short note thanking Miss Sloane for the clothes. Several times I tore up what I was writing and started fresh. I wanted to strike just the right balance between gratefulness and independence, yet I wanted to make sure I didn't sound as if I were lecturing her about making grand gestures to poor employees. I didn't want her to know I remembered the kiss. I worked on it over a couple days' time.

When my note was as right as I could make it, I took it into Marta one afternoon and asked her to present it to the mistress of the house.

"You can give it to her yourself," she said. She was counting wine glasses in a cabinet by the door to the hallway. "She wants to see you."

Did this mean I was supposed to go looking for her or wait to be called into her presence?

Neither. Miss Sloane herself appeared behind Marta. She was frowning and tapping a pencil against a leather-bound address book.

Upon catching sight of me, her lips turned further

downward, a real scowl of irritation. If she had wanted to see me, now didn't seem like a good time. I turned to leave.

"Don't go. Didn't Marta just tell you I want to talk to you?"

I obeyed and turned back toward her, staring at her now. No make-up heightened her cheekbones or bruised her lips. Her skin was nearly white, with just a dusting of light freckles under her eyes, making me think of those other young girls they'd hired for the party. Her clothes were less exotic as well. A simple white shirt was paired with tan wide-legged trousers. And she was sober.

"I was going to come looking for you, but here you are," she said, obviously tired. "You promised to show me your drawings. You never did."

"I didn't know when would be convenient, ma'am."

As soon as I said "ma'am," her eyes narrowed, and her cheeks reddened. She stared at me like she wanted to slap me. Oddly, this satisfied me. Bringing someone to the edge of that kind of anger is a form of vengeance.

She stole it from me. Blue eyes softened, widened. Her head tilted to one side, and she breathed out a sigh, the same sigh I'd heard when she'd first asked me to call her Ellie.

For a moment, I was afraid she would cry. Now I was made the bully.

I shifted from one foot to the other. "I didn't know if you'd really be interested, or were just being polite."

"Go get them now. I'll be in the sun room." She turned and left.

Marta called after her. "You are expecting that telephone call…"

"I know, I know!" Eleanor said over her shoulder.

Marta turned to me.

"The sun room is on the southern side of the house. Go in the front hallway, and it is the third doorway on the right, past the library and the dining room."

Wanting to obey quickly, nervous—or was it irritation that rattled me, I don't know—I ran to my room and retrieved my sketchpad. Should I change into some of the new clothes that she had bought for me? No, didn't want her to think I was trying too hard to please. I spit-combed my hair and took off.

In my rush, I forgot the original mission that had sent me to the kitchen. The thank-you note. I left it on my table.

My drawings under my arm, I approached the front of the big house a few seconds later. I'd yet to go in the front door, always being careful to show I knew my place by using the kitchen servants' entrance. Glancing over my shoulder to see if anyone had observed me, I slipped into the cool entrance hall.

My previous trip to the large parlor the first night of Miss Sloane's return had been with a guide, Marta. She'd taken me from the kitchen, which is on the southwestern side of the house, through several halls to the most northeastern corner. Now, I fully appreciated why it had seemed confusing in the shadow of night. The designer of this house didn't like straight lines.

The entrance foyer was a dark rectangle with doors on either side. Through one, I could see the long, tall rows of books of the library. Through the opposite door, I could see a grand piano and rich chairs and settees. Some other parlor.

Beyond the small foyer, however, was a very large, round room, a central hall from which other rooms led off like spokes around a wheel. Cutting into its perfect curve on the far left was a magnificent staircase that widened at the base. You couldn't look at it without imagining the owner of the household descending in a gown.

As if to prompt this thought, a huge movie poster hung on the right wall between two doors. It was a color drawing, almost cartoonish in its flatness, of Pauline Sloane in a flowing medieval-like gown, her eyes lifted up toward heaven, while the words, "She must choose — love or country" spelled out the simplistic plot line. "Daughter of Destiny" was the title of the show, and Miss Sloane looked very young in it, but I couldn't tell if that was because she had been young when it was made, or whether it was the artist's interpretation of her age.

The central hall floor was covered with red earthen tiles set in a pattern to mimic a primitive sunburst. In the middle was a round wooden table topped with flowers and a silver candelabra.

I walked past another door on my right, this one opening onto the dining room, and here my sense of place began to return. I could see through the long room to the narrow hall that led to our kitchen.

Beyond this were several doors, one behind the staircase that led to another narrow hall. To the right of this a door opened onto a light-drenched room that could only be the sun room. I went in.

"I was wondering if you'd come." Miss Sloane stood near the large windows that made up the walls of this room, looking out to the south where the vineyard began. Her hands still in her pockets, she rocked back and forth on her heels. In fact, she had an overall fidgety appearance about her. Her smile was almost too quick, her voice clipped, her movements speeded up. She seemed as nervous as I'd felt hurrying over, which put me at ease.

Before I could hand her my sketches, she pointed to a bound book of pages, a script lying open on a table.

"How does anyone learn all these lines?" She grabbed the script, only to throw it back onto the table with such force that it knocked over an ashtray. I picked it up. So it wasn't my drawings she was interested in after all. She merely wanted an audience for this latest drama. I shrugged off any disappointment—my amateur attempts at art weren't much to begin with—and looked at this as an opportunity to impress her with my knowledge.

"It's only ten minutes' worth at a time," I offered, trying to put things in perspective. "Stage actors have to learn much more—"

"Ten minutes is a lifetime before the camera." She glared at me.

"That's because they can't edit the take with sound attached. It all has to be shot in one long take—"

"Well, I can't be expected to give my all with the world seeing every pore on my face, every hair on my head, every eyelash flutter, for ten fucking minutes without some sort of... of... break... to recapture myself, my character." She spoke this all to the windows, not to me, as if the hills beyond were her audience.

I picked up the script. "It helps if you run the lines with someone. I can read the other parts." I'd seen how a director could coax an inflection out of an actress, or shift the way an actor delivered a line. I was eager to try my hand.

I turned the pages and read the leading man's line: "Madam, your boudoir is hardly the place for a gentleman."

She paused, breathing deeply as if preparing herself for the scene, then turned sharply, stepping into character. But it was a silent film character that strode toward me, a vamp rolling her shoulders and tilting her head back, using the only thing she had to communicate emotion — her body.

"What makes you think you're a gentleman?" she shouted at me.

She was a parody of the character, and I strangled a laugh before clearing my throat and saying the next line: "I hardly think you'd be the judge of such things."

She closed the distance between us and stood before me, her head still angled back so she was viewing me through slitted eyes. With an exaggerated "harrumph," she brought her hand up in a vaudevillian wind-up to a smack on my cheek, withholding the full impact.

Again, I had to bite the insides of my cheeks at this overdone performance. With effort, I continued to read: "I see. If that's how it's to be. I should leave."

She grabbed my arms and heaved a noisy sigh that would have played very well in a silent film, the audience catching the meaning immediately from the sagging shoulders. "No, don't! I didn't mean it!" she orated, then stepped close, her eyes heavy, her mouth opening, ready for the kiss.

I couldn't hold it in. I snorted out a chuckle.

And then she broke character and slapped me again, this

75

time for real.

"How dare you!" she said, her eyes watery with fear and anger. "I was saying my lines perfectly and now you've ruined it." She crossed her arms and slumped on the sofa in a pout.

"Sound has changed things," I said, rubbing my sore jaw. "I saw an audience laugh at an actor who played it like you did. All that stuff you do, that was fine when nobody could hear what you were saying. Now, all that stuff seems clownish."

"I'm a clown," she hissed. "A chauffeur's opinion — I'm sure you'll be advertising your services as an elocution expert very soon."

I ignored this jab. "That's how you should play the scene. Just like you're talking now."

She fumbled in a nearby lacquered box for a cigarette. I rushed to light it for her, stepping away as she blew smoke in my direction.

"That's what anger is like, not walking around and rolling your eyes the way you were before."

"Go away! I'll work on this on my own."

Fine. I wouldn't argue. I put the script down and turned to leave. I was nearly at the door when her soft voice carried across the room.

"No, don't!" she said. "I didn't mean it!" The exact words from the script but no longer ringing false. As if proving she could play the scene realistically, she glided across the room, arms straight by her side, until she reached me. I waited.

With no overplayed motions telegraphing her next move, she placed her hands on either side of my head and kissed me, soft and sure.

I didn't care if she was acting. I kissed her back in my own way, the only way I knew, the real way, my hands finding her soft waist, my hips pushed toward hers as she ripped desire from my gut.

But a tiny tremble of her body cued me to stop. It wasn't a shiver of longing. It was the shake of one who needed a drink bad. I'd seen it in my mother. I pulled away, my heart heavy for both her and me.

"That was much better," I said, swallowing hard and wanting to leave. And wanting to stay, to help, to tell her to stop.

She looked confused, as if she'd lost her place.

"Maybe I'll use you to run all my lines," she said at last.

A phone on the table pierced the air. She picked it up quickly, barely waiting for the first ring to subside.

"I was expecting your call," she said, her voice now ice. I thought maybe she was talking to a vendor for the party. She waited while the caller spoke.

"I did what you said. Went to every fucking party on the planet." She took a breath to continue, but the caller must have cut her off. As she listened, she shivered and rubbed her shoulders. "You told me you would talk to him. The schedule has to be moved up, goddammit. Garbo's lined up for her first talkie, and I need to be out before that. Did you hear—they're going to shoot it twice, once in English and once in German. You never had to do *that* with our films!"

As she pleaded with the caller to move her shooting schedule up, I remembered Leo's words about the price for such a change and, for a moment, wanted to caution her. But I stopped myself. Maybe she was willing to pay that price?

"Warner Brothers's all ga-ga over Kay Francis now, you know. That cow! She sounds like a tramp. But that's what they want—a bedroom voice."

She shook her head, as if clearing it. "Of course I miss you, darling. I've only been asking you to come home for weeks now. Weeks!"

Holding her hand lightly over the phone so that the caller would still hear, she said, in a completely different voice, this one honeyed yet false, as if she'd already absorbed the acting lesson I'd deigned to give her, "John, dear, could you get me my cigarette? Over there." She pointed to the ashtray where she'd left hers. "The new chauffeur I've hired. Very charming."

After giving her the cigarette, I watched her blow smoke in the air. "He looks a little like Cooper on his best days." She winked at me. "You might want to get him a contract before someone else snatches him up." Another puff of smoke. "In fact, maybe I'll do the snatching." She gave me a teasing grin and, again, I knew it was an act.

"Oh, no, my sweet, he's different. You'd better hurry home and see for yourself." She laughed and looked around for something. I recognized the look. She wanted a drink. Smoke, joke, and drink. That had been the pattern with my mother.

"In fact," she said, while standing, "I was just about to give him a dancing lesson." She pointed to the Victrola by the wall. "John, turn that on."

This was another game. But I obeyed. I put on a record, and the tinny sounds of horns and violins filled the room. It was a waltz, something I didn't recognize except in the remote way you know you've heard a song before, that it was popular when you weren't paying attention. The caller's voice, a man's, was louder. Its squawk competed with the din, but I couldn't make out any words. Only emotion—annoyance, maybe jealousy.

While she listened, she swayed back and forth and motioned for me to come closer, twirling the telephone wire around her finger. After putting down her cigarette, she placed her free hand on my shoulder and nodded for me to place my hands on her waist, while she held the receiver to her ear. Thus positioned, we moved back and forth together to the music, not able to go far because of the phone's cord. Her mood was joyful, victorious, and it didn't take much speculating on my part to know that I was being used—to make the man on the phone jealous. He was still talking. I could hear his voice. Something about "coming home" and "don't play with me." My face burned. I wanted to knock the phone from her hand.

"I'm having a party. We can always use an extra fellow or two!" she said into the receiver while looking into my blazing eyes. Seeing my irritation, she thrust out her mouth in a pretend pout that said, "Don't be that way, play along."

"Then, come home!" Although her voice was light, there was something desperate in it, a shade of a tremolo like the quick pulse of a gypsy violin. "You promised once already! You're just torturing me!"

Torture was *this* game.

After a few more minutes of conversation—from annoyance to coyness to pleading and back again—she leaned back and hung up the phone. I used that opportunity to let her go. Anger flushed my body warm. She was a quick study. Already she knew how to pretend in a natural way.

"You don't know how to dance, do you?" she asked.

Who the hell cared if I danced? I didn't. "We were given some instruction in the fine arts at Canfield, things to make us appreciate higher culture," I said. I remembered how Milqueton had introduced us to that particular teacher, a matronly woman named Bernadette Frost. He'd almost apologized to us, saying that the new oversight board had insisted we include these classes in the curriculum, and we should give Miss Frost our full attention and respect. Which we'd done, for the most part, because Milqueton would brook no mischief.

Eleanor walked over to the phonograph and put the record on again. Returning, she held out her arms.

"Then show me."

I almost said she didn't need my services in that regard now that her telephone call was over, but she interrupted me.

"Any man would love to have the great Pauline Sloane in his arms. Yet you resist," she said. "Do you think you're better than the rest?"

"I don't like being used."

"Nobody does," she said and grabbed my hands, placing them on her waist and shoulder respectively. "But we all do what we have to do, don't we? Show me how you dance, John Doyle, and then you can go."

Again, the playful tone. Disobey me, and I win, it said.

Obey me, and I still win.

I did as I was told, looking into her eyes, a thousand angry messages coming from mine.

I exacted my own personal reward. I drew her closer, pressing my hand against the small of her back, my fingers finding the little indentation where her spine nestled under soft flesh. I felt her breasts brush my chest. She didn't resist. As the dance progressed, her eyelids grew heavy, and she let her head loll onto my shoulder where I could smell her citrus perfume.

Jesus—she always won. My brow quickly coated with sweat. I was done for—weak-kneed and heavy—all because I had the great Pauline Sloane in my arms. She'd proven her point.

Forcing myself to concentrate on the one-two-three of the waltz, trying to think of Miss Frost's chubby lips counting out the beats for us young boys, I looked past Miss Sloane's face to the windows beyond, the rugged landscape, the real world that looked unreal. Nothing was true here.

The song ended, replaced by the hiss of the needle on the record's edge, but we did not stop. I thought of kissing her, of lifting her face to mine and playing the game she'd played with me, kiss and then pull away, laugh, leave. I saw myself doing it. I couldn't do it. I squeezed her hand more tightly.

The dog came bounding into the room, and I made a misstep, landing on Pauline's toe, the very foot she'd injured weeks ago. She pulled back with a start, but then laughed.

"You're right, John. You do dance just 'a little.' A little artificially, I might add." She laughed again, but her heart wasn't in it.

I let her try to wound me. "I hope I didn't hurt you."

"No. I'm a hardy girl. Can't kill me." She went to the sofa again and sat down. I was going to remain standing, but she waved me to a seat. "At this party, we'll hire some extra men to park cars. They'll be under your supervision. You needn't wear the uniform. In fact, now that I know what an acceptable dance partner you are, come in the tux. We can always use an extra fellow. The girls will fawn over you, I'm sure. I'll have to make sure no one steals you away."

She rubbed her head as if it ached. A hangover perhaps. But I'd not smelled alcohol on her breath. Hope, followed by quick skepticism, flowed through me.

I paid no attention to Eleanor's invitation to the party. I suspected she'd forget by the time it came around, and I'd be just as happy.

A rattling and bumping clatter somewhere above caught our attention. We both went to the central round hall, and she stopped and looked upstairs, nervously placing her hand on the banister.

"Marta! What's going on up there?"

The housekeeper appeared at the balustrade. "Cleaning, Miss Sloane. I have two girls working on the bedrooms and another in the attic. Is it a bad time? I can tell them to do it later if you want to rest."

"No, now is fine. But for god's sake, get that one out of the attic. No use cleaning up there. No one goes in the attic. No one." She completely ignored me and walked up the stairs, obviously intent on making sure that the attic was left alone.

 beginstyle

Yes, I dreamt of her that night. What man wouldn't after having her in his arms? She was an affliction whose symptoms grew stronger over time. She was a devil. She was ….

She was beautiful and seductive, and the dreams I had were of a carnal nature where our dance became much more, where she was frightened, and I was strong, where I dominated, and she didn't resist. I awoke in a sweat in the middle of the night when every problem is a crisis, every situation as stark as the black and white shadows of the night itself.

She'd deliberately seduced me—and for what purpose? Solely to revel in my discomfort! She had no intention of carrying through with her seduction, of jumping into the dreams I'd just left. She just wanted to see me suffer. I had to leave. And yet, you know I did not.

These thoughts clamped on me like the night air on my sweating body. Standing, I went to the window. Her light was still on. A single rectangle of gold in the silent darkness.

Do you believe in God?

Pete's voice, from the past, from his death bed. *Do you believe in a merciful God, John?*

I guess so, I'd said. I'd have said anything to keep him happy and alive. He was my only friend at Canfield. He was like me, contrary and wanting to be saved. Except Pete didn't need to be saved. He was a good boy at his core.

How can God be merciful and just at the same time, John?

Don't talk so much, Pete. Here, drink something.

When he'd arrived at Canfield, he was a good-looking, cheerful youngster from south Texas who'd fallen in with a bad bunch of thieving men. They'd gone to prison. He'd come to Canfield. He should have stayed a short while and then gone back to his regular life. He was no sinner, just a wayward boy caught up in something exciting. Clement took a liking to him, and when Pete didn't return the sentiment, he was regularly singled out for the headmaster's sadistic pleasure.

He'd been forced to stand all day in chapel, his hands out beside him as if nailed on a cross. He'd had meal privileges rescinded when he didn't smile the right way at old Brice; he'd had his teeth knocked out by a bully bribed by Clement to lure Pete into a brawl. After the fight, Pete was sent to the "hot box," a small shack in the middle of our yard that got as hot as an oven on a summer's day. He stayed there for three days and four nights, not uttering a peep. I was sure he'd suffered the same fate as my mother, but was surprised when he came out, nearly crazy from the solitude and temperature and lack of adequate food and drink.

It wasn't all those that killed him, though. He'd been slated for release on his fourteenth birthday. He'd talked about it constantly, told me over and over again how he'd write to me from Galveston, how he'd send me food and treats once he got back home.

Brice set him up the night before his departure. He had

three of the home's worst characters—boys beyond redemption, sunk in depravity and barbarism, avoided by the rest of us like the plague they were—sent to Pete's bed.

They did things to him.... I can't think about it now.

And I had been a coward, in bed a room away, covering my ears when he cried because helping him would have meant another beating for me, and I was still raw from the last one. I told myself it was my imagination, or just one of the regular criers, the ones who whimpered the night away and denied it in the morning.

Pete was accused of sodomy and sentenced to more time. He was whipped so hard he couldn't walk after that and was bedridden more often than not. But it was his spirit that really broke that day. He was never the same. Never. Even when Milqueton came. He was a haunted boy and died a day before his new release date on his eighteenth birthday.

I mean if God is just, he would punish old Brice. But if he's merciful …

You're out of breath, Pete. Let's talk later.

If he's merciful, he forgives Brice. Frantic eyes staring at me — *that means Brice'll be in heaven some day!*

Go back to sleep, Pete. God's whatever you want him to be. He won't let Brice near you again. You're safe from him now.

He was safe. He was gone. And I remained.

Milqueton saved me. Maybe he saved Pete as well, but it was a different kind of salvation, one that prepared him for death. I was too feisty to kill. I was prepared for life.

Gravel crunched, a car rumbled cutting through the gurgle of the fountain, drawing my attention away from the house and toward where the drive joined the plaza in front of the veranda. Who was driving up so late at night? Turning away, I grabbed my shirt and trousers, pulling them on as I hopped back over to the window. Headlight beams cut the void. Hurrying, I buttoned my shirt, wondering if I should call the authorities first to ward off this intruder.

A light came on downstairs at the big house, then the light on the veranda. The front door slammed open. Miss

Sloane — Eleanor — appeared in a silky robe that floated like the moonlight, her arms outspread.

"You did come! I knew you would!" She laughed as a tall, thin man exited the car and walked toward her. She threw her arms around his neck and kissed him. Their voices carried clearly in the night air.

"I came as quickly as I could, darling. No need for a fuss." He was foreign — a Brit maybe. He put his arm around her shoulder as they walked toward the house.

"You're a beast. You should have been here last week, Robbie."

"Didn't you get my gift?"

"What?"

"The necklace. I sent you a platinum and ..."

"Oh yes — I remember! Marta put it away for me."

"Didn't you like it?" His voice was high and hurt.

She laughed. "I loved it, darling. But you have to tell me about your call to Schulberg. What happened?"

He stopped, forcing her to stop, too, just before the veranda. "I convinced him. Your schedule is moved up. You'll release before Garbo."

She turned to him. "Robbie! I knew I could count on you. Thank god you're here!" With that, she leaned her head on his shoulder, just as she had leaned it on mine in the afternoon.

I walked away from the window.

Chapter Six

THIS WAS ROBBIE MORGAN.

I came face to face with him the very day after he arrived.

That afternoon, I'd set myself the task of looking at the Packard's gear shift which had been slipping sometimes when I put it into first, pushing out of my mind the dance, the kiss, the dream of working in the studios. Who did I think I was anyway? God almighty, even I was laughing at myself in the light of day.

The Packard was the most-used car on the estate. It's what I drove when taking Marta and Julia into the city, and even, on occasion, Miss Sloane herself. I loved to drive the Duesenberg but putting on the foppish chauffeur's uniform soured my joy. At least I only had to wear it at night when I drove Miss Sloane to parties.

As I lay on my back under the jacked-up Packard, examining the car's innards, I saw my employer's shapely ankles. Pulling myself out from under the car, I saw Robbie Morgan, too, standing next to her.

"John, I've been wanting to run some errands. But Robbie here said he'd do them for me. Would you drive him?" Her arm was linked through his.

"Of course he will, darling. He's the chauffeur, for god's sake!"

As I rubbed my oil-stained hands on my old coveralls, I took the measure of the man in full daylight. About my height, he was tall and thin. Even his head seemed elongated, with a skinny, narrow nose a little too long for his face, miserly lips, and small eyes. Above a high forehead, he had limp, dark hair, so dull it gave the impression that he was sickly. In fact, he did look sickly. His skin was pasty, and I noticed his hand, like Eleanor's, was unsteady as he took a drag from a cigarette.

Beyond that tremble, he was so confident and smooth that you'd only remember his attitude when you shut your eyes.

"I just need to change," I said. Placing the rag on a shelf by the wall, I headed for the narrow stairway to my rooms.

"No need for the uniform except in the Duzy," Miss Sloane called after me.

I assumed I'd be driving Mister Morgan's own car, a new Lincoln with snappy hood ornament and spacious interior. I'd washed it already that morning and checked out its engine.

I quickly went to the bathroom at the back of the loft and washed up as best I could. After stripping out of my soiled clothes, I grabbed a good shirt from the hook on the door and started buttoning it. I was about to pull on a decent pair of trousers, when I heard a sound in my front room, a low giggle, like a boy's nasty chuckle when he's making fun of someone.

I stepped into the front room. There was Mister Morgan, reading the thank-you note I'd never delivered to Miss Sloane. He didn't even look at me, but took a quick puff on his cigarette.

"'Your gift of clothes was most generous, and I am very grateful'," he read in mincing tones, "'I will be sure to put them to good use in the coming months, and your thoughtfulness will not be forgotten.'" He looked up at me, smiling wickedly. "Wherever did you learn to write such quasi-formal claptrap?"

Reddening, I did not answer his question. "That's my property, sir."

"Oh, don't get in a snit about it. It was on the floor. I picked it up." He giggled again. "It fell open."

I stood my ground and stared at him through hard eyes. After crushing out his cigarette on the wooden floor, he let the note flutter to the ground. "There, I've put it back. No harm done."

He wanted me to respond.

"We can go now, Mister Morgan," I said.

"Not yet, I'm afraid. I came up to tell you I've changed my mind. The Lincoln's been running rather ragged. We'll take the Duesenberg. I'll be on the veranda while you change."

When he turned to leave, I felt my hands curling into fists. Robbie Morgan was a type of fellow I'd come across before. A cowardly bully, too timid to fight fair.

I pulled at my shirt buttons, ripping one off as I struggled to undo them. Cursing myself, I slowed my pace. Let Robbie Morgan wait.

When I finally emerged a few minutes later, he was sitting in a wicker chair with his feet on the railing of the wide veranda that ran the length of the front of the house. Seeing me, his eyes widened in admiration, a look that made my skin crawl. I did not acknowledge him, but headed straight for the garage where I slid behind the wheel of the lovely new car.

The motor hummed, almost silently, and my own thoughts began to match its calm rhythm. So what if the uniform scratched my neck and made me perspire? This fine vehicle was a pleasure to drive. I'd focus on that and not whatever insignificant humiliations Mister Morgan thought he could foist upon me. Not responding would be my vengeance.

⋙

I had ample opportunity to observe Mister Morgan that day. And once he'd felt some measure of victory over me by forcing me to wear the uniform, he exuded a natural, if somewhat dandified charm.

On the way into the city, he talked without ceasing, his British accent making whatever he said sound more important than it really was. Mostly he gabbed about his errands. I got the impression that he was talking about them in order to make himself feel like he was a big man. He dropped names he thought I wouldn't know. Jack and Sam and Irving and Cecil. Gary and Lillian and Charlie and Errol. They flowed off his tongue like a list of "begats."

As he sought to impress me, he became smaller, even pitiable.

It didn't escape my attention that he referred to Miss Sloane by her given name, a name she said was only used by people who knew her very well. She was getting ready to start a new picture, he told me, one he'd "moved heaven and earth" to land for her since silent stars looking for good parts were as common as "Micks in a tenement house."

He was intent on making sure her film was shot and scheduled for release before that "Scandinavian witch" came out with hers. So he'd lied when he'd assured her that was a signed and sealed deal. Mister Morgan was sure that a few words here, a few pats on the back there, and maybe a *soupcon* of promises sprinkled on top for good measure would make everything right for "El" and she'd be as "giddy as a schoolgirl at holiday time."

Because her contract was with Paramount, we spent all of the day there, and he had me drive him from one part of the lot to the next while he waved to people he knew, and stopped to meet with directors or assistant producers or god knows who. I wondered if his big talk in the car was a cover for what he was really doing—prostituting Eleanor to get the schedule change.

Don't be hasty, John, I heard Milqueton say. *Don't leap to judgment.*

It was hard not to with Morgan.

As I sat and waited for him during these stops, parades of costumed actors walked by. The Duesenberg was just as much a rarity for them as their appearances were for me. A "knight" in heavy chain mail and cloth leggings even engaged in a knowledgeable conversation about how the manufacturer got the engine to run so quiet.

"Gary Cooper's got one, or is getting one, I hear," the fellow said, his southern drawl a far cry from the lordly character he was meant to portray. I let him look under the hood and admire the car's shiny engine. There both of us stood, he in his costume and I in mine, sweltering in the California sunshine. I felt like saying I'd worked with Leo Bartenstein and hoped to get behind the camera again soon, that I was acting now just like him.

He moved on when Mister Morgan returned, but I could tell that Morgan wasn't upset about the car's draw. If anything, he seemed to fancy it, which I suspect was the real reason he had wanted to take it instead of his own, still fashionable, Lincoln.

"Where to?" I asked, looking in the mirror after I'd held the door open for him.

"Mmm... just drive around. I need to think. Head toward Central Avenue."

Wondering if the meeting had gone badly, I glanced from time to time into the back seat, trying to gauge his mood. While I drove along narrow streets and open boulevards lined by swaying palms, he fidgeted and scowled, scrunched in a corner of the car as if the weather were frigid, and he needed to conserve his body heat. I, meanwhile, hated stopping at intersections because that's when the car trapped the heat and made the back of my neck feel grimy from sweat.

We drove like this for a half hour. When he didn't tell me to stop, I kept on going, down Central to the four-thousand block, a section with jazz clubs, speakeasies, boarded up stores, and open markets. I was about to head back toward a better section, when Mister Morgan perked up and stopped me.

"No, don't turn back. There, the Alabam" He pointed to a Nite Club a few doors away.

Nodding my obedience, I followed his instructions and pulled into a parking spot. Thinking that Mister Morgan must be confused, I turned to ask where I should head next.

He was already out of the car, not waiting for me to open the door for him. I watched him cross the street to a dilapidated building, a two-story squeezed between larger ones, that looked like it was vacant. He rapped its door while looking up and down the street both ways. After a few seconds, someone let him in.

It made me uneasy to sit in that neighborhood. The car and my uniform were an invitation to any bad sort who thought the way to wipe greed off the face of the earth was to punch a defenseless rich guy. Or, in my case, the rich guy's chauffeur. A couple of working women in gay colors strolled down the street, even though it was broad daylight, and disappeared into a second-hand store at the corner. A group of flashily-dressed men, Negroes and whites, walked by. From an upper-story window, the snake-like sound of a clarinet pierced the air, competing with the noise of the traffic and the laughter and talk of passers-by.

I considered driving around the block but was afraid Morgan would return to find me missing and have a fit of anger waiting for me to come back. He wouldn't want to be alone in this neighborhood.

I decided to take my chances and stay put. If I ended up mussing up the uniform having to defend this classic piece of workmanship, I'd consider it a rougher part of an otherwise soft job.

For nearly three-quarters of an hour, I sat there. I undid the buttons on my wooly jacket, letting what air there was evaporate the perspiration on my shirt. I glowered at a couple of roughnecks walking by, daring them to give me a hard time. And I fended off the attention of a talkative drunk who probably was looking for a way to waste time before his next bottle.

Drink was probably Mister Morgan's mission—a call on the local bootlegger in anticipation of the grand party. It was already clear he was as much a drunk as Eleanor. His breath told the tale, and his bleary eyes confirmed it.

From the drunken ramblings of my mother, I had learned many things. For instance, I'd come on the scene a little earlier than expected after a hasty wedding. My father had been the son of Texas wealth and would have done his duty in the Great War if a horse hadn't thrown him and broke his neck during a cavalry exercise. I hardly knew him before he died. I remember him as a distant man, tall (my height must come from him) with blondish hair and blue eyes. I only remember him hugging me once, before he left for a trip to see his brother in San Francisco.

His father—my grandfather—was a stern, silent man. Once my father was dead, his family would have nothing to do with me or my mother. She'd sung in honky-tonks to make a living, and we'd lived in rooms above bars. Rooms that would have fit right in in this neighborhood, I thought glancing down the street.

That had been a blow, moving out of our grand, rambling house in Austin, and into a fleabag set of rooms. Mother told me it was an adventure, and that it wouldn't be long before she earned enough to go back to school and become a teacher, which was what she'd wanted to be before meeting my father. She said it like she'd sacrificed a bright future for him.

She drank what she earned. And when Prohibition closed the honky-tonks, she married Earl Pickett, a sweet-talking salesman who promised her the world and me a better life.

I'd not believed him, even though my mother had. That's when I started losing myself in the local moving picture house, watching happy people live in another world. Even the sad stories were a comfort, reminding me others had it worse.

"Thanks, old boy. You're a sport. I wasn't gone long, now, was I?" Mister Morgan was back, his face flushed and bright.

"Where to?" I asked.

"Oh, I think home now. All's right with the world. Lots to tell Ellie. She'll be so pleased." He leaned back in the seat, but this time, his nervousness was gone, and his hands were steady as he lit a cigarette. And yes, he had been drinking.

ೞ

With Morgan in residence, lights blazed in the downstairs rooms to all hours, even after they both came home from parties together, and the sound of laughter and music drifted into the night. Sometimes it would be the sound of the phonograph playing, fast and raucous music that made the peaceful landscape seem cold in comparison. Sometimes it would be melancholy piano melodies played by Mister Morgan in the front room, the sound settling on me like a pall.

I imagined Miss Sloane dancing with him to the phonograph music. Shutting my window did not keep out the sound. It occurred to me that she'd avoided the fate of my mother and me, moving from comfort to penury, but at what cost? She had kept her station in life, but she was still paying a steep price for it.

Even though Robbie had his own car, they used my services to take them to the shimmering halls of other stars, Mister Morgan slouched in the back seat, drinking from a flask and talking nonstop about studio people, often vulgar tales of what stars did to get their headline parts. Glancing in the rearview mirror during those conversations, I saw Miss Sloane's mouth set grimly tight, her eyes staring out at the black night. Why did he torture her so? No wonder she passed it along to others. She was scared, like everybody else in this town, afraid to give up her little corner of fame and fortune.

Although she had expressed an interest in walking with me, it seemed to evaporate in the glare of Robbie Morgan's withering gaze. I walked alone that Sunday, but walk was all I did. No sketching. No stopping to admire a landscape that both fascinated and repelled me with its barbaric emptiness. No writing thoughts or words in my notebook. I wandered aimlessly, trying with each step to focus myself again on what had been my goal—to do well, to improve myself, to be my own master. I wished I knew where Leo lived—I'd have driven into town to visit him. Sure, I wanted to know how he was faring. But I wanted to ask him about Eleanor, about Morgan.

When I had been beset by challenges at Canfield, I'd turned inward and concentrated on the future, the most convenient escape from a difficult present. So now I forced myself to think of my goals and what I wanted out of life. I'd left Canfield when it ceased to offer anything to me. Milqueton had made it clear he expected good things for me and knew I was capable of them. I let myself hear his voice exhorting me to *honor my birthright*. No matter how low a man had been born, nor how low he'd sunk, Milqueton always hearkened to his birthright—the right to choose good over evil, to choose grace over sin.

Strange as it may seem, those choices were not hard at

Canfield once I'd decided to work toward freedom. Few temptations presented themselves when my size and station were enough to keep bullies and prevaricators away.

Here temptation floated in the air—the sound of her laughter or the scent of her perfume. It drowned out the whisper of the fountain and the voice that told me to leave. Fighting it meant fighting myself. That was one battle I'd never won.

To take my mind off her, I resolved to be more diligent—about everything. My job. My self-improvement. Even my recreation. On my afternoon off, I walked even further afield, carrying water with me against the effects of the merciless sun, and food enough to hold me all day. I often returned after dark had crept up the hills to the estate. Sometimes, when my feet crunched on the gravel, I'd see her glance out a window, quickly pulling the curtains closed if she noticed me looking her way.

I wrote letters to Milqueton and a few boys at the Home that he asked me to correspond with *to set an example, John,* of what they could make of their lives. I must admit I struggled with those notes. What would have been an easy task just months before became a slow, grueling assignment as I searched for words that did not hold the same meaning for me any longer. A fine job, I'd write, while thinking that I wanted more. A decent employer, I'd pen, while wishing I could talk with her again.

And I slowly convinced myself that my desire for contact sprang from a desire to prove that I wasn't under her spell!

This torment so consumed me that it only seemed natural to hear a sound one night that echoed my own suffering. Waking from what I thought was a dream, I heard a long, low sobbing, a sound almost inhuman in its keening wail. A sob of "no, no, no." And something else—something so pathetic it made me recoil with a shiver.

Disoriented, I sat up in bed and looked out the window into the blue night where a three-quarter moon cast all in ashen shadow, just as in my drawings. No color, only shading, and the fantastic shapes of the house and countryside looming beyond. I waited. Had it been a dream?

Just as I was ready to turn back into my bed, I heard it again. My heart raced. No combination of syllables could describe its piercing sorrow. It was a desperate cry wrenched from the gut of a dying soul, a long, harsh sigh, a plea for something I could not begin to explain.

No lights were on in the main house. No one stirred. Was I losing my senses? Had no one else heard?

In the distance, an owl hooted. A few crickets buzzed. Far away, a dog howled. All set against the undertone of the fountain.

Hearing nothing more, I lay back down in my bed. In a drowsy haze, I convinced myself it had been the dog, despite the fact that I knew better. I was too tired for mysteries. I drifted into uneasy sleep.

 C8

The next day I awoke stiff and tired. The noises in the night had left me restlessly dozing and now I felt as if I'd not slept at all. At breakfast, I asked Marta about the strange sounds I'd heard. She stood at the big stove, pouring herself a cup of the strong coffee she favored in the morning.

"It was probably a wolf in the mountains," she said. Almost imperceptibly, her mouth twitched. Creases lined her forehead.

"Marta, there are no wolves in California," I said.

"Then a coyote."

"But did you hear it too?"

"I sleep very soundly, *Señor* Doyle. Nothing wakes me."

This was a lie. I knew for a fact that Marta was a light sleeper. One of my first nights on the job, a wind had whipped through the estate and knocked a shutter from my window. Even though Marta's rooms, like Julia's, were in the main house, she'd come running out after midnight, dressed in her cotton wrapper, to see if I was all right. That small thump had been nothing compared to the wailing of the night before.

I turned to Julia, who picked absently at a roll while

studying a magazine about the cinema.

"Julia, did you hear it?"

She looked up, amused. Her lips curled into a smile. "*Non, monsieur.* It was probably a wolf in the mountains," she repeated.

It hadn't been a wolf, damn it. But had it been a dream? Had it come bursting from my soul, some remnant of my past at the Home, or from before? Had I dreamt of my mother's lonesome cries and thought I'd awakened when in reality I'd stayed asleep?

These thoughts plagued me as I went about my duties. Whether the cry had been real or not, it now became mixed with my mother's voice in memory. Over and over that day, I heard her weeping, begging my stepfather to leave her alone, to leave me alone. Assuring him she'd been faithful, that she'd be good, that I'd be good as well. Screaming, her hands crossed over her head, her face stained with tears.

I was glad to be busy that day, but sometimes my hands shook as I tried to push the memory back. I comforted myself with the cars, with the easy fixes of tightening screws and filling tanks. And even a trip into the city chauffeuring Mister Morgan in the Duesenberg was a welcome distraction, uniform or not.

When I brought him back that afternoon, "Ellie" was waiting for us. Her hands across her chest, she looked angrily out from the veranda as I dropped off Mister Morgan and put away the car. Although I heard them exchanging sharp words, I didn't linger to eavesdrop. By the time I had the car parked in the garage, he had gone into the main house.

But she came to the open bay, looking at me with angry eyes.

"I didn't expect him to take that car." She pointed to the Duesenberg. "Why does he take that one? Is there something wrong with the others?"

I didn't know what to say. Who was I to complain? Having to wear a uniform didn't qualify as hardship. But something in me was glad she'd noticed, was glad she'd come to champion me. It was rain after a dry summer.

"This is a beautiful car." I patted the Duesenberg's engine cover. "And he's your guest." I nodded toward the house.

"Robbie isn't a guest."

"Well, your agent."

From behind her, the door opened, and Robbie called over to her.

"El, would you like tea in the sun room?"

Without looking at him, she answered. "That will be fine."

He stood on the veranda waiting for her, but she did not turn. She was waiting, too. After a few minutes, he went back inside, letting the door slam after him. She jumped at its crash.

"Robbie isn't 'a guest'," she repeated in a rush, as if she had to hurry before being caught. "He's my stepbrother."

Chapter Seven

HER STEPBROTHER. Of course, why not? Nothing else was clear here.

I went to bed that night uneasy, so it was only natural that I'd awaken just as confused. Confused and frightened, in the blackness where even my panting breath seemed to belong to something else designed to torment me, I awakened to the blood-curdling cry I'd heard the night before. Sitting straight up, clammy from fear, I rubbed my eyes and then pulled on a shirt and trousers.

Damn it, I'd see to this. I'd not sleep another night wondering what ghosts were ready to strike. But as I came to the downstairs door of the garage, lights went on in Eleanor's bedroom, followed by the drift of angry voices into the air. No ghosts there.

"I told you already—nothing's going on!" Eleanor's voice, followed by a low mumble—his voice. But no complete sentences carried.

"He doesn't even like me, for crissake!" The scent of cigarette smoke floated with the words. And through my muddled mind, a thought permeated. She was talking about me. Blood rushed to my head, sharpening my wits.

"Oh, for god's sake, Robbie." She laughed, artificially. "I was just trying to make you jealous! You'd abandoned me. Don't be that way."

Anger smoldered through me, licking at my finger tips, beading sweat on my brow. Yes, I'd known I was being toyed with. But to hear her say it—that was something different, a fresh cut.

"Stop saying that! I *am* grateful!" Now her voice was

frantic and scared, the tremolo returning. But I felt no pity. I was still angry. I wanted to call out. I wanted to leave—again! And yet—I didn't—I didn't leave. Because I wanted to be avenged!

I hid in the shadows. I plotted. I'd watch and wait. The next time Morgan came out looking for me, I'd strike. I'd trip him first. Then when he was on the ground, I'd kick. And then I'd spit on him and laugh at him … and then I'd leave.

"Don't be silly, Robbie. I told you already—he's just the damn chauffeur!"

What was I thinking? It wasn't he who had wounded me! It was her! She was the one who played with me, like a dog, petting me and cuddling, only to abandon me later—no, worse, not merely abandon me—mock me, use me, humiliate me. No wonder the last chauffeur had left.

I was too warm now to sleep. And even though their conversation was ending, I stood stock still, afraid to move. Afraid that movement would make this all real when I wanted it to be a dream.

Give me the grace, O Lord, to forgive my adversaries.

The snatch of prayer from Canfield's daily service intertwined with the scent of cigarette and eucalyptus, with the drone of the fountain. Give me the grace.

Give me.

A few more mumbled words I couldn't make out, then Eleanor's light went out. A hall light flickered through to the window, then shut off. I went back to bed.

☃

The next day, the ferment of the night before continued. I worked with Marta getting the house ready for the party, which was now only a day away, and spent most of my time in the kitchen and beyond, helping her rearrange furniture, roll up a rug, pull silver and glasses from high shelves. Vaguely aware that Julia was missing, I asked Marta if she was ill. I wasn't content to passively wonder what was going on anymore. I wanted to know—who was where, what they were doing, and why—why she played with me, why the noises awakened me, why I ached when I should be content.

"No. It is her day off," she said with evident disgust. "On this day — when we have so much to do!"

"Then why'd you let her take it?" I asked. Again, I'd know.

Marta looked up sharply."I didn't. *He* did." Morgan.

In the afternoon, I nearly collided with Julia on the veranda where I was placing an extra chair. She clasped an expensive-looking bag, and her face was made-up, with dramatically outlined eyebrows and exaggerated red lips.

"I thought you were gone for the day," I said to her.

She looked startled and blushed. "I will be leaving soon."

"The party's tomorrow," I said. "We could have used your help."

"I have often thought the same thing on your day off." She pulled a mirror from her bag and examined her hair. Like Eleanor, she was dismissing me.

I hid my feelings and went back to the kitchen where Marta waited for me to move boxes of glasses.

Hours later, Marta told me she didn't need me any longer, and I was free to go. "Come back in an hour for some sandwiches." She smiled at me.

The air was warm and still, and I wanted to wash the sweat off myself and change, so I headed to the garage, only to hear Eleanor calling Marta, then appearing on the front veranda, calling after me.

"Where is he?" she asked.

Of course I knew she was referring to Morgan, but I'd not seen him all day, and it was nearly dinner time. I was hungry and tired.

"I don't know." I didn't even bother to look at her but continued walking across the gravel to the garage.

"Julia!" she called, and walked back to the door.

I stopped and turned. I'd take my revenge where I could get it. "She's not here."

She let the door slam behind her and turned back to me. "What do you mean she's not here? She has work to do!"

"It's her day off."

"The party is tomorrow!" She patted the pockets of her dress looking for cigarettes and found none.

If she asked me to fetch her one, I was prepared to say I was off-duty as well, that it was my dinner hour, and she could get her own smokes.

"Where did she go?"

"I'm not sure. I just saw her here, on the veranda about ... awhile ago."

She peered over to the open bays of the garage. "What car is missing?" She held her hand over her eyes to block the sun.

I turned and followed her gaze. "The Nash."

"He took it!"

She was probably right. Morgan had admired the sporty car and had even said he wouldn't mind taking it for a spin. He was missing, his car was still in the drive, but the Nash was gone — it didn't take much of a mind to put that one together.

"And he has that little...." She turned to me again. "What was she wearing?"

"What?"

"Surely you notice what a woman wears. What was it?"

I tried to conjure up the image of Julia on the veranda, waiting. I remembered thinking she looked like a little girl dressing up, like she was wearing clothes that weren't quite her style. Something was off about them.

"Green." There — I'd give out only what I had to.

"Oh come on — green what? Green blouse? Green trousers? Green night shirt?"

"A green dress," I said slowly. Let her feel what I felt — to wonder. "Something with a belt ... "

"That little bitch!" She whirled around and ran into the house, calling over her shoulder as the door slammed. "Get the car!"

I did as I was told, at first heading for the Duesenberg. No, I'd not get that car dirty with my sweat. I changed direction and grabbed the keys to the Packard instead. In a few moments I sat in the car with the engine idling right outside the veranda. I was enjoying her discomfort. To hell with wanting grace. This feeling was sweeter.

She reappeared quickly, a wide-brimmed hat shading her face and dark glasses over her eyes. When I stepped out to hold her door open, she waved me away and got in the front seat next to me.

"Drive," she said. "I'll tell you where to go."

As she pulled on her gloves, she told me to try the studio first so I headed down the hill. When I asked her which one, she thought for a moment, then said "Paramount. He'll start there. Then we'll try RKO."

We rode in silence into the city, and she was visibly impatient, clucking her tongue when I slowed down for a light she obviously thought I should have run. When we came to the studios, she directed me with curt commands — right, right again here, not there, this one, left, see that little driveway, turn there …

It was a whirlwind tour as we cruised by studio after studio. She had me drive around lots, around fake Greek cities and western towns, around a New York street and a medieval castle. While I drove, she stared out the window looking for the Nash. She didn't see it. We stopped only once, and it was my luck that it was near the soundstage I knew Leo was working.

While she stormed off to some office, chasing her paranoid fantasies about Julia, I left the car and sought out Leo. I had to wait, though, for a break in shooting to even enter the soundstage and see if he was free. When I opened the door to the still, sweaty warehouse of a room, an argument was in progress, and I was afraid at first I'd witness some humiliation of Leo's. But he was a spectator, like me.

"Tell me if you can understand them," the director simmered. His hands were on his hips as he sat on a high stool, one long leg extended before him. He faced a smaller balding man with a pencil behind his ear and some papers in his hand.

One glance up at the window of the sound booth told me

who he was talking to. The door was open up there, and it was empty. The god to whom the actors looked for approval at the end of each scene had descended to walk among them.

"The decibel levels are all wrong," the man said, haughty indignation making his voice rise. "You'll have to reshoot."

"But you could understand them, right?" The director mopped his sweaty brow.

The man tapped his papers. "And you could hear an echo when he dropped the book." He pointed to an actor who gulped and stepped back as if fingered for elimination.

"Books echo in rooms when they're dropped," the director sneered. "That's a natural sound."

"Well, still, the decibels. Like I said, they're not right. The studio pays me to get them right."

The director stood and crossed his arms over his chest. "Well, the studio pays me to make sure this picture makes money. The fellow in the audience could care less about decibels, Mister. Just answer my fucking question: Can you understand what they're saying?" His voice boomed into the space which was now as quiet as if shooting were taking place. Actors stared. Gaffers waited. Leo beamed.

"I... I..."

The director kicked over the stool by his side, creating a clap echoing like thunder even in this sound-dampened catacomb. The soundman jumped.

"Answer. The. Fucking. Question: Can you understand the actors when they speak?" the director bellowed.

The man's face flamed red. He grit his teeth. He spit out: "Yes."

The director looked up, stretching his arms out in gratitude. "Then we have a wrap on that. No retakes. Not when I finally had them saying their lines exactly the way I wanted to hear them!"

Someone giggled in the corner. Leo, I noticed, suppressed a chuckle.

"Get out of here!" the director said to the sound man. "We're shooting again in fifteen minutes."

With that, a hum of noise flooded into the studio, with actors and the crew buzzing about the scene that had just played out: *a director triumphing over the tyranny of the sound technician.*

Leo, who had just weeks ago dismissed this director as a stage-imported hack, now sung his praises as we walked into the light outside.

"Glory be, I never thought I'd see that day! He has balls, all right, Johnny. That man has balls! Going to be a great director, I'm sure."

He was so excited by the display we'd just witnessed that he didn't ask me why I was there, and, after a quick search for smokes (I pretended I didn't have any on me for the sake of his ailing lungs), he resumed his role as teacher, mentor, and informant.

"No jobs for you yet, son. But don't give up. They're making some good movies to release in Europe and places in the States not wired for sound yet. Maybe you can get work on one of those sets and really see how it's done."

I wanted work on talkies, but silents would do.

"Problem is," he said, "good fellas are looking for camera work, guys with lots of experience." His tone turned hushed. "Charles Rosher's out of a job," he whispered, as if it was such an embarrassment he dare not speak it aloud.

"Who's he?" I'd long since given up pretending I always knew who Leo was talking about.

"Was Mary Pickford's cameraman for nearly fifteen years. And she kicked him out when she couldn't pass the sound test! Looked her age, dammit, when she's trying to play young."

I could piece the story together even without the details. Rosher might have been right for Pickford in silents with their arc lighting and older film, but nowadays …. Like Leo said, she was no spring chicken. She'd need an expert in the new stuff to shoot her right.

The old arc lights of silents hissed, which meant they'd been replaced by incandescent ones on sound. And the less bright incandescent lights meant switching to film that picked up more of the light spectrum — panchromatic film. But Leo said it was the lights that you had to get used to. The old ones sent a wash of unfocused light over everything, meaning a dame like Pickford didn't need to worry so much about wrinkles or flaws. But the new stuff had to be focused more, bringing out flaws, every crease, even the make-up itself used to cover those things.

Hell, even The Jazz Singer had been shot with two types of lighting and film — orthochromatic for the silent parts and panchromatic with the sound ones — and you could tell, too, if you knew to look for it. That ham Jolson looked like a pasty-face freak with dark lids and clown make-up in the sound parts of the film.

Poor Rosher. Another casualty. With men like him looking for work, no one would be hiring inexperienced fellows like me.

I let Leo talk — between coughs, which were frequent when he was as riled as he was now — keeping my eye out for Eleanor. I wasn't heartened by his suggestion that there might be work on some silents slated for European release. C'mon, even I knew that Fox had announced that spring they weren't making any more silents at all, and I was sure other studios would follow. Leo might not admit it, but the director he'd both cursed and praised was the new Hollywood. He should learn to work with the likes of him. I know I wanted to.

Finally, when Leo was finished with his monologue, I brought Pauline Sloane into the conversation. I told him about meeting Morgan, about how he'd gotten her picture moved up, about how we were driving around town now searching for Julia, the estate's cook, and how I'd heard strange noises in the night.

In comparison to the world-changing event we'd just witnessed in the studio, my stories sounded like nothing more than small town gossip, though, and Leo offered few comments beyond a "that so?" or "watch out for that Morgan, he's a viper."

By this time, I saw the figure of my boss returning, and Leo, too, had to go back to work. He clapped me on the shoulder, his eyes bright, his face happy. "Take care and keep stopping by. Something will turn up. Something good that'll show you how it's really meant to be done."

Before I could say more, he was gone, and she was back, harrumphing into the back seat and urging me to drive home. Clearly, her visit to whomever had elicited nothing. Or rather, nothing she wanted. She sulked in the back seat all the way home.

"I should have known he'd take her for a *private* test. Of course. The bastard." She muttered something under her breath.

When we arrived home, the Nash was there, too, parked at a crooked angle in the garage. As I got in the Nash to reposition it, so I could pull in the Packard, I heard her argument with Morgan cut across the veranda and piazza. I worked quickly, cutting the engines fast once the cars were in place. I wanted to listen. They were in a front parlor.

"How could you!" A slap so loud it made my cheek burn to think of it.

"How could I what, El? Take a drive?"

"You were not taking a drive. You were taking her for a screen test! And she's in my fucking dress!"

"Calm down, El. There are lots of roles out there. You can't play them all, darling."

"Robbie, how could you be so cruel? You know I want . . ." She was starting to cry. I could hear it in her voice. I couldn't hear what else she said until a moment later, and now she clearly wasn't talking to him.

"Take off my dress!"

"*Oui, mademoiselle*, I will go change … "

"Now! Here!"

"*Monsieur* Morgan told me I could borrow it, *mademoiselle*. I did not mean to offend." For once, Julia sounded small and afraid.

"Take it off." Ice was in Eleanor's voice. "Give it back to

me. Now. It's not yours."

"*Monsieur*," Julia whimpered. But Morgan said nothing.

I looked across to the windows where shades made the scene play in silhouette: Julia slowly peeled off the dress, crossing her arms over her bare breasts.

"Marta!" Eleanor called. "Come here and take this dress away. Burn it! It has an odor to it!"

At this, even the stalwart Julia broke. She ran from the room, exiting the drama that continued to play out.

"I should fire her," Eleanor said, her voice now showing some contrition.

"She'd run right to Louella, and you'd deserve it."

"After I've been so kind to her? Giving her a job when you begged me to."

"If you fire her, she'll have no livelihood, pet. And then what will she do? Then she'll be knocking at Jack's door faster than you can say ... a star is born." I heard his fingers snap in the air.

"You bastard."

"Keep her around. I like her. And, in case you haven't noticed, she likes me."

"You're a snake, Robbie. You like her because ... "

"Because liking her makes you realize how valuable I am?" Sarcasm left him, and only honesty remained. There was something pleading about his voice, something that bordered on the pathetic. "How much you need me?"

"If she knew that was your rationale...."

"She just wants to get ahead. So does everybody. So do you."

"You don't really know what I want, Robbie. You never did."

Her voice dropped to a hush, and I could barely make out the words. I thought I heard him say he knew her better than she knew herself. I thought I heard him say he loved her, but the way he said it—there was something in it with the feel of groveling, like one of her fans craving a smile or a wink, a dog wanting a crumb.

And I thought I heard her respond with a mixture of disgust and fear. "Don't say that."

Then she came to the window and stared into the dusk, stared over to the garage where I wiped the dust off the Nash, and I could have sworn she stared straight at me when she next spoke. "I want what any girl wants — loyalty, devotion, love...and peace."

Robbie let out a surprised laugh. "Christ! Isn't that a line from 'Daughter of Destiny?'"

She turned back to the room, a different character, a different voice. "Maybe Julia won't want to stay."

"She'll stay. And she'll be your cook and pretend she's not. And everything will be happy, just like it was before. We'll all get along famously, won't we darling?" His voice darkened. "You won't disappoint me, will you? Not now, darling."

There was silence as they retreated to the far side of the room. Their shadows blended together. Robbie was comforting her, his arm around her. Their voices were murmurs in the dark, as rippling and incomprehensible as the fountain. I held my breath, wanting to hear more, and wanting to leave.

Just as I was about to, they came closer to the window, and Robbie handed her a drink.

"The shooting schedule came," Eleanor said in a more business-like voice. "I'm not happy with starting the day after the party. They weren't supposed to start with me."

"Oh good Lord, El. First you want me to move things up, now you're mad that I did as you wished! I moved heaven and earth ... "

"I know, I know .... but I'll be awfully tired that first day. Maybe we should cancel the party ... "

"No! Don't do that. They'll think something's wrong, that you're up to your old tricks. You need to show them just how healthy and vibrant you are, how ... ready!"

"Stop it," she said, but I wasn't sure what she was referring to. "I'm going up."

"We should go out."

"I'm too tired."

"Now, El, don't pout."

"We can go out another night, Robbie." Her voice was slow, as if speaking were an effort.

"Are you ill?"

"I have a headache."

"I can give you some aspirin for that. I have some in my bag."

Silence, then I saw her shadow cross the room, and in a few moments' time, light flooded from her bedroom window. Meanwhile, I saw another shadow join Morgan and heard Marta telling him that dinner would be ready soon.

"I'll be dining alone. Miss Sloane has retired for the evening."

"Oh. Is there..."

"She's fine, Marta. Just a headache. I'll give her something. Could you bring my dinner into the sun room? I'll listen to some music in there while I eat."

"Yes, *Señor*."

"And, Marta ....Take this cash and order some roses for me tomorrow, will you? For Julia. Here, I'll write down what the card should say...."

By now, I was no longer hungry enough to want to go anywhere near the big house. So I skulked upstairs to my own room and washed the day off my back.

In bed a little while later, I fell asleep with a copy of a Melville tale on my chest.

I awakened again to the sound of keening, but rolled over and buried my head in my pillow to shut it and this world out.

Chapter Eight

PERHAPS BECAUSE OF the nightmarish noises, I dreamt of Canfield and Brice Clement that night.

Brice was larger than life, his St. Nicholas-like face a glistening, laughing caricature. In my dream, it was one of my first days at Canfield, when I was still adjusting to the fact that I'd killed a man and was yet alive myself.

It all came flooding back in the dream, the sensations, the fears, the resentments. I'd resented that I was still alive. I think I'd wanted the State, or the "people," as the prosecutor in my case kept saying, to hang me. Then at last I'd sleep peacefully. I'd stop hearing my mother's screams.

My mother had been a dreamy woman, rescued from drudgery by my father, John Doyle, Sr. on a trip East, scandalizing his parents with a hasty marriage and returning with a bride they never fully embraced. When I was young, we'd lived in my grandfather's big house, with many servants, lacy curtains, and silence.

My grandparents were quiet, stately people who didn't like to make a fuss or to have one made in their presence. The only sounds I remember from their household were the tick-tick of an old clock on the mantelpiece in the crowded front parlor, and my mother's laugh. It echoed in the hallways and down the stairs, catching up with me wherever I was, like a playful wind that teases at the hairs on the back of your neck.

My mother had not been as beautiful as Miss Sloane's mother, nor even as lovely as Miss Sloane herself. But she had a liveliness to her that, when matched with her vulnerability, made her hard to turn away from. You wanted to protect her. She'd had darting blue eyes and a white face, and bright red hair that never seemed to stay where she pinned it.

Once my grandmother had scrutinized me after a bath

and pronounced, "At least you don't have that hair."

In my dream at Sloane Hall, my eyes burned with tears for my mother. Brice Clement stood over me laughing. He picked up a board— he was going to hit me with it. But instead he merely placed it on my chest. It read: "life," and the meaning was clear and horrible — a life sentence.

In streaming sunlight, I awakened sweating, sure that the noises at Sloane Hall had triggered the dream. Breathing heavily, I looked around as if the very walls could reassure me that it hadn't been real. But what had been the dream — the wail, Brice standing over me triumphant?

Rubbing my eyes, I brought myself back to the present. It would be a busy day with little time for reflection. Good. I washed up and headed for the house.

In the kitchen, Marta was already working, counting plates and silverware. Julia, looking as if nothing had happened the day before, was boiling eggs.

"Coffee is ready. And there is bread," Marta said distractedly pointing to the table.

"I'm all right. I'll help myself. Do you need to go into the city?"

"No. Too much here. The pool — I need you to fix it." She pointed toward the back of the house.

Pouring myself a cup of coffee, I sat down at the table. "What's wrong with it?"

"It has a fountain, too, at the very end. It's not working. You made the fountain here go, so..." She shrugged toward the front.

The fountain out front hadn't been broken, though, only turned off. But I didn't point that out to Marta. She had too much else on her mind. It felt good to be needed, so I quickly finished my breakfast, grabbed some tools and headed to the back of the house.

Edged in deep blue tiles, the pool glistened in the early sunshine. Below its surface, I could see the slender pipe of a fountain hugging one wall, extending to a corner where a sculpted fish waited to spew out babbling water. I looked it over and couldn't see the problem, so I had to actually wade into the water to take it all apart.

Stripping off my shirt, shoes and socks, I walked down shallow steps, getting my pants wet. Oh, it felt good, that cold slap of water encasing my body. The sun made me squint, so I took off my glasses and impulsively splashed water on my face to wipe off a coat of sweat.

This was just the kind of job I needed, a challenge in a challenging environment. For an hour, I tugged and pulled, using a wrench and a crowbar to take apart the pieces, laying them neatly one by one by the pool's edge. Finally, I came to the length of pipe that caused the problem and cleared out the mess that had clogged the system.

Unraveling mechanical mysteries is satisfying work. I think that's why I liked the camera work, too. It was clean and tidy. Lenses and pipes and gaskets and levers all have a way of fitting together neatly, unlike the moving parts of life itself.

I made far faster work of the reassembly—quickly screwing in the parts that I'd laid out in order on the cobalt tile. But I couldn't find the valve that would make the pump start. I felt the piping. I got out and walked around the pool, peering into the depths. Nothing. I got back in and waded to the fish. There I took a screwdriver and poked in the mouth of the sculpture, looking for a button or lever, or screw …

Water gushed out right into my face! Coughing, I jumped back, dropping the screwdriver to the bottom of the pool.

"You'd better fetch that," Robbie Morgan said from behind me, laughing.

I bent down and retrieved the tool, then wiped the wet hair off my face and squinted at him.

"The valve's over here," he said, grinning broadly. He pointed behind him, to a bench near some bushes. "She didn't want to have to get in the pool to turn on the fountain. See?" He took a step back, leaned over and twisted a knob. The fountain dribbled off. Then he turned again, and it cascaded to life.

Standing upright, he shoved his hands in his pockets and

chuckled with undisguised glee.

"Sorry, old man. I thought you were on your way out."

Ignoring his transparent lie, I slogged out of the pool. I'd walk by him, "accidentally" knock into him....

No. I wouldn't give him that. He'd laugh even more. I picked up my things and headed for the front of the house, away from him, saying nothing.

"I say, you really ought to speak to El about getting some swimming things for you too. I'm sure she won't like seeing you in those soaking rags any more than she liked seeing you in your other old clothes."

Responding would please him. That's what he wanted. Stony silence was the answer. I provided it with my back.

In a few moments I was in my apartment, stripping off the sodden clothes, drying my glasses, changing into dry trousers and shirt.

Changing gave me time to think. *Men hate you,* Reverend Milqueton had told me, *when they want something from you that they think you don't deserve.* That gave me comfort, that Morgan thought I didn't deserve something. And what was that—the affection of his stepsister?

Of course—he wouldn't think I was good enough for her. Here was another lesson, one that crept up on me. When thinking of Eleanor, I'd reduced our kiss to its most powerful element—longing—and I'd begun to believe in the dark corners of my soul that she actually did long for me, that somewhere in her silly talk about wanting love and devotion, she'd been making a plea to me.

No. She only liked teasing.

Combing my hair, I catalogued both assets and failures, Mister Morgan's and mine.

He was powerful. But I was strong. He was obviously wealthy. I was poor, but I worked for my living and didn't take it out of the work of others. He had some charm, was well-spoken, and even, in an eccentric way, had some looks. I, on the other hand, struggled to be couth, did not trust my tongue to articulate what was in my heart and mind, and had the nondescript looks of a field hand. But I … I was honest, and he was a liar. I was fair, and he was cruel. I was repentant, and he was a sinner.

It didn't matter. I might be better than men like Morgan, but I was playing the cruelest joke on myself to imagine for even a second that Eleanor wanted anything from me, or that he'd approve.

Finished with this scrutiny, I spun around to go back to the house and caught a glimpse of a figure in the high attic window across the way, moving quickly by the panes, someone I recognized from the tight bun on top of the head. Julia. She was in the attic that Eleanor so vigorously protected.

Had it been Julia's voice I'd heard last night? Closing my eyes, I tried to remember, comparing the nuances of the sounds I'd heard to Julia's own speaking voice. She was too stingy with her voice, however, and I didn't have enough to go on. The voice I'd heard could have been male or female. It was the voice of desolation, of abandonment, of self-loathing.

I rushed down the steps and over to the house. Not thinking, I entered by the front door only to see Julia coming down the stairs. Her eyebrows arched upward, a silent accusation of my impropriety. With new suspicion, I eyed her steadily.

"Does Marta need me?" I asked.

She shrugged in reply and vanished in the direction of the kitchen.

Marta showed up soon enough, appearing from the back hallway beyond the stairs with new chores for me to do. So the day went, with hardly any time to think, to rest, or even to eat. Throughout it, the memory of my bad dream echoed in my mind the way a muscle ache reminds you of an overly active day. I tried to shrug it off, but it caught me unawares at inopportune moments. It wore me out.

Late in the day, the hired servants began to arrive, and I showed them to the sun room to place their personal items there as if I owned this house, taking pride in its richness, and in my mistress' accomplishments.

Marta, too, was enjoying her role, completely in charge, ordering people here and there with an authority born of both confidence and experience. Several times she frowned and muttered something in Spanish or looked at me and rolled her eyes at some servant's clumsy mistake. "This night is very important," she said.

It seemed more important to her than to Eleanor who was nowhere to be seen.

Neither was Mister Morgan. I knew he was around because his car was still in the garage, but he remained out of sight for the remainder of the day.

The pace increased as the day shifted gears toward early evening. Unknown maids bustled in and out of the kitchen while Julia gave brisk instructions. The jazz orchestra arrived, and they put on their red-sashed uniforms and tuned in the great room. The valets, who had been hired to help park cars, came in as well and loitered by the garage in their matching red uniforms, laughing and joking. Marta strode from room to room muttering under her breath, checking and rechecking, consulting a card upon which she'd written notes.

At the Home, the biggest commotion we ever witnessed was the annual Christmas Eve dinner at which Milqueton handed us each a small present, usually something useful such as a muffler or new socks or a cap. The last year I was there, he had given me a dictionary and a pen knife, both especially meaningful gifts. The knife signified that he trusted me. The dictionary that he believed in me.

But those festivities were subdued affairs compared to this day. Even I couldn't resist its pull. I became excited as time wore on. I began to worry I wouldn't have time to wash and change, and with that worry I realized I, too, felt like I was attending this party. And with that realization came another — the memory of her inviting me to the party because they could always use an extra fellow to dance. And with that came yet another thought — the longing! It was always there, torturing me. I was the tortured one, not her.

At last, Marta released me, and I hurried back to my

apartment where I bathed and shaved. It was finally time to don my new tuxedo. I'd never tried it on since it had arrived, thinking that somehow doing so would be a sign of greed. Now I cursed myself for such false modesty. What if it didn't fit? There'd be no time to fix it, and I'd look ungrateful for not having taken care of it earlier.

No such problems befell me. The black pants and jacket were cut exactly right, and the stiff white shirt only pulled a little in the sleeves. The whole thing came with cuff links of black stone and button tacks that I'd never used before. In fact, assembling the suit took some mechanical prowess as I had to figure out how to affix the wide belt, tie the bow tie, and snap into place the studs and cuff links.

I ran the comb through my hair one last time, lingering over my reflection to once again remind myself— pinching a scar—that I had a job to do, that was all, that I shouldn't spend the night glancing over at the house looking to catch a glimpse of her, of what she'd be wearing. You notice what women wear, she'd asked. Of course I did. I noticed the perfect curve of their bodies, of her body. I noticed the welcome blush of their lips, her lips. I noticed, goddammit. And she'd forced me to notice her.

I stared in the mirror. I didn't consider myself a handsome man. I was passable, with plain brown hair and a squarish face, a chin that was perhaps just a little too prominent and eyes that were shadowed by heavy brows and hidden by my glasses. Nothing special.

The band's tuning escaped into the late day shadows. My three workers loitered in their ill-fitting uniforms by the side of the garage, smoking cigarettes, sometimes sneaking a drink from a flask.

Soon, before we were hardly aware of it, the party began. The first guests arrived, their cars were parked, the band started blaring out waltzes and tangos, glasses clinked, and laughter rose into the sky like smoke. The fuse was lit.

Each arrival brought glamour and stardom face to face. Everyone I'd ever heard of in the cinema was there and many I didn't know but vaguely recognized. Men in rich-looking tuxes and suits. Women in silks, jeweled chiffons the color of skin, satins, feathers, minks, their hair as bright and shiny as their costumes, their faces perfectly painted, smiles in place, eyes wide with curiosity and cynical pleasure.

The house became a jewel box for all these glittering diamonds and rubies and sapphires on display, their personalities as gaudy and as rock-hard as the stones they wore.

My own party began as the first guests arrived. Roland Maguire was among the crew, driving his boss's shiny Cadillac up the hill and around the drive. We'd run into each other occasionally at other parties, but because Eleanor only had me drop her off and not stay, I'd not had a chance to catch up with him.

"Quite a show," he said, after letting one of the valets park the big car. He walked over to me by the garage. "I don't think I've been up here before."

He unscrewed his own flask and drank. Everyone drank. The smell of alcohol seemed to be as heavy as that of the flowers and eucalyptus.

"Want some?" He extended the silvery flask to me.

In the distance, I heard Robbie Morgan's throaty laugh, and a kind of knifing despair hit me, the same kind of despair I'd felt when Jake told me I'd have to leave, the sense that I didn't fit in and never would, that it was all for naught, all the lessons Milqueton had tried to teach me. Standing there on the edge of the world, with the blue black sky reaching well beyond the artificial city, covering both murderer and victim, sinner and saint, I didn't want to know what was right or wrong.

"Sure," I said and took a swig.

It burned as it went down. But I didn't have enough experience to know whether it was good or bad liquor. Rubbing my mouth with my hand, I thanked Roland. Another car came around the curve, and I walked forward to direct its driver to a suitable parking space.

"Jesus," I said, looking at the driver.

He was so scrawny and short that he looked like a kid behind the wheel. He was having trouble backing it into the spot where I'd directed him, and some of the other drivers were beginning to laugh. The liquor made me laugh, too, even though he reminded me of Pete with his long eager face covered in freckles. I motioned for him to stop, and, shooing him over to the other side, I jumped into the driver's seat.

"Let me," I said, easily shifting the car into gear. "It's tricky."

"Gee, thanks, mister. I only just started. Don't know if they'll keep me—the Zukors, I work for. Don't know if they use a guy regular or just for these things."

After I had the vehicle safely maneuvered into a spot, we both got out. His uniform looked too big for him, and my guess was he'd lied about his age to get the job. Placing his hands on his hips, he stared at the brightly-lit house where the sounds of the party stole into the night.

"Holy Moses," he exclaimed. "That's some place." He turned toward me. "Say, do you have to bow around her?"

"Who?"

"You know, Miss Sloane. Her being royalty and all."

Roland snickered behind me.

Royalty? Robbie was British. Maybe they were both royalty and hadn't bothered to tell me. One more secret.

Roland came forward. "He only has to bow on special holidays. Opening day of the World Holy Fucking Cricket Cup and Empire Garter Crapping Day. Things like that," he said and handed me the flask again.

I drank. This time it didn't burn.

"Hank Grazkowski," said the young driver, offering his hand.

We all introduced ourselves.

"I've only been here a month," he continued, taking off his hat and rubbing his head. "I'm from Wichita, and..." He stopped as another car pulled up to the door and a young starlet with flame-red hair disembarked. "Hey—I met her last

117

week. At a gin joint near Vine." He whistled under his breath. "She was good!"

His exclamation led to a heated discussion among the other chauffeurs of who was the best fuck in town. Some claimed to have slept with big stars. Others with nameless climbers like the redhead Hank had drooled over. While I listened to their banter, I held my breath. I didn't want to hear, I was afraid to hear—her name. I was afraid, but I was waiting, expecting to hear it and knowing if I heard it, I'd feel foolish—foolish for what? For not sleeping with her or for wanting to? I didn't know.

"Give me another swig, Rolly," I said. I was liking the way it made me feel.

"Get a refill, will ya, when you go into the kitchen." Roland handed me the flask, which was nearly empty now.

Her name. Did someone say it? Did someone say "I screwed Pauline Sloane." Did he? No, I could breathe again. It was another actress. And another man outside this circle.

"They all do it," Hank announced. "That's the way they get their parts, you know. They call it the casting couch."

"You don't say, Hank," Roland murmured, but Hank missed the sarcasm.

I still had Roland's flask. I held it up. "More! And sumpin—somethin' to eat."

Into the night, onto the gravel, past the fountain, over to the kitchen.

Julia was alone arranging little tarts on a tray. Poor Julia.

When she saw me at the door, I held up the flask. "Empty," I said mournfully.

She laughed and pointed to some bottles on a sideboard.

"You got somethin' for us boys to eat, Julie baby?" I asked her.

"Wait a minute." While she handed the tray off to a maid who came into the kitchen, I filled Roland's flask, spilling some. Since it was too full to cap, I took another gulp and then screwed on the top.

"Here's some bread and cheese," Julia said, placing both

on a wooden tray with a knife. "And I have some roasted chicken." She went into another room and came back with the bird on a plate.

"Cluck, cluck," I joked.

For the first time since I'd met her, she broke into a genuine laugh. The good cheer of the party had even infected cold-hearted Julia. "*Monsieur* Doyle, you are drinking."

I laughed with her and gave an exaggerated shrug. "Yes, Mam'selle Nons, I am." And I bowed, sweeping the flask in front of me. Bowing. That reminded me.

"Miss Sloane," I said, as I righted myself. "Is she a princess or somethin'?"

Julia came to the sideboard and wiped up the spill I'd made earlier. Then she took the cloth and wiped a trickle of booze from the corner of my mouth.

"You're welcome," I said.

"Who told you that—about Miss Sloane?"

"Nobody." I didn't want to get Hank into trouble. Don't say nothin' that would get nobody else in trouble. That was the rule at Carfield. "Just thought, you know, since Robbie is."

"*Monsieur* Morgan's father was an earl," Julia said. "But his father is not Miss Sloane's father. *Monsieur* Morgan's mother, she died, and then his father married Miss Sloane's mother. But then he died, and she came back to America and married again—Miss Sloane's father. *Comprenez-vous?*"

Eleanor and Robbie were not related by blood. That much I "comprenezed."

Music and laughter drifted into the room from the kitchen door.

Marta poked her head in. "Julia, are the dessert forks in here?"

"*Non,* in the dining room. The chest by..."

"Oh yes, I remember!" With that, Marta was gone.

The music was a waltz. I grabbed Julia's hand and put my arm around her waist.

"Dance with me," I said.

She laughed again, but played along. "You will have a

bad head in the morning, *Monsieur* Doyle."

"Tell me about Robbie," I said. "About *Monsieur* Morgan. You like him, don't you?"

She blushed. "He is a very intelligent man."

One-two-three, the beat went. I guided her along the sideboard. One-two-three.

"He's an earl...."

"No, his father was."

One-two-three. "But she's not. A princess, I mean."

Julia shook her head.

One-two-three. Music, don't stop. Don't stop. Don't stop, don't stop, don't stop stop stop.

"He told everyone she was a princess." She nearly tripped over a chair. "He can make anyone a star. Anyone."

One-two ...

"But her parents are dead," I said.

"*Oui, monsieur,* they are dead." And she laughed. "But that does not make her a princess." "Many people," she continued, smiling at my drunkenness, "think *Monsieur* Morgan is not her stepbrother."

"Whadda they think he is?" I asked, dancing up to the door. I was a swan. I was fucking graceful.

"They think they are lovers." She giggled. "*Monsieur* Doyle, you are not a very good dancer."

"I've danced with her." Lovers. Naw. She'd not said that. "You have?"

"Just once. Just one time. But I've kissed her."

"Then you know she is a drunk." She smiled. Not a vicious smile. I don't think it was a vicious smile.

"Yes," I said. "But now so am I." I twirled around and nearly fell.

Julia laughed again. "Stop it, *monsieur.* You will hurt yourself and damage something. I have many things to do. I'll have someone take the food out to the drivers." She stopped mid-step, making me stumble again, and gestured at the trays.

Before I left, I helped myself to another drink from the bottle on the sideboard. I didn't want to use up all of Rolly's supply, after all.

On the way back, I heard it. It competed with the gurgle of the fountain. A laugh like that, uncaring, eternal, ungraspable. Up the scale and down again. *Don't be silly, John. You don't dance. do you? This is what you'd miss if you couldn't kiss me again. Love, devotion ...* When it touched my ears through the mixed-up blare of noises spreading around the house, I couldn't help but turn and peer up to the windows hoping to catch a glimpse of her. I hated myself for it. Like a dog waiting for scraps. Like...

There she was, on the veranda, her arm looped through Mister Morgan's. Her face was natural again with just a hint of make-up, a master stroke that made her beauty all the more striking next to so many artificial roses. Instead of a dress, she wore some sort of oversized trousers and matching blouse in a creamy silk fabric that seemed woven of butterfly wings. It moved fluidly as she walked, creating the impression that she was floating. She *was* a butterfly. A nymph. The girl in the fountain. Ungraspable.

She must have sensed my gaze because she looked over at me. Her smile turned brittle. Her eyes looked wounded, as if I'd abandoned her. And I wanted to rush over and ask why. what had I done, but I couldn't. Another Duesenberg crawled up the hill, and I wouldn't trust one of the hired valets to park it, so I rushed to the car instead, taking over from its driver and maneuvering the magnificent machine into one of the few remaining spots near the garage. By the time I was finished, she was gone. I went back to Rolly and crew and ate and drank with them. I played cards and craps. I heard her laugh in the fountain. Constant.

By eleven o'clock, the arrivals had stopped. And Rolly's flask needed to be refilled once more. I headed for the house. Past the fountain. Past the reminders. Wanting, longing. Breathing the same air.

Julia was at the stove cursing at a girl who looked no older than thirteen. A pot of sticky syrup exuded an acrid, burnt odor. Marta was pulling glasses out of a box on the kitchen table.

"What are you doing here?" she asked as she saw me come in. "You are supposed to be at the party. Miss Sloane was asking for you."

Julia stopped her cursing to glare at me. Her earlier good humor was gone.

"I've been busy. I came in to help." I burped. Julia laughed under her breath.

Marta looked as if she were going to protest and usher me into the party, but something made her think better of it. Perhaps she thought that sending me into that sparkling gathering would be like forcing a crow into a pen of peacocks. But I wanted to go in, I wanted to see her, Eleanor.

"All right. Come here. I need to get these out."

For the next hour, I worked with Marta and Julia, sometimes checking on the automobiles, but wanting to join the party now. My good sense was dulled by drink. By this time, I was sure I'd dance as well as a Russian ballet master, that I'd fit in. Let me prove myself.

Several times, I caught a glimpse of her dancing, once with a balding man at least twice her age, another time with Mister Morgan whose hands encased her protectively. I saw Morgan, too, with other women, but always his eyes flitted back to her, beseeching her to pay attention to him. They could have been my eyes.

And yet another time, I saw her smoking by the pool while some young starlet peeled off her clothes and dove in. A figure as beautiful as the girl in the fountain. A figure perhaps one of the other chauffeurs had fondled. A fluid sculpture, tempting lust out of every man in sight. As others in the crowd laughed and cheered, Eleanor's face turned cold and distant. Was she sizing up this woman as her competition? Was she wondering if she'd be required to doff her outfit and go in after her to prove she was capable of retaining her star status? Yes, dive in, Eleanor. Let me see you.

The rooms were full to bursting, and there was so much laughter, music, and chatter that it felt as if this were the first party of its kind after a long social Lent.

Snatches of conversation drifted past me as I went from room to room on my chores.

"She cried her eyes out after her sound test, I hear...."

"...drunk for half the shoot..."

"I know I don't sound like that—something's wrong with the damned machine. My agent's sorting it out...."

"Goat-gland movies, that's what they're making over there...."

"I'll insist they cast you as my co-star. Do you have to be home right away..."

"What do you mean by goat-gland?"

"Doesn't she have vodka? Vodka's the only thing that calms my nerves...."

"That doctor who put goat balls into men who couldn't..."

"This woman I work with is doing wonders. Even my wife notices it. Says my voice is deeper... certainly has improved her disposition, if you know what I mean."

"They're trying to give silents some balls by smacking sound on them. Goat gland movies, I tell ya...."

And Morgan in the corner, bent toward the band's trumpet player, a skinny man with a pock-marked face, vaguely familiar—like one of the men who'd passed us on Central Avenue—dark, greasy hair, bony hands, unhealthy looking. Morgan was giving him money, tightly folded bills passed from palm to palm so no one would see. But I saw.

I was just about to head back to the kitchen when I ran into Eleanor. She stood by the door from the parlor into the foyer, and when she saw me she moved to block my way.

"You said you'd come to the party." Her lower lip pouted.

"You invited me. I didn't say if I'd come." A joke accented by a lopsided grin. How clever I was.

"Marta can make do. You're a guest right now." Her words were a little slurred. Like mine. She took my hand.

I let her drag me into the room but then broke free and stood by the wall, clasping my hands in front of me, a guard on duty, a wallflower daring her to turn me into a prince. Across the room, Mister Morgan talked to Julia, who held a silver tray in front of her, and she was laughing, her face lit up with real mirth, as I'd seen it in the kitchen just moments — *moments, hours?* — ago. At one point, he put his hand under her chin and leaned close to whisper something to her.

"Dance with me." Eleanor put her glass on a nearby table and grabbed my hand. The music, fortunately, was a simple three-beat, and I'd already practiced in the kitchen. I was ready.

Stiffly pulling myself up, I put my hand on her waist and began the gentle dance. Up so close to her, I could smell again her perfume, I could make out the tiny line of sweat on her upper lip that did not repulse but attracted me, that made her look girlish and vulnerable. Her eyes blazed into mine. She was hurt, dammit. Hurt because Morgan was flirting with Julia.

I looked over my shoulder. Julia had left the room, probably summoned back to the kitchen by Marta. Morgan now stared straight at me.

All right. If this is what she wanted...

I moved my body closer to hers, digging my fingers into her tender waist and up until the edges of my hand felt the underside of her breast. She did not pull away. I nudged the hair away from her face and kissed her cheek. She didn't stop me. I placed my head next to hers and breathed into her ear profanities about what I could do if she were a willing partner, things the other boys had talked about, and what I expected her to do for me. She did not recoil.

And then the joke turned sour. The room, it swirled, it danced, it rotated so that my feet no longer had to move. The things I'd said — I wanted them. They were no joke — I really wanted them! I wanted them more than anything in the world. *Give them to me!*

Desire swamped me, pushing me under until I could barely breathe. I *was* a drowning man, gasping for air and finding only the waves of longing that broke over my body, cresting and falling with my thudding heartbeat and ragged breaths. I wanted to... *I had to...Please, let me...* The warmth of her body penetrated to my own, her scent filled my nostrils, strands of hair brushed my cheek.

"I..." *Please, please, let me...*

"I... love you."

Had I shouted it? Whispered it? Had I said it at all? I shook my head.

Morgan stood before us. I stopped.

"My dear. you must stop trying to give the hired help dance lessons!" he said to a tinkling of appreciative laughter. "We don't want our chauffeur running off trying out for musicals." He stopped and gave me a scathing glance, his cigarette held high next to his chin as if evaluating my performance. "Though, from the looks of it, I don't think there's any danger of losing him." More laughter greeted this remark.

But it wasn't his crude attempt at a joke that stung, nor the tittering that followed it. It was an overheard whisper, a dark, smoky woman's voice dripping with venom. "Gads, they get younger every year, don't they? Wasn't it the gardener last year? My god, he was just a boy."

"Thank you, Eleanor." I bowed ever so slightly and walked out of the room with a straight back, a good soldier, his duty done. Where was my reward? My ears and cheeks warmed from the blush that was exploding there. My face was hot, and I wanted, most of all, to disappear into the cool night and go back to the garage where I fit in. I'd have another drink— no, not another. I'd laugh and joke—no, not those jokes. I'd play cards. I'd suffer. Yes, I knew how to do that.

On the veranda, she caught up with me. "John, wait!"

I stopped without turning.

"To hell with Robbie. To hell with all of them," she said. She placed her hand on my shoulder. I turned around but did not look up.

She stroked my cheek with the back of her hand. "I would have liked you to stay."

Was she still teasing, still trying to make a point with Morgan? I looked beyond her and didn't see him. "I don't fit in."

"No, you don't." She looked down. "And neither do I."

Her hand lingered on my face. Without thinking, I closed my eyes and sighed. She was an instinctive woman, so she completed the sigh with her own, breathing onto my face as she bestowed a kiss on my cheek. But I was not to be treated like a puppy to be petted and cuddled. I had stronger needs now.

In the shadows of the veranda's roof, I pulled her to me and gave her a kiss, a hard kiss, not a soft imitation of one, but rather one where I pressed into her delicate lips all the longing and desire she had awakened in me. Take that, this kiss said. I hated her. I loved her.

After she pulled away, she smiled. "Meet me in an hour, outside, near the sun room."

∞

"Give me another," I said to Rolly. He passed me the flask.

"Hold on, fella. You don't strike me as the type who's used to drinking."

"I'll refill it. Don't you worry." I handed it back after a gulp.

Hank stood up after losing a round of poker.

"That's all for me. I'm cleaned out. Jeez, how long will this go on? Any more food, John? I'm hungry."

"Don't you worry," I said. "I'll go get somethin'. I'll get that little Julie to come out here, too. She's a firecracker. And she and Morgan ..." I waved my hand in the air. "They're a hot number."

"I thought Morgan didn't play that way," one of the other boys sneered. "I thought he liked 'em in pants." Snorting laughter.

Leaning against a car, Rolly looked down at the crew.

"Well, *she* wears pants," he said in a know-it-all voice. "At least tonight."

I stepped closer, felt my fists tighten. "She's his sister, for crissakes," I said with a dare-ya tone.

"Could have fooled me," one of the boys said.

"Where's that food, John?" Rolly asked.

I left. The hour was almost up. *Meet me by the sun room, John.* Should I go? *She wears pants. She's his sister. Not his blood sister, though. Where's the food, John?*

Into the kitchen—Julia was working with maids, arranging food on trays.

"Boys want some more, Julie," I said from the door.

She looked up at me and didn't smile. "They can wait. I'm busy." She went back to her task. "And do not call me that. My name is Julia. Julia Nons."

Not wanted there. Might as well go outside, by the sun room. Might as well. No harm in that. I'll just tell her that she needs to tell Julia to get the boys some food. That's all. She's the boss. She can order Julia around. Julie, Julia. What did it matter.

I stumbled in the dark, and found my way to the meeting spot. It was empty.

On this side of the sun room, the land sloped downward, which meant I stood on an incline where the ground was dark in shadow. You could feel you were on top of the world there, with the valley spreading below, the lights of houses and businesses making everything feel small and insignificant.

"Well, Johnny," I said to myself, "she's not here. What'd ya expect?" I turned to leave.

She appeared, a blur of white in the blackness, an angel floating from the void. Seeing me, she picked up her pace. The band music was faraway in this lonely little corner where the brightness of the party did not blot out the huge void of dark sky with its real stars and the city below with its artificial ones.

"John! Now you can dance with me. No one is here but us."

The music was a tempo I knew no steps for. It didn't matter. She crushed herself to my body. My arms enfolded her. I kissed her hair as we moved slightly to the distant beat of the band, pretending to dance when in fact we were ...

We were one breathing, longing body in the cool air, under the dark sky, feeling like the only thing alive, the only real thing for miles.

Chapter Nine

I WAS DRUNK.

For a little while, I forgot who I was. I was not John Doyle, son of a woman who'd drunk herself into a marriage with a wicked man. I wasn't the boy who'd murdered that man and paid for it with ten years at Canfield. Or the fellow who'd seen his friend nearly beaten to death there, and more like him mistreated in ways I'd forced myself to forget.

For a little while, I was only the man whom the great Pauline Sloane wanted. And that was enough for a lifetime.

We said nothing. We swayed to the music. I kissed her long neck, her cheeks, her ears, her nose, her mouth, each touch pushing me to press for more. She laughed — real happiness, nothing else — and kissed me back.

I didn't care that she smelled of alcohol, that she stumbled. I smelled of booze and stumbled, too.

This was something I'd never known, not caring where I'd fall as long as she was in my arms along the way.

The only time I'd never cared what came next was when I was in a fury to hurt someone — my stepfather, other bullies. This was a different kind of fury, sweet rather than bitter.

This was, it seemed to me that night, a reward for suffering so long in silence. I was not plain in her arms. I was not uncouth or lacking charm. I was not a killer. She saw in me what I most wanted to be, what I hadn't realized I wanted to be. A real man. A lover.

"John." She whispered my name.

I kissed it off her lips. She nuzzled into my neck and rubbed my back. She felt so soft, so fragile that I was afraid of hurting her. For the first time in my life, I was caught in a present tense I enjoyed, not wondering about the future nor worrying about the past. Only this moment existed, and I didn't want it to end. We had stepped outside time, she and I, into a world where... God, how I loved her.

"I want to feel your skin," she murmured and tugged at my shirt so that she could glide her hands underneath up to my chest, around to my back, kneading out aches I hadn't realized were there.

I was no stranger to strong desire. Like any man, I'd yearned for the touch of a woman. I'd craved to be consumed by the kind of flame she was now igniting in me.

"Ellie," I whispered.

"Say it again."

"Ellie. Ellie. El." I kissed her neck a thousand times, saying her name to the rhythm of my heartbeat. Each time I said it, she giggled with happiness.

"John," she said between kisses, "you're a good man. I know I can be good, too."

It was impossible for me to recollect exactly how long we stayed there. It seemed to last forever, yet it wasn't long enough.

And if you are wondering how I forgot how she had teased me, how fickle and cruel she had been, I have no excuse, not even the drink—because as soon as she appeared, I was shocked into sobriety. I had no excuse except raw hunger so powerful that it made everything but the present disappear—did I not already tell you I was a different man in her arms? I'd never held a woman like this. Never. I was lost. Already lost.

Time passed, and into our world, footsteps came, each one bringing reality closer. Pulling away, she continued holding my hand.

"There you are!" Robbie Morgan stood in a square patch of light cast from a window up above, looking like he was on a stage showcased in a spotlight. "The party's going fabulously, darling, but people are beginning to wonder where you are. Not good—having people wonder about you. Not tonight."

Although his tone was light, his eyes told a different tale. They stayed locked on where her hand grasped mine. Even when he brought his cigarette to his mouth, his gaze did not stray. After one last drag, he threw the butt to the ground and smashed it out with unusual vigor.

"Come along!" He held out his hand to her.

She obeyed, not saying anything to me. I thought of stopping him, of challenging him, of showing her (yes, a primitive urge) I could best him and win her love. A haze dulled my reflexes, though, so I stood fast.

I stood, breathing in the cool night air, trying to ease myself into the real world, to leave the place where she had led me, where she had bewitched me. Eventually, I awakened enough to tuck in my shirt and walk slowly back toward the front of the house. My legs were weak. I wanted to splash cold water on my face to awaken from this dream.

It was very late.

As I made my way along the south wall toward the kitchen, Julia met me. Hugging her arms to herself against the chill, she cried out when she saw me. "*Le voila!* I have been wondering where you were. I need you." She turned, expecting me to follow.

Not only was it odd she'd sought me out, but odder still that, when we reached the kitchen, she had no chore for me to do. Morgan must have told her to lure me away from Ellie. Maybe keep an eye on me. I hung around the house and didn't go back to the other boys.

For the rest of the evening, I felt like a different man. My skin seemed to prickle with fever, my heart raced with need. Even a few seconds when I wasn't occupied with a task would find me drifting to the deep waters of that kiss, that embrace. She had drowned me.

The party wasn't over for hours, and, even then, several stragglers lingered on the veranda saying endless good-byes. I watched from the shadows as Eleanor bade them farewell. I willed her to look at me. But she stood out of sight, slightly behind Robbie Morgan who did look at me, a chilling stare that contained its own brand of willpower — a vengeful kind.

After she herself had gone into the house, he threw

another spent cigarette into the bushes. His eyes never left mine as he tossed the smoke. His message was clear. He'd have loved to press out the glowing ash on my skin.

I ran back to the kitchen to offer my help to Marta, but in reality I still hoped I'd see Eleanor. Perhaps she'd come down to thank everyone. Perhaps she'd wander through a hall in search of a scarf, a shawl, a misplaced earring.

No rendezvous awaited me, and eventually Marta declared our chores over for the time being. We were to finish in the morning. Morning — dawn was not that far off.

By the time I crept into my bed, all the lights except Eleanor's were out at the main house.

Standing at my window, I whispered to her, wishing she was doing the same.

"Good night, El," I said.

Tomorrow I would have to try to place this in perspective. I'd have to remind myself again who I was and who she was. I'd have to detail the hopelessness of my longing and perhaps burn it from my heart.

But tonight, I would allow myself to dream of her. I slipped under the sheets with relief, not bothering to close my eyes, reliving every second of our dance in the dark, correcting myself when I missed a detail, taking pleasure in remembering an aspect that I'd forgotten — the tilt of her head, the moonlight on her hair, the sound of crickets in the background, the song the band played.

It was a still night, and an air of satisfaction fell over the house. I fell asleep.

○ঙ

Someone had put a vise around my head and was tightening it by tapping in a wooden screw. *Thud thud thud.*

"*Señor* Doyle."

Thud, thud thud.

"*Señor* Doyle."

"Go away," I mumbled and rolled over. Go away, Brice, leave me alone. Go away, go away.

"*Señor* Doyle! *Señor* Doyle! You must come quickly! *Señor*

Doyle!" My eyes opened. Not Brice. Marta.

My head exploded with pain as I sat up in bed. Steadying myself, I pulled on trousers and shirt, and then let Marta in. A long-fringed shawl covered her shoulders, and she was still in night dress, with a black hairnet over her head and a flashlight in her hand.

"There is a problem at the house. You must come!"

"What is it?" I mumbled. My stomach churned. The worst part of the liquor's taste was left, dry, metallic, sour. I needed to vomit.

"An accident! A terrible accident!"

"Eleanor?" I mumbled, my head throbbing.

"*Señor* Morgan. Not the *Señorita*. Come quickly!"

I followed Marta out, down the stairs and across the drive and lawn to the veranda, my pulse pounding in my ears, a hammer on metal. I must have only been asleep a short while. It was still dark.

Sobs came from the rooms above. Eleanor's voice! I forgot my pain and raced past Marta upstairs and into the front bedroom.

What a horror greeted me— blood on her creamy blouse, her sleeve, her hand! Eleanor sat on the edge of the bed, crying, rocking back and forth.

I froze. Morgan. Had he... ?

He didn't mean it, Johnny. Don't worry me by you getting riled up.

Marta brushed past me to go to her. The movement made Eleanor turn, but her eyes didn't focus. She didn't seem to recognize me. She didn't say my name or call out for me. I was no one. I was ... still with fear. Was she hurt?

Marta knelt before her.

"I'm sorry. I tried..." Eleanor said. When Marta touched her knee, she flinched, then rocked back and forth again. "I wanted to be good...."

"Hush, *niña*. Hush," Marta cooed. Then she looked at me and nodded toward the dressing room where the door was ajar. "*Señor*, in there!"

I took a step toward Eleanor, poor El. But Marta fiercely shook her head and pointed to the other room. "In there. Please."

I turned, with great reluctance, toward the other room, and here was a more grotesque sight still. Mister Morgan sat in the dressing table chair, his eyes half-closed, his legs sprawled out before him, and a six-inch butcher's knife stuck in his left shoulder.

"Miss Sloane, she found him. She tried to help him, but— *Madre de Dios*—she is not strong. She only managed to get him here...." Despite Morgan's horrible pain, I breathed more easily. He hadn't hurt her.

I examined him while Marta comforted Eleanor.

"Acc'dent," he mumbled, his eyes half closed. "Acc'dent."

"Remove it," Marta called over to me. Mister Morgan groaned.

"No, he's lost too much blood," I said. Already, he looked ashen. "He needs a doctor. Call one."

Marta went to the telephone by the bedside and dialed the operator. While she made the necessary arrangements, I felt for the man's pulse. His skin was still warm, not clammy, but his heartbeat seemed weak.

My head aching but clear, I rushed to check on Eleanor.

"I'm sorry," she said to me. It seemed the only thing she was capable of saying.

"You said you tried," I said, kneeling where Marta had been. "You tried to help."

I shivered. Tried what? No, she couldn't have. Not like that. Not like me.

Let her out, or I'll kill you! I swear it! Let her out of the closet, you fucking bastard!

I closed my eyes.

"The doctor's car— it is not running!" Marta turned to me. "You must take *Señor* Morgan to him."

I stood, glad to be rid of bad memories. "You'll have to help me move him."

Together, we went back to Morgan. After wrapping a towel around his shoulder to keep the blade from slipping, I gave Marta quick instructions on how to help me get him down the stairs. I swung his good arm around my shoulder and hoisted him to his feet. With a mighty groan, he managed to stand enough to lean against me. Marta went to his other side and kept her hands on his waist to steady him. Thus arranged, we started for the door.

When Eleanor saw us, she covered her eyes with her hands and wept again. *Please Lord, don't let her live through what I lived through.* Couldn't think of it. She couldn't have... no, not to Morgan. Why?

"I'll handle Mister Morgan on my own! You see to her." I shrugged toward Eleanor.

As I maneuvered Morgan out of the bedroom, I heard Marta consoling Eleanor. "I will draw a bath for you and wash up your bed things. Do not worry. You did your best. No one could have done more."

In the hallway, I could see the path Eleanor had taken with him from what must have been his room at the back of the house. A streaked trail of blood stretched around the stairs to the attic and led into her room.

In the car, a few minutes later, I expected Morgan to suffer in silence as I sped him to the address Marta had given me. Instead, he insisted on talking, wanting to make sure I knew how the awful event had happened.

"It was an accident," he gasped out. "An accident. I was with... Julia... and playing a game...."

"Try not to talk, Mister Morgan." I looked over at him. I'd propped him in the front seat of the Duesenberg, the fastest car in the barn, so that I could keep an eye on him.

"No. Important. It was an accident...."

Although it was difficult to tell exactly what happened, his tale seemed to indicate he'd been teasing Julia and had goaded her into throwing the knife at him, "like a circus act."

Even through my hangover, I could still reason. Why would Julia have a knife in his bedroom? No need to stretch imagination to figure why she was there in the first place — but with a knife? And why would he feel the need to make excuses for her if she'd really attacked him?

Peering into the darkness ahead, I found my way to the doctor's home, a small house at the bottom of the hill, just off of Franklin. A single light shone from the back, so I careened around the corner and screeched to a halt there. Helping Morgan out of the car was tricky business. He'd apparently stiffened during the drive and found any movement, no matter how small, excruciatingly painful. The doctor must have heard us arrive, however, and he joined us outside with a hypodermic needle in hand.

"Good lord!" he said, looking at the knife. "Here, this will help."

Ripping away some of Morgan's tattered shirt, the doctor administered the shot.

Morgan gave us both a sickly smile. "Just what I needed," he said, his speech slurred. "More please."

He was now able to be moved, and, together, the doctor and I managed to get him into the house and onto an examining table in the little office at the back. The doctor was small but strong, with a thick-muscled neck and square face, heavy white hair, and bead-like eyes.

As the doctor examined Robbie and removed the knife, he asked questions.

But even the effects of the drugs left him unwilling to change his story. It was just an accident, he repeated. "Julia did it. Always knew she couldn't be trusted" he said and started laughing.

"Stay still!" The doctor pulled sutures through the puffy skin.

"Damned French. Never trust a Frenchman, Johnny. Never trust 'em!" Robbie was silly from the effect of the drug added to the liquor he'd already consumed.

"You said she threw it, young man?" the doctor asked him.

"Yup. Straight as an arrow."

"Must be some woman. Is she a big one?" he asked.

"Oh yes. An Amazon," Robbie replied, laughing again.

Julia was no Amazon. She was small-boned and short.

"Had to be to throw a knife with that much force."

"She was damned angry, sir. Damned angry. Never make a Frenchie angry, Johnny. Makes 'em careless." Robbie twisted his head toward me.

The doctor was able to get no more information from him. But he did stitch him up quick and neat.

When the doctor suggested an overnight stay in the hospital, Robbie tried to sit up. "No, sir. No hospital for me. I'm right as rain." But he nearly passed out.

After the doctor let him rest for a spell, we both helped him back to the car. By now, he was snoring softly.

After Robbie was settled into the front seat, the doctor talked to me in the gray light of pre-dawn. "Ordinarily, I'd report this sort of thing to the police. That knife was pushed in with some force. Just missed an artery. But he's insisting it was an accident. Can't persuade him otherwise. Could be the shock, though. If he changes his mind, let me know."

He handed me a bottle of medicine for Robbie to take for the pain, and I was on my way back to Sloane Hall.

Robbie slept all the way there, leaving me time to think and wonder. As with the noises, I suspected I'd get no easy answers to this night's ruckus. They were all hiding something. Just as I'd begun to feel close to Eleanor, I was faced with evidence of some major fraud. Of course I wondered if she had stabbed him. She'd been bloodied. He was in her room. Had he attacked her?

If so, why didn't she just say so?

With little sleep after a tiring day, I was moving through an invisible wall of mud. Every action — shifting gears, looking in the rearview mirror — seemed to take longer. She'd feel the same and be in no shape for an interrogation. I'd have to wait

At the house, Marta helped me steer Morgan to his bed as the pink light of early morning began to signal another day. The first day of Eleanor's new movie. How would she find the strength to go to the studio? What a stupid idea to have a party the night before. Morgan's idea.

After getting Morgan settled, I stood outside Eleanor's closed door. I stood, tired, hungry, afraid. *Should I go to you – can I take that liberty?* It was a humiliation not to know. As I turned to leave, Marta appeared from Eleanor's room.

She whispered to me. "I will go make some coffee for you and for Miss Sloane. I must awaken her in an hour. No later."

"Is she all right?"

"*Si*, as good as can be expected." She pointed to the door which was closed tight. "I put her to bed after I cleaned up. I think having it all wiped away helped her. I had to roll up one of the rugs." She shook her head back and forth at the memory. "But at least Mister Morgan is not in danger."

A curious comment, I thought, if Julia had been the attacker and was still in the house. Which made me wonder where the cook was. Had she gone back to bed after the incident? Had she been frightened and run away?

Marta looked me over. My shirt was old and stained. My pants were ripped. And I wore shoes with no socks.

"You should go get cleaned up. You will need to drive her."

I headed back to the garage apartment to wash and change. My head was pounding now, a heavy dull ache behind my eyes and pinched around my forehead, as if my skull had shrunk and there wasn't enough room inside. I swallowed some bicarbonate of soda and nearly gagged it all up. I splashed cold water on my face and rubbed my eyes. I leaned on the sink and stared in the mirror. Pale as paste. Nothing to brag about. What did she look like now? What did she feel like? I resisted the urge to go to the window. I finished washing instead. But, after I toweled myself off, I walked to the window. Her drapes were still drawn.

By now, the sun's rays were casting the valley and hills in stark relief, making the landscape cruel and inhospitable, making us smaller and even more insignificant. Eerie stillness wrapped the mountains in blue shadow, but workers were rising somewhere. Somewhere they were drinking their morning coffee, grabbing lunch pails and leaving, slipping easily into something normal, something not like this, and that was a comforting thought.

I'd be driving her in the Duesenberg, so I grabbed the uniform, its scratchy wool choking me at the throat, pinching even more pain from my head. Cap in hand, I headed back to the house.

By the fountain, I looked up. The light was on in Eleanor's room. I paused. No answers came.

In the kitchen, Marta silently poured me coffee. Julia wasn't around.

No talk, just the gush of coffee from the pot to my mug, the scrape of my chair, the swoosh of water from the spigot. If we talked, it would be of last night, and we couldn't speak about that.

Light footsteps came into the hallway, and there she was, at the door. At last. My heart raced. I stood. I rubbed my hands on my pants and then quickly wiped a napkin across my lips. I started to say, "ma'am," just because I wanted to say something. But I stopped and let my mouth hang open like a fool. I was a fool. Marta jumped up and went to her.

"*Señorita*, let me get you some more café."

"No. I've had enough." She was a ghost of herself. Or a doll. Something mechanical. She wore pale yellow again, a color she favored. Some loose dress with a V-neck. Her hair was curled so carefully it didn't move when she nodded her head. And her face was painted like a canvas, pink on those high cheeks, red on those lips, something gray above her eyes. Eyebrows drawn with a pencil. She twisted gloves and hat in her hands.

I thought to grab my cap and place it under my arm, standing at attention.

"I'll bring the car around, ma'am." The word "ma'am" slipped out. But it was just as well. That word was a test of what was true and what wasn't, what I'd dreamed and what had happened. Before I turned, I saw her mouth open a half inch, and her eyes narrow. So I'd really held her after all.

Out front, she slid into the back seat without looking at me. In fact, during the entire drive, she stared at the window, sucking in her lower lip, even wiping away some tears.

As I drove, I glanced at her in the mirror. I think I wanted to see something in her face that would let me ask her things— how she was, if she needed anything, if she even remembered our kisses, and yes, what had really happened to Morgan. But I didn't see that opening. So I drove, my head pounding, my hands sweating in their kidskin gloves, my whole body screaming to get out of that uniform or out of the car. Better yet, out of all of this. I wished I could say this to her: I want to take you—and me— away from all this horror. But it sounded like a cheap line from a movie. That made me feel bad, too, that I couldn't think of anything better to say.

A few minutes before we reached the studio, she pulled out her compact and repaired her face. Along with the make-up, she painted on a bright smile, practicing it in the tiny mirror.

Finally, I found my voice.

"Are you in trouble? Do you need help, Eleanor? "

At the sound of her given name, she looked up, sharp and quick. "You are so good, John."

Did she mean it? I don't know. She didn't say more because we were in the city, and soon I was at the Paramount entrance, crawling up to the arch with its wrought-iron filigreed gate— the top of which, I'd been told, had been added to keep grieving fans out after Rudolph Valentino's death three years earlier.

She smiled and waved to the guards who greeted her like an old friend. Then she gave me directions in a flat voice, so low I had to strain to hear. Turn here and there, it's in the back, the building over there, past that circus set.

She leaned forward, her hand and elbow near my ear. "There it is. That building on the back lot." She sank back in her seat, letting out a slow breath of exhaustion.

After stopping, she got out so abruptly that I felt cheated.

I'd not realized how much hope I'd pinned on the chance of holding her hand for the few seconds when she exited the vehicle. I ran around to her side of the car just as she snapped her handbag closed and straightened her hat. Not able to resist, I reached for her hand.

"Don't worry, El," I said. "It wasn't your fault."

I didn't know whose fault it was. I only wanted her to be the woman she'd been the night before, in my arms.

She looked up, her eyebrows lifting in surprise. Uncharacteristically, she blushed. I wondered if I'd been too forward, calling her "El" in public, where someone might overhear. But she squeezed my hand in response, and a tear gathered in the corner of her eye. Wiping it away with her gloved hand, she squared her shoulders as if going into battle.

"I keep trying to fix things," she said. "And I just make them worse, John."

With quick strides, she was gone, disappearing into the large nondescript building that squatted in the California sunshine.

I went back to Sloane Hall, dragging myself up that hill in the Duesenberg, feeling like I was pulling the car with me. Worn out, I took off my uniform and sought out Marta to find out if there was anything she needed me to do. She was in the kitchen, sleepy-eyed over her own cup of coffee. Julia was still nowhere to be seen.

"You should rest now, *Señor* Doyle." She sipped her coffee. "While you have the chance."

"How is Mister Morgan?"

"He is sleeping. He took some of the medicine." She shook her head. "Too many medicines. Not good."

"That was a pretty big gash. He's probably in pain."

She snorted in disgust. "He should suffer like a man."

I ignored her comment and poured myself a cup of coffee from the pot on the stove. I was tired but restless, and by now I was used to my headache.

"You must go lie down. I am going to lie down. When Miss Sloane returns, she will need you. She will need us both."

After finishing my coffee, I did as she said. I slept away the morning, a black sleep where you're not even sure you're sleeping, and you don't feel any better for the rest when you finally get up. In the afternoon I worked on the Packard, looking at clocks every quarter hour, thinking more time had passed, thinking of Eleanor working, wondering when she'd call for me.

When Marta finally did come to fetch me to tell me that Eleanor had called for the car, it was sunset. I threw on the uniform and cap and sped down the road, but I still had to wait nearly forty-five minutes outside the studio building before she appeared. I passed it thinking of what I'd say, going back and forth between a friendly sort of inquiry for her health to a more intimate level of conversation. I got more bothered the more I debated myself.

I kept telling myself, too, that I'd wait five more minutes before going in to see about her.

Wind blew dust down the studio street and against the building's colorless walls. People walked by, talking, laughing. Doors slammed, engines started. Shadows drained the color from the day. Muted grays and musty tans took over the world. Rest beckoned. And no rest came—neither for her in the studio finishing her day's work, nor for me, waiting uneasily outside. I leaned against the car, watching the door, a hunter watching.

The door opened. I straightened. Several people left, calling cheerful farewells to each other. A lull, then more exits. Finally, she came out, a handsome man kissing her good-bye lightly on the cheek. Although she smiled at the gesture, her eyes were hollow.

Pulling on her gloves, she did not look up to see me. Her face was white, without makeup, her hair mussed, and her gait slow and wavering. As she headed for the car, I became afraid that she would faint, so I ran to grab her, holding her under the elbow. She shook like a willow. She said nothing, but let me settle her into the back seat.

Driving away as fast as I could, I kept glancing at her.

Gone was the depression of the morning. In its place was just the misery of the sick. I began to wonder if I should stop at the doctor's on the way home, the same doctor I'd taken Morgan to in the wee hours of the morning. But by the time we reached that point, she was asleep, her body trembling with chills as she curled up like a baby on the seat.

Marta took over when I got to the estate, hustling Eleanor off to bed with promises of broth and tea. Eleanor murmured something to Marta I did not hear. But after getting Eleanor settled in the house, Marta came over to my apartment and gave me a message.

"She wants to see you. Let her rest awhile. Then go to her. As long as her light is on, you can go to her."

Her room, however, was dark for most of the night. I know because I sat on my bed staring outside, watching as other lights in the house were turned out one by one, as Marta closed up for the night, as lights came on and were swallowed up in the void of the valley below.

In the quiet, voices whispered to me, her voice last night, Robbie's at the pool, my mother, Pete, Milqueton, Jake, even my stepfather taunting me. *You think you're a little man, don't you, Johnny? You think you can fight me?* It made my throat dry and tight.

How could I think with a head that still throbbed? Resolved: never to drink again.

Worn down, I stared at her room, as if, as if it held the key, as if her light going on would make my past disappear. At one point, I even considered going over to her, thinking of an excuse to offer. "I thought I saw your light." Or, "Marta said I should come by." I could hear myself saying it. I practiced it, whispering against the window pane, my courage disappearing as the mist on the glass evaporated. I did not move. I was caught in the present now, all right, one I didn't like, a punishment for no crime.

I closed my eyes. After my mother had married my stepfather, I became convinced she didn't want me around. He certainly made no effort to hide his feelings in that regard.

Why does the boy have to eat with us? Why does the boy have to sleep down the hall?

And when my mother finally did take up for me, I ended up wishing she hadn't. The first time he'd beat her was because she'd refused to let him punish me. He'd wanted to keep me from eating dinner because I'd not polished his shoes. She'd stood up to him and told him I was not a servant, I was her son. And she had set a plate in front of me with a wave of her hand.

He'd flung the plate to the floor with one stroke, then flung the back of his other hand against her cheek. As it turned out, this was the mildest of his tirades. Once he'd tasted brutality, he couldn't get enough. And the surest way for my mother to provoke him was for her to take up for me. My eyes closed tight, I tried to remember her. Exactly what she did look like. The memory is faded. I saw no full portrait. Only expressions. Sad eyes. Gash of a mouth.

When I opened my eyes again, Eleanor's light was on.

I rushed into the darkness and flew up the front steps and into the house, to her room. Everything else, including dim memories and gloomy fears, receded.

∞

She rested in bed, pale but less sickly. She wore white satin, with something feathery at the wrists and collar.

"I was so hoping you'd come." She whispered it.

I hurried to her side, sitting on the edge of the bed and grabbing her hand. Her voice was the voice of days ago, the teasing voice of confidence carried on the breath of brandy — an empty glass was by her bed. I didn't care.

"How could I not come?" I kissed her hand, then her neck, and then her cheeks. "El."

She reached over and turned out the lamp.

In the ghostly silver light of the moon, I was in her bed.

Chapter Ten

A CONFESSION: I'D never been with a woman before.

Sure, boys at Canfield liked to brag about their experience, just like the boys I talked to at parties here. But I was never sure how much was boast and how much was fact. I suspect that most of the boys who'd been at Canfield as long as I had been were just like me — with no opportunity to act on their lust. And when I'd left the School, I couldn't bring myself to spend money on prostitutes. Not that I hadn't considered it. Yes, I'd thought of seeking solace in the arms of a working woman, if only to remove the stigma of virginity. But I'd always decided against it, not wanting to part with my few dollars for what I was sure would be a fleeting pleasure. And afraid, yes, afraid I'd be so green and ignorant, that I'd be laughed at.

So my night with Eleanor was a line in my life. I was a man now. A man — yet it made me feel weak, as if under a spell. How could that be? After that night, I couldn't stop thinking about her and wanting that night to happen again and again.

To this day — Jesus! — my breath stops when I think of that night. And everything — *everything!* — from the tilt of her head to the tone of her voice to the flick of her hand in the air, everything now became an affirmation or denial of my love. I had entered a world of coded messages.

I wanted to stay with her all night and the next day, to make love in the cool shade of her bedroom, in the white hot blaze of noon, in the lazy shadows of afternoon, never to leave the nest of wrinkled sheets and overlapping limbs.

This was new to me — the desire to linger.

Ever since I'd been a boy in my grandparents' strict household, in my stepfather's mean home, in Canfield, I'd always been thinking of the next place, the next time. Next time it will be better. Next place will be finer. Next time, life will be easier. Next time, next time... there will be hope instead of despair. I'd forgotten about this time. This moment. I'd forgotten how to enjoy it.

If only we could have lingered. As dawn's mist intruded, I considered how it would look for me to be in her bed in the morning. Kissing her lightly, I rose and began to dress. She stirred.

"Do you have to go?" she asked, sleep still in her voice.

"I think it's better for you if I do."

"Better for me." I heard the smile in her voice. "You are so sweet, John. Such a good man. Good for me."

I remembered her words when we'd first embraced. She wanted to be good, too. Maybe I was to provide the example. I'd try.

I kissed her again, an embrace that threatened to make my will to leave crumble, and made my way to the door. After softly closing it, I was startled to see Mister Morgan's door ajar and a light coming from his room. As I crept down the stairs, a shadow crossed his threshold.

A few hours later, Eleanor was coifed and dressed, ready to go into work before I was even finished my breakfast. I snapped to attention and ran to get the car.

Dark glasses covering her tired eyes, she sat in the back of the Duesenberg in a shiny gray dress and tight-fitting hat. She scowled so much, I began to fear she regretted our rendezvous. Then, just five minutes away from Sloane Hall, the source of her irritation became clear.

"I want you to burn that uniform," she said. "I never should have ordered it for you."

I said nothing.

"And I hate sitting in back here. Stop the car."

I pulled over to the side of the empty road so that she could get out of the back seat and switch to the front.

"That's better." She reached over and curled her fingers through mine.

☙

As I drove back to the estate that morning, I lived and breathed every moment of the night before, becoming so distracted that I nearly ran off the road on a long flat stretch by letting the Duesenberg creep up to the high speeds its manufacturer bragged about. But when I returned to Sloane Hall, the smell of burnt wood hanging in the air snapped me out of my dreamy thoughts.

Marta came running at the sound of the tires on gravel.

"Good thing that our little Julia has such a sharp nose. She smelled something. Miss Sloane must have been smoking in bed, *Señor*. The whole thing is nearly gone. We managed to put it out with blankets and water from the bathroom...."

This cut me, this bad omen. I deserved at least a single day free of worry. Just one day—one day to think it all through and remember. Her bed. The bed where we'd... I rushed upstairs with Marta behind me, the bitter smell of smoke growing stronger with each step, fueling my own temper.

She hadn't been smoking. Not when I'd left her that morning.

"Where's Morgan?" My voice shook as I went to the door of his room. The son of a bitch. My muscles tensed. To hell with his injury. He'd have to take his punishment. Pushing the door open, I was met with the lingering aroma of his cologne but nothing else. He was gone.

"He left this morning." Marta followed me to the door. "After you left for the studio."

"His arm..."

"When *Señor* Morgan wants to do something, he does it." She clucked her tongue. "She will not be happy."

I turned to her. "What do you mean?" My voice was too harsh. Too obvious.

Marta looked down. "*Señor* Morgan fixes things. Keeps things in the newspapers and things out. And he'd made sure that she had this part."

"Maybe she needs another agent," I said.

Marta looked up, her mouth in a weak smile. "She needs many things." And unspoken, hanging in the crystal air, was the question, "Are you what she needs? Show me."

"I need your help," Marta continued, "moving Miss Sloane's things into this bedroom."

"Why not the front guest room — or the other rooms?"

"The roofers are repairing the front room," she said, impatiently. "They arrive today. And the other rooms are dusty and unready. Can you help me move some of her things?"

"Of course." I followed her into the bedroom I'd just left a few hours ago. It wasn't the same room. The bed itself looked bad enough, a charred mess of smoldering sheets, but ash had also licked up the wall, creating a black stain. And the room no longer smelled of us — Eleanor and me. It smelled of smoke even with all its windows open to the morning breezes.

I helped Marta carry boxes of clothing downstairs to air outside, and then went back upstairs to tote a crate of personal items to the guest room — a carved wooden jewelry box, bottles of perfume and cosmetics, silky scarves, a hat, and several pairs of gloves.

Just as I crossed the threshold, the crate gave way, scattering its contents on the floor. I bent to pick them up, drinking in the scent they gave off, her scent, the odor of flowers and oranges overpowering the sharp smell of burnt wood and bedding. The jewelry box lay open on the floor, yielding a strange treasure trove. It contained a secret drawer, which had sprung open when the box had fallen.

A single newspaper clipping rested there. It was an obituary.

"Basil Griswold dead at 25," the headline blared. I read on:

"Son of wealthy railroad tycoon George Griswold, Basil Griswold died at his home yesterday. He was twenty-five. Basil was the Griswolds' only child, and husband of Eleanor Brickman Griswold…"

My hands went cold. Married — she'd been married. The

rest of the story talked more about the Griswold family than Eleanor and her ill-fated husband. The only reference to her was the date of her wedding, a mere fourteen months prior to her husband's death.

"John!" Marta called from the stairwell. I scooped up the jewelry box and replaced the clipping. "Make sure you close the door when you are finished. I do not want the smell to travel to that room now."

"I will!" I stood and arranged the things in what was to be Eleanor's room. It was not nearly as large as her bedroom and still held his smell, his sickly cologne. Something too sweet for a man.

I grabbed one of her perfume atomizers and misted the room with her scent.

႒

By the time I picked her up late in the day, Eleanor was so exhausted she could barely speak. So I did not tell her about the fire. Silence connected us to the other silent moments we'd shared earlier, and I was selfish enough to want to taste those memories even on the drive home. Sitting next to me in the front seat, she curled up and fell asleep, her head on my shoulder. Arranged thus, I could pretend during the drive home that she was more than my secret lover, that she was my girl, that I was capable of protecting her, that I could take her out and show her off as mine.

When we arrived at the estate, she was ill again, complaining of fever and headache. I called for Marta to help get me get her into the house. As we went up the stairs together, she asked why it smelled like smoke.

"There's been a fire," I told her. "It must have been a cigarette."

She straightened and trembled—so much so that I was afraid she was having a fit of some kind "I wasn't smoking... I didn't smoke." She turned to me. "What was burnt?"

"Your bed. You'll have to sleep in the guest room."

She collapsed onto the stairs, sitting with her head in her hands.

"No, I can't sleep there. Not there." She shook her head back and forth.

I sat next to her and placed my arm around her shoulders. "It will only be a little while. Marta said she has ordered a new bed for you. She said it would be delivered by the end of the week."

By now Eleanor was crying, her face buried in my chest, murmuring about how tired and sick she was, how she didn't want to sleep in that room. When her sobs subsided, I gently helped her up and headed up the stairs. Although she didn't fight me as I guided her into the guest room, she stiffened at the door and took a deep breath, holding it for a few seconds before crossing the threshold. Marta settled her in bed, and we let her sleep. This was not the time to ask her about her marriage or her husband's death. Or even about whether I'd see her again as I'd seen her last night.

Later, I asked for the privilege of taking a tray of broth and tea up to her, and was troubled by the sight that greeted me.

Although she sat upright, she shook with chills. Her lips were chapped and dry, and she watched me with red, haunted eyes.

Looking at the tray, she wrinkled her nose. "I need a drink to calm my nerves. Something... a scotch. A whiskey. Soda and whiskey. Tell Marta."

"You're not well. You shouldn't—"

"Tell her!" She interrupted me in the voice of the mistress of the household. The same look she'd given me her first night home. It was plain—I was the servant.

Fine. I'd be the servant. A servant doesn't care if his mistress drinks herself to sickness and beyond. So I rushed to the kitchen and sloshed whiskey in a glass myself as Marta looked on from the stove.

"Where is Julia?" I asked. Although Marta had mentioned her that morning, I'd not seen the cook since the party.

"Away. For a little ... holiday."

I trudged upstairs with the drink, and Eleanor sipped at it

hungrily, her mood shifting as she took it in. She became calmer.

"Julia's gone away," I announced. "With Morgan."

I assumed this. And I assumed it would hurt her to hear it. I wanted to wound, to test the depth of her feeling.

She stared at me over the rim and finished off the whiskey in one long gulp. Holding the glass out to me, she asked for a refill.

"You shouldn't—" I began, the angry preacher now, and again she cut me off.

"Don't lecture me." Her eyes filled. "It calms my nerves. It's not poison."

But it was poison. It blotted out everything. I took the empty glass and did as I was told, each step downstairs a step away from what I'd thought was mine.

When I returned to her room, I sat silent while she drank, and then while she sipped half-heartedly at a few spoonfuls of broth. When she'd had enough, she pushed the tray aside and scooted to the edge of the bed.

"I have to get out of here," she muttered, reaching for her robe.

I placed my hand on top of hers, stopping her. She was no longer trembling. "Your room is unusable."

"Then the other one." She gestured to the front of the house.

"Marta had the roofers here today. They're not finished."

"Then another one. What's the matter with the other ones?"

"They're not cleaned..."

"I pay Marta enough money to make sure they're clear! Get her here. Tell her I want them ready. Tell her to get Julia...."

"Julia's gone," I reminded her.

"I don't want to stay in this room!" She looked at me wild-eyed. "Not *his* room!"

She pushed past me to the hall and over to her room. The bed had been removed, but the wall still bore the stain of the "accident."

She hugged her arms to herself, rubbing her hands up and down. "He must have been very angry," she whispered to herself. Then she giggled, as if she were pleased.

I stood behind her, and I placed my hands on her shoulders. I'd have that at least, the feel of her, the grazing of her hair on my knuckles.

"You should go to bed," I told her on a sigh. "You have to get up early."

This all felt so familiar and so unfair.

After a few moments, she turned and went back to the guest room where she got back into bed. Not once did she reach out to embrace me or treat me as anything but a servant. Yes, I was disappointed, but I told myself it was because she was ill, and the true test of our bond would come when she'd fully recovered. Acting my role, I took the tray away and left the room.

In the kitchen, I found Marta at the table sipping coffee.

"I think Miss Sloane should see a doctor," I said to Marta. "I could fetch the doctor who fixed up Mister Morgan."

"She does not want to see a doctor. I've already talked to her." Marta shook her head. "If you can convince her...."

I had little hope of that. "Maybe we should just have one come."

"She would refuse," Marta said. "Give her a few more days. We will take care of her."

"She has to work every day. She has the picture." I stood before the table, next to Marta. "How can she continue like this?"

"She will pull through. We will help her."

"We can't help her if she keeps drinking."

Marta stood and put her cup in the sink. "I have known her for a long time. She is strong and works hard, for all of us. She is a good girl. And she will do the good thing. But not if we try to be her nanny. She is grown up now." She looked me in the eye. I was the outsider here.

Frustrated, I left the room, not even returning for

something to eat myself. I lay on my bed worrying, occasionally looking out the window across the way, as if I could detect from the front of the house what she was thinking and where I fit in. But now that she was in the back bedroom, I couldn't even content myself with a glimpse of her light, which at least let me into the rhythm of her life.

"Damn," I muttered into the silence, angry at myself for putting up with this ambiguity. I should go to her and demand to know — am I servant or lover?

Anger led to fatigue. I fell asleep still dressed. When I awoke hours later, the room was dark, and a soft California breeze teased at the curtains. Something else had awakened me, some noise that had crept into my consciousness while I dozed. Adjusting to the darkness, I lay still and listened. Gentle footsteps sounded outside on the drive, coming toward the garage. I sat bolt upright and shouted.

"Who's there?"

After a pause, the answer came, a tiny, tired voice, her voice. "It's me. El."

I scrambled to let her in, wrapping her in my arms to calm her chills, leading her to my bed.

When we lay together, she rested her hands on my chest. "I couldn't sleep there. Not there," she whispered.

ଓ

In the morning, she returned to her own bed just after dawn's unsentimental glow began to fill the room with muted light. This time I was the one begging her to stay with me, but she merely smiled and kissed my forehead before leaving.

Thus began the pattern of my continued humiliation. Nights in bed together — hers was replaced soon enough with a new, extravagant one. Days as her servant. Surprised by new secrets and disappointments.

Morgan and Julia were gone, but Eleanor tried incessantly to reach him, to "fix things" for her. We argued when I refused to get her a drink. We made up in bed. We argued when I suggested she fire Morgan. We made up in bed.

The week passed thus, with only one incident bringing

cheer to my soul. I managed to slip into the soundstage one afternoon to watch her shoot and saw yet another director arguing with the sound man. He wanted to get Pauline's dialogue while she was walking, since she looked so "fluid" when she moved, and he wouldn't take any guff from the sound fellow on why it couldn't be done.

I wanted to race to tell Leo, but I didn't know where he was. When I mentioned this to Pauline later, she offered to ask about him. This kindness touched me more than it should have. I wanted to believe she wanted to please me. I wanted to believe she loved me as desperately as I loved her.

Chapter Eleven

"WHY DO YOU KEEP calling Robbie?" I spit out after ten minutes' silence on the ride into the studio the next day.

She didn't answer right away. Her grim look and set mouth told me she didn't like the question. "He's my agent," she said at last. "And he fixes things."

I snorted with disgust. "Fixes them how? By offering you to studio heads?"

She said nothing but glared at me from the back seat. When we finally arrived, she waited for me to open her door, then hissed at me: "Thank you, darling, for your limitless faith in my talents." And she left.

I felt like the transgressor now.

What did I know of her world and how she navigated it? Nothing. This picture would wrap in eight weeks' time, and she'd need another one, another victory to help her seal her success. Crowds might throng to see the first talkie a silent star made, but it was the second picture that told studio heads if curiosity or talent drew audiences in.

I drove back to the estate to collect Marta who'd asked me to take her to church that day, even though it wasn't a Sunday. Marta was quiet during the drive, but before she left the car, she said, "I light a candle for her. Every week, I light a candle for her," so softly I wasn't sure if she was speaking to me or thinking out loud.

To pass the time while Marta was in church, I went to the post office and picked up the estate's mail. There was the usual crate of fan mail, as well as bills and magazines, and also a thick envelope for me — from Milqueton at the Home.

Actually, there were two letters, one from Milqueton that was short and, as usual, to the point.

"My dear boy," it began. "This arrived at Canfield today,

and I only wish I could have passed it along to you myself the instant I read it. If you hurry, you might be able to respond in time, especially since you are in the same state. I hope you are well. Please write when you are able...."

The other letter, addressed to him, was on stationery that read "Samuel Marks Doyle," the name of my grandfather, but it was signed by "Constance Moran Doyle," a name I was only vaguely familiar with.

> "*Dear Reverend:*
>
> *From previous correspondence, I know you had a boy at your home who is related to my family. His name is John Doyle, and he is my nephew. Although the family has been estranged from John, John's grandfather lies on his deathbed, and I would very much like to have the boy see his father's father before the man goes to his reward. If John Doyle still resides at your home, or if you know how to contact him, please let him know that he is welcome in my home, where his dying grandfather awaits heaven's trumpet. His grandmother, I am sorry to report, passed away a year ago. This will be John's last chance to see his grandfather, and the older man's last chance to see his grandson..."*

Enclosed in the envelope from my aunt was a generous amount of money to pay for a train ticket to San Francisco, where she lived.

Milqueton mentioned in his letter that this was not the first contact he'd had from Constance Doyle.

"Your aunt wrote while you were at the Home, but only to inquire on your progress. I replied with a report that was both honest and complimentary."

I smiled. It was just like the Reverend to make sure I understood he'd not been trying to do me favors but just say what was true. And it was just like him to tell me, without saying it, that Constance Doyle had had the opportunity to reach out to me in the past, yet had not taken it. He was warning me to be careful.

I put the letters back in the envelope, and my heart was lighter. Yes, lighter at news of my grandfather's impending death! I had a reason to leave Sloane Hall and Eleanor. No more torment. I'd be free. That seemed infinitely better than having my grandfather recover. After all, I'd not really known him, and he'd kicked out my mother and me after my father had died. Why shouldn't I use his deathbed as a way to get rid of this burden?

I rolled down the car windows and unbuttoned my jacket. I rubbed the sweat from my brow and neatened my hair. Marta would let me go. Julia had plenty of holidays – she was on one now. And Marta wouldn't refuse me the right to visit a dying relative. I bent low to look out the passenger window. People were coming out of the church, slowly making their way down its wide stairs. There, in the back of the crowd, was Marta clutching her rosary. I got out, my letter in hand, and waved her to the car. When she came over, she pulled off her lace mantilla and looked at me with worried eyes.

"Is something the matter? Is she all right?" Her first thought was of Eleanor.

"I just wanted to tell you I got the mail." I held the door for her, then hurried to my side of the car. "And I have to leave Sloane Hall."

As I drove I told the tale of my aunt's request, and she listened in silence. When we arrived home, she shook her head. "It's not a good time for you to go. With everything so, so..." she searched for a word, "...so upset. With Julia gone. With..." I knew what she'd meant to say. With Robbie gone. All the more reason for me to go, too. "When will you leave?"

"Tomorrow," I said. I'd have left that afternoon if I could have arranged it.

She sat in the car as I let the engine idle. "Miss Sloane's family is from San Francisco," she said, absently folding her mantilla.

"I know. In shipping."

"*Si*. Herbert Brickman. Brickman Steam Lines."

"You worked for them. Is there any family left?" I might as well take what information she was willing to give.

"No. Herbert Brickman had one sister, Eugenia — Miss Sloane's aunt — and she is gone now. Very sad."

"How so?"

"Miss Eugenia died very poor. Miss Sloane's mother was not very wise with the money. Nothing was left when her parents were lost. Nothing but debts. Miss Sloane tried very hard to help her, but she was not the famous star then."

"How did Miss Sloane survive after her parents died?" I expected a bad tale — the kind the drivers told behind the garages at parties, or a story like mine.

Marta paused, as if considering how to answer. "She was only fifteen."

"Did she live with the aunt?"

"No. The aunt was very..." She tapped her temple, indicating the aunt was not of sound mind. "Eleanor... well, Mister Morgan does not like us to talk about it. He worked so hard, you see, to get her this." She waved toward the house. "I must go see about dinner. You don't stay away too long. Miss Sloane needs you here."

The estate was so quiet now with Julia and Morgan gone, with Eleanor working. It was like it had been before she'd returned. But then the silence had been full. Now it was empty.

I didn't have anything else to do that day, so I went into the city again and picked up the train schedule, then packed and waited for Eleanor to call.

When I picked her up that evening, she was angry. Instead of slumping in the seat next to me and falling asleep, she immediately pulled out a cigarette and started nervously smoking and talking.

"He said I was looking ugly today!" She shook her head in fury. "In front of the whole cast. He said he couldn't get the lighting to work for me!" Her foot twitched.

My impending departure made me bold. "It's the lights,"

I said, remembering the story of Pickford's cameraman. "And the new film they use. Makes you look older than your years."

"Oh, really? Well, that makes me feel so much better."

My faced warmed from sudden anger. "At your service, ma'am."

"Wonderful! Now you're sulking!"

I glanced at her and raged. "I'm just damned tired of being in your bed at night and doing nothing but driving this fucking car during the day."

She remained mute while we rounded a curve, bracing herself against the door as I let the car gain some speed.

"You're tired of being in my bed?" she said at last in a low, steely voice. "So soon?"

At the house, the first thing she did was ask Marta to help her find Robbie. He would know what to do, she kept saying. I hoped to God I never heard those words again. I went back to the garage and kicked a tire on the Packard so hard I made the car shake. Damn her. Maybe I'd leave that night and take the sleeper car.

But after dinner that night, she called me to the house, and I went to her. It was my own illness, my own drink. I told myself it was because I wanted the satisfaction of telling her about my trip. But even that was stolen from me, as she spent hours on the phone trying once again to locate Robbie. I had no time to read to her, let alone explain my plans. As soon as she put the receiver down, she'd think of someone else to try — an acquaintance, a friend, a business associate, even a hotel she knew he'd stayed at once on a trip to Mexico.

I sat in a chair across from her, silently witnessing this desperate struggle and growing smaller while it progressed.

After each unsuccessful try, she'd put down the receiver and smile at me.

"That reminds me," she said after one call, "I asked about your friend Leo. He finished his film and went to visit his son."

A son? I'd not known about this.

"Where?" I pressed.

"San Francisco."

This uplifted me. I seemed destined to go there now to see my grandfather and perhaps to see Leo, too.

I told her of my travel plans.

Now my satisfaction. Her mouth fell open and she leaned back. "No! Why?"

I told her about my grandfather.

"How long will you be gone?"

"I don't know. Maybe a couple weeks."

"That's too long!" she exclaimed, and my heart leapt at the fear in her voice. Here at last was what I wanted. "A week. You should go for only a week. They abandoned you, didn't they?"

"They abandoned my mother."

"And you forgive them?" Aware of how imperious this sounded, she softened her tone. "I seem unable to forgive a slight, let alone something that serious."

"I'm not sure I forgive them." I'd not even thought of forgiveness. Now I'd ponder it. "It's curiosity that draws me." And the desire to wound her by leaving!

She sighed and stared at me. "The fact that I can't let go of others' transgressions makes it difficult sometimes not to transgress myself. Isn't that strange, John?"

This confession could easily have been my own. She might swat at me because she couldn't beat down others who hurt her. I knew what it felt like to be in that place. I had made such a business of not turning the other cheek that it made me stiff-necked and rigid. Like my mother's family. I still had a long list of sins to atone, and I added to them every day. I rose and sat on the bed, cupping my hand over hers, as warm and fidgety as a baby bird.

"I *have* to go," I whispered.

"They have no claim on you."

"Do you?" I asked.

She looked down and blinked fast. "You never come to me unless I ask you," she said, a soft voice about to crack. "And already you are tired of me."

No, Eleanor, not tired of you. Tired of...

The phone rang, startling us both. She picked it up quickly and identified herself, then listened for a few moments. She spoke softly, as if she didn't want me to hear.

"Do you know where he is?" she asked. And after a few seconds, "I know he's been in touch with you! For god's sake, if he told you not to tell me, I can make it worth your while...."

She was willing to pay for information on Robbie's location.

I slipped out of the room and headed back to my own bed, shame growing with every step.

The worst humiliations are like this — small omissions, invitations not extended, kindnesses not offered. They creep up on you, their effect not fully measured until the pain sinks deep.

Later, she tried to convince me to stay by coming to my room. At first, I pretended to be so dead to the world that I was unaware of her feather-light fingers on my arm, of her lips on my shoulder. But my body betrayed me, and I welcomed her into my arms. She smelled of brandy.

"You think I'm just playing with you," she said, after we'd made love. "You think I'm like this with every man."

"Yes."

"That hurts me." She kissed me, reminding me she was a drunk. "I don't know what I'd do without you."

"You have Robbie. You have others." I lay on my back with her head on my chest. The cool night air came through the window, drying our sweat.

"No! You don't understand." She traced a circle on my chest, and I started to want her again. "None of them really know me. They know Pauline Sloane. But you ... you only want the real me, Eleanor. Eleanor is like you, just like you. Still trying to find how to be good. We can do it together."

Even Marta, who'd known her since childhood, called her "Miss Sloane." Did I know her more deeply? Maybe. Neither of us could let go of something. For me, it was my rage. For her... I'd yet to learn.

"Promise me you'll come back in two weeks. No longer than two weeks."

I promised.

Chapter Twelve

I BOUGHT THE more expensive ticket for the coastal route. It would take me away from Eleanor faster than the San Joaquin Valley train with its lumbering crossing of the Tehachapi mountains. I bought it because Marta had forced money on me, on orders from Eleanor, before I left.

When I sat on the train watching the scenic landscape roll by, I tried to talk myself out of my anger at her presumption that I couldn't pay my way, that I'd need or even want her money. I reminded myself that money means only what you make it mean.

Money is powerful. But I did not subscribe to the notion that it was the root of all evil. It was merely a tool, used by good and bad alike to achieve their ends. Even bad people could use it wisely, and good people could be stingy for the right reasons.

It had not been money or lack of it that had led to my mother's decline. It had been her other sins, perhaps most notably a general untidiness about life, an unwillingness to organize her needs and determine what sacrifices would be necessary to fill them.

I'd seen money's good side, too. It was stinginess that had led to Brice Clement's ultimate comeuppance. Specifically, county regulators' desire to make sure the "people's" money was handled frugally. A new county auditor had been the first one to notice irregularities in the Canfield books. From that tiny crack, the entire lid was opened, letting out the slimy, dark secrets Brice had thought would always be buried there. Thank god for that regulator's parsimony.

One by one, the county folks had questioned us, stern-faced bespectacled men in clean suits. *Don't talk to each other about this, son,* they said. *We're trying to get to the truth.*

And so I sat, in a straight-backed chair in an empty room, in what should have been a classroom. But its desks and chairs had been broken up for firewood the winter before when Brice had used the coal money on other things.

Maybe new clothes. He'd looked especially dapper that year, I recalled, with a pinstripe suit and shiny gold watch chain across the vest, a fur-collared greatcoat, and embossed boots. He'd had women out to the School that year, two at once. He introduced them as his nieces, and they'd giggled when he'd said it. That had been one of the nights he'd tried to get Pete to visit him. One of the girls—a flashy redhead with a birthmark painted near the corner of her mouth— had asked Pete to stop on by after dinner. He'd looked down at his feet and not responded.

I'd been surprised. Naively, I couldn't think of a reason why he shouldn't go. "You'll probably get some cake from them," I'd said. "Or even candy."

But Pete was wiser. "Hell, John, you are one dumb sumabitch. Didn't you see ol' Briny jabbing her to ask me. I'm not goin' within a mile of that house."

Shortly after that, Pete's stay was extended at Canfield.

And then the auditors came. And each of us had wondered: are others telling the truth, or will I alone say what happened here? And then will Brice stay and dole out to me more fearsome punishments than what I've already seen?

To my shame, I did not speak right away. I sat silently staring at the empty blackboard in the empty room with its dusty plank floor, its fogged windows, its smell of sweat and coal dust.

Until finally, one of the inspectors, a thin man whose suit looked too big, said to me, "Is it true that Mister Clement told you boys to burn the desks in this room to keep warm?"

And then I'd known that at least one boy had talked and had given this detail of the winter before, of a January cold as Satan's heart, when our hands and feet were swelling from chilblains, when even Brice became afraid that he'd lose too many of us to pneumonia and be looked at too closely.

So he'd shrugged at us in class one morning and said, "Coal delivery is late. You might as well burn these desks, boys, since you're too dumb to learn anything, anyhow."

Remembering, I'd said, "Yes, sir," to the thin man questioning me, still afraid that my small words would lead to large wounds.

The man had knelt beside me. "What else?" he'd asked.

And so, I'd told him. Everything. I'd been surprised at how much I'd remembered. I told it all in a low monotone, even the parts about Pete.

A week later, Reverend Milqueton arrived and Brice Clement was gone. We never saw him leave, which was a disappointment. I'd wanted to see him taken away in handcuffs and striped uniform. I'd imagined a hundred times his humiliation, even his death at my hands. He was the only man I could stare at with my murderer's eyes and not feel ashamed.

૪

By the time I arrived in San Francisco, I was tired and cross and wondering if I'd done the right thing. I thought of discarding my responsibility to my aunt and grandfather and seeking out Leo instead. I'd found out where his son lived and figured on calling on him at some point.

But I was wrung out from fighting myself by journey's end. I still thought of her, of what I'd say, what she'd do, how I'd get back at her (for what I wasn't sure—for not loving me enough).

This is why I despised hope. Against my will, it tossed me so high into the air that pain was inevitable, and she was the one who made me hope, hope for a smile or a kiss or a cooing word. I wanted to shake hope free. Surely a deathbed would kill it for me.

I had no illusions about a grand reunion with my grandfather, filled with emotional pleas for forgiveness or declarations of long-suppressed affection. If anything, I expected to find the same crotchety man I vaguely remembered from my childhood. These suppositions were borne out when I finally arrived at the Doyle household on Nob Hill. It was an imposing house, with many silent servants. Constance Doyle, my aunt, greeted me with gushing enthusiasm.

"You came! How wonderful! Oh, do come in, do come in. Are you hungry? Thirsty? Jean, bring him some lemonade. And some cookies, too. Have you eaten dinner? Are you tired?"

She pounced on me with years of unused maternal instincts. She was a solid woman with broad shoulders and a thick waist. Her face was soft and round with large ruddy cheeks and small eyes. Dark hair was parted and pulled back into a braided bun near her neck. She wore a gray dress and heavy black shoes.

"Your grandfather is sleeping now," she explained after she showed me into the parlor, a dark room crammed with heavy furniture and thick, gold-fringed drapes, and a musty air—a sense that life lay strangled somewhere in the thin space between the daguerreotypes and the walls. She gestured to a green-brocaded settee, and I sat down while the wordless Jean brought in the treats and placed them before my aunt.

"I can't tell you how happy I am to see you here." She choked up as she passed me a glass of lemonade and reached for a lace-edged handkerchief in her pocket. "I was so afraid you wouldn't come."

"Does my grandfather know you contacted me?"

Her eyes flitted down to her hands resting in her lap. It was clear he didn't know. She'd arranged this visit as part of some misguided sense of mission. The lemonade stuck in my throat and made me cough.

"He's ill. Half out of his mind with pain most of the time. He needs to be reconciled with the Lord."

And I was to be the instrument for this deathbed salvation. I sighed and placed my glass on a table next to me. I would not be foisted upon him, no matter how well-meaning the gesture.

"I will see him after you tell him about me," I said, staring at her and speaking firmly so she wouldn't mistake anything I said to suit her plans. "Tell him everything. Even about Canfield."

She did not flinch, but her lips pursed, and she smoothed the skirt on her lap as if it needed ironing.

"Well, I... I myself don't know everything." She bit her lip. "I know you were there. I found that out from Mama Doyle before she died. Before that, all I knew was what my own beloved Sammy told me." She looked over at an oval sepia picture hanging on the wall above the fireplace. A heavily mustachioed man glared at the room, his right hand on his knee. My uncle. As stern and forbidding as my grandfather. I remembered meeting him once. It had been so long ago, and I'd forcefully forgotten most of it after it was clear my mother and I couldn't reclaim that life.

"I murdered my stepfather," I said simply. "They said I accidentally killed him when I tried to keep him from beating my mother again. But it was no accident. I meant to kill him."

"Oh, my."

"That's why I was sent to Canfield. I was too young for prison."

"But you're better now." She said it as if Canfield had cured me of my sickness, smiling with satisfaction that all had worked out so well. Her grand scheme to salvage old Doyle's soul through me would not be set back.

I let her think what she wished, and told her where I was working now, and what my plans were, or what they'd been before meeting Eleanor. She nodded throughout my recitation, obviously grateful to be on more familiar ground—the territory of the reclaimed soul.

"I should now tell you about us," she said after my monologue. "Sammy— your uncle—moved us to San Francisco after the earthquake, before your parents married. Sam invested in building. We did well, well enough that I've wanted for nothing even after Sam's death...." She rambled on at great length about her own background, which had little to do with mine. She must have been lonely since my uncle had died just a year after my father.

She'd been alone for more than ten years. During that time, she'd become heavily involved with her church, a new Pentecostal denomination with a preacher she spoke of in hushed tones. On the rare occasions when my grandparents visited her in California, she told me, she'd tried to interest "Mama Doyle" in joining to no avail. During one of those visits Mama Doyle, my grandmother, had revealed I was in reform school.

"She knew you'd been sent away. She wept when she told me. 'Poor Johnny's been sent to Canfield,' she'd said. And she had to stop and gather her wits about her before continuing. 'For a long time,' she'd said, 'a long, long time.' I asked her if she'd tried to contact you, and she said she'd sent you a letter that you never answered."

"I never received such a letter. We didn't always, in the early days, get things that were meant for us."

"I'm sure she would have tried again, but the General didn't tolerate talk of his sons after they were gone, and it would have been hard for her to go about searching for you." The General was the family's name for my grandfather, who'd ruled his household with military-like precision even though he himself had never worn a uniform. In fact, it was probably my grandfather's reverence for military life that had inspired my father to sign up when war broke out in Europe. I knew the General saw it differently—he'd thought my mother had inspired my father to join.

My great-grandfather, however, had served in earlier conflicts, a fact that had been omnipresent in the Doyles' rambling Texas house. It had been filled with mementos of the Civil War— a saber hung on the wall, an old regimental flag, even a few daguerreotypes of unflinching soldiers whose hollow stares told me more about war than any schoolbook could.

Part of my grandfather's antipathy toward my mother was borne of the fact that she hailed from Boston and was a Yankee, a term he used to describe only the lowest forms of human life, said with such withering scorn that he sounded like Lucifer pronouncing a sentence.

All these memories came back to me in this cushioned parlor as I sipped lemonade with my aunt, a stranger to me in youth and now one in spirit. As kindly as she was now, it did not escape me that she herself had made no effort to save me from Canfield when it was clear she'd be hampered by my grandfather's unforgiving nature. My aunt had not interjected herself into those struggles, yet now she wanted to throw me into the last struggle of a dying man.

"When did my grandfather become ill?" I asked.

"A year ago. He'd been ailing before that, of course, ever since suffering the influenza after the war. He never really regained his strength...." She looked away, her eyes filling with tears. That was how my uncle had died — of the Spanish flu. My grandfather'd survived, probably because he refused to be felled by some foreign pestilence. I knew this from the ramblings of my mother. Poor creature. She'd tried to get back into the Doyles' good graces even after they'd kicked us out.

"He fell and broke his hip and then had pneumonia." She shook her head. "It was horrible. I went to take care of him, but I didn't like being away from my home and my church, so I arranged for him to come up here."

"That must have been difficult."

"Yes, he is a bit stubborn." She managed a weak laugh. "He'd fired half his staff because he didn't like the way they cared for him. When I came to see him the first time after his accident, he was in an awful state. No one was cleaning him properly, or turning him in bed." She wrinkled her nose at the memory. "His misery was enough to persuade him. I only had to mention it once or twice."

Or a dozen times, I thought. Whatever it took, she'd managed to get him to her house where she could care for him and have her minister visit him regularly. Despite myself, I smiled. If you defined hell by those things you most despised, my grandfather was in it. Whatever he'd done to me by cutting off my mother, he was being repaid.

"You said you weren't sure how long he'd last?" I prompted her.

"The doctor was just here yesterday," she said. "He says his heart is weak, and his lungs are diminished. Sometimes, he can hardly breathe. It pains me to listen to him."

"Perhaps you should go to him now and tell him I am here?" I didn't want to come all this way and have the man die before my aunt had a chance to finish the plan she'd started. Besides, now my curiosity was aroused, and I wanted to see him.

"Oh. Not tonight, dear. He gets quite... perturbed... if his evening rest is upset. And the doctors are so happy when he has a good night's sleep." She smiled at me. "First thing in the morning, I'll take you to him. You must be very tired yourself!"

I could have protested and insisted on seeing him then and there, but I was too run down, too eager to lose myself in sleep, too, where Eleanor would be blotted out. At least, I hoped that would be so.

My aunt led me to a bedroom on the back of the house, a small room with narrow bed, dresser, and rocking chair. It was so spare that I wasn't sure if it was a servant's room, now unused. I didn't care. I threw myself on the bed after undressing and fell fast asleep.

And in the morning, I awoke panicked, not remembering where I was, going through the possibilities one by one and eliminating them—the various apartments in which I'd lived with my mother, the home she died in, Canfield, Sloane Hall—until my memory caught up with my body and awakened as well.

After washing up and dressing, I joined my aunt for breakfast in a sunny lacy room off the kitchen. When she lingered over her coffee, admiring birds and butterflies in the garden beyond, I grew anxious.

"Perhaps you should take me to him now," I told her.

"Oh, yes. Yes, a splendid idea."

She stood, but from her hesitation, I could tell she

thought the idea not very splendid at all. She was afraid to tell him about me now that I was here in the flesh. The idea that had seemed so perfect when she'd penned her note was now beyond her control. It bothered her. I could see it in her smooth face, and I wasn't angry. Just impatient.

"Why don't I go up with you and stand in the hall," I gently advised. "You can just tell him that you'd sent for me, and I'd responded."

She nodded her head eagerly at my suggestion. That was it — letting her off of telling him my history. She wouldn't have to be the bearer of bad news, only good.

"Yes. And then I'll just leave and usher you in." She strode out of the room, expecting me to follow. Now that she had a plan she was comfortable with, she moved forward forcefully, presenting a picture to me of how she'd probably been in life so far. Reticent, then impulsive.

I walked after her into the wood-paneled main hall and up the staircase. The morning light was shining through the leaded-glass windows on the front door, casting rose-colored shapes onto the wall. Through this fiery spectrum of color, we moved rapidly to the second floor and down a long hallway until we came to a closed door.

"I gave up my room for him," she explained before knocking softly, then cheerily announcing her presence as she opened the door.

"General, are you awake?" she asked as she walked into the room.

He surely would be now, I thought. I heard a grumble but made out no words. She said her part exactly as I recommended and retreated back to the hallway so swiftly that I'm sure the man barely had time to comprehend what she had said.

"Go on," she told me, her eyes wide and a little frantic. "I've told him now."

I walked in.

In spite of the gravity of the situation, I had to struggle to suppress a chuckle. The room was another aspect of a hell designed especially for him, papered in a flowery print, the bed a ruffled canopied bier. Lacy curtains let in yellow light, and sentimental paintings, some religious in nature, were on the walls, along with a sampler embroidered with the Beatitudes. "Blessed are the poor in spirit" stared my grandfather smack in his rich-spirited eye.

He was but a shell of the man I remembered, and when I looked at him my thoughts turned somber, turned to more serious Biblical lessons, the one about dust to dust, ashes to ashes. He seemed to be decaying before my eyes, the once lion-like head now thin, the skin stretched over his bones making his cheeks hollow, his eye sockets large, his nose sharp. His whole body seemed to have shrunk, making but the least perceptible lump under the embroidered covers.

He did not turn to me, so I walked further into the room, into his line of vision at the end of the bed. The room reeked of the scents of old age and of death. Sweet and putrid all at once, overlaid with the floral perfume of my aunt.

When his eyes finally focused on me, he quivered for a second.

"John? John?" He thought I was my father.

The moment passed, awareness returned. Even now, I was destined to disappoint. I was not my father.

"John Junior, sir," I said in hushed tones.

"Come closer. I can't make you out. No wonder I thought..."

He said it as if I'd deliberately deceived him. He tried to lift his right hand to wave me in but could only muster the strength for it to move a half inch from the sheet, the bony fingers gnarled into a distorted claw.

I moved to the side of the bed, close to his head. He looked me over from head to toe as much as he could see. His mouth hung open and drool collected at the corners. Seeing a cloth on the bedside table, I picked it up and wiped him clean.

"Take off those glasses."

I did as he requested, squinting at his face.

"You look well," he said, a pronouncement that was

probably intended to assure himself he'd not harmed me.

"I am well, sir." After replacing my spectacles, I drew up a nearby chair and sat beside him. "Aunt Constance says, however, that you have been faring poorly these days."

He snorted, which brought on a coughing spell. Standing, I put my hand behind his back to raise him sufficiently to clear his lungs. His frame felt so light I feared I might unintentionally hurt him. When he was recovered, his breath was shallow and rapid. Between breaths, he gasped out words.

"She would like... me to be worse than I am.... " At these words, I heard a soft clucking noise from the hallway. My aunt was listening there. "...so that damn snake oil preacher of hers... can get his hands on my money...." He coughed again but not as severely.

I gave him water to drink from a pitcher on the table.

Ah, so that was it. I was not just to be used as a tool to save my grandfather's soul, but also as a way to pry his money from him for my aunt's pet ministry.

"What happened to you?" he wheezed out.

I recounted, in brutal simplicity, the tale of my life. He smiled when I told him of my stepfather's death at my hands. The thing that would haunt me the rest of my days was the thing that would make him proud of me.

"Where are you now? What do you do?"

"I'm a chauffeur and mechanic. For the movie star Pauline Sloane."

"Sloane? I've seen her. Wicked woman," he grunted, and I wasn't sure if he was giving me his opinion of Eleanor's feminine charms or naming one of her movies, not all of which I was familiar with.

"Not a job for you," he whispered. "Get something else." He closed his eyes.

Thinking he was going to sleep, and my duty was done here, I stood. I was mistaken. Sensing the movement, he instructed me to stay.

"Close the curtains. It's too damned bright in here."

I did as I was instructed as best I could, but the lacy drapes still let in enough light to make lamps unnecessary. I sat with him the remainder of the day, even feeding him soup at lunch, delivered by an unsmiling maid. Each time I tried to leave, he pushed me back, either with words or with a movement of his hand.

When my aunt came in with the evening meal, I finally made my escape, stiff and drained. But the visit was already starting me down the path I'd sought. No longer did I think of Eleanor every waking moment. My grandfather's death struggle was the eclipse I'd searched for, blotting out all other emotions, providing me with fatigue and numbness, making me immune to any desire beyond the need for a meal and a comfortable bed. And for this, I was grateful!

The meal came soon enough, served in a huge dining room this time that made me feel inconsequential by comparison. Dark, with golden walls and shadowy paintings, it was so shut off from the world I couldn't tell if it was night or day.

"He really likes you!" My aunt rang a bell signaling the maid to clear away the dishes. "He wanted you to stay with him. John, this is going so well."

I knew better. In those hours at his bedside that afternoon, I'd learned something about him and about myself. We were alike in this regard—resistant to sentimental emotions, stubbornly refusing to even feign kindness or affection when we felt none. Where we differed was in the practice of these principles. He sought to actively cut himself off from those he disdained. I merely passively ignored them.

No, he didn't have any affection for me. If he asked me to stay with him, it was because I was a less offensive companion than my effusive aunt. Even I had cringed at her sing-song entrance announcing it was "time for the evening feast," in tones so bright my own spirit growled in response.

Not wanting to cast a pall over her idealistic vision of my grandfather's world, I changed the subject to one I should have avoided. And as soon as I uttered the words I knew I was gone, that hope had betrayed me, had pressed me to commit a treachery against myself, to undo what the day's monotony had succeeded in doing.

"Did you know the Brickmans—of the Brickman Steam Line?" There, my hopes rose again. Talking of Eleanor's family made me a familiar. It granted me an intimacy. Even hundreds of miles away I was caught up in this thinking.

She tilted her head to one side. "I didn't know them well. I do remember seeing her at some balls. Quite a handsome woman. Not my type, though." Not the Reverend's type either, I suspected.

"Eleanor?" As soon as I said her name, I was lost even more. My pulse quickened, my face warmed! *Eleanor. Eleanor. Love me, Eleanor.* "I've... I've run into her in Los Angeles."

"Really?" My aunt brightened. The possibility that I could be rubbing shoulders with someone from her social world was a delightful coincidence, one that I'm sure she attributed to the grace of God and that reinforced her opinion that the Canfield School for Wayward Boys had been merely a convalescent home.

But then her face darkened. "Yes, I remember. That was in... let me see... ? Oh dear, I can't recall exactly what year. But it was a huge scandal. In all the papers." She nodded to the maid who silently served the coffee.

First, she poured from a silver urn. Then, replacing the urn on the sideboard, she picked up a gold-rimmed tray with a cream pitcher and sugar bowl. Offering them to my aunt, she only stepped away after my aunt had put her spoon on its saucer. The maid then moved to me to perform the same ritual, and I nearly brushed her away—she was taking too long, dammit! I needed to hear my aunt's tale out of the maid's earshot. But I accepted coffee, telling myself that this after-dinner conversation would be prolonged if I had some in front of me, that the tale could be spun out as long as liquid stayed in my cup. I was lost!

"What was a huge scandal, Aunt Constance? The death of Eugenia Brickman?" I said at last when the maid disappeared behind a swinging door. How foolish to think it mattered if the maid heard or not—but I knew, even before my aunt spoke, that whatever I heard about Eleanor would cut me to the core, and instinctually I wanted to experience that pain without the maid nearby. The maid was my equal, after all, and she would surely guess, unlike my aunt, that I was besotted with Eleanor, that my questions weren't idle conversation. The maid would know.

"What? My goodness, no. Although that was a very sad story. No one could have done anything, though. She was a pathetic creature. Half out of her mind. Living at the St. Francis in rooms she couldn't pay for. Of course, by then, it was well-known that the Brickmans couldn't pay for anything. Because *she* had run up so many debts."

"Eleanor?"

"What? No! Lillian, her mother. Eleanor was a lovely girl, so beautiful. So many beaux. That was her downfall.

"She had a face like an angel. And her hair—oh my, it was a golden brown. And she wore it up before her coming out party. She wore all the latest fashions, too. Scandalous things. Went to every party in town. She was a wild child." She leaned into the table and whispered, "She drank...." I'd noticed that my aunt's house was a dry one, and I didn't doubt for a second it would remain so even after Prohibition was lifted.

"But when her parents died, it was time to really face the music." She shook her head. "She had to sell the family home. It's just three blocks away. Lovely old mansion. Used to belong to a railroad tycoon. Rebuilt after the earthquake to its original specifications. Italianate is the style."

I breathed easier. Perhaps high scandal in my aunt's world was merely being unable to hold onto one's wealth. "What happened to Eleanor after she sold the house?"

"She disappeared for awhile. Went on the Grand Tour to Europe. Oh, no, wait, that was after it happened, not before."

"After what?" My fingers clamped on the fragile handle of the porcelain coffee cup.

"After her husband killed himself."

"How sad." Again relief—I already knew of his death. Now I learned it was a suicide. Perhaps that was all. Perhaps there was no new pain here. Perhaps I was free. This is what I had sunk to—relief over the news of a man's suicide.

"Oh yes. It was quite horrible. His parents were beyond grief. They blamed it all on her. She'd refused to settle down even after she married. And such a wonderful family, too. The Griswolds. Basil Griswold was his name. They were married about a year. What a lovely wedding, too. Photographs in the society section of the paper. She looked like a child with those big eyes. She had fourteen bridesmaids, and they had to hire two bands to play because there were so many guests, they couldn't fit them all in one hall...."

While my aunt showered me with details I had no interest in, I tried to imagine Eleanor young and carefree, a "wild child" with a hundred beaux. She was used to being loved. Why had she chosen this man, Griswold?

"...and then there were the parties! So loud that the police were called out on more than one occasion. I could even hear them over here, and I'm at least five blocks from the Griswolds' home. Basil's home, that is. The elder Griswolds still live near Telegraph Hill. In fact, I think he's been elected to the symphony board. Or maybe it was the opera. They didn't do much after their son died. Oh, come to think of it, Basil and Eleanor *were* married a year. Did I say under a year? Well, it was more than that. Apparently—and I must say I'm uncomfortable even talking about this—he came home early to set up a little surprise party for her. The only problem was he was the one who was surprised." She let out a sharp laugh, then quickly placed her hand over her mouth as the inappropriateness of her joke dawned on her.

"So Eleanor was unfaithful?" Yes, I said it as calmly as if I didn't know her. As calmly as if we were discussing a movie star's life. Of course. A movie star's life. Not the life of someone I knew, of someone who had lain in my arms. My hand brushed my cup, rattling it against its saucer, so I placed my hands in my lap. There, they wouldn't betray me.

"Not just unfaithful," my aunt said. She shook her head solemnly, making up for the unsettling levity of the moment before. "Unfaithful to a degree that would make one faint. The rumor was—and I don't know if I should be repeating this at all—but the rumor was she was there, when he came home to surprise her, with two men. I do not like to even contemplate it. It's horrid. Sinful. The Griswolds thought she had done it— shot him, that is. But the police made quick business of clearing her of *that* crime. Wherever she is, I'm sure she is getting her just rewards."

Blood raced to my cheeks, so I sank back in my chair searching for shadow. Was this worse than I'd imagined or not as bad? Were two men better than one? With one there could be devotion and fidelity, something pure. With two—this implied mere lust and pleasure, nothing deep, nothing that signaled true betrayal. Perhaps there was hope ...

But you know I was doomed! I was searching for good news in the small print of an obituary. She had to die in my heart. Isn't this why I came here—to grasp death and make it my own?

I looked up at my aunt daintily sipping her coffee. She was so cut off from anything but her home and church that she had no idea that Eleanor was being rewarded lavishly for her grand passions. What my aunt considered sinful, the cinema celebrated by showcasing Eleanor's sultry eyes, her come-hither look, the very sensuality that had driven her husband to his grave.

"She was torn up by the death?" I asked. My throat was dry. I sipped coffee as well, struggling to keep my hand from trembling.

"Even the most cold-hearted woman—and clearly she was one—would be torn up, as you say, by having her husband blown up in her lap. And apparently that's how he did it. Walked in on her, got the gun, stood right over her and... " My aunt shuddered, but I believed some part of her enjoyed this gruesome tale, just the way a child enjoys a good scary story from time to time.

"She was under a doctor's care for months before she eventually left for Europe. Very badly shaken. Rumors of a nervous breakdown. The Griswolds paid for her care. But little else. Considerable wealth, too, but Basil had little of it on his own, it turned out. They weren't heartless, mind you. They paid for her Grand Tour. Quite frankly, I think they'd have loved to see her stay in Europe. Maybe that's where she is. Oh wait, no. You said you'd seen her. Where was that, dear?"

Considerable wealth. Was that why she'd married him? To try to save her aunt, her home, her life as she'd known it? So she had gone to Europe, come home and reinvented herself as Pauline Sloane with Robbie keeping the scandal of her husband's death, the whisper of blame, from her fans. She'd mentioned making bad choices. Was Basil one?

No longer hungry or thirsty, eager to be alone, suddenly afraid that my aunt would find out that I, too, had fallen prey to Eleanor's charms, I placed my napkin on the table.

"I... I saw her in Los Angeles, Aunt Constance. Do you mind — I'm very tired — I think I'd like to retire now."

"No, go right ahead. You've had a long journey. I'm so glad you came. I really had no right to expect it. No right. The General really lit up when he saw you."

The General had done no such thing. And if my grandfather had received the same grudging treatment he'd visited on me that afternoon, he would have left my aunt's house with a surly farewell. But I was not him. So I resolved to stay as long as necessary, if only to prove that I was not the man that he was, or that he might think I had become.

Chapter Thirteen

THAT NIGHT, I sat in my room at my aunt's house, still dressed in my best shirt and tie—the one that Marta had knotted the first night I'd visited Eleanor—my elbow on a dark green upholstered chair. I stared into the shadows resigned and bleak, mulling over what I'd learned and forcefully pulling myself back to the truth. She'd married a man for money and been untrue. Was she now just as false?

I remembered how eager she'd been in my arms. I was different than the others, she had said. She needed me. And we were alike, were we not? Both "trying to be good."

We had both tasted bitterness and horror. She'd witnessed a violent death. I'd caused one. Our parents' deaths had left us vulnerable to these tragedies. I had changed. Couldn't she? Hadn't she? Perhaps her husband's suicide had been her Canfield—an experience designed to rehabilitate.

For hours, I centered on that thought, creating a world in which we were both reformed, and try as I might, it felt every bit as artificial as the movies she worked in.

I went over my own history at Canfield and what I'd learned. I reminded myself of how different I'd become. Wasn't I here in my grandfather's house, tending to him in his dying hour, even though he'd betrayed me? Would I have been able to do that if it had not been for Canfield? Surely Eleanor's husband's death had had the same effect—bleaching out a bad past. Surely she was new and fresh. Forgiven.

It crept up on me like that. It tempted me. Being away was worse than being near her. Away, I could conjure her up to any specification I desired—I could see her as reformed, as a victim, as betrayed, as anything, anything that made her into a woman capable of loving me. At least in her presence, I was face to face with her faults. Here, hundreds of miles away, I had only a phantom.

CB

To clear my head, I sought out Leo the next day. My aunt, once she learned I had a friend in the city, was effusive in her desire to help me find him, showing off her skill at talking to the telephone operator, eventually locating his son's rooming house near Chinatown. I left a message for Leo and was surprised when he called back within the hour. My aunt insisted I invite Leo to tea, even making it clear this would be a "gentlemen's meeting" upon which she would not intrude. I took her up on the offer.

And so it came to pass that Leo Bartenstein, learned man of the cinema, came humbly to my aunt's abode, hat in hand, worn coat on his shoulders, that very afternoon.

He looked small. It wasn't his sickness that shrunk him but his being removed from the studios. There he was teacher as well as friend, looming over my inexperience like a titan. Here he was … spent and sad, an equal. And, I suspected, as bereft of affection as me. He'd probably come to San Francisco to seek it — in his son's home. It pained me to see him thus and made me regret inviting him to my aunt's home.

"Come on in," I told him, showing him to the over-decorated parlor.

He gawked as we moved through the hallway. "You didn't tell me your blood ran so blue, John."

"It doesn't," I said, urging him to sit. "Have something to eat."

Here, at last, I could be of service. After the briefest of hesitations, he began eating the finger sandwiches the cook had prepared, washing them down with a large glass of cider.

We talked of Hollywood — I told him of Eleanor's director and his rebellion. Leo nodded at this story, wiping his mouth as he laughed. Even as I told the story, though, the real reason for my need to see Leo ripped at my heart. I wanted to talk about Eleanor, and here in my aunt's parlor, with no interruptions or distractions, with her food and comfort providing the fee for his information, I could feel free to throw question after question at him.

But I didn't.

Now that it was clear how pathetic I'd become, I'd be damned if I place it on display. So I tried only asking a few questions that wouldn't give away my obsession, repeating the stories I'd heard from my aunt.

Leo wasn't fooled. He listened with a half smile, finishing off the plate of sandwiches and reaching for cookies. I was glad to feed him. When I was done, he wiped his mouth.

"I don't blame you, my boy. She's a looker," he said as if I'd just confessed to our affair. "All I'm saying is keep your eyes open. Morgan is vicious. Word is he had a man roughed up who looked the wrong way at the great Pauline Sloane. He's particular about her 'friends.'"

This information led me to tell the story of Morgan's own knife wound.

Leo sat back and wiped his brow. "No kidding," he said. "Now, that's something. Maybe somebody come to avenge themselves? Somebody who'd felt his wrath? You should be getting out of there if it's come to stabbings in the dark." And then he'd laughed at the preposterousness of it all.

I asked him about his health, but he was vague, sweeping the air with his hand to dismiss my concern, telling me doctors didn't know nothing, and he was putting his trust in the Almighty who at least never promised that life on this earth would be easy.

But I knew then and there that his trip to see his son meant he was losing hope. It came over me as suddenly as darkness. And I regretted again asking him for such selfish reasons to this house of death, where my grandfather was on a sad journey to the grave.

I shifted our conversation back to familiar territory, to the greatness of directors like Murnau, Griffith, and Vidor, and let Leo go on for a half hour on his favorite subject—the way these men had used their own personal vision to create a world, how a silent script presented a director with a thousand options and talkie scripts had only the writer's ideas with no room for a director's imprint, with how the best days of Hollywood were gone.

"One man, one film is what it should be," he said, shaking his head. "One vision. That's all over now, though."

I nodded my agreement, letting him go on.

"The man who started all this," Leo said, referring to the talkies, "died before it came to pass, you know."

"The guy who invented Vitaphone?" I asked. Vitaphone was the sound system that had shifted the earth under Hollywood's feet.

"Naw, Sam Warner. He's the one who pushed his brothers into the Jolson picture. He's the one who wanted sound with a feature-length film. He died the day before the movie opened in New York."

I didn't know if Leo was feeling sad or victorious over this irony — Sam Warner passing away before The Jazz Singer and all it unloosed had appeared. It saddened me.

He laughed, but it was forced. "At least when I go, I won't be missing some big new thing I want like heck to see. What's worth seeing is past now."

But he would be missing something — the rebirth of the cinematographer. I could see it happening, little by little, now that I'd witnessed directors wresting control of their films back from the tyranny of the soundman. The shackles of stationary cameras, airless camera booths, stagey dialogue, and uninformed directors were being discarded. All was changing into something else, something that promised to be just as good as that which Leo mourned. Leo couldn't see it. I didn't point it out to him now

I changed the subject back to the new lighting, wondering if I could pick up some information that might help Eleanor as she dealt with cinematographers and directors who, like Pickford's cameraman, didn't know how to use the new equipment well.

But Leo offered me no advice, lapsing instead into reminiscence.

"When you headed back?" I asked Leo, as his

monologues started to fade.

"In a week maybe."

I told him to let me know, that maybe we could travel together. And I asked if he'd mind if I stopped by his place so he could teach me, maybe even "apprentice" me whether he had a job or not.

He started to shake his head, and I waited for the inevitable "no work available" talk.

Instead, he paused and looked up into my eyes, his own glistening. "I've heard that Raoul Walsh might have something up his sleeve. You know the fellow?"

Embarrassed, I said no. I'd heard of him but had never met him or even seen him.

"Played Booth in Birth of a Nation, went on to direct...." Seeing no recognition from me, Leo continued: "Lost his eye filming In Old Arizona?"

That conjured up a picture. I'd seen a man with an eye-patch on the studio lots. So that was Walsh. I nodded.

"It's early, but I heard he's going to do another western. I can put in a word and get you on it. It'll be easy as breathing. Just stoop in that booth, and point the camera, keep the lens focused.... Yeah, look me up when you're back in town. The job'll be yours if I say so, and maybe it's time you moved on from Sloane Hall. You'll like Raoul. He's a tough one."

I couldn't shake the sense that Leo was offering me a job he himself would have taken had he not been so sick.

⑃

My grandfather rallied for a few days. Every day, at his demand, I went to him. I knew his requests for my presence did not represent some mawkish attempt to reconcile by staying as close as possible during his final days. All he wanted was company, someone who wasn't my aunt who would listen to him complain. I could have been a companionable manservant and served just as well. As soon as my aunt would leave the room, he'd waste the best part of his breath grumbling about her and "that wretched warlock she calls a priest."

The "warlock" himself, Reverend Walter Thistle, came to call one morning while I was there, and once again, I had to stifle a chuckle as I realized the reason for my grandfather's nickname for the man. Although made of the same overly-cheerful stock as my aunt, he sported a moustache and goatee that did, in fact, give him a devilish, or, at least, rakish, air. With thinning brown hair and small eyes, the only thing that kept him from looking sinister was his constant smile. He was either guileless or contrary. All that was missing were pitchfork and horns.

Ignoring my grandfather's uncharitable ranting, the Reverend Thistle intoned prayers and psalms and patted my grandfather's hand assuring him that a "better life awaited him," to which my grandfather truthfully replied that "anything would be better than this." My poor aunt stood in the hallway during this visit, a habit of hers, I came to learn. She could not tolerate uncomfortable scenes.

When the Reverend left the room, she stood in the doorway and crooked her finger at me. After telling my grandfather I'd return, I went to her.

"Come join us," she said, beaming. "For tea. I'd like you two to get to know each other."

I followed them downstairs into the airless living room where we sat while my aunt rang for Jean to bring the refreshments. She must have made prior arrangements with the maid because Jean appeared within seconds bearing a tray with a heavy china teapot, cups and saucers, and other treats.

She served Rev. Thistle first, and obviously knew his customs—she put sugar and cream in his cup before handing it to him, but asked me how I preferred mine.

"Plain," I said and took the full cup from her. "Thank you."

There was no sugar for tea at Canfield under Brice and certainly no cream. I'd developed a taste for strong, unflavored tea.

Rev. Thistle sipped his tea and stared at me over his cup with a sickly smile that made me think of the visitors to

Canfield when Brice was there, coming to "inspect" the premises and feel good about "society's efforts" to reclaim our lost lives. They saw only what they wanted to see.

"Have you lived here all your life, Reverend?" I asked politely while nodding away the cookies the maid offered me.

"His family's in New York." Aunt Constance looked at him for approval.

"Yes. They're still there. I came west ten years ago."

"To set up a church?" I asked politely.

"Partly." He put his teacup down and reached into his jacket pocket, pulling out a leaflet. Leaning forward, he handed it to me. "This was the other reason."

Fair wages, fair treatment, fair share, it read on the cover. Inside was a description of an organization called Liberty's Children. It was written in exaggerated prose full of high-minded goals and fiery rhetoric about the "working man's plight." Through the jumble, I determined it was a cross between a unionizing effort and a mission. My confusion must have been evident on my face because Reverend Thistle immediately took up the cause.

"Men are working eighteen hour days in dangerous conditions for not enough money to put food on their tables. It's shameful."

My aunt clucked her tongue in sympathy. "It's terrible, John. Just terrible. No wonder the country's doing so badly."

"What men are you talking about?" I asked calmly. I put the leaflet on the table in front of me, where Thistle snatched it up quickly.

"Any working man! Longshoremen, builders, bricklayers, people who work with their hands." His voice gained strength as he preached a sermon he must have been using for years. "Meanwhile, the wealthy live in palaces with servants and luxury. They are resting on the sweat of the working man's brow!" His voice echoed in my aunt's own luxurious palace, where a servant hovered out of sight waiting to be called in to replenish our tea. My aunt was smiling. The irony was lost on her.

"You mean people like my grandfather," I said dryly. "He's wealthy."

"No, not like the General, John," Aunt Constance said, amusement in her voice. "He was different."

"How so?" I asked.

"Well, for one thing," she continued, then paused, looking for the "one thing" that would make him different from the exploiting tyrants that Reverend Thistle held in contempt. "For one thing, he made his money through farming." She sat back, proud to have thought of it.

A memory came back to me: my mother sprawled in a chair, her feet up because they were swollen from standing all day behind a store counter, her hair disheveled and her speech slurred. *John, your grandfather owns three mines – coal, silver, and I don't know what. You ever need money, you go to him.*

"I thought he owned some mines," I said, taking a last sip of tea before setting my cup on the table.

"Oh, that." She waved her hand in the air. "That was something he didn't really handle. He had a manager for that."

I looked at Reverend Thistle. "Would you say that exempted him?" I asked, smiling.

To his credit, he didn't shrink from the truth. "No," he said firmly.

From the corner of my eye, I saw my aunt move back in her chair, her face a mixture of worry and fear. She bit her lower lip.

"But that's the reason your aunt is so committed to having him seek salvation, isn't it, Constance?" When he beamed at her, her worried face transformed into a smile.

"Yes, of course," my aunt agreed. "The Reverend's work is so important. And support is so hard to find. I've given all I can." She gave an embarrassed laugh. "Without making myself destitute, of course! That would hardly help matters."

"And you yourself," I continued pleasantly, looking at Thistle, "Is your family among the downtrodden?"

He was unruffled, smiling at me as if he knew the point I

was making and didn't care. "They own banks."

"I see," I said, nodding. "They helped set you up?"

"As a matter of fact, they did."

"He has a trust fund, John," my aunt explained, happy to be on familiar ground. "Barely enough to keep a roof over his head." She shook her head back and forth at the awful thought that Reverend Thistle had to worry about shelter.

I thought of asking him where he lived but restrained myself for my aunt's sake. His well-groomed hands and face told me he didn't live in a shanty. The roof over his head was more likely made of Italian tile than cheap tar paper.

"Which is why we're always looking for help." He finished his tea and set his cup down. "The work requires continual support, especially if we're to influence those in power to make the necessary changes."

"If your grandfather were well, I know he'd be impressed with the Reverend's work," my aunt offered. "School programs for girls, soup kitchens, *scientific* farming— it's wonderful. All to help correct the mistakes of generations."

I don't like bullies, not even ones who bully to try to do good.

"I'm very tired, Aunt Constance," I said. Standing, I nodded to Reverend Thistle. "I'm sure we'll meet again." Without waiting for a reply, I left the room, walking up to my grandfather's bedside.

He was asleep and didn't notice me. I looked at his fine profile and thought of the men he'd probably hired throughout his life to do jobs he wouldn't have had his own sons do for him. I thought of the men who'd probably died in his mines or sacrificed their health for his good fortune. But my grandfather, for all his faults, didn't say he knew what was good for another man. He only knew what was good for himself. There was no pretense in that. Rev. Thistle, on the other hand, was sure he knew what ailed the world and how to fix it, and he would force his will on everyone because of it.

Silently, I reached for my grandfather's hand.

ೞ

Before consciousness slipped from my grandfather entirely, he sent for an attorney, a sign my aunt hopefully interpreted as meaning he was redoing his will. His call for a lawyer came right after another visit from Reverend Thistle. Knowing my grandfather, he'd planned it that way just to plant a false sense of anticipation in her bosom.

She couldn't help but be optimistic. It was in her nature. She confessed to me that evening that his old will left everything to a distant cousin named St. Claire in Devil's Rock, Montana. She didn't want the money for herself, she assured me, but for the church. "It seems a shame for him to bestow his gifts on someone who's never even seen him or helped him."

My grandfather lingered on in a way that tortured us all. While his own suffering was apparent in his trembling breaths and intermittent moans, ours was visible in shadowed eyes and shuffling feet. We set up a vigil, taking turns through the long night, sitting in the chair by his bed, waiting for death to carry him away. As a consequence, we were never fully rested and had little energy for anything beyond the basic functions of eating and dressing and bathing. We said little to each other during this death watch and would catch each other napping in chairs in the parlor during odd hours of the day. This helped me push Eleanor away.

He passed away on a foggy day in late summer, when the darkness he craved in the room now crept into his very soul. For two days, he'd lain asleep, unable to speak or see. If he heard, I do not know. I read to him, tales of adventure from my own collection, not the Bible stories and morality books that lined the shelves of my aunt's house.

His breathing became continually ragged, often startling us into thinking he'd gone. But the final death rattle was a prolonged, wrenching sigh that, after it was over, left no doubt his body was at last without a spirit.

I did not betray him to the end. I did not whisper that I loved him, nor even held affection for him. This resistance, I am sure, would have made him proud of me.

189

My aunt, on the other hand, let out a wailing lament. "The General's gone! He's gone!" she sobbed while standing by his bedside, her hands clutching a handkerchief to her bosom. "And the reverend wasn't here for him. Oh, my. Oh, my!"

I realized she had cherished the hope that the General would pass away while Rev. Thistle was in the room, so that she could feel she had attended to her father-in-law's spiritual needs at the very end. Although Rev. Thistle had prayed and blessed the man a dozen times while I was there, I'm sure my aunt was always worried about my grandfather backsliding into moral oblivion as soon as the holy man left the room. Poor Aunt Constance. She sensed what I knew — that Grandfather cursed a blue streak after the Reverend left the room, a willful dare to the Almighty to strike him down whilst sinning words were on his lips.

It was over. And I was changed but not precisely in the way I had envisioned.

I was right about my grandfather's will. He'd altered it before he died, and it did not include my aunt's charity, the Reverend Thistle's mission. In fact, my grandfather put in his will an especially cruel twist. He was leaving half his estate to Constance, but only on the condition that she swear in an affidavit not to give a penny of it to Thistle and any of his endeavors. He was presenting her with a struggle of conscience that was sure to bedevil her for the rest of her days.

The remainder of the money, I was shocked to find out, was going to me. It was not a huge sum, a surprise to both of us. We'd assumed chests of treasure were hidden in his past. But it would be enough to allow me to realize my dreams of independence.

I had reached, through no effort of my own, the goal for which I had strived when I first set out for San Francisco. To be free. I no longer had to work for Eleanor or any man for that matter. I could go my own way.

And in this newfound freedom, I discovered just how deep my affliction went. Before coming to my grandfather's bed, I'd tricked myself into thinking that staying at Sloane Hall was a matter of practical consideration, and that I'd have to learn to live with my obsession and suffer its torments because I had to bide my time, after all, before returning to the studios. Under the current circumstances, I'd be a fool to give up good work.

Now, I would be a fool to keep it. Yet, I wanted to keep it! I sat in my aunt's house, spending days going through the details of death with her, finding comfort in her discomfort because it meant I had to stay, I had to put off the decision that now loomed before me as surely as the end of life had loomed before my grandfather.

I helped sort out my grandfather's papers, I contracted with a solicitor in Texas and instructed him to sell the General's house there, and I wrote letters of recommendation for the few remaining servants who cared for his property. I did all this as if I were a fat squire of a country estate, smug with good sense. In reality, I had no senses. They'd been stolen from me.

My old pretense stolen as well, I had to devise a new one. Oh, it didn't take me long. In the hours when the drawing room clocks ticked away my excuses, I found what I needed. I'd go back, I'd call on Leo there. I'd let him teach me. And while I learned, I'd work for Eleanor, giving her time to hire someone new. After all, I couldn't just run off without giving her *the chance to...* because she had been so good to me.

The chance to... the chance to tell me to stay. Wasn't that what I really wanted? Of course it was clear — in the part of my heart not blinded by my obsession. But the rest of me, caught in the fog of indecision and grief and caught in the crawl of time that made details nothing more than isolated atoms, not part of a whole, not part of a larger map that would have given me direction —

To me, the only clear thing was to return and hope that she would love me. In spite of the fact that she had no history of real love. That I was not even as interesting or good or colorful as the men she'd loved before. That I was merely a worker among many.

I would go back. I would curse and rail—and pretend! Nothing could kill hope. It was a weed that grabbed at my feet whenever I tried to walk away.

Chapter Fourteen

I'D BEEN TOO late for the Sunset Limited. And since the Lark had no coaches or chair cars, I'd retired almost immediately after boarding. There, alone in my compartment, I'd felt like screaming with the engine whistle — *let me go, let me go. Look up Raoul Walsh*, Leo had said. Yeah, I'd do that. But first I'd go back to Sloane Hall. Let me go.

I was a walking ghost when I disembarked in Los Angeles on a hot, cloudless morning. Pulling at my shirt collar to loosen it, I made my way through the crowds to Alameda. I should call Marta, tell her I was back in town. I should... do something.

I stood on the corner for a good quarter hour rooted to indecision.

Hunger and thirst wore me down. I snagged a taxi and made my way back up to Sloane Hall, slumped in the back seat just as morose as Eleanor when I drove her into the studio.

ᘓ

I arrived just after noon when the air around the fountain was motionless and hot, the gurgling water a rude interruption to this still life. I stared at the house, and, when no one came out to greet me, I wiped my face and headed to my apartment. On this hot day, the plan formed. I had no money yet. It would take awhile for my grandfather's estate to unlock that treasure for me. So I'd have to stay until then. Besides, I wanted to look up this Walsh director, like Leo said. Money or not, I wanted to work in pictures. I'd stay until then, until I could get work or money or both.

She was probably filming today, so there was no rush to share these plans. I'd tell her later, if she was interested in seeing me.

As I put my things away, Marta called up to me from the bottom of the steps. I'd have preferred some time alone to think and plan. More plans. Endless plans. But I walked down the steps to greet her, forcing a smile as I went.

"John! I am so glad you are back!" She came toward me and wrapped her arms around me in a motherly embrace. "Come to the kitchen. I will feed you."

I did as she said, all the sadder as I remembered how good I'd felt after I'd settled into Sloane Hall for the first time.

In the kitchen, she fed me a piece of pie and served me tea, pulling from me the story of my grandfather's demise and my aunt's home. I did not tell her of my inheritance. It was *my* secret.

Julia was nowhere to be seen.

"We have missed you," Marta said. She poured me another cup of tea. "Miss Sloane misses you the most." She said it seriously, as if there were more to tell. "I will tell her you are here."

"She's not on the set?"

"She's sick today."

"She has Mister Morgan to keep her company."

"They are still quarrelling." Marta put the tea kettle on the stove with an emphatic thump. "And he stays away."

She turned to the stove, busying herself with some pots and pans which led me to wonder if Julia had been let go.

However, just a few moments later, Julia showed up, sauntering in, not through the servants' entrance on the far end of the kitchen, but from the dining room door. Marta scowled at her.

"I wanted you to make her a custard tonight. Now it won't have time to chill."

Saying nothing, Julia grabbed the sauce pan. Into it, she sloshed some milk and then reached for some eggs.

A few seconds later, a bell rang from somewhere in the house, a bell similar to the one my aunt had used to summon her servants. Surprised, I looked at Marta. The Sloane estate did not use bells. Whenever Eleanor wanted us, she usually came looking.

"Miss Sloane," Marta said, before scurrying away.

Julia didn't look at me. "She is drinking again."

"What do you mean, 'drinking again?'" As far as I was concerned, she drank all the time.

Shrugging, Julia continued cooking. "Too much. Sick with it."

I pressed her while I had the chance.

"Why?"

Again, she shrugged. "Robbie not staying." She moved her pot off the flame and reached for some eggs. "You leaving. I do not know. It is always one thing or the other."

Marta came back in the room, and I stood, looking at her anxiously, my hands rubbing my legs. I wanted to do something. See Eleanor. Or leave. Something.

She looked at Julia, busy cooking, and twisted her hands before her. "Make some coffee, Julia."

"Why? She will not drink it." Then, under her breath, Julia murmured, "Unless you put rum in it."

Marta looked up at me. "She wants to see you. But wait a few minutes."

"What's the matter with her?" I demanded.

Julia looked up, surprised by my tone. "I told you—the drinking."

Marta frowned. "The studio. They want to fire her. It was in the papers."

No wonder Julia was acting so smug. She saw her chance. She was just biding her time—"pretending" to be the cook, as Robbie had told Eleanor—she was waiting for Eleanor's fall to be complete.

"Why do they want to fire her?" I asked.

Julia answered with a bark of a laugh. "Because she is a drunk!" she said, as if I were the stupidest man alive. "Because she is a—"

"Shush!" Marta interrupted. "She drinks because she is unhappy. And the studio people, they are the ones who make her so unhappy—all their demands! She works so hard, and so long, and tries so much to be what they want her to be." She wiped her eyes.

I remembered what Leo had told me about some of the silent stars. They'd made a hundred thousand or more a picture. Now that sound was bringing new stars to Hollywood, studios were conveniently finding reasons to let the higher-priced ones go. Eleanor was helping them get rid of her.

"And you have no place to criticize," Marta hurled at Julia, "you and *Señor* Morgan. You think I do not see. But I see. I see *everything!*"

"Then fire me." Julia smirked.

Marta opened her mouth to speak then closed it. Julia laughed at her.

I looked at Marta. "Why don't you fire her?"

Marta remained silent, but Julia spoke as she stirred the pot on the stove. "Because I see everything, too, *Monsieur* Doyle. Everything."

"What do you know?" I asked Julia.

Julia stopped and smiled at me. "I know things *Monsieur* Morgan has worked hard to bury."

"About her marriage? Her husband's suicide?"

Julia's smile faltered, and I knew I'd hit a mark. "Yes. All that. All that and more."

"What more is there?"

Her smile dropped. "Surely you know it yourself, *Monsieur* Doyle. You have slept with her, have you not?"

I felt blood rush to my face.

"I'll..." Fatigue swept through me, and I ran my fingers through my hair. "I'll see her now." Yes, that was it—to take liberties, to show Julia I was not one among many, that I was different, that she, that Eleanor... I don't know what I believed. I just wanted to sound confident.

"Wait, let me see if she is ready." Marta rushed off to the other room.

I hesitated, then marched through the central hall into the parlor, looking into the dining room, the library, the sun room.

Finally, I slid open the doors to the great room, and here, I saw her hand lying on top of the sofa. Marta leaned toward her, holding a compact. She was trying to make herself pretty.

When Marta saw me, she straightened. I walked into the room and around the sofa, facing her. Eleanor's efforts were in vain. Her hair was disheveled, and her salmon robe was stained. The place reeked of alcohol. I'd seen her drunk before, and I'd seen my mother drunk and looking worse with the same sallow skin and slack mouth. And now I had the same reaction—a mixture of pain and disgust, of pity and disappointment.

She hobbled to her feet, swaying, her arms outstretched.

"John, John, you're home at last. Thank God!" She hiccupped and began to cry. I let her fall into my arms. I felt her tremble and weep. "Why'd you leave me? Cruel boy, cruel..."

"Help me put her to bed." Marta said, standing.

Gritting my teeth, I picked Eleanor up as if she were a child. Her head fell on my shoulder, her breath caressed my neck.

Marta clucked behind me as I struggled up the stairs. Eleanor felt like a cat in my arms, a wounded cat.

The cat spoke. Twisting her head to see Marta, Eleanor giggled. "See," she lisped. "He came back."

My face grew red from embarrassment and the effort of the climb. Eleanor continued talking in a slurred, hushed voice, as if she were talking to herself.

"He does love me, yes, he does. Not like Basil. And not like..."

Panting, I reached her bedroom and pushed open the door with my foot. Marta rushed ahead and turned down the bed.

"I will help her bathe in the morning," Marta said to me while Eleanor continued to babble.

"You came back, you came back," Eleanor said, like a child happy with her new toy. She kept her hands around my neck as I laid her in the bed. Her gaze locked on mine as if

197

afraid I'd disappear should she blink.

"Why did you go? Don't go!" Eleanor grabbed my hand and held it to her cheek, her joy now turning to sorrow, tears running down her cheeks. Marta came over and pulled the blankets up around her.

"Don't go!" Eleanor cried out when I tried to move away. Now her voice was colored by anger. She moved toward the edge of the bed. "You go and I'll, I'll..." She pointed to the window. Her meaning was clear. Anger turned to giggles. She covered her mouth with her hand.

"I'll stay with her," Marta said quietly.

"No, not you, Marta!" Eleanor tried to push herself up in bed by balancing on the bedside table. But she swayed and fell back, her arm swinging wildly, knocking over a lamp. When it shattered on the floor, Eleanor sobbed. "Lamp's gone, lamp's gone," she said in a sing-song voice while I bent to pick up the pieces.

"I'll get a broom," Marta said, leaving us alone.

Then, with more intensity, Eleanor sounded panicked: "Have to get another. And 'nother. And 'nother picture. He's says 'nother picture..." She sobbed more, deep wails that had nothing to do with a broken light. She spoke, but it was slurred and incomprehensible. She asked for a drink again and again. She pleaded, begged for one in a sad and repulsive way, and, then, before I could catch her, she tumbled off the bed, right on the pile of glass, crying out as her knees and hands were cut.

"Eleanor, get back in bed," I said, tired already.

She stared at me, eyes angry at my lack of sufficient pity, mouth set. She crouched on the floor like an animal.

"You don't lub me," she growled. "No different than..."

"No different than who?"

But she didn't answer. She looked at her hand where slivers of glass lay embedded. She heaved a trembling sigh, and quick as lightning, she sprang up and stumbled toward the bathroom. Something glinted in her hand. A piece of glass! Sharp and ready to cut.

I ran after her.

She tripped over a chair leg, sprawling just in front of the door, still clutching the glass. When she looked up and saw me just a step away, she slithered backward, moving her body like a snake while she took the glass and started to rub her wrist with it, her eyes locked on mine.

"No!" I roared, falling on my knees beside her and grabbing her hand. She wouldn't punish me for sins I'd not committed, dammit. I was not like the others she'd betrayed!

But her anger made her strong, and she pulled away. Her eyes were slits, her mouth thin and furious. She pushed harder against the tender flesh, raising a bead of blood.

"You stupid bitch!" I yelled.

She wouldn't relinquish the glass. I grabbed the other hand and pulled them both apart. She leaned toward me with a groan of effort and bit my arm, forcing me to drop her hands.

"Don't stop me!" she said with new clarity. Hair covered half her face, but one cheek was wet with tears. "Don't!" She renewed her effort to slash away her life, while at the same time she slid into the bathroom, shoving the door closed with her foot.

But I would not stand for it. This was all for my benefit, a performance I would not applaud.

I kicked the door open and flung my arm back, slapping her hard on the cheek. It was a strong enough smack to make her body jump, dislodging the glass from her hand. And god, it felt good to hit her because I wanted not only to stop her from hurting herself— *I* wanted to punish her for trying to punish me!

No! I wouldn't be that.

"Shit," I whispered. I scooped up the glass and tossed it out of sight.

She bent forward sobbing, and I knelt and stroked her hair, sick at heart.

At that moment, Marta returned, broom and dust pan in hand.

Dropping them, she ran to us. "What has she done?" she cried.

Still sobbing and gulping for air, Eleanor placed her hands on my knees.

Marta squatted next to us and placed her hand on Eleanor's back. "My little *niña*," Marta cooed. "Why can't you be happy, eh? Why can't you be happy?"

Without words, we both helped Eleanor back to bed. Except for shallow cuts on her knees, hands, and the one wrist, she wasn't hurt. Marta brought a pan of water to the bedside and washed her while I swept up the debris. When we were both finished, Eleanor murmured my name. Marta looked at me, nodding to the bedside. After she left, I sat by the bed and took Eleanor's offered hand.

I had thought of her every day I'd been away. Jesus, why couldn't she be... who I wanted her to be?

Closing my eyes, I leaned forward. Cascades of memories filled the void in my heart. My mother promising to make things better. *This is Earl, John, your new daddy. We're moving, Johnny, to a better house. Tell the grocer I'll pay him next week, Johnny, when I get my pay.*

Was Eleanor so bad for wanting to avoid that kind of life? She'd had others depending on her — her aunt, Marta, debtors to be paid. She'd tried to be good, she'd told me. And she kept making mistakes. I, of all people, knew what it was like to make a mistake.

Eleanor turned her face to mine and stared at me in silence for a long time. We stayed thus all afternoon, into evening, as shadows engulfed the room, as sounds of the world returned, the distant hooting owl, rustle of leaves, the brush of branches against a window. Life came back in and with it remorse.

"I'm sorry," she whispered through dry lips.

I said nothing, and she turned her head away.

Her shoulders shook. "You know prison. How did you get out?"

She wasn't talking about how I'd served my days. She

was talking about how I'd managed to leave it behind. But I hadn't. I had no advice to offer.

I kissed her forehead. "Try to sleep."

ଏ

I was stiff and sore in the morning, and she was already beginning to shake as the liquor left her. She thrashed about the bed and asked for another drink, but I wouldn't give her any, and I suspected this was a struggle that had started before I'd come home. Marta came into the room as dawn broke, carrying a tray with coffee and toast.

"Get some rest now, *Señor*," she said to me.

But I wouldn't leave. Standing, I stretched and looked out across the gravel to my own rooms, the view she saw. Had her longing matched mine? I couldn't imagine her standing there, looking out as I did. My room seemed so small.

"No, don't want any," Eleanor said as Marta tried to get her to sip coffee.

"You must eat, *Señorita*. You must have some coffee. Or perhaps some juice? Here is some orange juice."

I heard a bump and turned around. Eleanor had knocked over the orange juice glass, and liquid pooled on the tray.

"I'm so cold. I need a drink to warm me up. A brandy," Eleanor said through chattering teeth.

"She needs a doctor," I said flatly. "She needs a place to dry out. A sanitarium."

Marta looked at me and shook her head. "A sanitarium — they would find out."

I knew what she meant — Louella Parsons, the Hollywood press. If they got wind of the fact that Eleanor had the drunken shakes and was in a sanitarium somewhere....

"*Señor* Morgan kept it out of the papers last time," Marta said. Had that been when I'd arrived at Sloane Hall? Had that been where she'd been?

Eleanor hiccupped and started to gag. Marta and I quickly propped her up and held her straight while she vomited, only emitting a foul-smelling drool. Looking at her in the early light, I noticed she was thinner, and her eyes were sunken in her face. She had to have a doctor's care.

"A hospital," I said as we eased her back onto the pillow. "We should take her to a hospital."

Marta pursed her lips and was about to respond when another seizure overwhelmed Eleanor, this one worse than the first. Her body shook convulsively, and her gagging kept her from gaining breath. I was afraid she was going to pass out.

"I'll call the doctor!" I said, now awakened to the fact that something horrible could happen here, that leaving one deathbed did not make me immune to experiencing another.

I reached for the phone, but Marta put her hand over mine. "I will do it," she said, and took up the receiver.

While she placed the call, I did what I could to ease Eleanor's suffering. I placed her in a sitting position and swaddled her in a cocoon of blankets. I sat with my arm around her shoulders and stroked her brittle hair. Her breathing calmed, her head fell on my chest.

"He will come immediately," Marta said after hanging up the phone. She looked at us both and twisted her hands before her. "He will probably send her to hospital."

"Good," I whispered.

"And then what will we say, *Señor* Doyle? What will we say when they call—when the newspaper people and the studio people call?"

I started to say, "The truth," but closed my mouth. Eleanor moaned lightly and trembled in my arms. I swallowed and closed my eyes. There was no way around it. It had to be done. Shit.

"Tell Julia she has to find Morgan, or she's fired."

Marta understood and left immediately to find the cook.

Alone in the room with Eleanor, I rocked her slowly. "It's all right, El. We're going to find Robbie."

Chapter Fifteen

AS I SUSPECTED, Julia knew how to find Morgan, and he was back at the estate by late afternoon. In the meantime, the doctor came and confirmed what we already knew — Eleanor was suffering from withdrawal, from alcohol poisoning, and needed to be hospitalized. We told him we'd make the arrangements ourselves and waited for Morgan to return.

By the time he came, Eleanor had fallen into an uncomfortable sleep, hallucinating and shaking uncontrollably. I stayed with her the entire day. Any time I tried to leave, she'd cry out. I was used to vigils by now and slept in the chair most of the time, numb from the effort.

Morgan breezed into the room a little before four as I was dozing.

"My god, she looks like a little *hausfrau*. We have to get her prettied up!" he said with false cheer. I gritted my teeth. Marta went to Eleanor's closet and pulled out a white satin robe — the one she'd worn in bed that night, the first night we'd made love! And Morgan came over to the bed, not even acknowledging me. I'd known it would be like this.

"I'm here, darling," he said as he went to her.

Her eyes fluttered open, and her lips pricked up in a half smile.

"I know what you need." His voice was low and tender, almost sad, stripped of bravado for a flash of truth.

He brushed by me and picked up the phone. He called a sanitarium and reserved a room. He must have made this call before.

Over his shoulder, he asked Marta, "Where's her make-up? She needs some rouge and lipstick. And her perfume. It smells like a tomb in here!"

Then he called the great Louella Parsons and gave her the

story. "She's collapsed, Lou! They've worked her to the bone!" His voice quivered with emotion, and he spoke so low, she must have asked him to repeat himself. "We're taking her to... well, I can't say. Her fans would mob her. I'll let you know in a day or two. Don't breathe a word until I call you. I'll give you an exclusive—and another bit of news as soon as I get this all settled." He sounded as if he'd break down crying.

He stayed on the telephone with her for a few more minutes while Marta wiped Eleanor's face and applied make-up. I got up and stood out of the way. I had to admit he was good at this, taking charge of her life, making everything go.

After Robbie was off the phone, he looked at Marta. "Let's get her changed."

While Marta untied Eleanor's robe, Robbie brushed past me again, not saying a word to me or even noting I was in the room. I don't know why I stayed. Maybe because I was tired, too. Too tired to decide anything, even moving beyond my spot on the carpet.

A few moments later, he returned, holding a glass of golden liquid.

"What's that?" I asked, suddenly on edge. I knew what it was. I could smell it.

At first, an almost-imperceptible sneer lifted his lips. Then he glared at me.

"What do you think it is? She needs it. A quick one to get her into shape. One can never be sure if photographers will be around, despite the best precautions."

My blood started pumping again, and fury swept over me. I was too tired to be careful. My hand struck out and toppled the glass from his hands, spilling the brandy onto the carpet. Marta quickly turned toward us but said nothing.

"Damn it, boy. Now you'll have to get her another one," Morgan said. Then, in a lower voice, a whispered hiss, "You've really fucked this up, haven't you? You should have called me sooner. I know what she needs."

"She doesn't need a drink."

He stared at me. "Get it, or you're fired."

"Then I'm fired." I turned and walked out with slow precision, down the steps, and over to my rooms. I knew without even looking at him that he'd be smiling.

The weight of fatigue made me feel like I had chains around my ankles and gauze around my eyes. I was too tired to think straight, or to care, and it occurred to me that this problem had had the effect I'd sought at my grandfather's deathbed. It had numbed me. It had made me capable of leaving. And now I had no excuse—Robbie had fired me. Perhaps I should have thanked him.

I slowly packed my duffel bag again—placing back in it the few items I'd removed since returning from San Francisco. I looked over at her window while I packed. They were undressing her there, removing the silky robe, touching her soft flesh, slipping the white satin over her breasts.

A voice broke my thoughts. Julia. She stood in my doorway.

"Marta wants you to get the car. The Packard." She looked at my bag but didn't say anything about it. She was as sullen as I was— her dreams were gone, too, now that Morgan was pumping life back into Eleanor.

"I don't work here anymore."

"Marta said to make sure you know you are not fired."

"No, I am."

"*Monsieur*," she said slowly, "I do not care if you are fired or not. But if you do not get the car, Marta will have to drive."

Marta hated to drive. Julia actually felt sorry for her. And now I had to ante up my sympathy as well.

"All right." All right. I'd drive them to the sanitarium. And then I'd leave.

After she left, I sat on the bed and closed my eyes, trying to steal some of the rest I'd lost the night before. Nothing moved. I sat for days. Minutes. Seconds. I didn't know. I heard the door to the big house creak open, so I stood, moving slowly, swimming through heavy water, grabbing my bag. Below, in the garage, I threw it in the trunk and pulled the car around to the front of the house. There, Morgan stood with

Eleanor in his arms, looking smugly heroic, carrying the damsel in distress. Marta had "prettied her up," and she looked as gay as a corpse. She was calmer and half-smiling, no doubt as a result of the brandy Morgan had given her. In fact, her arms encircled his neck in much the same way they'd encircled mine the night before when I'd carried her to bed. She grabbed on to whatever life raft was available. We were interchangeable.

After Morgan settled her into the back seat and sat next to her, Marta got in next to me, clasping a rosary in her lap.

The drive was silent and long. With Morgan giving directions, we raced into the mountains, up the same road where I'd met Eleanor for the first time. Eventually, after nearly an hour's drive, we came to a long, low building surrounded by bright flowers and big bushes, and fountains to mask the fact we were in arid hills. It all looked expensive and strangely cold.

I waited in the car while Morgan and Marta settled Eleanor in. He seemed to know the place, and I suspected Marta had been here before as well. Neither Morgan nor Marta suggested I accompany them in, so I leaned back in the hot car, and I closed my eyes, drifting into a half sleep where ghosts roamed my dreams.

As clear as the sky, the thought came to me that Eleanor was doomed. With Robbie's management and Marta's weak resistance, Eleanor would drink again and eventually die from it. Maybe not in a dark, locked closet like my mother. But somehow, somewhere — in a gutter, behind the wheel of a car, in a hospital bed while her body shook out the life within her, and while Morgan looked on, mourning her loss. I couldn't save her from that. Only she could.

This thought roused me, and I smacked my hand against the steering wheel, cursing.

Do you believe in God, Johnny?

Pete's voice, piercing through the thin, hot air.

I was with him at the end, but only at the end. When he fell ill, I avoided him, angry he was sick, always sick, that he didn't take care of himself. What did he expect when he worked outside in the cold without his jacket, when he didn't wear a hat in the rain? What did he expect when he dared to be struck down?

I'd pulled away, not sitting with him as often as I should have, not being available to read to him in the evening.

"Oh, that's all right," he'd say when I came in late from the yard. "It's too nice a night to be cooped up in here with us chickens."

I was the chicken, too scared to care. When Pete passed on, I'd actually felt a small measure of satisfaction in my grief. It could have been worse, I'd thought, it could have been worse if you'd grown closer, been a better friend. As it was, I managed to choke back any tears and didn't shed a one as we gathered around his grave on a windy, dusty September morning.

It could have been worse.

It was after his death that I talked to Rev. Milqueton about leaving. I'd followed him into his office, quietly closing the door behind me and asking if he had a few moments.

"Sit down, boy." He'd gestured to the chair in front of his desk while he took his own seat. His desk, like his office, was clear of clutter or adornment. A ragged-edged ink blotter covered most of the desk, a paperweight made of Texas rock on the left, holding down no papers. Those would be filed away.

The only decorations were a plain wooden cross and a line drawing of St. Paul on the road to Damascus. When talking to Milqueton, you couldn't avoid staring at the drawing, which hung just above his chair. St. Paul was on the ground, his head turned toward blinding rays, his mouth a cavernous open cry of shock.

We were all on the road to Damascus when we came to Canfield. And I suspect Milqueton thought of us as prospective St. Pauls, being led to personal epiphanies, being struck by the light.

"I—I would like to resign." I'd leaned forward, as if I

were going to leave at that very moment once I'd made up my mind.

Milqueton didn't say anything at first. He was not a man to be hurried. He clenched his jaw and then crossed his hands on his desk.

"Pete's passing has been hard on you," he said.

I whipped my head up to stare at him. "Not at all. It's just time."

He winced. "It's your right. I can't bind you here, now that your time's served." He stared at me and I looked down. "But you should give me notice. A few weeks is usual. I would advise you take a little longer to get your things together, perhaps secure another position."

Relieved that he would not fight me, I looked up and saw sad eyes crowned by a furrowed brow. "I'll help you with that. Finding a position," he said.

As it was, I stayed almost another year. Milqueton wrote to several schools and churches he knew seeking employment for me, but no one had a position open. Finally, I'd told him I was going regardless of my prospects. He didn't stop me. He wrote the recommendation letter, told me not to dwell in the past, and asked for me to drop him a note now and then.

And here I was, exactly where I'd started when Pete had died. Eager to get away.

"We can go home now." Marta's voice, tired and low.

Doors opened, they slipped in. I turned the engine on. No one said anything. I didn't ask. How is she. How long will she stay. What should I do.

Morgan quickly fell asleep in the back seat. Marta pulled out her rosary again, but her fingers didn't move over it. We were all stuck.

By the time we arrived back at Sloane Hall, I didn't know who I was or what I was doing there. My duffel bag was still in the trunk. What had I intended when I threw it there?

Marta lingered by the car while Morgan shuffled into the house.

"She will be there for at least a week," she explained.

"And then they will put her in the hospital in town. *Señor* Morgan says that is the best way. The press can see her there — at the hospital. We can visit her there."

I rubbed my eyes. The sun had set, and the sky was darkening, with just a ribbon of scarlet on the far horizon.

"What does that matter to me? I'm leaving."

"You are not leaving," she said, anger creeping into her voice.

"Mister Morgan fired me."

"*Señorita* Sloane did not fire you."

From inside the house, we heard the telephone ring, and Morgan's voice cut outside as he picked it up in the front parlor.

"I was just about to call you. You worked her nearly to death, goddammit. And don't think her fans don't know. She's already got a room full of flowers.... Yes, I can be there. Mm-hmm. All right...."

I looked at Marta's pleading eyes. "I was going to leave anyway," I told her. "I have my bag in the trunk."

She stepped back from the car as if stung.

"You are going no place tonight, *Señor* Doyle. You cannot keep your eyes open. Tomorrow you will speak with me. And we will talk about this leaving you want to do."

ભ

All right. I slept there. I was tired, like she said. I was going to leave in the morning.

But I didn't. Marta was sly. When I talked to her after breakfast, she didn't try to argue me into staying on. Instead, she just asked me to stay until Eleanor was home from the hospital. In that way, I could look for something better, she could look for my replacement, and I could tell Eleanor myself that I was leaving.

It is a measure of how easily I fooled myself that I accepted this arrangement, even though I never saw Marta actively seek another chauffeur — not one phone call about it, not one advertisement posted, not one mention to shopkeepers in town or other stars' households.

Meanwhile, I searched out Leo, now intent on learning more about the Raoul Walsh film he'd mentioned, looking forward to the moment when I could tell Marta — no, Eleanor — I'd landed a job as a cameraman and wouldn't be staying at Sloane Hall any longer.

On the lot of the studio Leo had worked on last, I had a fright. A medic, black bag in hand, was rushing to a soundstage. My first thought was that the old cameraman had collapsed. But when I followed the crisis, I discovered it was just an actor needing smelling salts. He'd forgotten he was on a sound set, stood too quickly, and bumped his head on the heavy brass microphone hanging just above.

Leo was on no set that I could locate, but I did manage to find out where he lived — in a sad one-room not too far from the Central Avenue digs I'd visited with Robbie. Leo was coughing and smoking when I arrived, and I insisted on going out to fetch him some soup.

Once back with that, I pressed him on the film he'd mentioned to me and on the idea of "apprenticing" to him whether working on a film or not.

To this he warmed considerably, his cough subsiding and his need to feed it fading as well. He picked up the old camera he'd rescued and went through each of its parts from lens to aperture to shutter. He teased me about my mistake of loading the film in the cartridge the wrong way. He explained how the cinematographer more than the director decided how to use focal length to determine how large an object or subject loomed in the audience's vision.

"This is all mechanics, though," he said, as I handled the old camera, looking through its lens. "That's stuff any car repairman can figure out."

I ignored his jab at my skills and let him continue.

"The thing that's hard to teach is looking at the world like you're seeing it through a camera. Not even directors can do that right. They get the space all wrong in their heads. They don't know how the light affects things, especially how it can surprise you. They don't realize how much they're relying on what they see here." He moved his hands along the sides of his eyes while keeping his gaze straight. "They have an idea for a tracking shot that sweeps through a room, getting the looks of actors along the way and keeping a steady line like a dancer... but the cameraman, he's the one who has to figure it all out—the space, the light, and the speed that make it possible." He laughed. "You see, John, most people's imaginations tend to sort of float. A cameraman has to anchor all those ideas to the reality."

He asked me for the time and jumped up when I announced it.

"Gotta go. Can you drop me at the studio?"

Surprised that he might have a job to go to when I thought he was home sick, I asked him where he wanted me to take him.

"Warner Brothers," came the quick answer as he jammed a cap on his head and made for the door. "I'm meeting King Vidor to go scouting a location for him." Vidor, he explained, always took a cameraman when looking at locations because he understood that a cameraman knew light and would know the best time of day to shoot.

Location shoots were rarer now that sound was everywhere. But directors still used them, overlaid with music or sound effects, to set a movie's tone. And some directors were taking the bulky booths on location, too, to film in the desert.

That reminded me to press Leo again about the Walsh film, which I did as we drove in, and to ask him why he wasn't signing up for it.

He smiled, his hand on the door handle as we pulled up to the Warner lot. "You need a chance, kid, and I've got other things lined up. Big things."

With that, he left and I had no excuse but to head back to Sloane Hall.

◌ঃ

The first week that Eleanor was gone, Marta made sure I was too busy to think of leaving. She enlisted me to help her sort the star's fan mail, which arrived in ever-increasing amounts once word leaked of Eleanor's hospitalization.

Every afternoon, I'd bring boxes of it into the kitchen, and the three of us—Julia, Marta, and me—would sit at the table opening and filing it. Requests for autographed photos in one pile. Get well cards and wishes in another. Pleas for help (money, starting a career in Hollywood, even for a place to stay while visiting the city) in another. Then I would be directed to take the sorted piles to a secretarial service in town that Eleanor employed for responses.

Marta kept a small pile of letters to show to Eleanor personally.

> *Dear Miss Sloane, I lost my husband last year and was near despair when I saw you in "The Prince and the Commoner." You made me smile again....*

> *Dear Miss Sloane, I once saw Sarah Bernhardt on the stage, but your performance in "Daughter of Destiny" was just as good, maybe even better....*

> *Dear Miss Sloane, You are so beautiful that it's unfair to the other actors and actresses in your films – we're always looking at you when you're on the screen....*

"Take these to her, John," Marta said, tying a small pile in a blue ribbon. She pushed them across the table to me.

I looked up, surprised. But yes, my heart beat faster. I wanted to see her.

"It's a long drive. I'm supposed to take Julia to the market," I said, nodding in Julia's direction.

"The hospital is not too far," Julia said. "Fountain Avenue."

"The hospital?

"She's been transferred there," Marta said. "Cedars of Lebanon."

So she was well enough to go to a hospital now, and no

one had told me. Why should they, I reminded myself.

I scooped up the letters Marta had pushed my way and stood. "All right. Just tell me where."

Marta wrote down the address and gave me directions. She told me I should not take the Duesenberg or the Nash but something more nondescript, the Packard or the Ford. There was still an air of secrecy about Eleanor's whereabouts. No doubt Morgan had some plan that was playing out, some plan that I wasn't allowed to know.

Once Marta knew I'd take the letters to Eleanor, she told me to forgo taking Julia to the market until the next day. Marta seemed eager to get me to the hospital, and I flattered myself with the thought that it was because she knew Eleanor would be cheered by my presence. And because I had a task to perform, I could fool myself into thinking that my eagerness to see Eleanor was merely part of my duty.

At the hospital, I parked the car in a rush and stuffed the packet of letters into my pocket. Then I hurried to the doorway — an arched one like a church, like the studio — at the base of a tall eight-story rectangle of a building with two shorter wings reaching out at angles as if to embrace the sick and those who cared for them. Once inside, I scanned the lobby until my eyes lit on the elevators.

As I walked toward them, a man's voice called after me.

"Son! Where do you think you're going?"

Turning, I saw a guard sitting at a wooden desk to the side of the doors. A sign above him read: "Visitors, please check in first."

"I'm here to visit a patient," I said, standing before him.

He was pudgy and cheerful-looking, too much like Brice Clement.

"Which one?" he asked.

"Pauline Sloane."

His eyebrows went up, but he didn't say anything. Instead, he flipped through a notebook, slowly scanning the names on each page.

"She's not here."

"Then try Eleanor Brickman," I said, impatient.

He repeated his routine, taking even more time.

"Sorry. No one by that name."

"I know she's here. I..."

"Are you a relative?"

"No, I'm..." What—I inwardly screamed—exactly what am I to Eleanor? "I'm her ... friend." I held out the packet of letters. "I have something for her."

The guard scrutinized me, his gaze moving from my head to my trousers as he sized up whether I fit the "friend of a movie star" category. Unsure of the verdict, I decided to leave and try another route, perhaps a back door, when he spoke again.

"Leave your name," he said. "If she does check in I can see whether she'll see you."

After giving him my name, I turned to leave. Out of the corner of my eye, I saw the elevator opening. Robbie Morgan stepped off.

His hands in his pockets, his gaze was intent on the floor before him, as if he were distracted by troubling thoughts. When he finally did raise his head and see me, a sickly smile spread over his face.

"John, is the car out front?" He said it loud enough for the guard to hear, sending the clear message that I was nothing more than a hireling.

Not wanting to make a scene in the lobby, I merely nodded and headed for the door. But Morgan called after me.

"Hold on, John!" He caught up with me as I stepped outside. Angrily, he pulled at my shoulder.

I shrugged his hand off.

"You needn't be so touchy, boy," he said, laughing at me.

"You have your own car with you," I said.

"Ah, yes. I forgot. Saw you and just thought... only natural, you know."

"Why can't I see her?" I asked through clamped teeth.

"She needs rest."

"Marta told me to bring these." I held up the letters.

"I'll take care of them. You've done nothing but upset her since you arrived on the scene." He grabbed the letters from my hand and slipped them into a pocket.

"How is she?" I had to know, now that I was denied the opportunity to see for myself.

"As well as can be expected." He patted his pockets searching for a cigarette. Finding one, he stuck it in his mouth, then pulled out a match which he struck unsuccessfully several times.

"What does that mean?"

"She's just high strung. Something you wouldn't understand." He tried again to light his smoke but couldn't do it. He held out the matches to me. "You want to be useful?"

His eyes laughed at me. I reached up to take the matches, then impulsively smacked them out of his hand instead.

Surprised by my action, he smiled, but his eyes were dark slits. "I wouldn't do that again," he said, low and sinister. The smile disappeared.

"Why? You gonna fight me?" I knew he wouldn't. His amused self-importance vanished, replaced by red anger.

"I'm not a fool," he hissed. "Go back to wherever you came from. Ellie doesn't need you. She doesn't want to see you."

"That's not true."

"I fired you."

"She didn't fire me." So now the truth came out, revealing itself to me. I was defending my right to stay when just a week ago I had been glad to have it decided that I would leave.

He smiled again. "I'm in charge, Johnny boy. I always was."

I wanted to hit him. I wanted to beat him again and again. My fists clenched. I closed my eyes. When I opened them, he was walking away.

ଔ

Now I stayed as a rebuke to Morgan. If he thought he was in charge, I'd show him. I'd prove that it was Eleanor who controlled my fate.

Eleanor. Morgan. Marta. Even Leo. Everyone controlled it except me.

Marta kept me busy with the fan mail, trips to the market, to her church, to shops for new furnishings, and she was quick to point out even the smallest tap or squeak in the cars so that I'd spend my spare time working on them.

No one talked about Eleanor, so I resorted to reading *Variety* about her status, picking up the newspaper from the post office and scanning it before taking it in with the other mail.

She was rumored to be suffering from tuberculosis, to have had a nervous breakdown, to be sick from food poisoning, to be starving herself to look as svelte as Harlow, as gaunt as Garbo.

Studio executives were quoted gushing with concern, but gossip columnists wrote that enough footage was in the can that the film could be finished without her. Her contract could be scuttled, and the movie wouldn't suffer. When unknowns were being hired to play leads for less money than the established stars, she was hardly secure. Morgan couldn't fix everything. This consoled me, even though it was at her expense.

It was a sunny Thursday afternoon. After placing the mail on the kitchen table, I looked at Marta. I looked at her sitting there, sipping her coffee, waiting. Waiting for Eleanor to get well. To what end? Just so she could keep things the way they were? Eleanor drinking and then not drinking. Morgan lolling around like the master of the manor. Just so we could all get our paychecks each week?

In that was madness. I felt like I was going mad myself, staying there. Jesus Christ, I wouldn't be imprisoned again. Not even one of my own making. If Leo couldn't find me something in the studios soon, I'd take any job. I'd go back to Jake's and see if I could be a car mechanic while I waited for my grandfather's money to roll in. That's how bad I felt.

But the next day everything changed again. With just a

sentence. Just four words.

Bring the Duesenberg around.

That's what he said.

It was a bright, shimmering morning touched by the cool resignation of fall that whispers in the background: it's over, it's over, you know it's over. Dew was on the ground, and I was on my way to the main house to see if Marta needed me.

As I walked by the fountain, the front door opened, and Pilot bolted out ahead of Morgan. Hands in his pockets, Morgan stood on the veranda, smiling. He waved to me to come forward, and right away I felt a cold fear creep up my spine.

"Bring the Duesenberg around. We're picking her up. Oh, and be sure to wear the uniform. She said I should tell you." Whistling, he turned and went back into the house.

Bring the Duesenberg around. Bring her back. Forget about Jake's. Forget about Leo. It's over.

In an instant, I went from idle to racing speed. Breathing hard, I rushed to my room and pulled out the uniform. My hands trembled as I buttoned the heavy jacket into place, as I brushed my hair and dusted lint off my trousers. She was coming home.

After shoving the cap on my head, I backed the car out and drove up to the front door, where I waited a maddening half hour for Morgan to appear. Just as I was about to go searching for him, he finally sauntered out.

I wanted to ask him if she was really well, if she was going to finish the picture, if... and not one question could I ask! Because if I did, Morgan would burst it all with a sneer or a snicker. He'd burst the fine, good feeling of a prayer answered, of grace bestowed. Of course I was glad she was coming home—that meant she was well. And I wasn't so heartless I didn't want her well.

I drove silently, my hands gripping the wheel like a life preserver as I glanced at him from time to time with darting eyes — if I moved my head, he would notice I was looking, and he'd know I was searching for answers in his face. He slouched, smugly serene, in the corner of the back seat, staring hard into the passing scenery.

Three blocks from the hospital, he made me stop at a florist where he picked up a large bouquet of roses.

At the hospital, I saw the reason for the flowers and for Eleanor's request that I put on the uniform. The entrance was swarming with press, their bulky cameras ready to flash pictures in the shadowed doorway with rapid-fire speed.

"Drive around for twenty minutes or so," Morgan said before he got out. "We'll be ready by then." I reluctantly did as instructed, preferring to sit and wait, my eyes trained on the entrance like a camera blocking out everything but the star.

In ten minutes' time, I was back in place, and fifteen minutes after that, Morgan was pushing her wheelchair through the door. She was pale but sunny, all dressed in white, with the brilliant blood-red roses in her lap. Her head was adorned with her straw sun hat, her eyes shaded by dark glasses.

As Morgan wheeled her to the car, she waved a gloved hand and smiled and answered a few friendly questions tossed her way.

"Miss Sloane, what was the diagnosis? What happened to you?"

"Just exhaustion, boys. Nothing serious. Sorry to disappoint you."

"When will you go back to work?"

"That's up to my doctors."

"Is it true that you are ordered off the picture if you don't show up by Monday?"

"I wouldn't dare to presume to speak for anyone, especially if they were to say something as nasty as that!"

"What do you think of Garbo's first talkie?"

"I think she's a wonderful actress."

"Aren't you disappointed you weren't offered Karenina?"

"Boys, I was born disappointed!" With that, they all laughed good-naturedly, and she was ready to get in the car. Mister Morgan went to help her, but she reached for my outstretched hand, and the flashbulbs burst with light, making my eyes blur.

Once in the car, Morgan kept up a steady flow of conversation while she said very little in return. He complimented her on her performance with the press, especially her line about the studio letting her go. She looked at me — yes, I know she was looking at me and not straight ahead, I felt her eyes on my back, my neck. I didn't care if Morgan noticed — I looked back at her in the mirror, and I tried to say in my eyes that I was sorry, that I'd waited, that I hadn't betrayed her, that I wasn't serious about leaving.

"Let him try to fire you now, darling. He'll look like Scrooge."

"Robbie, he likes looking like Scrooge."

"And saying you were 'born disappointed.' My dear, how do you think of these things? Even Harlow couldn't have come up with that one."

"Poor Jean."

She was changed. Pale, gaunt, but less excitable. Her cheeks were hollowed, and when she removed her glasses, I could see dark tired circles, like bruises, under her eyes. Gone was the nervous tapping, the twitching of her leg. Even as she talked to Morgan, she looked out the window, her mouth a relaxed self-satisfied smile. She was a different person. Maybe it was possible.

At the house, Marta fussed over her and insisted I help her to her bed. When Morgan tried to insert himself, Marta shooed him away.

"No, *Señor* Morgan. Your arm is still not strong enough." But of course, it was.

Eleanor was quite capable of walking on her own, however, and Marta gave up the pretense of aiding her when we were halfway up the stairs. With Morgan standing at the base of the steps sulking, we made the rest of the short walk together, my hand under Eleanor's right elbow to steady her.

Once we were in her room, her shoulders sagged. She let out a long, weary sigh.

"Close the door." She walked to her bed as I did as she instructed. After tearing off her hat and shaking her hair, she lay down on the coverlet and beckoned me to her.

I sat on the edge of the bed, waiting, longing to touch her, to kiss her. She looked at me, studied my face, and waited as well. And then, she sighed and put her hand over mine.

"Why do you play this silly game?" she asked.

"What game?"

"Always waiting for me to make the first move." She stroked my hand, my arm.

I moved closer. I embraced her. No scent of alcohol. Only her perfume.

"El," I whispered into her hair.

"Tell me you love me. Say it." She kissed my ears, my neck.

"I love you, El. God I missed you."

Chapter Sixteen

WHEN I LEFT THE house a half hour later, I was filled with hope again, and Robbie Morgan was quick to smother it. Standing on the veranda, leaning on its rail, staring into the sky as if searching for something, he didn't even look at me when he spoke.

"She's still a drunk, you know," he said. "That sort of thing doesn't just disappear. And she's damned lucky to have me around to fix it all up for her."

I turned away, heading for the garage.

But he followed me there. It made my skin crawl, to have the taste of her still on me and Robbie sniffing around.

"I need to go into the city." He put his hands in his pockets. Ah—so I was to drive him, and he would thus put me in my place.

"I thought you'd fired me."

"Well, you're still here, though, aren't you?" A quick smile. "Unless you'd rather stay fired?"

I said nothing.

"Have to try and straighten out this mess. It's not over yet." From the smell of his breath, I could tell he'd been drinking. How did he expect her to stop if he didn't?

"Always pulling her out of messes, you know," he said. "That's my job. I shouldn't be called her agent. I should be giving out cards that say 'mess cleaner.' Fucking mess cleaner."

Not wanting him to stay, I said nothing. I opened the Duesenberg's hood and started examining the engine, not for any reason in particular, but to lose myself in something and to send the signal that he should leave and get ready if he expected me to drive him somewhere.

"Of course, I wasn't around when she got into that big

mess up in 'Frisco. Damned slut. She is a slut, you know. Oh yes, you do know. Don't you?" He sounded desperate, as if he didn't really want to hear the answer to that question, or secretly hoped the answer wouldn't be what he knew was the truth. And it was only this discomfort on his part that kept me from downing him with a few quick blows.

I threw my energy into twisting caps, checking the oil, focusing on the hard shiny surface of the powerful engine in front of me, its coldness, its ability to perform unhampered by anger or despair. But my hands shook.

"Poor Griswold. Thought he'd found the perfect mate. When in reality he'd found the perfect little tramp. If the papers got hold of that one now... her morals clause would have her out on her ear. Never work again."

A cap slipped out of my hand and landed below. Gratefully, I slunk beneath the car, glad not to have to see him.

"That's what I'm for. Keeping all of that under the rug. Nice and clean. The mess eraser. So, old boy, I'll just run into town and do some more clean up, all right?"

"I'm ready. The car's ready," I hissed at him as I stood. "Get in." I held the back door open.

"Let me just get my jacket."

I got into the driver's seat and pulled the car out and around to the front door where I waited. And waited. Nearly a half hour later, he appeared, his jacket over his shoulder. This was another ploy, one he embellished by standing and lighting a cigarette by the door I held open for him. When his smoke was finally glowing, he scooted in, and I slammed the door behind him. Now I hoped he did smell Ellie on me. I hoped it choked him.

Halfway down the hill, he told me where to head. Once we got into the city, he directed me to a café near the Biltmore where he met an attractive woman dressed in a shiny blue suit and large matching hat. I was to come back for him in an hour.

I drove for that hour, out past the city into open land, the window open and my cap off, and I let the motion build on the euphoria I'd experienced in Eleanor's room. She'd wept for me. She'd kissed my hand and told me she was never going to drink again, that I'd rescued her, that it was I who had pulled her back from the brink, that it was I who had saved her from everything foul, that she'd learned her lesson, that she would be a "good girl" now and love me the way I deserved to be loved.

Yes, she said she loved me!

And she told me to come see her that night after everyone else had gone to bed, and when I'd protested and pointed out she'd be tired, she had put her finger on my lips and said, "No, you must come. I won't fall asleep until you come see me."

So I had a rendezvous to look forward to.

When I returned to the spot where I'd dropped off Robbie, I still had to wait another hour before he reappeared. I knew he probably deliberately gave me times to appear that were well before the time he'd need me, but I had Eleanor, and he didn't, and that was all that mattered.

His meeting must have been successful, however, because when he got in the car, he was in good spirits.

"Have you been to the post office yet to pick up the mail?" He lit a cigarette and blew a quick gust of smoke out the open window.

"Yes, sir."

"Well, drive me to the pharmacy. I need to pick up some medicine for poor old El. And then to that place on Central. You know. The art dealer." He giggled.

So it was an art dealer he saw in that section of the city. No, I didn't think so. And I didn't want him visiting some bootlegger when Eleanor had just gotten clean. After we'd picked up the medicine, I asked him if he also needed to get to the studio.

"No. No studio today. My work is done."

"Then I think we should head home. There's something wrong with the engine," I said, "and I'm afraid it'll break down."

In the mirror, I saw him scowl, but he didn't say

anything, and I drove him silently back to Sloane Hall. At least no new liquor would enter the estate that day.

As soon as we arrived at Sloane Hall and I'd put the car away, Marta came looking for me.

"Miss Sloane has been asking to see you," she said anxiously.

Victorious, I ran up the stairs to the big house and into her room, not caring where Robbie was or if he saw, even hoping he would see.

Propped up by pillows and surrounded by flowers sent by well-wishers, she looked tired but still beautiful. Her hair was no longer wavy but frizzy now, encircling her head like a soft cloud. She wore her salmon-colored robe, now clean and fresh, and it nearly matched the fleshy golden tones of Pilot, who lay by her side on the floor.

As soon as I walked in the room, I caught sight of my reflection in a mirror above her vanity.

My hair was uncombed, my face sweaty. I was a working man. It cut me.

"Come here," she said, patting the bed beside her. Pilot interpreted her gesture as meant for him. He jumped up onto the bed, his tail wagging.

She pushed the dog away. "Go on, girl. You're not leaving any room for John." When the dog obeyed, she tilted her head to the side, waiting.

I went to her. I sat on the bed as I'd done earlier in the day and wondered if she'd called to tell me she was too tired to see me later.

The corner of my eye lit on something different in the room, something out of place. I turned to look at it. A steamer trunk lay open, a few silky undergarments already folded inside. Now I knew why she'd sent for me.

"You're going away." I whispered.

"Yes." She lowered her head, not able to look me in the eye. "The doctor thought it would be best ... "

"The movie?"

"I won't finish it. Robbie can't fix it."

"He thinks he can." For once, I found myself taking up for him.

She shook her head. "No. It's too late. They have enough to finish without me. They'll pull my contract." She looked up and over into the light pouring through a window beyond me, fixating on it. It was cheerful light, yellow and bright, the last burst of afternoon before the day's promises died.

Taking a deep breath, she went on, as if she'd rehearsed it. "I'll be gone like John Gilbert, Pickford, Clara... all the rest..."

What would happen to her? How would she support herself now?

She bit her lower lip. "Aren't you going to say anything?"

"I... I'm sorry." I didn't know what else to offer.

" 'Stay' would be nice to hear," she pouted.

"Then stay."

She didn't answer, which was my answer.

"Where will you go?"

"A house in Mexico—someone Robbie knows is letting us use it. It's something of a palace," she replied.

Robbie. Us.

"Is he going with you?"

She wouldn't look at me. "He's going ahead to make arrangements...."

I remained silent.

Her head flew up, and now she glared at me, anger spitting from her eyes.

"I thought you'd be happy—to get away with me."

"A moment ago you wanted me to beg you to stay here with me."

"No, no! I just want..." She shook her head, confused. "I thought you wanted me." She grabbed a lace-edged handkerchief from the bedside table and wiped the corner of her eye. The gesture looked so smooth and calm, just like from a movie.

"When will you leave?" My voice was steady.

"In another week if we can." She leaned forward and

stroked my hand, but I pulled it away. "John, John, listen — I want you to come with me. I want you by my side. I will be completely well in just a little time. I know it. I've not had a drop to drink, and I don't want any. I only want you. And peace. I just need to go away, and everything will all be right again, back to normal."

What did she think normal was? A depressing scenario played out in front of my eyes. Driving them all to Mexico — even Morgan, who would surely delay his departure to accompany her — driving them all in the Duesenberg perhaps, in the uniform. And carrying their bags to grand rooms while I drifted off to my corner, something decent no doubt, but still something not equal to her, and then waiting, waiting, just as I'd waited here for her call, for her kisses.

A shiver went through me. Nothing was changed. I'd played the fool again. I had a lot of practice. I studied her face. She was pale. A tray of uneaten food sat by the bed. What would lead her to take the first drink — would it be Robbie, the smell of liquor on his breath? Would it be something she read in the papers about herself? Would it be when she realized the studios simply wouldn't pay the salary she wanted any longer?

"Well?" she asked, her voice trembling. "My god, I didn't expect you to have to think about it!"

The great Pauline Sloane. Any man would be happy to have her in his arms — isn't that what she'd told me?

"I... I can't go."

"Why not?" She retracted her hand.

"I... I might have a job. Cameraman for Raoul Walsh."

"One-eyed Raoul?" she asked, sounding flabbergasted. You could have the great Pauline Sloane, her tone suggested, and you choose a deformed director instead.

She looked at me as if waiting for me to embrace her, to tell her I loved her, to say no job could take her place. But loving her came at too steep a price — subservience. I wanted to hold her in my arms — of course, I did. I wanted to feel her light body against mine, feel the passion rise in me and be answered by her. As an equal! Not like this, like Pilot being called to her side. I wanted to...

It was warm in the room, and my uniform chafed. And I now felt cheated — when she'd said she wanted me to see her that evening, I'd naturally assumed it was because she wanted to make love. Not to tell me she was leaving. Damn it. Standing, I wiped my sweaty hair back with my hand.

"Will that be all, ma'am?" I asked.

Her mouth fell open.

"Ma'am?" she whispered, full of hurt and indignation. "Call me El. Ellie."

Her eyes filling with tears, she waved a hand in the air.

"Go! That will be all!"

☙

I went to my own room. I tore off the uniform and splashed water on my face. She would leave. She would leave, and so would I. Damn it. I reached for a pair of clean trousers and shirt and dressed. I ran downstairs and grabbed the keys to the Packard. I'd drive into the city again — I'd go to Leo's, I'd beg him to get me a job, even if it was sweeping the soundstage.

I'd forget her — and in the movement of car down the road, I felt that rush of victory, as if I were driving toward forgetting her, each mile signifying an emotional distance from her, from my past with her.

In town, I sped around corners and rushed through lights. I went to Leo's room first and knocked so loudly a neighbor appeared.

"He ain't in," she said, pulling a stained robe around her. "In the hospital, I think."

☙

I had no trouble getting past the security guard at Cedars this time. Leo wasn't in a private room but a big ward filled with white-sheeted beds and quiet nurses. I was relieved to find him happy and lively — and pleased to have a visitor.

"Just here for more treatments," he told me. "Will be back out soon."

I didn't want to fill his ears with my troubles but couldn't stop myself when he asked me how I was doing. I told him about Eleanor — Pauline Sloane was the name I used to him — losing the picture and going the way of the silent stars whose careers were crashing against the rocks of sound. I expected Leo to join me in crowing over "the mighty being brought low," but his previous pronouncements now softened.

"Oh, it's terrible, terrible," he said, shaking his head. "The studio chiefs don't give a damn about anything but big, big money. Especially now that their boards have got bankers and electric company men calling the shots."

My recitation of Eleanor's troubles prompted Leo to offer help before I asked for it.

"Walsh isn't ready with that film I mentioned to you. But if you're looking for work, go see..." and he spit out a list of names, some directors I recognized, others cameramen I didn't, so fast I had to struggle to keep them all straight.

I visited with him until his next meal came and promised to stop by and see him once he was out. When I left, he was wolfing down a sandwich with some soup, and I suspected he liked being cared for after having to fend for himself alone for so long.

In the next few days, I started going through Leo's list, which I'd written down as best I could remember as soon as I'd left the hospital. I freely used his name, which elicited admiration and concern wherever I went. Leo was well-liked, even respected, not a bad legacy. I was eager to tell him so and to tell him I now had leads on a few projects. It was just a matter of time now before I'd be set free.

Marta, however, did her best to dissuade me when she learned I was looking for other employment at the studios.

"You should stay and wait for us." She stood in the kitchen one evening, folding towels.

"I have other things to do."

"She has not had one drink since she's been back. Not one."

"What does that have to do with me?"

She turned to look at me. "Everything, *Señor* Doyle. Everything."

If I was such a strong influence on her, you'd never know it from the way she treated me the last week before her departure. Or, to be more accurate, the way she didn't treat me. She avoided me. If I happened to be around where she could see me—from the sun room or the veranda or a window—she would quickly leave, hurrying out of sight. And if I came upon her around the estate—which was rare, because she stayed in her room most of the time—she turned and nervously left the scene.

This angered me, that she couldn't bring herself to look me in the eye. As my employer, you'd think she could muster the strength of character to wish me a kind farewell, to thank me for my services.

Two days before their departure, I was sent into the city on various errands—to buy last-minute supplies, to pick up the mail, to drop Julia at the market. When I was on my own, I used the time to get ready for my own new plans. On this errand, I secured a room in a boarding house, and I talked with more filmmakers, even mustering the courage to seek out a director or two.

My grandfather's money had still not started to flow my way, but, when it did, I'd already determined to place a fair share of it aside for a rainy day. I didn't want any reason to be as desperate as I'd been these past few months.

I drove back to the market and waited for Julia to finish her grocery shopping. As I sat in the car, I opened the daily copy of Variety. Ignoring the industry business that covered the front pages, I flipped inside to the gossip columns.

"She might have been ditched off her latest movie, but Pauline Sloane is ready to swim to more pleasant shores," the column read. "Rumors are swirling about her upcoming trip to parts unknown. Will she meet a certain director there for quiet nuptials? A director who could restart this talented, but misused, actress' career? The beautiful Miss Sloane has been unable to work because of unidentified ailments. But sources tell us that she's really lovesick, and this trip will surely affect the right cure."

The photograph of the columnist was familiar. Closing the paper, I thought back. The woman Robbie Morgan had met at the café. That was her, the gossip columnist. He'd planted this story, which presented a flattering picture of Eleanor. It might not be enough to persuade studio chiefs to keep her on, but it would keep fans happy, and the fans would in the end decide if she continued to reign as a princess of Hollywood. I slammed the newspaper shut hot with humiliation. That's why she was avoiding me. She had another man—of course! The great Pauline Sloane could have her pick of men. She could ask us all to come with her, to meet her, and choose which of us would be worthy of her treasure. If I said no, there would always be some willing soul ready to say yes. Morgan probably helped set the poor soul up. She could have told me to my face, goddammit. I wondered who else knew—Marta, Julia?

I was angry, too, at being denied the opportunity to hurt her with my own leaving. Why should she be hurt if she had another man's arms to run to?

In a few minutes, Julia cut short my fuming by showing up with bags in both arms. I put them in the trunk, opened the passenger door for her, and we began our silent journey back to Sloane Hall.

Oh, I had done it again, held fast to hopes I didn't even know I'd had. Thinking I would get on with my life! I'd secretly been hoping she would come to me and beg me to stay!

The heart is a saboteur, planting lies, encouraging small false hopes, hiding the details of the reality that will crush us in the end.

I wasn't dropping her. She was leaving *me*.

છ

At dinner, with Julia absent, I finally told Marta I would submit my resignation and would be gone before they returned from Mexico. She was not happy. But what did she expect, I pointed out, when Morgan had already let me go.

Marta ignored the reference to Morgan and concentrated instead on what she knew was the true reason for my departure—Eleanor.

"She has been very sick." Marta leaned into the table. "You should not leave her when she is so sick, *Señor* Doyle."

"She told me she's on the mend." I stood and took my plate to the sink. Marta soon followed me.

"I thought you were a sensible man," Marta said. "Are you so blind?"

"She has many people to take care of her. She can hire more."

"She needs *you!*" Marta shook her head. "You cannot go. *Señor*. You just cannot."

"She doesn't own me."

Wiping her hands on her apron, Marta stopped and turned. Her face was twisted in sudden anger. "Of course she doesn't own you. But you and she—one would think, one would hope that two people who have been so close..." She struggled to say what she didn't want to admit knowing, that we had been lovers. "One would think you would be a gentleman and stand by her."

"She herself is leaving. She is not standing by me." I crossed my hands over my chest.

"*Señor* Doyle, if you only knew, if you only knew..." She shook her head and plunged her hands back into the sudsy water.

"Knew what? What should I know?"

"It is not for me to say. Not for me." She refused to look at me.

Now leaving would be easy. Not only would I be away from Eleanor, I'd be away from Marta whose mysterious talk only made me feel still more subservient. Even Marta was let into secrets to which I was not admitted. After several moments of angry silence, I changed the subject.

"Where is Julia this evening?

"Julia," she said with an unusual sneer, "thinks she can

have something she cannot have. She is with Mister Morgan."
She placed a dish in a drying rack with such vigor I was afraid
it would shatter.

She might as well have been talking about me. I thought I
could have something I couldn't have—Eleanor. What made
me any different from the cook? I looked down on her, just as
Marta did, for her clandestine meetings with Robbie Morgan,
for the affair they were obviously having. No wonder Julia
sneered at me. She knew we were both alike, yet I refused to
acknowledge it.

I took the dishes from the rack and wiped them dry,
placing them carefully on the table for Marta to put away.
Rubbing her hands on a towel, Marta turned to me.

"You will tell her?" she asked in a clipped voice. She was
still angry.

"I'll write a letter of resignation. I think that's how it's
done." Milqueton had gone over with me the finer points of
employment—how to get a job, how to keep it, how to bid it
farewell.

Marta let out a grunt of dissatisfaction. "No, you will tell
her face to face. Like a man."

Brushing past me, she moved to the table and started
putting away the plates.

With nothing more to say, I left. A light rain began to fall.
It matched my mood.

Later that night I sat at my table and did sums. I
estimated how much money I'd need to get by until my
grandfather's money came in or a steady paycheck arrived. I'd
saved a bit so I had a cushion. I calculated everything to the
last penny, and for a little while it cheered me as I basked in
the sense of independence that this move would give me.

Yet as soon as I was finished, the good feeling
evaporated. And this made me angry, that Eleanor could spoil
activities that months before would have filled me with
contentment.

In frustration, I swept my hand over the little table,
knocking my notebook and pencils to the floor. Burying my

head in my hands, I sat still and breathed shallowly. Then I picked up paper and pen and began my resignation note.

"Dear Miss Sloane" — how could I call her anything else now?

"I will leave your employ as of today. Thank you for the opportunity you gave me as well as the gifts of clothing. Thank you for allowing me to use your library."

I did not write what I felt. I did not write, "Eleanor, you have ruined me...."

After folding the note, I went to my bed and did what had now become a custom — I stared at the house, waiting to see her light go on and then later, off again when she went to sleep.

❧

The next day, I awoke determined to hand in my note, but not, as Marta wished, in person. I would not let my heart subvert me again by building up a heady anticipation of seeing Eleanor. I would hand the note to Marta and let her deliver it. If that made her angry with me, so be it. Before heading over to the house that morning, I packed my bag and cleaned up my rooms. It would all be over soon. Thank god.

As it turned out, I wouldn't have been able to get Eleanor alone anyway. In the morning, the doctor visited her, and for the rest of the day, Robbie Morgan was omnipresent, a guard dog, more ferociously protective than Pilot who, more often than not, scampered merrily up to visitors, even strangers.

Marta, however, was busy that day with the repairmen who were finishing the work on the roof in the guest room, so I didn't give her the note immediately. She even recruited me to help, asking me to supervise their work and make sure they were not "taking advantage of la *Señorita*." After giving me these instructions, she narrowed her eyes, then added, "And you can give her your news, eh?"

While I watched the workmen, I wondered if Eleanor was still in her room or had gone downstairs. My answer came in a few minutes when I heard voices coming from her room. Robbie was there.

"I've rung up Bordoni's," Robbie said.

"What on earth for?" Eleanor responded.

"To have one of their gals come out for a fitting. A wedding dress."

"Robbie! I don't need that!"

"Don't fuss. Of course you do. Every new bride deserves a new wedding dress." He laughed.

"In the first place, I'm not a 'new' bride. In the second place, I'm..."

"There is no second place, darling. Just leave it to me. I've already made the arrangements."

"I'll feel silly."

"Then feel silly."

"Oh all right. I don't have to get something white, do I?"

Robbie chuckled again. "You can get flaming red for all I care. Just something bridal. They'll be by this afternoon."

"Oh, Robbie, I don't have time. We're leaving tomorrow."

Their voices disappeared in a symphony of hammering as the roofers nailed tiles back into place. The hammering could have been the fury pounding in my heart. She'd wanted me to stay — for what? To be her lover while she wed another man? Even if that marriage were for show, how dare she think I'd tolerate such a humiliation? What that said about how she thought of me — it stabbed me.

When the roofers were finished, I rushed downstairs and over to my apartment. Fetching my resignation note, I raced back to the house and the kitchen. A bleary-eyed Julia was there alone, drinking tea.

"Where's Marta?"

"By the pool."

Knowing I wouldn't run into Eleanor there, I strode outside and around to the gleaming water. Marta was talking with a gardener about pruning back bushes for the winter. When she saw me, she finished and came my way. I held out my note.

"You give it to her."

Shielding her eyes from the sun with one hand, she

accepted the note and quickly read it.

"I will not do such a thing." She handed it back to me.

"You have to."

She started to walk away from me. "Why? It is your letter."

Running, I caught up with her. "You are the housekeeper. This has to do with household staff."

She stopped and put her hands on her hips. "I will not do your dirty work for you, *Señor* Doyle." Her voice rose to a pitch where Eleanor would hear her clearly if her windows were open. "You must tell her yourself that you are leaving." She stormed off toward the kitchen, letting the door slam behind her as she entered.

I continued to the front of the house, unsure of what to do. As I rounded the corner, I heard a car engine starting. It was Morgan in his Lincoln, going out, probably to the bootlegger to get enough booze for the journey. It was a good time to leave.

At the same time, Eleanor opened the front door and came out onto the veranda. Hugging her arms around herself as if chilled, she looked down at me.

"Did you want to see me?"

My pulse galloped. Her dress was something sheer and floral, something that made you want to touch it.

"Come inside," she said.

I followed her, note in hand. Marta glowered at me from the hallway, then disappeared into the kitchen as Eleanor and I went in the parlor.

She sat on the divan. I stood. Without a word, I handed her my note.

As she read it, I heard the workmen piling their ladders and hammers onto their truck outside, talking with an end-of-task ease. Their voices were filled with good cheer, and I could imagine them stopping for a sandwich on their way into town. I wished I could join in their ordinary conversations, their ordinary lives.

In a few moments, their engine rumbled to life, and the

gravel crunched under their wheels. Silence filled the air after they'd left. Even the fountain was off now, shut down so that Eleanor could sleep better.

She looked up from the note.

"You can't even wait until I leave. You have to let me know you'll be going." Her eyes narrowed; her voice shook.

I stared at her, my own anger rising. "What do you expect of me?"

"What do I expect?" She laughed bitterly. "Nothing. I expect nothing of any man. Especially you."

No, I wouldn't let her heap denunciation on me. She was the offender here.

"Don't you mean men can expect nothing from you? No loyalty, love, or devotion?" I said.

"So you're cruel, too. Bravo."

"Like your husband was cruel? Like the men you... you..."

Her face, already pale, turned whiter.

"Fucked? Is that the word you seek?" she asked. When I didn't respond, she went on. "You don't know anything about me."

"I know you had enough lovers to drive him into his grave." I wouldn't let her do the same to me.

"You know nothing about it," she said, her voice and her body like stone. "Are you reading old gossip columns about me?"

"No!" I told her about the newspaper clippings I'd seen and about my aunt's tales. It was a relief to tell her. It had felt like my secret rather than hers.

"Did your aunt tell you all about Basil," she snapped out, "or only about me?"

"She said the Griswolds were a good family."

"Ha!" Her voice split the air. She searched a nearby box for a cigarette but found none. "Where are the smokes? Marta!"

"Don't bother," I said. "Marta thinks smoking is bad for you."

"So you're both conspiring against me."

She drummed her fingers on her arm. "Let me tell you a thing or two about Basil Griswold, John. He was no saint. If you think I was bad—he was worse. For every lover I took, he had two. He was a fraud, a cheat, and a bully, too."

I remembered her words when she'd first interviewed me, when she'd asked about the man I'd killed. And I remembered how she said we had something in common. Maybe Basil hadn't died of his own hand. Maybe... blood rushed to my face.

"Then why'd you marry him?"

"I think you already know."

"Did you kill him?" I asked.

"What?!"

"Is that why you went away? Did you kill him?"

"Just because you did away with a despicable man doesn't mean everyone does it, my dear," she said.

"You married him for money, didn't you?"

"Yes." She looked me straight in the eye. "Did you expect me to lie? Yes, I married him for money. I was destitute. My father left me with nothing but debts—debts *she* had accumulated over the years. Furs, diamonds, gold jewelry, our house. And my aunt Eugenia was a madwoman. It broke my heart to see her in a pauper's room. I would have done anything to change that."

"So you married Basil and cheated on him."

"So I married Basil because I thought he loved me. In addition to being rich." She looked around the room again, searching for a cigarette or a drink. "But he didn't love me. And it didn't matter that he was rich because he didn't leave me a penny when he did himself in."

"But he did himself in because he caught you..."

"...fucking another man. That's it—say it again. I think you like it. Imagining me with other men. Does it excite you?" she said loudly.

"You..." Slowly, I shook my head from side to side. She was a monster.

"I admit it. I was unfaithful. I thought I had the right when I learned he was unfaithful, too. And had never really loved me."

She stared at me, daring me to interrupt, to accuse. I wouldn't give her the satisfaction.

"Yes, he caught me. And he was so devastated, so crushed, so beyond hope..." She searched for a cigarette while she talked, pulling open drawers, looking in boxes, patting down her dress pockets. "Because I'd managed to find the one man who made him insanely jealous. The one man whom he couldn't bear to see me with. The one man that *he* loved." She walked to the window and stared outside.

I stepped back.

"Poor Basil," she said in a soft, faraway tone. "His parents thought him a saint. If they'd known... they would have cut him off completely."

"You never told them?"

"No. Even I couldn't do that." She snorted out a quiet laugh. "He was a good son to them. It would have just broken their hearts all over again.

"Thank god for Robbie," she continued. "He kept all that buried." She turned around, flushed with anger. "Get me a cigarette! Tell Marta I must have one now. It won't hurt me! And tell her I want a small glass of brandy. Just a sip. To calm my damned nerves. Tell her I'm upset—that you upset me."

Oh, God, no. She was slipping already. "Not on your life," I said, unsure of what to make of this new secret revealed, if it mattered, if it changed things. No, it didn't. Not if she was still to be married, once again for convenience, and especially not if she was still drinking. I turned to go.

"That's right. Leave now. Just go without another word. How courageous."

"Your courage shames us all," I countered. I stopped at the door. "You said you wanted a brandy, ma'am. Perhaps I'll just wheel in the whole liquor cart instead?"

"Damn you."

"Cursing makes you cheap."

"So now you're my teacher. When you walked in this room, I thought you were my lover. Then you became my enemy. What will you be next?" Her eyes, cold blue marbles, froze on me. "Do you think you're the only person who's suffered?"

"Nobody suffers as much as you," I retorted. "You've made that clear."

She stood motionless, not breathing. Her eyes lit on a porcelain box on the table near the sofa and she picked it up, looking for cigarettes. Finding none, she let out a growl and threw the box on the floor where it shattered near my feet.

I went over, knelt and picked up the pieces, placing them on a table next to her. When I was finished, I stood, so close to her now that I smelled her perfume, and my anger could have easily shifted to something else in that moment of temptation. I steadied myself by looking at the broken box.

"I'll fetch a broom. Will that be all, ma'am?"

She looked into my face, her eyes registering hostility and disappointment. Slowly at first, then swiftly, she brought her hand up and—smack!—she slapped me across the cheek. The movement was so quick and her hand so light, it hardly stung.

"You ungrateful bastard," she hissed. Her voice was choked with hurt, vaguely familiar, the sound of an animal wounded in the wilderness. "You never, ever came to me unless I called you. Not once! You always made me come to you. Did that arouse you in some way? Having the great Pauline Sloane always asking you for it? You made me come to you like, like some common..." She looked away. "That's all I was to you—a tramp, a whore. You used me, you bastard."

Her eyes filled with tears. "I was a fool," she said. "I won't be made a fool of."

"You made the fool out of me! I loved you—really loved you!" I would give back as good as she gave. "You're getting married. Did you expect me to stay your lover after that? Is this the pattern—you marry for money or station or work and take on whomever you like on the side?"

"Where did you... ?"

"Your wedding dress. Aren't you being fitted for it today?" It felt good to fling the truth at her, so she could feel its bite as I had.

"My wedding dress?" Her mouth opened. A cruel smile licked at her lips. "Bordoni's. You overheard." She sank onto the sofa, her elbow on the armrest, her fingers cradling her chin. "There is no marriage."

"But, the papers. They say..."

"That I'm in love," she snapped. "Robbie thinks that fans will love a Pauline Sloane who is in love herself."

More pretense. More lies. None of this comforted me.

Her face was drained of color, as if this discussion had used up all her energy. She opened her mouth to speak but said nothing. She sighed, twisted a piece of her dress, sighed again, looked at me, waiting, waiting. I would not say a word. She looked down and spoke lowly, with no inflection, as if startled to come upon this truth and unable to completely grasp it. "I'd hoped you would wait. That's how stupid, how silly I am. I actually hoped that you — of all of them — would wait."

Her voice was small, so defeated that I wasn't sure I'd heard her. Then she changed, shaking herself free of stupor, regaining the control of the great actress she was.

"You'll make me ask *you*, won't you? You'll make me beg you," she said. "All right then. Stay, John, please stay. You say you love me. I love you. Aren't we alike, you and I? Haven't we both shared sorrow, and tried to make things better? I'll never find another like you. Wait for me. We can be together. We can go on as before, only better. We can stay in one another's arms forever and be good for each other. Oh, John, if only... if only we could..." She straightened, looked me in the eyes, and then, in a rush, like a schoolgirl discovering some forgotten lesson: "*We* can marry. Something simple. You'll take care of me. I know you will. We'll hold each other up...." Her eyes were wild, watery, on the verge of tears. This was the woman I wanted to love, someone vulnerable, willing to expose her heart to me. What she'd said was true. We were alike. We were both searching for redemption. And yes, I weakened.

When I didn't respond immediately, she closed her eyes. "I'm sorry. I shouldn't have asked." And I looked at her and thought...

What *did* I think in that moment, that life-changing moment, I don't know anymore. Perhaps I thought I had a chance to have something I'd always wanted, that I better grab it fast and make it my own. Perhaps I thought I could save her, that we could "hold each other up," as she suggested. Perhaps I was in a stupor myself, yes, I know I was, confused, angry, hurt, and aching with longing even then for her soft touch, to feel her once more against me, to believe the lies I'd told myself. To stop time.

I went to her and held her tight, breathing her, feeling her, wanting her. And not knowing what I'd do or say until the words were out of my mouth. "No. *I* should have asked."

Her eyes stayed closed. She shook in my arms, the tears flowing freely. "I... I..." She gulped for air, her head hanging low. I gently pulled up her chin.

Eleanor. My Eleanor.

She held her breath.

"My darling," I whispered. "Will you marry me?"

Her answer came on a sigh of relief. "Yes."

Chapter Seventeen

I'D DREAMT SHE was marrying someone else, and she was marrying me.

Everything wrong that had ever happened to me evaporated in the sunlight of this new day, the day that Eleanor accepted my proposal. Even Canfield seemed to be a bad dream in that moment.

Now when I look back on it, I flush with embarrassment at how naïve I was, how willing to suspend belief—after all, just seconds before I'd blurted out my proposal, I'd wondered if she'd been drinking! I still wonder. I even saw her that very evening, silhouetted against the window of the parlor, her hand stroking what appeared to be a bottle, struggling, fighting—had she lost or won that battle?

Immediately after my proposal, Marta came into the room to ask about the shattered glass. Eleanor's eyes glowed as she told Marta of our engagement. Marta, who just moments before had scolded me for wanting to abandon Sloane Hall, was strangely subdued. She offered quick congratulations and then advice: "Go somewhere quickly to marry."

I interpreted her counsel to mean she didn't think it wise to alert the press.

"We don't need anything fancy," I said, to reassure them both.

Eleanor picked up on my theme. "No, something small. And secret."

"Our secret," she'd said before kissing me good-bye, "Don't tell anyone—not your friend, Leo, not anyone. And I won't either." By this I knew she meant Robbie.

Robbie left that night—to go to Mexico before the rest joined him. I was in the garage when he said good-bye to

Eleanor on the veranda.

His bag in hand, he paused and looked uncomfortable. "Maybe I should stay and bring you down with me," he said. His voice was strained, and I knew he was waiting for her to tell him to stay.

"No, Robbie," she said, standing. "You go ahead and open up the house. I'd hate to get there and not have everything in order." How easily she lied.

"I'll be at the train station, then, when you come," he said.

"That's right. You can pick us up. Since John won't be there." I knew she threw that in to make him comfortable with leaving.

He paused, and my mind screamed at him to leave, to get it over with, not to change his mind …

"Uh, there's a bit of sticky business you could help me with, El."

"What?"

"Well it seems Julia has this idea — don't know how she got it in her head, poor girl — that I was going to take her with me." He said it in an incredulous voice, as if Julia were a madwoman.

"I thought you were!" Eleanor said.

"No, I've hired another cook for you down there. Some local woman. Marta will love talking to her in her native tongue." He shifted his weight. "Would you be a dear and slip Julia a few dollars for me so she can buy herself a pretty frock or something? That should make her feel better, don't you think?"

Irritated, Eleanor inhaled sharply. "A frock?" Her voice tightened. "She's getting cheaper, isn't she?"

"A frock, a coat, whatever you think suitable. I'd do it myself, but I'm a little short right now. Had to go downtown, you see, and visit an old friend. You know him...."

"All right! I'll make sure she's taken care of," Eleanor said in a high voice. She turned completely away from him and returned to her chair.

He bent over and kissed her on the head, then put on his

hat and walked to his Lincoln on the drive.

After he was gone, I came out of the shadows and over to Eleanor. She knew why I was there.

"Marta will send a telegram in the morning," she said, leaning over the rail, "and tell him we were delayed."

છ

Eleanor didn't come to me that night, and I didn't go to her. I didn't expect us to be together now, not until we were married. As soon as possible, she'd made me promise. She'd arrange everything. It would be at Sloane Hall, not away, as Marta had suggested, so Eleanor could have the wedding she really wanted.

In the morning, Marta greeted me at the kitchen door, wiping her hand on a towel tucked in her skirt. She was bothered by the morning sun, her creased face hiding from me whether she was happy or distressed. "I will help you. I will make everything work."

When I went inside, she waited on me. While she poured my coffee and set out a roll and butter, she listed what she'd do, in a quiet voice, with many glances over her shoulder to make sure no one was eavesdropping.

Get a justice of the peace. Buy the flowers. Fix the wedding breakfast.

"And I will make the train reservation for you. For the honeymoon," she said. The honeymoon. I didn't even know where we would go.

"I can do it," I protested.

"No. It will be easier for me to do. The phone..." She gestured to the wall. "And besides, I can make sure that we keep this a happy secret to ourselves, no?"

Everything fell into place, which added to my sense of ease. Obstacles disappeared, the road was clear, nothing seemed capable of drowning our happiness. Even Robbie was securely off stage. After I drove Marta into town to send the telegram, we received one in return later in the day saying he'd look for us in a week, he had plenty to do anyway. At the end of that week, when we were safely on our honeymoon – a trip to Arizona, somewhere Robbie would never look—Marta would send another telegram, telling him of the marriage.

Even though I drove Marta and continued to handle my responsibilities, I ceased being Eleanor's employee. Oh, I still acted the part so as not to arouse suspicion. But I refused wages. At last, however, I received a check from my aunt's lawyer, my grandfather's bequest. I'd never seen such a large number of digits on a check before and stared at it for some time before heading into town and depositing it. It seemed like destiny to get that check. I'd be able to take care of Eleanor even before I landed a job.

Music filled the house now as Eleanor listened to old phonograph records. When I heard those recordings floating out into the still afternoon air, it was as if she were by my side. All I thought of was the day when she would be mine forever. And so I swept aside doubts. I even saw her fixing me dinner, tending our child, enjoying simple things... and, of course, not drinking.

The story Morgan had planted in the trade paper had the effect of galvanizing Eleanor's fans. Flowers arrived daily, and she started receiving many more letters, usually from women congratulating her on her upcoming wedding. Now those letters had new meaning, and Eleanor would share them with me over tea in the evening.

Marta informed me that the justice of the peace was contacted and that Julia would fill in for the second witness, but she would not be told until shortly before the ceremony.

Because of Marta's fast work, the ceremony was only days away. She'd greased some wheels (probably with cash) to get the licenses and justice of the peace in record time. This race to the altar didn't bother me—I was eager to get it done now, too, and to move on to a more secure place in our lives.

When I tried to talk to Eleanor of the future, though, she shushed me with kisses. "Let's not think of that now," she said. "Let's talk about our honeymoon."

The days telescoped in, the wedding rushed toward us. I refused to worry, to fear. I concentrated on happy tasks. In town, I bought Eleanor a wedding gift—a delicate strand of pearls. Wrapping it in white paper, I left it on the table in my room, planning to pen a loving note to go with it.

I felt as if my suffering until this point had been worthwhile, and now I knew its true value. Here, at last, was what it paid for—an eternity of love and affection. It was worth the price. I thanked God for sending me that suffering if this is what it bought.

The day before the wedding, a storm whipped through the hills, a raucous wind making shutters bang and curtains blow. We'd not had such a storm since my first days at Sloane Hall.

Returning to my room after bidding Eleanor good-night, I was shocked to see an open window above my table, the thin drapes soaked with rain and my box for Eleanor on the floor. Oddly, the paper had been ripped off, and the box opened. The lovely strand of pearls was broken, the individual beads rolling around. It was not the work of the storm that did this, but human hands. I could think of only one suspect. Julia.

Swallowing my disappointment, I collected the pearls and placed them in the box, telling myself I'd have them re-strung. I shook free of ill feelings and went to the estate to help with closing up the windows.

Julia was in the kitchen when I arrived. She pointed to an envelope on the table.

"Special delivery. I looked for you. But couldn't find you."

Picking up the envelope, I stared at Julia. She stared back, daring me to accuse her.

"Did you go to my room to look for me?"

"Yes. Of course." She smiled wickedly. "Why?"

"I had some things that were damaged."

"Many things are damaged, *Monsieur* Doyle, that we can do nothing about." She turned back to the stove where she stirred a pot.

The special delivery letter was from my aunt. She'd solved the riddle of conscience my grandfather had left for her with his bequest. She was sending me her inheritance as well. "Since I'm forbidden to spend it on the one thing closest to my heart and can't bear to think of spending it on myself, I've decided that I should simply give it to you. Enclosed is a check..."

I was a wealthy man! Surely this was God's work.

"Thanks for holding this for me," I said and took pleasure in the confused look on her face. I could afford to buy Eleanor a new strand of pearls if I desired. I need not worry about the expense or irritable cooks.

Chapter Eighteen

RAIN FELL, STEADY and bleak, as I awoke that day. Later, I realized it was the very same kind of weather that had greeted my mother on the day she married Earl Pickett.

My mother had only been seeing Pickett for a couple months. She was working in a five-and-dime in downtown Austin, her third job in a year. Pickett wasn't a customer, but a salesman come to visit the owner about introducing a new line of women's perfumes and men's colognes. He always smelled of men's cologne, a too-sweet smell for a man, a smell that made me distrust him from the first moment I met him.

By that time, I'd grown protective of my mother and knew her failings, and knew I wouldn't change them. She spent our household money on gin when she could get it. She forgot to buy me new shoes for school forcing me to wear old ones that cramped my toes. Except for an occasional dinner, she wasn't much of a cook—I often cooked for us both. But I had grown used to our life such as it was.

When I first met Earl Pickett, he gave me a gift. A peppermint stick that he said "came from the best confectionery in the city, La Bonne's on Dogwood Lane." He was lying. It was the same kind of peppermint stick sold in the store where mother worked. He either thought I was a fool or easily bought. It set the tone of our relationship from then on—with me skeptical and him scornful.

I hadn't expected her to marry him. She had been out with other men since my father died. Like Earl, they were good-looking and sweet-talking. Usually, they ignored me. Earl was the first one who paid me any mind, which I came to realize might have been one of the reasons my mother said yes to his proposal. I know at least one of her other beaux had asked for her hand. She'd told me one night when she'd been drinking. "But he didn't want children, John. Imagine that!"

I'd thought at first he didn't want new babies. I realized later he didn't want me.

She didn't tell me about Earl's proposal until right before the wedding. She always dressed for work as if she were going to see the queen, taking an hour to do her hair, powder her face, and set her hat in place. She was putting a beaded pin in a black hat when she said, nonchalantly, "Tomorrow's a big day, John. You're going to have a new daddy. Mister Pickett and I are getting married at City Hall. And then we'll be moving to a big house on Walter Boulevard. Oh, don't forget to buy bread on your way home from school. Put it on credit and tell O'Malley to speak to me if he has a problem."

With that she had gone to work, leaving me to ponder whether I should run away before or after the ceremony. I had no illusions about Earl Pickett. I knew he was a slick con man who'd won over my mother by promises he had no intention of keeping. There was no big house on Walter Boulevard.

But I had grown so used to looking out for her that I couldn't leave her on that important day. She dressed me in my best suit—a too-tight brown wool that made me sweat—while she wore a dark purple silk dress with lace at the collar and a new hat with a shiny feather.

We were to meet Earl at City Hall. He was late. As we waited, I secretly hoped he wouldn't show up. I even started planning how I'd comfort my mother, suggesting we get an ice cream on the way home.

To my disappointment Pickett did show up, carrying some ragged flowers that looked as if they'd been purloined from an unsuspecting homeowner's garden.

After the ceremony, we went back to our apartment, and Earl said he'd be moving his stuff in that day, although "there wasn't much." My mother didn't say anything, but I knew what she was thinking— what about the big house, the house on Walter Boulevard?

There was no house. At least not there. We did move that month to a ramshackle old home on the edge of the city, a far walk to anything, and we had to walk everywhere because we had no other way of getting around. Mother had to continue to work because Earl's salesmanship was so poor he lost his job pretty quick. And, of course, not long after that he was dead at my hands.

These gloomy memories, thank God, did not cloud my mind on my own wedding day. They were to rumble up later.

My wedding was to be at noon, in the parlor, and I was eager to make myself useful, so I went to the big house straight away and offered to help Marta.

"You should do nothing today, *Señor* Doyle, except to get ready for your bride. I should be helping you!" She shooed me out of the kitchen, telling me not to come back until a few minutes before noon. She even had Julia bring me over a mid-morning snack of oranges and biscuits which she delivered with her usual silence. Before she left, she made a curious comment that I took as just one more barb.

"It's too bad you have no groomsman to stand up with you," she said.

By eleven, I was dressed and ready and spent the time alternating between pacing and staring out the window at Eleanor's room trying to catch a glimpse of her preparations. All I could make out, however, were shapes crossing in front of the window. It made me happy to know she was preparing for our moment.

At eleven-fifteen, the justice of the peace arrived. To make myself useful, I rushed to help park his car, but Marta was there before me, pointing to an appropriate spot by the door.

Lamenting the fact that I had no gift to present to Eleanor, I decided not to waste any more time nervously waiting and headed for the house to meet the justice of the peace.

Marta was talking to him in the parlor which was decorated with banks of flowers — white and yellow mums, and other flowers whose names I once would have eagerly searched for in the library's books.

"This is the groom, John Doyle. And this is Mister Herbert Clement."

As the man held out his hand, my heart turned cold. Clement. Surely he wouldn't be related to old Brice. He certainly didn't look like him. Where Brice Clement had been squat and fat, this man was tall and bony, with a long face and sparse gray hair around his ears. Like me, he wore glasses and smiled so warmly that I forced myself to concede that he bore no relation to the cruel headmaster at Canfield, and his selection as the minister at my wedding was nothing more than unhappy coincidence. Marta wouldn't have known.

As the noon hour approached, we made shy conversation. By now, even the unfortunate name of the minister could not dampen my gladness. The room was beautiful, I could smell good things in the kitchen ready for our post-wedding meal, and Marta was dressed in dark blue with an orchid pinned to her collar.

Even Julia looked pretty. Instead of her usual gray uniform and white apron, she had changed into a sleek red dress that accented her figure, and her hair was no longer pulled back, but framed her face in an explosion of curls. She even wore make-up, her lips painted a deep rose. She looked so glamorous, in fact, that someone coming upon the estate might be hard pressed to determine who was the movie star at the house—she or Eleanor.

Julia flitted about in the foyer, waiting for the moment to alert us to Eleanor's descent from upstairs.

At last, looking strangely disappointed, Julia nodded her head to Marta who arranged us near the piano. I was on the right, Marta beside me. Julia walked in, or rather, sauntered in, holding a few long-stemmed roses in front of her in such a detached way that she almost looked as if we were taking her away from something else she'd rather be doing. But once she was in the room, my own beloved appeared, and all other thoughts vanished from my mind.

Eleanor stood for an instant in the archway leading to the parlor. I remember her dressed in white, ribbons around her waist, smelling like orange blossoms, flowers in a circle on her head holding down a gossamer veil. Her face, I could see beneath the veil, was only lightly powdered, with the barest shimmer of paint on her lips. Her hair combed in graceful waves.

My childish grin was answered by her own sweet smile. In a few moments, she was by my side. I hooked her arm around mine and held her hand in both of mine while Marta took her bouquet. Julia helped her with the veil, lifting it over her face where I could see Eleanor's blue eyes flashing at me. Her lips trembled.

The minister began by talking to us about the seriousness of marriage, but I heard little of what he had to say. I was listening to Eleanor's eyes which stared into mine, telling me far more important things, telling me she was changed, she was better, she was different—and we would stand by each other.

At last, the minister opened his book and started the ceremony. As he intoned the age-old words, I was vaguely aware of a sound outside, the sound of a car pulling up. But even then, I pushed aside that sign, thinking it was a delivery of some sort, something that Marta would handle once the ceremony was over.

As the minister began to say the vows, the front door slammed open, its harsh thud a hammer breaking the fragile porcelain happiness I had built there in my foolish heart.

Chapter Nineteen

FROM BEHIND US, a sinister voice oozed into the room.

"Didn't you forget something?"

Eleanor straightened as if touched by an electric wire.

I turned, knowing from his voice who would be standing there, knowing as the door slammed open who it was, knowing deep in my heart that this moment was inevitable.

Robbie leaned against the doorway, his face waxen, his lips sneering. His clothes were disheveled, his hair appeared uncombed, and even from my distance I could smell the liquor on his breath.

Julia looked at him and smiled. She had been the one to summon him. My "groomsman" that she'd arranged. She went to him, but he ignored her. Her victorious smile froze in place.

"You forgot the part where you ask if anyone here has an objection, or has a reason, or whatever the bloody hell it is. To stop the ceremony. You didn't say that part." Robbie pointed at the justice of the peace.

Marta uttered a soft, insistent "*Madre de Dios!*"

Clearly not used to this kind of interruption, the justice of the peace appeared dumbfounded. I turned completely toward Robbie, shielding Eleanor from his gaze. She, meanwhile, dropped her head to her chest. Her body trembled, and she moaned faintly, almost inaudibly, a distant "please, don't."

Please. Don't.

It was like a bell tolling, those two syllables. As soon as she said those words, I intuitively knew that Robbie would triumph, that it was over.

Perhaps it was from years of experience, of interpreting the quick unusual gesture, the raised voice, the syrupy tone as preludes to dark events. My stepfather had always become quiet before a storm. Brice Clement had exuded an oily good cheer before meting out his capricious punishments.

And now Eleanor's "please, don't" signaled bad things to come. They found me wherever I went.

Her words, her tone, they were filled with fear. Fear and grief. I was afraid, too. She was fragile and needed protection. Robbie could try to hurt her. Would it come to this? My hands sweat as I clenched them. My throat ached.

Yet I mustered my strength and acted my part, as if acting would make it real. We were all acting. Standing in a movie star's home upon a stage.

"Robbie, I think you should leave." I stepped toward him. Oh, I was the hero. I was the protector.

But he didn't back off. Instead, he moved farther into the room, pulling a flask from his hip pocket and taking a swig before continuing. Julia remained behind, her smile now faded. Her plan was not working as she'd hoped. *Damn you, Julie. Damn you.* If her intention had been to lure Robbie back with the news of Eleanor's marriage in the hopes that she could reclaim him, it was now clear as a noon sun that Robbie's protectiveness of Eleanor would not let any other woman intrude. He made my skin crawl.

"Or what, old man? Are you going to challenge me to a duel? Twenty paces at sunset?" He laughed, a mirthless sound cut short when he noticed Eleanor's noiseless weeping. Staring at her back, his eyes became wild with rage.

"Look at me!" he shouted at her. "*Look! At! Me!*"

As if hypnotized, she turned to face him, her movements jerky and automatic. She might know how this scene was to play. I had no clue. But my pulse still raced, my breath was short. No good could come from this.

Please, don't, she had sighed. *Please, don't.*

"How could you?" Robbie said to her, his voice now trembling like a woman's. "After all we meant to each other?"

Answer him, Eleanor. Tell him to leave. I waited, but she said nothing.

Tell him you love me. Tell him everything you whispered in my ear.

Where were those phrases? Where were her promises of fidelity, devotion, love? Oh Jesus, it stabbed me, that silence. Those beautiful, perfect lips. Silent.

Her mouth opened, and she stared. At him, not at me. Perhaps she was wishing him away. Perhaps she was too shocked to speak. I could only hope.

I'd fight her battle. I was supposed to fight it, wasn't I? I stepped into her line of vision and faced Robbie once again.

"Leave. Or I shall force you to go. In your present condition, I don't think it would be a fair match. And I don't think you want your sister to witness it."

Robbie raised his eyebrows in surprise and giggled. "Oh, my, you are priceless. I can see how Ellie was taken with you He's a charming gallant, El, just charming…"

"No!" Ellie finally spoke. "Leave, Robbie!"

The justice of the peace found his voice as well. "Perhaps you should do as the lady says, Mister…"

"Morgan. Robert Morgan, stepson of the same bitch who whelped the bride, isn't that right, El?"

"Really!" the justice of the peace exclaimed.

"Robbie, please, don't talk that way…." Ellie whimpered.

"Why not?" He spat out the words. "Lillian was the one who left us impoverished, squandering my father's estate and your father's fortune. She was the one who drove us to this life…." He waved his hand in the air and nearly lost his balance. "Even to—"

"Stop it! Please, oh god, just stop it!"

A grin painted Morgan's face. A god-awful sickly grin, like the grin on Brice's face after he'd decided how to hurt us. *Oh Christ.* He straightened.

"Oh, so he doesn't know, does he?"

Doesn't know what, I wanted to scream, but I stayed mute. Sometimes it was better not to know. I hadn't wanted to know about Pete. I hadn't wanted to know about my mother's failings. Later I would know. Later. Whispered in my ear by angels. I. Didn't. Want. To. Know.

I just wanted this to end. With a sense of doom I had not felt since my days under Brice at the School, I knew I was headed for unjustified punishment. And no matter how well I prepared myself for it, how many bromides I made my mind swallow to accept the bad news, it would still sting as sharply as the flick of the reed on my shoulders. Already I winced, not wanting to hear more. I couldn't escape it. It would find me, yes sir.

Even as I stood rock still, my legs wanted to move. To walk away. In my mind, I saw that scene. I'd walk away cold as ice, not feeling a thing, not even the wind on my face. Gather my things. Go down the road. Never see the estate again. I should have forced him to go, but I couldn't. That would be taking the next step, the one that led away from here.

"Robbie..." Eleanor pleaded.

No one spoke. No one moved. Even the dust in the streaming sunlight seemed stuck in air as we waited. Taking a long, deep breath, Robbie continued.

"How did you hide it, my dear?" he whispered. "There's no costume mistress, no make-up man in one's bed."

Eleanor stared at him and shook her head "no."

He looked at me. "You see, old man, this woman you want to take as your bride—she's already married. To a savage beast who tolerates no competition." He looked at her. "Isn't that right, El?"

I looked at her, but she stared at the floor, her body shaking like a willow. So fragile. So easily broken.

So capable of inflicting deadly wounds on my own vulnerable heart. I wanted to get her alone, to hear her laugh and say, "Robbie is a fool, isn't he? Wasn't that quite a show? And yet here we are, darling, nothing's changed, I still love you more than life, more than anything."

Not more than anything. Something was in the way. Something.

She remained mute. She reached out to Marta who

steadied her.

The justice of the peace broke this silence. "Look here, sir," he said, "If this woman had been married before, she wouldn't have been able to get a license."

Robbie laughed, a wicked cackle that echoed off the halls. Staring at me, he grinned.

"Didn't you wonder what those noises were at night? Didn't you want to know? It was your beloved, paying homage to her other master."

"No, Robbie, that's all over now." Eleanor spoke softly, to herself more than to anyone else in the room. "Not one drink. Not one..."

"I think you need to leave," I repeated, but the authority had left my voice, replaced instead by doubts, doubts that Robbie Morgan was all too astute to notice.

"Don't believe me? Come see for yourself!" He walked out of the room and headed for the hall and the stairs. As if jolted by lightening, Eleanor ran after him, screaming "no!"

Once he knew she was behind him, he quickened his pace up the stairs with us all in pursuit.

When he came to the attic door, he pulled a key from his pocket and unlocked it, rushing up the ladder-like steps to the chamber above. We all followed. To me, it felt like a funeral procession in quick time.

The unfinished attic was dusty and warm, muted light pouring through its high windows. A small space to the left of the stairs held nothing but old boxes and trunks, but Robbie had turned to a larger area on the right.

Expecting to see some lunatic husband—to find Basil Griswold still alive and haunting her in the flesh—I was relieved when nothing but a near-empty room greeted my eye. An old sofa was pushed against the eaves, some newspaper clippings sat in boxes—some, I could see from the headlines, were reminders of Eleanor's tragic past, detailing her husband's suicide, her parents' deaths. Had she come up here to mourn her past?

I breathed out. Was this all there was? Remnants of her

unhappy first marriage, her parents' demise? Was this what he meant when he said she was already married — that she could not let go of these torments?

Now ready to throw out Morgan with renewed courage, I squared my shoulders. But Robbie wasn't done.

He walked over to a corner of the sofa where my gaze fell on a thin wooden box. It wasn't dusty. It was —

Robbie must have been waiting for me to see it. With melodramatic flair, he picked it up and opened it, holding it out for me. "*Voila!* Here, at last, is the evidence."

And before I even gazed at its contents, I knew. Of course I knew. She wasn't just an alcoholic — god, no. Some inner voice had secretly hoped, all this time, that that was all she was addicted to. Just liquor. And that inner voice knew, and kept me from seeing, that there was more, there were worse things.

The box was lined with red velvet. Two old needles lay in a neat row, point to point, by the clasp. In back of these was the hypodermic, and in back of that, closest to the hinge, were the vials for the heroin. Yes, I knew what it was. You didn't go through a place like Canfield without knowing.

And I realized — so many realizations now that I could no longer hide from the truth — that this inner voice, the one that had known all along that alcohol wasn't her only demon, had hoped she would only be addicted to cocaine or marijuana, like the jazz musicians in the clubs like the Alabam. That inner voice had known and put the thought aside for another day. Another day to deal with that problem, after we dealt with the booze.

I looked at Eleanor, but she would not look at me. Her face was red with a rash of tears. Her veil was hanging off the side of her head, held in place only by a corner of the flowery garland. It was ripped near the hem.

While she stood stock still, Robbie walked over to her and pulled up one of her sleeves, revealing the bruising and scarring of needle marks. She did not protest or try to stop him. She was like a store mannequin, not real. No longer the person I knew. She was the person she'd always been.

"She's an addict. Just like me. Sobs like a wild animal when she can't get her next fix. She'd do anything for it. *Anything.*"

Long sleeves. She always wore long sleeves. Even in the hot sun. I'd assumed it was to protect her pale skin from the brutal rays. The first day I'd met her, she'd been wearing long sleeves. She never used the pool because she didn't like to disrobe. And in bed — in bed, shadows made everything black and white and gray, just as in her movies. And I hadn't wanted to know anyway.

I had seen what I wanted to see. Always, it was this way. I saw what I wanted to see until it was too late, and I had to face the truth. She was the same as my mother. She had not reformed. She could not turn away from pleasure, from bright lights, from wealth and comfort. Why had I thought...

"That's over," she whimpered. "It's been over since... since the night... " She slumped against Marta.

"Since what night, El?" Robbie stared at her with a malevolent grin, as a zealous prosecutor would pounce on an unsuspecting criminal who's opened the door to the truth.

She just shook her head. Yet, still I knew that this was not the worst of it. Like an animal sensing danger, I knew that more was to come. My hands were sweating. My collar cut into my neck. Breathing was difficult. I felt like I was suffocating in the close, musty air. I had to leave. *Please, Lord...*

Where was the door? I couldn't stay because if I did I'd be forced to hurt someone, and I couldn't hurt her.

"Tell him what else we've shared besides a taste for this, Ellie dear. Tell him what we shared the night of your party."

Ellie froze. Even her breath seemed to stop. She clutched Marta's arms. She squeezed them.

Marta held her fast and nearly spit at Morgan.

"Leave her alone. The doctor just saw her. She is with child."

My eyes fixed on her. She looked away. I died. No, I wished I'd died. Because I knew...

Robbie stepped back. His grin left him.

"With child?" he whispered. He advanced toward Eleanor, his arm outstretched toward her.

Julia uttered an oath and left the room. Whatever satisfaction she'd hoped for was now gone.

Eleanor shrank behind Marta as Robbie stopped in front of her.

"*My* child?" he said. He sounded like he would cry.

No! Not this! Yes, this.

"I don't know," she whispered.

Oh Jesus. Not this. Yes. This.

The justice of the peace gasped. Marta exhaled sharply. My mind went blank, pushing out images. Not that. Not with him. Bile clogged my throat.

Then, silence. No one moved.

At that moment, I longed for the past, even a past that included my suffering. The limits of that suffering were known, like the foibles of a testy friend. That pain, remembered through the veil of time, was now comfortable and familiar. This pain was fresh and its depths unplumbed. How far would I sink through its scraping, slashing sorrow? How much would I have to endure? She had betrayed me even before our marriage. *And with her own stepbrother.* My god. My god. She wasn't human.

Robbie was talking to me.

"She was so desperate for a fix that night that she would have done anything. And she did do anything. Anything I asked."

"That's a lie!" she shouted at him. Her sobs poured from her throat. Like a little girl blubbering, she said, imitating him, "Just give us a little kiss, El. Just a little kiss..." And more sobs wracked her so hard that Marta had to hold her upright. "Just a little kiss..." she whimpered. "But you took more...."

I could not leave. I was caught here in my own private "hot box," far worse than any device old Brice Clement could have put together to punish us boys at Canfield. Even Brice couldn't have conjured up this particular hell. Even he would have had a hard time imagining such depravity. Nothing was real. This was some strange dream I'd wandered into. Surely I'd awaken soon. And never have known her.

My hands clenched and unclenched. Who could I hurt, who could I hit now? Not her, not when she was with child. Yet I wanted to hurt her! I wanted to bloody her face and make it ugly to anyone who gazed at her. I saw myself pulling back and hitting her, just as my stepfather would hit my mother. And I could see the red-blue lump it would cause near her eye, the swelling that would disfigure her. If I hit enough, I'd ruin her perfect face forever. She was nothing but a stupid, stupid bitch! She didn't deserve to be so beautiful!

Couldn't strike her. Not her. Not a woman carrying a …

Whose baby? Whose baby? Robbie, so smug, so sure, so evil. It was his fault. Always his fault. He'd forced her. Did it matter? And now this, now this horrible thing. The room was hot. I was sweating so much a drop fell from my brow to my shirt, staining it. And this too seemed like Robbie's fault. He'd brought us up here. He'd interrupted our wedding, my perfect day, the day when I'd finally get something sweet, something I could keep, something mine forever. He'd ruined it!

I ran toward him and swung hard, beating him over and over again, taking the same satisfaction I had experienced when I'd pummeled my stepfather to death. It came back to me, and I liked the feeling, I liked knowing I was crushing the life out of some insect who should never have been born, whose very existence sullied all the lives of those he touched, the shit who'd forced my El... her... the woman who...

I was hot and sweaty and unaware of anything but the satisfying righteous rage that turned my hands into weapons, that filled me with peace when I viewed the object of my fury, bloodied, cowed on the floor, groaning. Take that, you bastard. You shit. You...

Marta and the justice of the peace pulled me off of him. Someone was crying. It was Eleanor.

"Good Lord!" The justice of the peace exclaimed.

Robbie licked his bloodied lips and leered up at me.

And behind all this, as background music, was her sobbing, a wail really, the same wail I'd heard coming from this very attic.

"I should have killed you! I should have cut out your heart!" she cried, her words barely understandable through her weeping, her hands twisting her gown. "I hate you! I can't stand to be around you! I hate..." She ripped a piece of silk on her skirt and dissolved into tears.

Marta put her arm around Eleanor's shoulders.

I did nothing. I did not feel part of this scene.

Robbie touched his cheek and mouth and viewed the blood on his fingers.

"I should have killed you that night," she sobbed again, "for what you did to me."

"You did it to yourself!" Now his voice changed, and he looked at her with the desperate eyes of unrequited love. My eyes! My god, he had my eyes—we were the same, yearning for her, longing for her. A lone tear made its way from his right eye down his cheek, mingling with the blood. This I couldn't bear. I turned away.

"I just loved you. The way I always have." Robbie sounded like a hurt little boy.

Sobs rumbled through her body. She shook her head from side to side. Marta and the minister held her, a tortured doll on display.

"I hate you," she whimpered, sliding to the floor, Marta kneeling beside her. She rocked back and forth, her hands pulling at her satin ribbons, her embroidered flowers, as if rending them would tear away her own skin, revealing someone new."I hate you." But her words lacked conviction. Maybe she hated Robbie. But she hated herself more.

"Whose baby are you carrying, Eleanor? It is mine, isn't it? Oh, El, it has to be. I love you so." The words seemed wrenched from him, an agonized sob. He was a wounded animal, wanting what he felt was his, what I thought had been mine. And for a moment, a terrible moment, I felt sorry for him. He was down, beaten, begging. And all he wanted was her affection! Didn't I myself know that pain?

I was a stranger here. The world as I knew it had crumbled under my feet, and if I took the tiniest step I would fall into oblivion.

His anguish now mirrored my own. The words he'd spoken could just as well have been mine. *It is my baby, isn't it? It has to be. I love you so.*

His words created a rhythm that allowed my feet to move. Slowly, I walked from the room. *It is my baby, isn't it?* I climbed down the ladder. *It has to be.* I walked down the stairs. *I love you so.* I passed Julia on the veranda who blew smoke into the distance.

"She is a whore, *non?*" Julia called after me. "They are both whores. Both of them! Full of the big promises they do not keep."

On the drive, Eleanor's voice carried to me, a distant but familiar wail of heart-rending anguish that had filled the nights at Sloane Hall. But now it voiced a name. My name. "John! John! John! Please!" until it petered out into sputtering sobs.

Chapter Twenty

THE RAIN PUMMELED me as I walked forward, not knowing where I wanted to go, only knowing I wanted to leave the torment I was in. I could not stop the images. Over and over, I saw her that night at the party in my arms and then... then I saw her with him.

Closing my eyes would not stop it. Running would not blot it out. Even crying—yes, I cried, I cried like a child—wouldn't bury it. I thought I'd had something, and it had been stolen away.

How could I be punished like this? I'd saved my mother, hadn't I? I'd tried to! I'd killed the man who'd beaten her. I'd tried....

I called out for her, something I'd never done since leaving the Home. And this opened the floodgates, the tears streaming down my face until my eyes and throat hurt. Unashamed and alone, I sobbed. "You made me who I am! You gave me this burden! If it hadn't been for you..."

I'd never have killed. I'd never have tasted the sweet, pure essence of revenge.

And who could I avenge now? The baby was not mine. How could it be when nothing good was mine?

Miles from the estate, I stumbled and fell to my knees. It was then that I realized I was on the same dirt road where I'd first encountered Eleanor months ago. And I hoped that my mother would hear and weep for me, that she'd be sorry she had left me to turn my anger into the mortal sin of murder, that she was the one who'd branded me, with her love of laughter and fun, she was the one who'd made me into a killer, haunted and never at peace. I wanted her to suffer—even in heaven, she should suffer!

Gray clouds stared immutably back at me, offering no answers, only the illusion that evening was close at hand.

I don't know how long I stayed there. I only know that by the time my tears were dry, the sky had increased its own. The rain was harder. I stood, letting the rain wash me, drench me, take away my feeling.

And yet, I still felt.

And yet, I still ached.

And yet, and yet, and yet ... I could not escape. I could not escape who I was. *Sin brings only misfortune.* My sin of long ago could not be paid for in years spent in a reform school, in youth taken from me. It could only be paid for in pain, the kind that now cut out my heart.

If I could have physically cut out my heart at that moment, I would have.

The image of Robbie stabbed, blood gushing from his shoulder, Ellie frantic. What had she said? "I'm sorry."

She had tried to kill him. It was no party joke gone awry, no hidden malefactor who'd crept onto the grounds unawares. It had been Ellie, trying to kill her sin by killing he with whom she had sinned.

Did it matter that he'd forced her? Had he forced her? If he had, why hadn't she told me? I didn't know. This is what stabbed *me*. That I couldn't be sure...

I wish I had killed you.

But she had killed the wrong person.

She had killed me.

I was dead inside, the tiny flame of life that had begun to flicker after leaving Canfield now gone.

I heard Reverend Milqueton's voice intoning across the miles, his throaty rumble, the very rumble of the heavens. *You cannot escape yourself,* he had once told me. *You can run from everyone but yourself.*

Thunder roared. Lightning flashed. Rain and wind whipped my face. If ever I had wanted to die, it was at that moment. If ever death had seemed a better place, it was then.

I had no grand illusions of heaven. I had no dreams of

soft clouds and welcoming angels. Death at that moment was nothingness. And yet I craved it. Even the void would be better than the sheer agony that seared my soul.

I had loved her. And she had deceived me.

Even Brice had not done that. His corruption had been visible, bared for all to see. There was a strange morality to that. A morality that not even Eleanor could live up to.

My wanderings took me far afield. For hours, until dark covered the valley, I strayed. Foolishly, I thought that if I could suffer enough in body it would replace my suffering in spirit.

I would have walked all night if it hadn't been for Marta. Hours later, a car pulled up beside me and stopped. It was one of the estate cars, the Ford. Marta sat at the wheel waving me inside.

"Please, *Señor* Doyle," she yelled through the open window. "Come in. You cannot keep walking like this. I have been looking for you for a long time." She sounded like she was going to cry. I considered not going with her, but I had no energy to argue. So I got in the car, not looking at her, my hands between my legs.

"I forgot that you drove," I said when I sat down. What a strange thing to say. As if nothing had happened.

"You must get dry. You will get the death of pneumonia. Miss Sloane is worried sick."

Marta did not talk while she drove home. The regular beat of the windshield wipers was the only sound. If Marta needed comforting, I had none to offer.

She drove very slowly, so it took us a good half hour or more to come back to the estate. By this time, darkness was all around. Out of habit, I looked up at the big house and saw a single light burning in Eleanor's bedroom window. Immediately, I looked away.

"I will make you some coffee," Marta said as she waited for me to get out at the garage. When I started to protest, she interrupted. "I'll bring it to you. You won't have to come to the house."

After I got out and went up to my rooms, she drove the

car around to the kitchen so she wouldn't get wet.

The rain created a sheet of noise on the roof of my apartment. I sat in silence at the small table in the anteroom, my head in my hands. My tux was ruined. I was happy it was ruined. One less reminder of Eleanor I'd have to destroy.

Thinking of her, I began to worry that she would come over to see me, now that I was back. Quickly, I switched off the overhead light and sat in darkness. When Marta returned a little while later, she scolded me.

"You would make me fall with no light," she said, placing a tray of coffee and broth before me. She switched the light back on and clucked over my wet clothes. While I drank some coffee, she went to my bedroom and brought back a blanket that she wrapped around my shoulders.

"Don't worry," she said. "She will not come to you tonight. I told her you were here but too tired to talk to her."

I said nothing.

"Miss Sloane is like my daughter. I raised her, not her mother," Marta said to me as I drank. She spoke in a low, sorry voice, apologizing for this "daughter" who turned out so badly. "Robbie has been no good for her, no good. You were good for her. She was getting better with you."

I was good for her? Not good enough. "Where's Mister Morgan?"

She looked down, pulled in her lips.

"He is in the big house." Her head snapped up. "But he will go tomorrow. When the rain stops."

"Will he take Julia?" I had a sudden sympathy for Julia and began to think of her fate as linked to mine.

Marta cursed in Spanish. "Of course not! Julia dreams."

Julia dreams. I dreamed.

Marta looked at her hands, clasped in front of her on the small table. "She did not even know him until she went to Europe. After her husband's death."

I knew she was talking of Eleanor and Robbie. I said nothing, letting her continue.

"They both shared something. A hatred of her mother.

For abandoning them, for leaving them penniless."

"You were there?" I asked.

"She took me with her. *Si*." Marta looked into my eyes, pleading Eleanor's case. "At first, I thought Mister Morgan was good for her. He was her stepbrother. I thought she'd find some happiness after the bad marriage, the gossip. The Griswolds—they treated her so badly. They would have had her put in an insane asylum if they could have." Marta shook her head back and forth at the memory. "She was beside herself, not knowing what to do, not able even to get up in the mornings, so sad was she.

"And when Mister Morgan suggested the movies, when he said he knew someone in Hollywood, I thought this was something good, something to keep her thoughts off other things, to give her life back to her. I did not know how else he was making her forget." She sniffled and rubbed her nose with a handkerchief.

"When he came here with her," she said lowly, not looking at me, remembering, "he made everything new. It was as if ... as if nothing bad had happened to her. He was like, it was like he had a magic wand." She swooped her hand through the air. "And he made it all go away. He conjured up Pauline Sloane. Pauline Sloane was a princess who'd given up her throne to be like everyone else. Pauline Sloane was kind and gentle, a woman who wanted a family." She broke down again. "Pauline Sloane was a good girl, the good girl I used to know...."

"How could you stand by and let her..." My voice was pinched, and my hands shook. I was afraid if I said too much I'd actually weep in front of her.

"When I found out, I did what I could. I said I would leave, and she begged me to stay, she told me she would stop with it. That was right before you came here." She reached over and touched my hand with her fingers. "When you came, from the very first I could see you were good for her."

I pulled my hands back. "So you let me think that she was normal."

Marta matched my anger with her own. Her voice rose, and she gestured wildly as she talked. "What is normal, *Señor* Doyle? Heh? Are you? Was your life so 'normal' that you can judge her?"

Pushing away from the table, I stood and turned away.

Marta rose, too, standing behind me. "She told me that in the pictures, you have to be so natural. The camera picks up everything. She was nervous, with the stage fright. Robbie gave her something to help her." She cursed, and I realized she was crying. "She is my daughter in everything but blood. Please, *Señor* Doyle. She needs you. Help her."

"I'm not strong enough for what she needs." I couldn't stop myself — I looked across the way to see if her light was on. Her room was dark. "I can't love..."

Another man's child. I turned back to face Marta whose anger was now replaced by sorrow for us both. "I can't even think straight."

"I will take these away in the morning." She gestured to the dishes. "You will let her see you then."

"I need to rest."

She hesitated, probably afraid of what I would do, afraid I would leave. She had to know I was thinking of it, but she said nothing about it.

"I will pray for you to do the right thing. Good night, *Señor* Doyle."

"Good night, Marta."

◌

After she left, I lay on my bed for an hour, unable to comprehend the events of the afternoon. Rising to the peak of happiness, dashed against the rocks. Better not to try for happiness.

That night, I waited. I waited to hear her keening, now knowing that the sad laments of the past had been her struggles against the drug that held her fast. There was only silence. And darkness. Not a single light blazed from Sloane Hall after Marta left my rooms. The moon hid behind heavy clouds. I drifted in a half-sleep where only demons lived.

When they threatened to overcome me, a voice spoke softly in my ear.

Leave Sloane Hall. Now.

I roused myself and washed, feeling the stubble of a new beard but forgoing the razor. My tuxedo was in a damp heap in a chair. I placed it in the trashbin, wishing I could place my worries there as easily.

After pulling on clothes, I dragged my rucksack from a closet and began to fill it with my belongings. There weren't many. I would not take anything she'd given me.

I signed over the check my aunt had sent me to Leo Bartenstein and placed it in an envelope to the old cameraman with a short letter telling him I'd come into some money and wanted him to have it, that I was going away for awhile and would contact him soon.

Chapter Twenty-One

FLEE TEMPTATION.

Clear as a bell, Milqueton's voice whispered in my ear. *Flee temptation.*

I was still too new to manly pleasures to fight her pleading seduction if she should beg me for forgiveness. How would I be able to resist her if she came to my bed that night? My body would want to forgive. It would betray me. This would not help her. And it would destroy me.

I glimpsed a light go on in the big house. It was inevitable that she would seek me out, no matter what Marta said. She was too weak-natured to wait. I could not let my longing for her cloud my reason. *Flee temptation.*

And yet another voice urged me to stay, the voice of the snake, the voice that said everything would be all right, that I could have her and happiness too, that honesty was not the most important virtue, that mercy was far more noble, that in the depths of mercy all wrongs are made right.

Do you believe in a merciful and just God, John?

No mercy. Only justice. I only believed in justice.

Pity bred lies. The kind of lies my mother told herself. If I stayed with Eleanor, it would be because I felt sorry for myself as much as for her. She would soon lose respect for me when she figured that out. But not before I'd lost respect for myself.

Quickly, I penned a note of farewell for poor Marta, thanking her for her care and for offering me the job. I left it on my bed next to the envelope for Leo.

Knowing Eleanor could look out and see the drive, I slipped out and around the back of the garage, walking along, but not on the gravel, careful to step where my feet would make no sound. It was steep there, and part of me hoped I'd fall and find release.

Rain poured steadily. It fell over the brim of my hat onto my chin and quickly drenched my overcoat. It spattered my glasses.

My plan was to head into the city and hitch the first ride I could find. Direction was no priority as long as it would take me far away.

In fact, I knew more of where I didn't want to go than of where I did want to head. Not back to Texas. I couldn't face that. Nor back to San Francisco. She'd look for me there. Perhaps East. Or South. Not to Mexico. Nor Arizona.

I had exactly ten dollars in my pocket. With a grim smile, I realized it was more than I'd had when I first came to Los Angeles. I'd already decided it was too risky to wait for the banks to open in the morning to draw on my account. As soon as she realized I left, she would look there. I'd have to make do until I could settle somewhere and then write to the bank.

I reached the end of the drive and looked up and down the road, choosing a direction. As I thought, I saw Eleanor in my mind, turning on her lamp, coming to my room, begging for forgiveness, encircling me with her arms.

I picked up my pace. As the rain beat steadily into the ground, I chose the northbound route. For hours I trudged, feeling like the only man alive. I wasn't even sure I really was alive. Perhaps I'd died and was now in hell. Perhaps the Lord exacts his punishment no matter how clean you try to make your heart. And I'd not tried very hard at all to wash away my sins, so eager had I been to commit new ones.

It was a strange night, with the landscape lit by an eerie light. A full moon hid behind dark clouds, creating a pinkish hue on the underside of cumuli to the south, while an ominous blackness filled the north. As I walked away from the moon-tinged clouds, it seemed as if I were walking into the jaws of hell, wandering through the thudding rain away from earthly joys and temporal beauty, toward permanent darkness.

It was a journey that had a sense of inevitability to it. It was as if I'd have to make it sooner or later, one I'd put off with Eleanor's love, a way station, a transient pleasure before the shadow enveloped me.

The earth smelled sour and damp, with the rotting aroma of fields recently gone fallow. The rain's drops were a hundred hoofbeats pounding into the ground, an army on the march, ready to strike me, an already vanquished foe, to the ground.

I was scared. To console myself, I tried to remember snatches of prayers we'd learned at Canfield, Bible verses or hymns, but nothing stuck with me or gave me peace. My mind replayed images—of Rev. Milqueton lecturing us, his eyes turned toward heaven, his hand on his Bible against his chest, his beard quivering as he declared the Word. *If you are penitent,* he had said, *the Lord will hear your call. Pride is a sin. Sin brings only misfortune.*

As dismal as those memories were, I struggled to retain them. Far better than the ones of Eleanor that flit through my mind, surprising me with their vividness and color in this oppressive blackness.

For four hours I walked until a car finally drove my way. Peering into the darkness, I could tell from the set of the lights that it was not an estate vehicle, so I stuck out my thumb. It went on by. I was not on the main road, because I didn't want to be found.

By my reckoning, it was well after midnight when a truck pulled up and a swarthy-faced driver asked me where I was headed.

"Where are you going?" I shouted through the rain's din.

He mentioned a town whose name meant nothing to me.

"That's where I'm headed." I hopped in and threw my rucksack on the floor. He was a small farmer heading back home after the funeral of his brother.

"He was such a happy fellow," the man said. He smelled like he had been drinking and confirmed my suspicion when he reached for a bag that held a bottle.

"I'm sorry," I replied.

"So young, too. Just twenty-five. An accident on his farm. His tractor fell on him. New tractor."

"Very sorry."

"You want a nip?" he asked and held out the bottle to me. It stank. It smelled like gasoline and vinegar and made my stomach turn. Get it away from me, I wanted to shout, but I just shook my head no.

"And his wife such a pretty young thing. Just getting started they were. If I could have gone in his place, I would have. I have no wife." He took another swig and veered to the right as he did so. He was drunk. The whole world was drunk. Liquor was prohibited, and yet people everywhere were acting like children denied a favorite toy, doing anything they could to get it. I wanted to get out of the truck. To hell with a ride. I'd walk. Who needed this? This stinking, sweating drunk. Maybe even this fellow's brother. Maybe that was what really killed him, not the accident.

"Here, son, will you hold this?" He thrust the bottle at me while he grabbed the gear shift on an incline. I rested it between my legs, not wanting to touch it, but he looked over at me and urged me to join him.

"It's good for what ails you," he said, nodding to the bottle. "Go on, have a sip. Won't hurt nothin'."

It would hurt everything, I wanted to shout at him. Everything. It destroyed. It melted away good, healthy lives. It devoured happiness. The bottle seemed to burn my thighs. I felt myself gagging as I grabbed it, being careful to hold the bag, not the bottle itself. Swiftly, before the driver could protest, I rolled down my window and chucked the bag and bottle into the rain soaked field.

"Jesus Christ Almighty!" He screeched to a halt. "What the hell'd you do that for?" Looking over his shoulder, he reversed the truck to the approximate spot where I'd tossed the bottle. His eyes were wide and afraid and angry. As he slammed on the brakes, I grabbed my duffel bag. He didn't even look at me as he left the truck, and I said nothing to him as I started on my way down the road ahead of him. I heard him cursing through the beat of the rain, as he searched the field for his precious bottle.

He was a disgusting animal, rooting in the earth for bad

seed. "Fuck you!" I yelled into the air, knowing he wouldn't hear over the rain and his own mad cursing. I was already a half a field away. "Fuck you, Eleanor!" I screamed.

My shoulders shook. Damn them. Not fair. Never fair. Damn them all, even the driver who gave me a ride. The driver who'd lost his brother. Do you think you'll find him in that bottle, sir? Do you think he's somewhere in that haze that mutes the world after you're drunk and falling down and smelling like yesterday's garbage? Do you think it's easy for people to help you there, to clean you up, to pretend...

I wiped my eyes.

To pretend they love you.

I sniffled and shook my head back and forth. Behind me, I heard the truck engine rumble to life. Either he'd found his treasure or he'd given up the hunt.

I took care of you. I was the parent. Not you.

The truck slowed beside me, and he called through the open window.

"You ungrateful son of a bitch!" Then he turned the wheel toward the shoulder of the road, and I fell to my knees on the embankment to avoid being hit. As he screeched away, I yelled at the fading lights.

"Damn straight I'm the son of a bitch!"

And then I sobbed into the earth for I don't know how long. Long enough to be drenched to the core. Long enough not to care about what happened to me. I should have stayed in the truck. Maybe I'd have been dead by now.

Eventually I trudged on.

Hours passed. Just before dawn, I came to a town nestled in hills, with only one store not yet open. I continued on my way, past closed houses that looked unwelcoming.

The rain was now a fine mist that left me damp even under cover.

At the edge of town, I picked up a main road again and headed north once more, walking until I stumbled and fell into a culvert by the road, sheltered a little by a ledge of muddy earth. Taking this as a sign that I should rest, I pulled my hat over my face and closed my eyes.

Fatigue so overwhelmed me that when I awoke, I felt as if I'd lost several hours and had not rested at all. I was living outside of normal timekeeping, someplace where time crawls over the sharp-edged rocks of painful memories and races through the moments of respite.

When I awoke, the sun blazed in a washed-out sky. While the night before had left me cold and wet, the sun made my damp clothes hot and steamy. I shed my coat and unbuttoned the top of my shirt. What I wanted most in the world at that moment was a glass of cool water. This comforted me. A physical longing that could blot out all else, all other longings.

By midday, I stumbled into another town and went to the gasoline station where I asked for some water. The attendant eyed me suspiciously, but I didn't begrudge him his harsh judgment. With mud-stained clothes, a day-old beard, and parched lips, I must have looked like a bum. I pulled out my money and offered him a nickel for some water. That loosened the strings of his heart and made his generosity pour out. In a moment, he was back with a grimy glass filled with lukewarm water.

It was enough to revive me. Not wanting to waste more of my money on anything else he had to offer, I moved on.

After another hour of plodding, I at last heard in the distance the sound I'd been waiting for. The lonely hoot of a freight train cut across the land. Listening carefully, I reckoned where it came from and headed cross country in that direction.

It took me several more hours to reach the track, and by this time, I was weak from hunger and regretted not buying anything to fortify myself. The train I'd heard was long gone, leaving me with two choices. Either I rested and waited for the next one, or kept moving down the line until it came.

Not wasting time on self-pity, I continued, following the tracks eastward, listening, waiting, hoping a train would come before I'd lost the energy to hop it.

Night fell and still the tracks did not hum. Not able to go an inch more, I dropped where I was, crumbled into a ball and prayed God to take me swiftly if this was my night to die.

Some time in the night, I was awakened by the roaring sound of steel and engine blasting through the void. Disoriented at first, I rose quickly, making my head swim. I mustered all my strength and ran alongside, keeping a good pace, looking for an open door. At last, at last, there was one, the slatted door open just a crack, just enough.

With a mighty heave, I hoisted myself—no, threw myself at the car. For a few moments, I dangled half in, half out. A pair of greasy hands reached out and hauled me aboard. Another hobo, just like the one I'd become. He wore threadbare pants and a plaid shirt ripped at the elbow. He smelled of sweat and old beer. His eyes were empty in his taut face.

We exchanged no words. He went back to his corner where a jacket was spread on the wooden floor. I nodded my head to him and went to the opposite corner.

My rucksack and coat were gone—I'd not had time to grab them when I'd made my pitch onto the train. All I had were the clothes on my back, my hat, and the money I still had left. To reassure myself, I patted my pocket. Too late, I realized it was ripped. The money was gone.

Sighing, I sat down and stretched my legs out before me, leaning against the rumbling boards of the car. Now I had less than what I'd had when I started out for Los Angeles.

❧

For three days, I rode trains. Famished and thirsty most of the time, I survived by grabbing fruit from the vine or bread left to cool on an unsuspecting housewife's window.

In fact, if it hadn't been for my hunger and other primitive needs, I would have stayed on that first train wherever it took me. The comfort in motion was all I had.

With my eyes closed and my head leaning back against the rattling boards, I could imagine all manner of things, including that I had never been to California at all. The clacking of the wheels, the pull of the cars, the steady jostling of my body on splintery floors all had a rhythm to them, like the rhythm of a cradle being rocked. When the train stopped, peace was shattered.

To keep myself from going mad during the lonely nights when no train came or when the one I was on stayed stuck on sidings, I came up with the plan to seek out my relatives at Devil's Rock. It gave me a goal that kept me from drifting into oblivion. It made me think, once again, that I had a life to be lived beyond the prison of Canfield and the new walls of heartbreak. I asked other hoboes about Devil's Rock. I asked townspeople the same—had they heard of Devil's Rock, Montana and the St. Claires who lived there? Some knew of the former. None of the latter.

I thought of looking for work, but most of the time I was so weak from hunger that I could barely muster the strength to wander far from the tracks. Food, drink, and directions to my cousin's house occupied all my time, a grateful relief from thoughts of Eleanor and our aborted nuptials. Occasionally, I could not stop the thoughts, and I would relive the careening moment of joy when I first saw her enter the room in her wedding garb to the chasm of despair when Robbie revealed their night together.

Self inflicted wounds. Yet I could not stop myself from pulling out these memories, laying them all in front of me and examining them, trying not to feel but only to think, as if analyzing this problem could yield a different solution. Where had I gone wrong?

My throat was often dry, but whether it was from lack of water or the bile of betrayal, I do not know. I only know if I stared too long into the darkness, my eyes would well with tears and my mouth stiffen from a jaw locked in rancor. More than once, fellow hoboes would scoot away in a car when that look came over me. Who could blame them? I felt like a wild creature ready to pounce on unsuspecting souls, trying hard to suppress the rage I had hoped I'd conquered.

The weather turned cold. Snow and hail replaced rain. And the air held the crisp, clean sting of the north. Why hadn't I headed here when I first left Texas? The blurred moral edges of California were left behind. Cold and heat. Right and wrong. That was what Montana seemed to offer. I embraced it.

From an open door, I could see the mountains disappear and the landscape stretch unyielding to the horizon, brown, tan, gold — all color washed out as winter approached. Few houses were in sight. Occasionally, a farmer walked an empty field.

For a day, I'd shared the car with three unnamed hoboes who stank and cursed and kept to themselves like some incestuous clan. When I jumped this train, I figured I'd keep to myself too, but their smell — like rancid grease and piss — and their ugliness was too much of an affront. I began to look for ways to irritate, to probe. One of them, a small stoop-shouldered fellow in his 30s, pissed on my side of the car. I looked at him through half-closed eyes, wondering when I should fight him.

But then a taller fellow, friendly and congenial, tried to get me talking, and I felt myself anticipate what was to come, like the calm stillness that precedes a storm.

"Where you headed?" he asked in a low mumble.

"Devil's Rock."

"Not too far."

"Glad to hear it."

"Where you from?"

"California," I said, not wanting to tell the tale of Canfield and Texas.

"See any movie stars?" he drawled, a smile flickering around his grubby lips.

"I worked for one. Pauline Sloane."

The two other men looked up, startled, and when he saw their awe-struck glances, he knew he had to knock me down.

"You're puttin' us on."

"No, sir, I am not," I said forcefully, already knowing this was the line that would be drawn and feeling my heart race as I got ready to step over it. "In point of fact, I did more than work for Miss Sloane." I stared at him. "I fucked her."

"Naw!" The other two's eyes were buggy and wide. They

moved a little closer.

"Don't give me that baloney, fella. I'm not in the mood for tall tales."

"No tall tale. Lordy, was she ever good, too."

He stood up. He'd been drinking. Even across the car, I could smell his breath and his clothes, the sour stale smell of bad liquor. Swaying with the car and his own inebriation, he came over to me. "Stand up!" he said. I obliged. We were the same height.

"She's a fine looking woman. Wouldn't be with a man like you."

I could have taken the first swing then. After all, he had insulted me. But I didn't. I held tight. I swung with words, not fists.

"You mean to say she'd never be with a man like you," I said slowly.

As it turned out, it wasn't my words that pulled the trigger. It was the low snicker of one of the other men. At that provocation, the bully sucker punched me hard in the gut, taking the breath right out of me. I'd thought he would be a sissy fighter. But he must have had practice. Before I knew it, he was hitting me again. And as soon as I returned fire, he let out a howl of protest that brought his friends to his side. They used fists and knees and feet. They punched and kicked when I was on the floor, and it didn't take long to get me there.

As soon as I fell I knew that I was a goner. I only put up token resistance, enough to let them think they had to keep going, while a small voice deep inside me whispered, *get it over with, let it end now*. I felt grateful that this opportunity had been given to me, that I didn't have to make the move myself to end it, that I could let these angels of mercy do the deed.

I was numb to the pain after the first blows fell. I was deep inside somewhere dark and small, only aware that my body was moving first to one side and then the other as their heavy shoes hit their marks on my torso and legs. I heard the dull thuds of their blows, the little grunts they made when they swung and kicked, and felt the trickle of sweat and drool that dropped onto my face.

I was not there. Already I'd left, and there was a lightness in leaving, a peace I'd never known, not even in Eleanor's arms. At the thought of her, a tear escaped my eye, and it didn't matter. They'd think it was from the beating. It would bring them pleasure and make them want more.

I tasted blood in my mouth, and my ears rang. Eventually, one of them slid open the door and cold air cascaded my pain to life, making my body a stinging mass of hurt, like acid had been poured in each joint and muscle.

"Devil's Rock," one muttered. "He said Devil's Rock's where he was going."

"Then let's help him out," the small one shouted. They dragged me to the door, and I felt immense relief. So this is how it would end at last, rolling down an embankment along the tracks. I thought of Milqueton and how disappointed he'd be, and I whispered a prayer to God to let the Reverend know he'd done what he could.

One of them patted me down for money and cursed when he found none. Then another grabbed my feet, while two held my hands and swung me, scraping my back against the floor twice before eventually letting go.

I rolled. I hit branches, scruffy bushes that clawed at my hands and face. I heard something snap and electric anguish jolted my left arm.

It hardly seemed fair to have to suffer like this at the end. But it had been my life so far, to suffer unfairly. Why should death be any different?

The trick, the voice said, was to let go. The more you hold on, the harder it is, the more it hurts. So I breathed out, willing myself to let all of it go, and the pain miraculously disappeared. I was rolling through cold clouds, weightless and light. And by the time I stopped I was so weightless that I had disappeared.

Darkness surrounded me. An animal howl cut the night. The train whistled far away, as far away as I was outside this body, looking down at a misshapen figure yards from the tracks. Who was that boy, and why was he so hard up, so sad? *Forgive me, Reverend, I tried, I really did. You couldn't have done better by me. Pete, you lucky fellow, you knew it was like this. You were the good one. The good die young …*

Forever encased me. Was I breathing? Shadows drifted around while I waited. Drowsiness overtook me. Sleep, a final sleep, was but shallow breaths away …

In stillness, in freezing cold, I heard a voice below. I saw a light coming upon my body, an *ignis fatuus* — an apparition, mist across a marsh, dancing to and fro. It was a single light, set all around by darkness, and as it neared my body, I returned to greet this visitor, hearing myself moan as I throbbed with pain.

"What's that? Dear Lord."

"Take him to the preacher."

"I'll fetch a board. Put him on that."

"And a blanket."

"He won't last. Did you see his arm twisted like that?"

Onto a board, the night stars shining directly on me, beckoning.

Come closer, stars, come to me, lift me high, take me into the void whence I came, floating so free and light. See me through, stars, don't betray me now, see me through.

Black night. White pins of stars. Pins of pain. They have betrayed me. They've turned me back.

Pins of pain, burrowing deep. Into my arm. My leg. My face. Throbbing. Something aching in my side, stretching my skin. Each move a knife.

Let me go, let me go!

Let me go to her….

Blackness, at last.

Chapter Twenty-Two

My eyes wouldn't open all the way. One felt swollen, and it was a struggle to move the lid beyond a slit of light. Here was the camera-vision Leo talked about. I could only focus on an object or two at a time, my aching head moving only slightly to take in my surroundings. I saw, first, the slanted ceiling just above me, whitewashed clean. Then a window frosted over with ice. Finally, I saw her, a fuzzy image of a woman, young and soft in outline, fulsome figure, pinked cheeks, lips moving. Now the sound was clear. She was reading from a prayerbook or Bible of some sort.

"Each day, He comes and asks for His servant. And each day, I answer, I am ready, Lord."

So the establishing shot told me I was somewhere cold, in a clean house inhabited by believers, one of whom sat by my side, caring for my wounds.

Thus, this part of my story began.

Pages breathed closed. She put the book down next to my bed. With a rough muslin cloth and soft hands perfumed with apples, she bathed me, stripping me bare with no shame. When she removed the cloths holding the splints in place, I flinched, sucking in my breath so fast that it caused another pain, a slashing ache on my cheek, and I could tell from the feel of something wet that I'd opened up a gash there.

"That's it," she said, gently moving the damp cloth down my legs. "Don't fight it. Let it out. Let all the hurt out."

When she moved into my vision's range, I could make out more of her, a young woman with honey hair and a buxom figure, the kind of woman who wasn't fashionable any longer. A chill came over me, and as it shook me, my arm ached so bad, I almost cried like a little boy.

"There, there," she cooed. Pulling the bandages back into

place with feather-like fingers, she quickly tucked a blanket around my body. "The fever's not quite gone yet. I'll get you some tea while you're awake."

Was I awake? I was in some half-sleep, some gray life in the shadows. I'd been there forever. I remembered waking, hearing voices, feeling pain and wanting to die so I wouldn't feel it. I remembered a doctor, this woman, another man...

He's malnourished. Wait and see. Pray awhile. Make some strong coffee. Don't waste time trying to get him to talk now. See if he can sit up in a day or two.

The spirit is a perverse captor. I had been ready to die, had accepted it, had dared God to take me. "Why not, you have taken everything else," I'd cried in the depth of my soul. "Take the rest of it. It's no good to me."

Now that death was within my grasp, my spirit would not let go. While I wanted to be rid of my grand sorrow, it fought for simple pleasures — the promise of a cup of tea, that woman's comforting voice.

She came back and sat by my head, cradling it with one arm while I sipped. Her breasts were soft pillows. I closed my eyes.

"Where..." I whispered.

"You're in Devil's Rock. And I'm Kate St. Claire. My father's Ezekiel, the local minister."

St. Claire. My cousins. The bums on the train had not thrown me to my death, they'd thrown me to my salvation.

"How long..."

"A week," she said with no fear. "It was not certain for awhile. But I think you're on the mend now." She gave me another sip.

"A broken arm and a sprained leg," Kate continued. "You might walk with a limp, I'm afraid." After helping me drink a half cup of tea, she tenderly laid my head back on the pillow and wiped my mouth.

"John Doyle," I whispered.

"That's enough for now, Mister Doyle. Maybe you can take some broth later."

I fell back into a sleep where dreams returned, dreams of home, of my aunt, of Eleanor, of Canfield. Dreams that left my hands squeezing in painful fists. Every aspect of my life was served up in twisted variations, some frightening, others joyful with happy endings replacing the real sorrows I'd suffered. When I awoke and realized they were not true, those dreams were more painful than the nightmares.

As consciousness returned, so did a sense of time. For another week, I lay in bed with Kate tending me and her father Ezekiel looking in from time to time. He was a short, muscular man with angular features and graying hair, the look of a prophet in his eyes. For the most part, they left me to myself, and I was still so weak that too much conversation was beyond me.

But with recuperation, restlessness returned, and, after five days had passed, I took it upon myself to get up. Using my good arm to slide my legs toward the edge of the bed, I managed to turn myself toward the door. With a giant heave, I stood, balancing myself by reaching out for a nearby chair. Kate came into the room as I stood unsteadily, biting my lip to keep from yelling in pain. It rushed up my leg and my bad arm. The joints seemed to explode.

"Really! You shouldn't have on your own." Kate hurried to me and draped my arm around her shoulders. "Come on, then. It's a good sign you want to be up and about. Let's see how you do."

I didn't do very well. I hobbled to the door and could barely move, afraid I'd not be able to make it back to the bed and would have to burden her to get me there as best she could. Kate was undaunted.

"You've started it. Let's finish it. To that chair by the fire." She nodded her head in the direction of an upholstered chair. It seemed miles away, but, with her steady help, I managed to make it. It must have taken us nearly a half hour. I had to rest after every hobble forward.

"My spectacles," I gasped out after I made it to the chair. "Were they found?"

"Oh!" She rushed back to the bedroom and in a few seconds reappeared, holding the wire-rimmed glasses. "They were found the next day, right by the track. Just scratched. You're lucky!"

"Thank you." I put them on. It was more than a scratch. A thin crack cut the bottom of one lens. But it wasn't enough to impede my vision.

She went to the wood stove in the corner and brought back coffee, then stoked up the fire. It was dark outside, evening was upon us. Soon, Ezekiel came through the front door, letting in flickers of snow. He stomped his feet and smiled at me as he took off his coat and hat.

"You're up! Thank the Lord!" But he didn't press me for more, and I dozed, my head nodding onto my chest, while Kate worked in the far end of the cabin near a woodstove.

That night, I joined them for dinner. They moved the table from the corner of the room to the front of the fire, so we could all sup together. Ezekiel reached for my good hand while Kate placed her hand on my damaged one, and we bowed our heads so Ezekiel could intone the grace.

"Thank you, dear Jesus, for the gift of food. Your bounty never fails us, and your grace is always a prayer away. Thank you, too, for mending your servant. Lead him on the path toward wellness and mercy. Amen."

While they ate ham and potatoes and pie, I drank coffee and broth.

Ezekiel told me of his work. How ironic it would have been had my grandfather left his money to Ezekiel, his second cousin, instead of to my aunt in an attempt to thwart her from giving it to Reverend Thistle.

My cousin, Ezekiel St. Claire, was himself a minister, a preacher who now made his home in Devil's Rock after a youth spent moving from one place to another. His wife and a son were dead, and his daughter Kate helped him with his work.

My first impressions of her now filled out. She had long golden brown hair, coiled in braids at the nape of her neck.

Her clothes were equally out-of-date, a dark skirt and blouse, covered with a gray-striped apron almost as long as the skirt itself.

They didn't question me that first night I joined them at table. They let me watch and eat in silence. When Kate helped me back to bed, I was exhausted.

My room was tiny, on the back of the small house. The bed took up almost the entire length of the room; its width was hardly larger. The roof angled sharply, too, creating a low ceiling that made me feel as if I were in some doll's house.

Everyday, Kate ministered to my physical needs while her father tried to account for my spiritual ones. She bathed and fed me and walked me to the front room. He read from the Bible and prayed.

At dinner at the end of that week, I finally had the strength to reveal to them our distant familial connection, and Ezekiel was wild with joy, a joy that made me feel uneasy. Would he expect too much of me?

"Praise the Lord! He must have sent you to our doorstep that night, John. He sent you to us! I'll have to preach a sermon on this!"

I wondered if Milqueton used me in his sermons as well, the tale of the saved penitent.

Kate didn't comment when I told my tale, leaving out the stop at the Sloane estate, but keeping in the story of my mother and Canfield.

"That would make us second cousins once removed?" she asked, her face aglow from the light of the fire.

"I'm not sure," I answered.

"Something very distant, though," she said softly. "Nothing too close."

"No, not too close," I said, thinking she might be ashamed to have me, a former resident of Canfield, as a relative. "Hardly related at all."

She brightened and continued eating.

But Ezekiel put his fork down and leaned toward me, intently staring at my face. Was he looking for remnants of his family there, evidence that I was, in fact, related to his cousin? He himself had only the hint of the Doyle make-up. Although angular, his face was longer than my grandfather's, and his eyes dark. His face was tanned from the sun, and he looked more like a farmer than a preacher, with strong hands and arms and a no-nonsense air that was a part of the Doyle character.

"You saw Samuel before he died?" he asked.

"I was with him at the end."

"Did he reconcile with the Lord?"

Looking at the eager man's shining brown eyes, I at first wanted to tell him he was a fool if he thought stubborn old Samuel had cared about the Lord at all. Samuel Doyle had reconciled something, perhaps, with me or with himself, but with the Lord? I was too tired for the truth.

"I think so," I lied.

Ezekiel bowed his head and closed his eyes. I was sure he was murmuring a prayer of thanks. Maybe I hadn't been lying. How could I know what my grandfather had said to the Lord before he'd met him, or if he'd met him at all?

"It's getting cold fast," he said, at last. "Too cold to travel in your state."

"I can fix things. I can work on cars." It seemed a silly offer, especially in my weakened condition. And I doubted many people owned a car in this rough territory. "I can do anything handy."

"What made you want to leave California?"

"I was looking for you," I said, thinking of Sloane Hall. My Canfield history I'd grown used to telling. This other humiliation would take some time to grow comfortable on me.

He thought about that for a few moments. If he had doubts about my real reason for seeking out such distant relatives, he said nothing about them then.

"Can you do carpentry? Build a house? Raise a roof?"

I had some carpentry skills and was sure I could learn more. "Yes."

He leaned back, satisfied.

"Then you can help me finish the meeting house when you're better. Before winter bears down on us." He rubbed his eyes and a smile slowly brightened his face.

∞

His need for help hastened my recovery. Eager to occupy my hands, I managed to accompany him for an hour's work the following week. Kate tried to insist that I was not ready, but I'd have none of that. I was now anxious to lose myself in labor, to find solace in the repetitive work of driving nail into wood, blade across lumber, posts into ground. It created an emptiness in your mind, that kind of work.

Ezekiel started me on easy tasks. The meeting house, as he called it, was to be a combination school and church serving the small local community and whatever Crow Indians he could entice. He'd managed to lay a foundation and get up a frame, but everything else needed to be done or he'd have to find a way to keep the lumber dry and safe all winter. Besides, the Lord had provided him with the gift of the materials through the bequest of a parishioner, Ezekiel told me, and it was his duty not to squander it.

As you can well imagine, I was not up to any real work with one arm still in a splint and my leg muscles sore and weak. I managed to do little more than hold wood while he cut it. After that, exhaustion won out over determination, and I was forced to limp back to the cabin on my make-shift crutch. It was less than a mile away, but it took me nearly an hour. The air was brightly chilled. My hands and face were ice by the time Kate let me in and fussed over me in front of the fire.

Since I had no other clothes, Kate found some things that belonged to her father and made me try them on. A pair of heavy pants. A flannel shirt. A corded vest. All needed alterations to make them fit, and she nervously made the adjustments with pins and measuring tape. It reminded me of Marta taking my measurements for Devlin's. I was glad those clothes were gone, the tuxedo ruined in the rain, other things deliberately left behind or lost in the trip. I took a grim satisfaction in knowing I had no mementos of my experiences at Sloane Hall. And in my lowest moments, I imagined Eleanor finding the sopping tuxedo and realizing I was gone for good.

After the session with Kate, I napped and then asked if I could help in the kitchen, but she would have none of it.

"It's good to see you up and about. But if you do too much, you'll end up in bed again," she said.

She forced me to sit in front of the warm, roaring fire and gave me a book to read when I expressed an interest in such things. It was a copy of *Meditations on the True Way*, the cover to which had wrapped a contraband *Huckleberry Finn* gift from Pete Salerno when I was at Canfield. I'd had it on the train to California, false cover and all. Here was a reminder of my journey to Sloane Hall. Putting it aside, I stared into the fire.

I was a recuperating patient and the St. Claire household was a convalescent home. I allowed myself to be healed by it, both physically and emotionally. Upon arrival at the Sloane household, I'd felt grateful for my good fortune. Now wiser, I offered no thanks.

"Would you like more tea?" Kate asked me, rubbing her hands together on her apron.

I smelled something warm and tasty, something of cinnamon and apples. "No, I'm fine. Thank you." I took off my glasses and rubbed them clean.

"I should get myself some of those." She pointed to my spectacles. "Have trouble seeing some things far away."

"You get used to how they make you look."

She blushed and looked down at her feet. "I'm not so vain, Mister Doyle, that I consider myself a beauty. It's that they're expensive, and we haven't the money now."

"What makes you think you're not pretty?" I stared at her, watching her redden from unaccustomed compliments. False modesty was as irritating as pride. When she didn't answer, I moved on. "Is there a place nearby, a town, where you could get them?" We were miles from Billings or Helena.

"Papa says by this summer we should have enough, and we can go to Collingswood to see about it."

"I could take you by then. My strength should be back." Well, this was news to me –that I'd even considered staying until the summer. I had no plans. Hadn't even begun to make them. But your heart makes plans even before your mind curls up around the idea of tomorrow. Already I was starting to get comfortable. What did I tell you before – how the devil steals your soul with comforts, not with riches?

She smiled, said nothing, and returned to her cooking, humming as she went.

When Ezekiel came home later, he was grinning broadly. The work had gone well, and he was now sure the building would be up before the weather turned real bad.

"Thanks to you, boy," he said, clapping me lightly on the shoulder. "You're a godsend."

I did not feel like a godsend, and I knew he was saying that to make me feel wanted.

That night, Ezekiel, Kate, and I joined hands around the table while Ezekiel spoke the grace in clear, confident tones. As usual, he thanked God for my presence among them.

"Thank you, Lord, for the blessings of this day. And also for the gift of your servant John. Thank you, too, for the food we are about to receive. All good comes from you, O Lord. We are but your instruments. Amen."

That night, I slept soundly, a dreamless, serene sleep, the first I'd had since leaving Sloane Hall. In the morning, the sun streamed through the cabin windows, and I awoke rested and at peace.

α

The entire time I stayed in Devil's Rock, I felt like I was saying good-bye to it, that as peaceful as it made me feel, I'd eventually be bidding it farewell. It was a way station, someplace to stop on the road to forgetting, to becoming someone else.

In the next few days, I shed my makeshift sling, and a week after that, I was able to walk a few steps without my crutch. Eventually, the crutch wasn't needed at all, but Kate was right – I walked with a limp.

I was able to do more each day. From time to time, Ezekiel had other helpers—copper-skinned Indians or young boys, in cloth shoes even in the cold. Sometimes even Kate came by to hold up wood while we hammered it into place. The work was good for me. There was no time for conversations about my past. And the noise effectively shut out all attempts at thought. Time crept by, placing distance between the now and the before and the yet-to-be.

As far as I could tell, the St. Claires existed on the charity of their neighbors and on the output of a small farm, tended by Kate, that stretched to the south of the cabin. She'd grown tomatoes and potatoes, corn and cucumbers, carrots and cabbage, and even saw to a few cows and chickens. While Ezekiel and I worked on the construction, she finished putting up the vegetables she'd harvested, spending all day in the kitchen boiling and bottling.

There was no lack of food. Each night, we'd sit at a rough-hewn table by the cabin's woodstove. After Ezekiel intoned the grace, we supped. Meat was often the result of a gift, and for one week we feasted on a ham from a neighbor five miles away. I still remember the taste of that good ham, salty and mild, the best I'd ever had before or since.

By this time, I'd become aware of the fact that I had displaced Kate from her room. The cabin only had three rooms—the large front one that served as parlor, dining room, and kitchen, and two tiny bedrooms on the back, built like lean-to's, one for her, one for her father, separated by a small bathroom, a luxury for this kind of dwelling. After learning of her sacrifice, I insisted she go back to using her room while I would bunk as best I could in the large room. She protested mightily but eventually gave in when her father asked her if she preferred the great room because it was closer to the fire.

After dinner, Kate would clean up the dishes while Ezekiel stoked the fire to life. Then we'd gather there to read a Bible story or two. Kate always read the stories, while her father listened and stared into the fire. Then followed silent reflection and discussion. After reading the story of Abraham and Isaac one night, Kate surprised me with her comments.

"That is my favorite story," she said. She refilled her father's cup of coffee and offered me some.

"Why is that, child?" Ezekiel asked. He took a long draw on his pipe, then sipped his coffee. "It's a hard story—God asking for the sacrifice of Abraham's only son. I don't know if I could do it—give you up if God asked." He shook his head. "I've already been found wanting there." I assumed he was talking about his lost son and wife.

"But Father, just think of how Abraham felt in that instant when he found out that if he was willing to sacrifice everything, he'd have his faith rewarded—he'd never doubt again."

"Rewarded?" I asked.

She turned to me. "His son brought back from the brink of death, and his own hand stayed from committing a murderous deed."

Sometimes Kate would sing after these discussions, usually at her father's insistence, accompanying herself on a stringed instrument she held in her lap. Her songs were always religious in text but haunting in tune. Other times, she'd knit or sew, her brow creased as she pulled thread through cloth or clicked needles as yarn grew into sweaters and scarves.

The wind howled at the door and rattled the windows, but inside that cabin all was warm and tranquil. Kate, in particular, exuded a quiet calm. She had a natural beauty unadorned by makeup or jewelry. In spite of her dowdy clothes, she was an attractive girl. With bright green eyes, hair that shone even in the dimmest light, and clear skin slightly tanned by the sun, she gave the impression of someone healthy from the outer layers to her very core. She matched her father's seriousness with a light and playful character, often chiding him to smile, lest he "scare away those you wish to lure to your pulpit."

When I was around her, her brightness managed to blanche my sorrow from me and left no room for self-pity.

Was I happy? No. Some part of my soul still beat out a thousand what-if's. What if I had stayed with Eleanor? What if I had never let her come to my bed? What if I could just forget and forgive? What if I was the father of her child?

The last question always ended my debate. Of course it wasn't my child. How could that one thing go right when so many other things had gone wrong? I would not be fooled again.

In weaker moments, though, I struggled with the idea of forgiveness. The devil's voice—or was it God's, they seemed intertwined to me now—would urge me to forgive and go back. I resisted. Forgiving would turn me into a hypocrite.

If I'd forgiven Eleanor, I'd be slipping back into territory where people saw what they wanted to see and avoided the unpleasant truth.

My grandfather had resisted until the end accepting the truth of my paternity. My mother had not accepted the unpleasant truth that she loved drink and high times more than she loved herself. Or perhaps even me, I suppose.

So if I was to remain honest, I would see Eleanor as a weak woman who'd sell her body for drugs, who'd lie to me about the child she bore, who'd hide from me the ugly facts beneath her beautiful surface, and who could probably no more be true to me as she was to herself. And once I accepted those realities, I could not stay with her.

Thus, I'd have to turn my head away, close my eyes, blot out the memories whenever I heard Eleanor's voice calling to me or her image renewing hope in my heart.

This was a tough chore. Tougher than anything Ezekiel had me do. Tougher still when a few days later, Ezekiel came back to the cabin from a trip into town and handed me an envelope.

"Someone must know you're here, boy," he said.

I recognized her handwriting. And felt as if—

As if the snow was crashing in on me, roof and all.

As if the sun was melting everything into bloom and blossom.

Chapter Twenty-Three

IN THE DIM LIGHT of the fire's dying embers, after Ezekiel and Kate had gone to bed, I read the letter.

She contacted my aunt to get this address and hoped her letter would reach me. Robbie didn't know where she was, and she wouldn't let him find her. She wasn't drinking.

Was that the truth or another lie? Just let me go, goddammit.

I wondered if she'd thrown away that set of needles in the attic.

She wasn't doing anything that would harm herself or the baby, she wrote. But she was afraid of what would happen if Robbie found her. She was giving up acting. She was going to sell Sloane Hall. She was—

The letter was filled with a thousand resolutions, a child's list of "I'll be good" promises. And it all sounded as desperate and false.

I leaned on my arm and thought. If she'd sent a one-page note, instead of the five I had in my hand, that said nothing more than she understood why I had to leave, and she hoped I would find peace in my life, then maybe I could begin to believe her. Maybe.

I thought of reading it again. But I decided that was the beginning of seduction. So I poked the thin pages into the coals. It burned up quickly.

But even that fire wasn't enough to satisfy my burning rage. I grabbed paper and pen and wrote a quick letter back: *Please don't contact me again. John.*

଼୦

That Sunday, I listened to Ezekiel preach.

I approached preachers with a fair amount of cynicism. At Canfield, we'd been exposed to many traveling reverends who used our chapel's pulpit to rain fire and brimstone on our heads. And who could blame them for their melodramatic warnings of hell? After all, there surely would be few occasions in their lives when they'd come upon an audience of convicted sinners.

After awhile, fiery sermons ceased to move, let alone hold your attention. A steady diet of even the best ruins the appetite for more of the same.

Although a capable speaker, Rev. Milqueton himself was not a brilliant preacher every Sunday. What made him interesting at all was his ability to vary his delivery more than his actual content. You never knew if he would approach the Word with fire in his belly or with honey on his tongue. So, you were made attentive by curiosity, eager to see what technique he'd use that particular week.

The preachers that earned our scorn the most, however, were not those who bored or thundered, but rather the ones who used the pulpit as an excuse to write their own biographies large across the broad canvas of our captive minds.

These ministers always had a story to tell that involved their own experiences. And while they might start out in these narratives as groveling sinners, by the end they were approaching sainthood after going through the life-changing lesson they were generous enough to share with us poor souls on Sundays.

So when I sat on the rough-hewn bench of the new meeting hall for the first time, I did not expect Ezekiel to inspire me or even to hold my interest. I merely hoped that he would not offend. I sat politely, a Bible in my hands, provided by Kate who sat next to me in rapt attention. The invigorating scent of newly-cut wood filled the room, a fire crackled in the stove in the corner, people coughed and squirmed. A child wailed while her mother shushed.

After the hymn singing and the praying, my cousin stood in front of us with no props. His own Bible was on a desk in back of him. He wore his "Sunday best," a dark blue suit that looked thin from too many cleanings. Superbly confident, he began, using the text of the day's reading as cue. It had been from the Gospel of Matthew. How often should I forgive, Peter asked Jesus. And He replied: seventy times seven.

"Forgiveness is easy, isn't it?" he said slowly.

I sat upright. This was not what I expected to hear.

"A man wrongs you. You can do nothing about it. Over time, you decide to forgive. Perhaps you offer him your forgiveness outright. Perhaps you hold it only in your heart."

Ezekiel's voice was clear but conversational. It held none of the rumbling force of Milqueton or the other preachers who'd paraded through Canfield.

"And before you know it, you are proud of yourself. You feel like a righteous man."

Ezekiel paused. Looking down at his feet, he smiled Softly, without staring at us, he said, "I knew a man, my friends, who fell into this sinner's trap."

And here I expected him to wander down the road of the Canfield preachers, telling us his own personal tale of redemption so that we might not only learn, but admire him, in the same lesson.

He did not take that path. Instead, he gathered us all together for another journey.

He looked up again, and continued in a more forceful manner. "He had the most precious piece of him stolen by the carelessness of a neighbor!" he shouted. "His only son's death was caused by the acts of this neighbor's own son!"

I could feel the crowd repulsed by such a sorrow.

"And yet within a day, this man had forgiven the neighbor." His voice became singsong, and he stared at the rafters, the good book clutched to his chest like a shield.

"But had he?" he whispered. "For when this neighbor was in dire straights, calling out for help, a man incapable of helping himself any longer... his friend turned away as if it were God's will that this father of a killer be struck down. As if offering him help would be against the divine plan."

People nodded their heads.

"We know only one thing of God's will for us—that he

requires us to love our neighbors as ourselves. As..." He thumped the Bible with his fist.... "Our. Selves.

"Beware, my friends, beware. How often, when we forgive, we are overwhelmed with a powerful sense of well-being we think is grace. It is not grace." He paused. "It is pride. We see the transgressor as a lesser soul."

He shook his head slowly. "We think we forgive. Instead, we are only interested in being seen as a forgiving man, being admired, even by God, for our virtue. True forgiveness must begin with forgetting. Locking away the grievance. Never to be taken out. Even when the devil himself offers us riches along with the key!"

His voice now rose to the emotional level of preachers I was long used to. He had us all riveted as he thundered away.

"He will tempt. He will beckon. He will entreat and bribe. What is the bribe he offers? Self-righteousness, my friends. You can look at those transgressions, he whispers in our ear. You can hold them in your hands and gaze at them with no bile because you are a forgiving man. You have put the past behind you. You have buried the hatchet, given your neighbor your blessing, absolved him of his sin.'

He paused and slowly looked around the room. "How many of you think you can absolve another man of sin. Don't answer me outright! Only in your heart."

The room was silent as we all made our answers.

"Who gave you that power?" he blasted, his voice a roar of indignation. "How dare you *think* you have the power to absolve another man's sin? Only the *Lord* takes sin away. Only the *Lord* washes clean our hearts. How *dare* we think we can take from the Lord what is only His to give?"

He took a deep breath.

"Forgiveness," Ezekiel said softly, slowly, "is not something we bestow on others. It is a gift God bestows on us. It does not naturally spring from our breast. What does spring forward is a desire to be loved. Do not ask the Lord to bless you for forgiving your neighbor. Ask the Lord to give you the *grace* to forgive your neighbor."

For twenty minutes more, Ezekiel preached in this vein, and I was held spellbound by a message that seemed tailor-made for me.

I could not forgive her. All I could do was desire to be loved. This desire still created an ache. Not a day went by that I didn't feel its twinge of pain, like a splinter buried too deep to remove.

෮

Kate explained the sermon to me that week. Her brother, Daniel, she said, became fast friends with a neighbor family's boy of the same age, Claymore. Claymore was a scalawag, always in trouble, as mischievous as an imp.

"Not a bad boy," she said, smiling as she peeled potatoes one afternoon. "Just curious as a cat and filled with boundless energy."

Her mother didn't like Daniel to go off with Clay too much because of the trouble they'd get into, but Ezekiel often overruled her worries and let him go. One cold spring morning, Clay decided to go ice fishing on the lake. It was too warm for that. The ice cracked, and he went through.

"Dan went to help him. Fished him out, too," she said, stopping her work and staring straight ahead. "But he himself went under."

Clay lived. Dan died. Kate's mother never was the same again, and Kate suspected she held it against her husband until the day she died.

"Clay's father was shot in a hunting accident," Kate said, no rancor in her voice. "His family came calling asking Father to go tend to him, give him a blessing and the like. But Papa wouldn't go. Said Mama was too ill to leave."

"That's when she passed on?"

She shook her head. "She recovered from that storm. Died almost a year to the day later." She looked up at me. "Clay's father went that night his family came by."

So Ezekiel had not truly forgiven the man and had found an excuse to deny the poor soul a last blessing before leaving this earth. He still lived with that sin. He'd not been able to forget.

Forgetting became my occupation. It is strange the way the heart remembers. Not grand moments or the thrall of passion. No, it is more likely to be a small gesture, a word, a scent that makes you ache for the past. My cousin Kate, as far from Eleanor in personality as one can get, might laugh and sing, and the very differentness of her sound would make me long for Eleanor's melodic giggle as a starving man wants bread.

The afternoon light would amplify the scent of pine, and for a moment I'd be transported back to the drive up to Sloane Hall, lined with eucalyptus trees, their heavy perfume exaggerated in California's sunlight. I'd remember then the sense of anticipation I felt every time I rounded that last bend toward the Hall, hopeful that I'd see her. How I longed to see her, her face framed by Sloane Hall's windows.

While I spent my time trying to bury the past, its stinging ashes found me. I could turn my mind away, if I tried hard enough, from thoughts of our lovemaking, from holding her tightly, from the cooing words of intimates. I could place those things in the box that Ezekiel talked about and shut it tight.

But she wrote again. This time, it was the note I'd thought I'd wanted. One page. *John, darling, I was so glad to at least know you are alive. All I want now is to know you are well. Send word by Marta if you can't stand to write to me. I am so sorry I hurt you. So very, very sorry. Please forgive me. Your loyal Eleanor.*

I thought long and hard before burning that one and cursed that I'd responded to the first. An honest forgiveness wasn't in my heart at that moment. The Lord had yet to bestow on me that grace.

All I had left were distractions. The way a terminally ill man might try to concentrate on other things to keep his mind off dying, I focused on my new routine to keep my mind from her.

I was busier than I'd been since Canfield and dead tired every night because of it, a blessing. A blessing to be in this small farming community, too, as things grew dark everywhere else. Stock market crash, the papers called it. It put folks on edge as prices began to fall and wages with them. Eventually banks closed, and I hoped Leo was the kind to stick cash under a mattress instead of in a bank. The one I'd used for my grandfather's other check had failed I learned and I'd only managed to write and withdraw a little of my money here in Devil's Rock. The rest was lost. One more reason not to return to California.

When I was fatigued, I fell into dreamless sleep. Dreams were not good for me.

When winter finally settled on us, it was the worst I'd ever experienced. Temperatures here dropped below zero on most nights. Struggling to keep the little cabin warm took up a large part of each day as I split wood and brought it in, stoked the fire and the wood stove. I never seemed to get warm enough, no matter how many shirts Kate forced on me, telling me to layer them over each other to capture my body's own heat.

By this time, a little corner of the main room was set up as my own space. It held a new cot and overturned box as a bedside table. In front of it, strung diagonally across the ceiling, was a clothesline upon which was hung an old blanket. I closed this at night for privacy.

Kate became a dear friend to me, making sure I had clothing, cutting my ragged hair, looking out for me. In this latter regard, she worried that Ezekiel would work me too hard.

"He's not our slave, Father," she told him one snowy night when the wind howled at the door, and we sat in front of the fire.

Ezekiel had just laid out in detail the next day's work. He wanted to hike into Collingswood, a nearby town, to buy ink and paper for the school and to spread the word about the church. Kate didn't want us to travel. And she used me as an excuse.

"John's already split near a cord of wood today. And fixed the roof as well as carried a basket of food to Mrs.

Atherton." She clicked knitting needles furiously.

"I don't mind," I said. "I like to keep busy. And to earn my keep."

"You more than earn your keep!" Kate said. She seemed irritated. Her lips puckered together and her brows furrowed.

"Then I'll go to Collingswood on my own," Ezekiel announced, taking a long draw on his pipe.

"You'll do no such thing in this weather. It can wait, Father."

"We can't wait for every fine day, Kate. The Lord expects us to make do, come storm or sunshine." He stood and warmed himself in front of the fire. He might be used to the cold winters in Montana, but that didn't make them any easier. I saw the telltale signs of chilblains on his hands and more than once had worried about frostbite on his face when he'd stayed too long outside or traveled too far.

"I'll go with him," I said. "As long as Ezekiel thinks it's safe to travel, I'll go with him. I'm strong enough now."

Not looking at me, Ezekiel smiled slowly. "Thank you, John."

Kate gathered her knitting together in a basket and went to the stove where she rattled a kettle while making tea. She was not pleased. With her back to us, she fussed at her father.

"You get more reckless every year." Tears and exasperation were in her voice. "You can't do everything."

"That's why we have John here," Ezekiel countered. "To help."

"John can't protect you from yourself. And your behavior will put him at risk. Just last year, Donny Templeton nearly died in a blizzard. Wouldn't have been found, either, if the Porters' dog hadn't sniffed him out."

"I have no intention of suffering that fate, nor any worse."

"Listen to you. *You* have no intention. As if it were all in your power. Isn't that what you constantly tell us? That it's not in our power? It's in His power?" She pointed upward.

Ezekiel just chuckled. "All the more reason to do what I have to do. If He wants to call me, He will call me — in a snowdrift or sitting warm in front of this fire."

Kate pulled a cup out of the cupboard so sharply it slipped from her hand and crashed on the flagstone floor. "Oh my!" She bent to pick up the pieces and cut herself. "Oh."

I went to help her. "Put something on that." I pointed to her cut finger. "I'll take care of this."

Tears glistened in her eyes.

By the time I'd cleaned up the glass and she'd tended to her cut, Ezekiel had gone to bed. While she fixed herself another cup of tea, she brooded silently.

"Your father is not going to do anything that endangers this mission," I said.

She exhaled sharply. "You don't know him."

"Why would he risk his life needlessly? He wouldn't leave you alone." If there was one clear thing in the world, it was how much Ezekiel loved his daughter.

She looked up. "Ever since my brother and mother died, he's been like this. Sometimes I think he rushes toward death, he dares it to grab him. He wants to be with her--and Daniel—still." Indignation tightened her fingers around her cup.

She stood close to the wood stove basking in its warmth, but her face was red from anger, not from heat.

"How long has she been gone?"

"Eight years."

Eight years. A life sentence. Closing my eyes, I thought of my own sentence. At Canfield, and now after Sloane Hall.

"Ezekiel strikes me as a man who loves life." I spread my hands in front of the stove to warm them.

"He tries." She shrugged. "But sometimes … sometimes I see his eyes light up with an idea. An idea that he's found the invitation."

"What invitation?"

"The one that says, 'you are cordially invited to see your wife and kin again, signed Jesus Christ."

Turning, she walked back to the chairs in front of the fireplace. With a poker, she tamped down the fire for the night.

"You're his kin." I followed her.

"I remind him of her, of both of them." She said it sad and low, as if she felt she didn't measure up. "I am only one person. He had a lifetime before me." She looked me in the eyes. "It would be the greatest kindness, if you would watch out for him. Keep him safe."

I nodded my head. "All right." Maybe an invitation waited for me.

☙

In the morning, the skies were gray and heavy with clouds, so low they made you feel claustrophobic, a strange sensation in this wide open land. After breakfast, served silently by Kate, Ezekiel and I dressed for our journey.

"We'll be home by nightfall," Ezekiel said to Kate as she stood in the door with her arms crossed over her chest.

Wearing a dark red cardigan over a black skirt, she stared at her father with thin lips pressed together and her foot tapping slowly.

I waved farewell. "We'll be careful!"

We *were* careful, but it was a hard journey, the snow making each step double work. By the time we reached the town, we were both panting. I was glad to be there, looking after Kate's father for her. It made me feel useful.

He introduced me to some friends—storekeepers he knew—and bought some supplies.

After a few hours in town, we started for home in silent companionship. If I'd hoped to use this exertion to once again scour my mind of Eleanor, it was not to be. The empty drudgery as we walked slowly through the snow left my mind free to wander as well. And wander it did, back to warmer days on her veranda, in my garage apartment, in her bed. And with each step, with each heavy trod through snow, through ice, I shouted into my mind: Leave me alone! Leave. Me. Alone. Free. Me.

Did God hear?

The silent whoosh of snow answered me, so I conjured instead an image of my grandfather on his deathbed. I thought of him in heaven, in a vaporous state looking down on me. What did he see? Would he be disappointed?

Yes, he would be. He'd tell me I was a sentimental fool, that a Doyle could have better and should expect better. He'd tell me that I should move on with my life and find a suitable woman capable of bearing me fine children and standing steadily by my side as grandmother had stood by him.

I could even hear his voice issuing these stern fiats. Get a good wife. Settle down. Don't dwell in the past.

Just like Milqueton. *Don't dwell in the past.*

I hadn't thought of them as kindred spirits, but, I suppose, in some ways, they were.

On the edge of town, we took a diagonal street back to the main road. It hooked around a stand of lonely trees, now painted white with the day's snow. Just beyond these was a clearing surrounded by wrought iron fence. A graveyard. Ezekiel asked me to wait while he went through the gate. He carefully brushed snow off two stones in the far corner, then stood with his hands folded and head bowed for ten minutes. The snow had stopped, and the clouds were lifting. Cold sunlight streamed through the trees, dappling the white-blue snow, unbroken except for his tracks.

His dark, stooped figure blended in with the crooked trunks of the trees beyond. All were still as death itself. What prayers did he offer, what conversations did he have with them?

"Nothing will keep Zeke from Collingswood," one of the storekeepers had said to me in town.

This trip had been no tiresome march for supplies. It had been his private pilgrimage to visit his dead wife and son. Ezekiel was still mourning. Still hurting. How long did it last?

When we started back into open fields, light was filtering through the far end of the cloud cover, a muted late-day light tinged with blue. I'd keep my promise to Kate. We'd be home before nightfall. As we entered Devil's Rock, I looked over at Ezekiel and saw a man refreshed. Despite hours of tough walking through snow in frigid temperatures, he looked as if

305

he'd just stepped outside. Eyes bright. Half smile. Serene face. No, he'd not gone to Collingswood for supplies. He'd gone for peace of mind, a fix as necessary as any Eleanor had been addicted to.

Chapter Twenty-Four

I turned twenty-two that December, but shared the date with no one. Kate and Ezekiel were more than generous at Christmas, however, the cheeriest I'd spent in a long time. To my surprise, they both presented me with gifts. Kate had knit a downy blue muffler for me, a present all the more dear because she'd worked on it in secret, stealing moments to finish a row while I cut wood or ran errands.

Ezekiel presented me with a Bible, but not a new version from among the small stock he kept to give out to fresh converts. This was a worn, leather-bound edition that was inscribed with the name "Rebecca Doyle," some distant relative to both of us. At first I protested, not wanting to take from him what must have been an old treasure. But he insisted. "I have plenty of Bibles, son," he said to me. "This has your family name in it. It belongs more to you than to me."

I had no books with me, so that Bible became my storybook, and I must admit I sometimes opened it just to view the strong, sloping handwriting of "Rebecca Doyle." After all these years, I felt a part of a family, connected over time to someone I didn't even know.

When they set their gifts out for me that Christmas, I realized too late I should have made something for each of them. Embarrassed, I told them I was "at their service" for any job, large or small, that needed doing. Ezekiel pat me on the back and said he wouldn't mind it if I would accompany Kate into town each time she went, since he worried about her walking alone. Kate, blushing red to the roots of her hair, looked at her shoes and said nothing when I made my offer.

My gift to myself was a letter to Leo. I'd not written him at all because I associated him with my painful time at Sloane Hall. But the generosity of Christmas made my stinginess with affection all too apparent. I owed him my news and my friendship. Cold cash didn't replace those. So I penned a note, letting him know I was staying with relatives in Montana and urging him to write to me because I wanted to know how he was getting on.

The winter wore on, and with it, I became more deeply enmeshed in the St. Claires' lives. It was impossible not to fit snugly into their household where everything was close and the work constant and shared. To my relief, I had no more letters from Eleanor. I alternated between thinking this was because she'd lost her resolve and started drinking again, and believing she might have stayed clean and moved on. Depending on my mood, each vision could bring either relief or dismay.

I did, however, receive a letter back from Leo, thanking me profoundly for my parting gift which he had, in fact, kept safe from the "robber banks." This gave me great joy — to realize he was still alive — and I laughed as I read his usual complaints about filmmaking. He'd managed to do another film with some fellow from Cal Tech named Frank Capra. He told me the hot box camera booths were being replaced by cameras with "housing units" that encased only the machine and not the man, but he still saw no future in the talkies and reminded me how producer Sam Bischoff had proudly proclaimed that "Columbia will never make a sound picture," even though, of course, that prediction had already been proven false. And then he ended his letter with an invitation:

"...and I hope you remember that film I told you about that Raoul Walsh is going to do. I hear he might be filming in the spring, and my offer still stands. I will get you on that set and behind the camera if you want to do it. It's a western and should be fun for a young fellow. He's using an unknown in the lead. His real name's Marion but Raoul is changing it to John something...."

Another new actor replacing the more expensive silent bunch. Another identity sculpted from the sands of fantasy into a new Adam. I saved Leo's letter but wrote him back with no promises, only news of my life with the St.Claires. I had resolved to make no false promises to anyone.

Each morning, I cut firewood until my muscles screamed, becoming stronger from the effort. If it wasn't too snowy, Kate and I would hike into the small town to buy supplies. Remembering Ezekiel's request, I was quick to respond. If she reached for her coat and hat, I reached for mine.

I enjoyed the freedom of walking, and Kate was good company.

Even in the worst weather, it only took us a little over three-quarters of an hour to tramp into Devil's Rock. Staid and serious the rest of the time, Kate became playful and girlish along the way. She'd throw snowballs at me and run ahead and hide, ambushing me from behind a tree as I came into sight. One day, when the snow was wet and heavy, she made me stop to help her roll together a snow man, a huge buffoonish character with pinecone eyes and sticks for arms.

She'd race me down the last hill to the town, laughing and breathless when she reached the bottom, and always claiming victory, no matter whose foot was first over the imaginary finish line.

She was a different person on those walks, a person who transformed immediately back to the respectable preacher's daughter as soon as she was within sight of the town's few buildings. It never ceased to amaze me how quickly the change took place.

In those moments of playfulness, I felt I was seeing the true Kate, a girl of spunk and energy and immeasurable possibilities.

After one outing late in the day, she dared me to race her back up the hill. Usually tired by then, she'd climb the hill silently and then talk amiably on the rest of the way home. This time, though, the sun had finally peeked through dark clouds. It made me feel like sighing and saying, "at last." At last, the sun is here if only to tease us for an hour with its thin rays, an hour before it fades beyond the horizon. Just that tiny sliver of sun in so much cold and snow was enough to make you feel like you owned the world. Infected by that joyfulness, she opened her eyes wide as she looked up the small hill.

"C'mon," she said. "To the top! We can see the sun there!"

She took off before I had a chance to reply. Clambering after her I slipped and slid, but so did she. We were laughing so hard from falling in the icy snow that we both made it to the top at the same time, in a prone position as if we'd been mountain climbers wedded to a cliff front.

Her eyes closed, she lifted her face to catch the weak rays that cut across the land from far in the distance.

"It's leaving us. We must say good bye," she said simply, like a child. "Farewell, brother sun. Until tomorrow!"

"You sound like a pagan, talking to the sun."

"Maybe I am one."

I sharply turned my face toward hers. She smiled an impish grin, dimples appearing on either side of her mouth below rosy cheeks glowing from the cold.

"You're your father's daughter," I said.

"If you mean I've got his faith, you're wrong." She stared up at the sky. "I used to have it. Until my brother and mother died."

"But you help him with his work. You like the Bible stories you read."

"They're good stories! And we all have to do something, John. He's my 'something.'"

I looked at her. I'd made false assumptions. "You don't believe in God?"

"Oh, I believe in God. I just don't know if He has a plan for us. I believe that I've got a choice — to help my father or not. And each choice means a sacrifice. I've made my choice. I'm happy with it." She laughed. "So you see, I could be a pagan!"

"I think not, Kate."

"Sometimes, I wish I could be."

"Why?" I leaned on one elbow in the snow, studying her.

"I wouldn't have to work so hard to be so good."

"What makes you think pagans were all bad? I'm sure they had some rules they couldn't break."

She sighed. Her good cheer left her. "There are always rules."

"What rules bother you?"

She stood and dusted the snow off of her skirt. "All of them." Shivering, she rewrapped her wool scarf around her neck. "Oh, that's not right. Only some of them."

"Which ones?" I persisted. Now standing next to her, I brushed snow off her back and shoulders.

At the action, she turned to me. With a curious look that mixed confusion with fear, she tipped her head up and quickly planted a kiss on my cheek. "That one. The rule that says a girl can't do that."

I felt my cheeks flush, but I didn't know what to say. Her gesture touched me. It stirred me fully to life again, making me realize I'd been holding back. Life was so hard to kill.

Clearing my throat, I suggested we start for home. For awhile, we walked in silence, and I knew Kate was smart enough to know what that meant—that I wasn't ready to return her kiss. As we walked, however, I began to question my reserve. Why shouldn't I return her kiss with equal vigor? She was young and attractive. She liked me. She wanted to be kissed. Maybe more.

"Why don't you tell me what other things you wish girls could do?" I asked after a while.

She answered immediately, as if the kiss had never happened. "I wish I could do the things Father does. Build a church. Lead. Even preach."

"Preach in your pagan church?" I laughed.

"Maybe if I preached it, I'd believe it more," she said, a smile in her voice. "Maybe all it takes is practice."

"There are some women preachers, you know."

She snorted. "Confidence men. Or should I say con women?"

"Well, there's nothing that says you can't do other things.

Like help with the building."

"Not when there's mending to do. Or food to cook. Or teaching to be done."

"Maybe you could get someone else to do those things."

She stopped and stared at me, the smile returning to her eyes. "Are you a volunteer?"

"What?" I laughed. "You don't want me cooking for you."

"See what I mean? Someone has to do those things. That someone is me."

"Maybe that will change."

"Not any time soon." With grim determination, she strode forward.

I ran to catch up, nearly dropping the paper-wrapped package of cloth and thread we'd picked up in town.

I grabbed her elbow to catch her. "You're angry with me."

I enjoyed having her like me. And I wanted to touch her again, to feel a woman's lips pressed on mine. I tugged at her elbow and whirled her around to face me. Then I bent down and kissed her properly, on the mouth. Her lips were cold but soft. She smelled of camphor and wood smoke.

She was not Eleanor, but she would do.

When we pulled away, she looked up at me, her gaze piercing my eyes, her own eyes a searchlight peering into my soul. I stared into the distance.

"I'm not angry with you," she said slowly, at long last. "Should I be?"

"No," I lied. Not if she didn't mind a man who used a poor girl's fancy.

She reached out and put her gloved hand through the crook in my arm. We'd never walked thus, even when the terrain or weather was bad. Always Kate walked alone, stolidly facing the elements on her own terms.

By the time we reached the cabin, the light had faded to blue shadows, a different blue from that which covered the valley at sunset in California. That shadow heralded secrets, this one invited you to find warm hearths within.

When he heard us approach, Ezekiel came to the door, pipe in hand. Although Kate dropped my arm at the sight of him, his gaze immediately went to where her hand had rested in my elbow. From that distance, I couldn't tell if he was pleased or annoyed.

"It's getting late. I was beginning to worry." He ushered us in and shut the door.

"Exactly how I feel when you traipse off." Kate uncoiled her scarf and stomped the snow off her boots. "I'll get dinner on."

"The kettle's still warm. I made some tea." Ezekiel walked to the fire and took his place there, a Bible by his side.

Although we didn't speak of it, we changed that evening. Ezekiel, with his fine intuition, sensed that Kate was different. Perhaps because he knew what this signified, he stiffened toward me.

After that walk, Kate effected an overfriendly shyness around me, a strange combination of both congeniality and timidity. She laughed a little too loudly, expressed too much concern for me, became moody and downcast in a melodramatic way. Ezekiel had little patience for these affectations, even telling her to "shush" one night when she'd giggled too long at a silly observation I made concerning the weather.

She was preening. Always neat in appearance, she now took longer to braid and pin her hair each morning and occasionally expressed displeasure at not having a better wardrobe. Not a more fashionable one—she was still too much the preacher's daughter to hanker after flashy new clothing that would pass as quickly as a summer storm. What she wanted was simply more variety. A tan skirt instead of black-and-brown. A spring dress for Easter.

When she mentioned these yearnings in front of the fire, her father set his jaw but did not protest. Instead, he sucked on his pipe and said he'd perhaps go to Collingswood in a week to see what they had. It was enough to quiet her. Late winter storms still snowed us in and came roaring in so quickly a man on the road could be in trouble fast. He'd made his point. Good things come with risk.

Curiously, I felt no guilt for leading her on. We all hunger for tenderness. She offered it. I took it with no regard for its consequences. Sometimes, my conscience spoke to me and urged me to pull away and offer no more affection. I ignored the call. I was still recovering, I'd convinced myself, and Kate was a convenient salve. And I was giving her what she wanted — my attention — without making any commitments of any kind.

Whatever I gave her, the St. Claires returned a hundredfold. For slowly and surely, just as slowly and imperceptibly as the seasons change, they began to rub from me my burden of rage. Perhaps it was Ezekiel's preaching, gentle and sure, and always filled with new insights. Perhaps it was merely the normal, regular routine of their lives.

Whatever it was, it made me feel like I was welcome inside the kingdom instead of standing outside gazing in. I still did not share their conventional religion. Although I came to appreciate their love of the Bible and prayer, and even the sense of losing oneself in hymn-singing, my relationship with the Almighty was still tentative and distant.

If I found Him anywhere, it was in the wide open skies of Montana, the crisp, cleansing air, the companionship of family life. For these, a constant prayer of thanks hummed in my heart.

Winter gave way, ever so tentatively, to an early March thaw that teased us with warm days melting the snow like rivers, making us get comfortable, making us forget our fears that cold was yet to come. As soon as we reached that blissful state of contentment, the wind screamed and threw ice against our snug home.

It was during the thaw that we were treated to the most glorious day yet. All the snow was gone, the earth brown and tinged with the green of new shoots of grass and bud. The sun shone in a blue, blue sky with cotton clouds merrily skipping across the void. The wind blew fiercely up above, pushing the clouds across the sun, hiding it, letting it free, hiding it, letting it smile on us, a faraway battle that left us unscathed.

It was a Saturday, and Ezekiel asked me to accompany him to the barn to make an inventory of farm equipment for the spring planting, to see what was rusted and broke beyond repair. Walking the little way to the ramshackle barn was a walk through life itself. The air was as soft as baby's breath, the sweet touch of early spring kissing your cheek. The sun when it peeked beyond the clouds was warm on your shoulder. But there was no shade. The trees were still bare of leaves, casting strange shadows across the land as if another battle had been fought there and razed the field.

Wordlessly, Ezekiel opened the creaking door. Musty air greeted us.

"Seems a shame to go inside on a day like this," he said, leaning on a fence rail while he stared into the distance where the fields met the heavens.

"We could pull the equipment out here to look it over. We'll need the light anyway."

"Or we could put it off to another day," he said.

Ezekiel was not a man to put things off. When he set out to do something, he took care of it then and there, not waiting for better times or a more willing spirit. Thinking he was eager to enjoy the morning sun, I went to the barn door and looked inside.

"Wait here. I can drag a few of these out or look them over in the light of the door."

Before I had a chance to head to a rusty tiller, he stopped me. "No. Come here. I want to talk to you."

My eyes narrowed. Slowly, I walked over to him and stood beside him. Both of us stared ahead, not at each other.

"It's time for me to be moving on," he began, startling me. "To China. To preach and set up a mission. I've felt a calling for some time now, and I've stayed here too long because of selfish reasons."

His wife and son's graves had been holding him back.

"When would you go?"

"I've been thinking of it and planning for awhile. Before you came. Before we started building the new meeting hall."

"Does Kate know?"

"Yes." From the way he said it, I could tell she did not approve. "I don't want her to go with me."

If Ezekiel didn't want his daughter to go, it was because the trip would be too dangerous. Kate was right. He embraced danger.

"Do you want me to talk to her?"

He gave me a swift look, almost angry. "I can talk to her on my own," he said. He scrutinized me, looking me up and down as if we'd just met and he was taking the measure of me. "It would be easier on her if she had a good reason to stay here."

His gaze did not leave me. I knew what he was saying. He wanted to know if I'd commit to Kate, if I'd offer her the reason to stay. I didn't say anything but picked up a dried limb fallen from a nearby tree.

After awhile, he sighed and looked away.

"Those letters you got—if you have no intentions for Kate, you should make that clear."

Eleanor's letters. Leo's letters. His latest had arrived just a day ago, reminding me of the Walsh film, The Big Trail, about to start filming. It was a short letter, and I'd planned on answering it this afternoon, unsure of what I'd say. He'd also included several hundred dollars—he told me he'd used what he needed of what I'd sent him and didn't want to think of me hurting due to an "overgenerosity of spirit." I'd shared with him the news of my bank's collapse.

Ezekiel filled the silence, picking up fallen branches as he talked, "When I married my Joan, I thought of her as a good helpmate, someone who'd assist me in my life's work." He broke the limb in two. "Then I came to love her."

I said nothing. We both continued picking up deadwood for kindling. It hadn't been our original task, but it would serve.

"Perhaps I'll do the same again," he continued. "Widow Perkins comes every Sunday and has asked me to stop by for afternoon coffee."

"You'd take her with you to China, you mean?"

"If she'd have me."

"But you hardly know her."

"I hardly knew Joan." His arms were now full of the dried wood. Mine were nearly full as well. He looked me in the eye. "Kate's like her. Solid. Dependable. Good. She's got her feet firmly planted. Once she says she'll do a thing, you don't need to wonder."

"I know."

"When I go, I'd like to know Kate's taken care of. I've not asked much of you since you've come here."

This was true. Any work I'd done had not been at his request but at my offer.

"But I ask this of you: Think about what I just said."

ଔ

I did think about what he said. I spent virtually every day thinking about it after our conversation. Ezekiel reinforced his words by visiting with the widow Perkins several Sundays in a row. He was setting an example, showing me that he could court a woman he didn't love, so I should be able to do the same.

My thoughts about Kate, meanwhile, drifted into a less noble avenue. I found myself watching her, the way she moved, the way her bosom swayed as she whipped batters, the way her skirts hugged her hips. I did not think of loving her the way Ezekiel wanted, but I did think of loving her. I wondered how she'd be, compared to Eleanor. I know it was a bad thing to compare like that. But I was a man, after all. And it was a kind of victory to have those thoughts after Eleanor had busted me up inside.

Kate, meanwhile, was unabashedly opposed to her father's wooing of the Widow Perkins. It wasn't that she disliked Ida Perkins, she told me one afternoon when her father was gone. It was that she felt he was "leading her on."

A curious choice of words considering that this could have been what I was doing with Kate. She was comfortable enough now with our friendship to share her hopes and dreams on afternoons while she sat outside peeling potatoes or apples or tending the garden. She was comfortable enough to reach for my hand as we sat before the fire at night, after her father had gone to bed.

She wanted to see the world. She wanted to leave Devil's Rock and lead a school, or even study to become a doctor. She'd heard about women becoming doctors instead of nurses. She had a healing touch—I remembered it from my first days there. Always Kate dreamt of leading, not following, of striking out against the wind.

I tried to follow Ezekiel's example. Kate *was* a good woman, and attractive too. Why shouldn't I fall in love with her, soul as well as body? I looked forward to seeing her when I came in from working with Ezekiel. I enjoyed her talk, her music, her company.

Ezekiel could be right—thinking of love like the seeds we planted, to be harvested later.

Throughout the days of quickening spring, I tried to imagine myself settled down with Kate. But, more often than not, my thoughts drifted to settling in the bedroom with her. Beyond that, I saw no life together. No Kate by my side, fighting the battles of the world. No children at our feet. Those images would not come, and if I forced them, a terrible emptiness clawed at me.

All winter, I'd avoided writing Milqueton, afraid I'd start to write things I shouldn't, things that would bring him sadness, that would make him think I'd been backsliding into the dark path. On a day when sunshine wouldn't let sadness live, however, I finally sat down to write in the quiet of the afternoon.

Leaning against the side of the barn away from the cabin, where no one could see me, I told him I was well and in "God's hands, or more specifically, the hands of one of His servants." I wrote about Ezekiel and Kate, telling Milqueton I knew he'd like them. I told him I'd helped build the meeting house and hoped to help more. "Beyond that I am not sure where my travels will take me."

As soon as I'd penned those words, the wind rattled the window. My pulse quickened. My travels — who was I fooling? When I thought of traveling, it was back to California, to her. But here, there was only one "travel" to be talked about in the St. Claire household, a distant journey fraught with peril. It would be the ultimate crusade, as far away from my past as I could get. Why not?

My barren heart would not give bloom to love for Kate, but my mind took hold of this seed and coaxed it into a wild plan. I owed the St. Claires a debt for taking me in.

What on earth held me fast where I was?

Only one thing, or rather, one person. Now I longed for her to write, damning me to hell. That would have cut my ties completely.

Folding the note to Milqueton, I closed my eyes and offered up a wordless prayer. Eleanor had no claim on me. She had to let me go. God help me — help me let *her* go!

For a long time I sat and waited for a voice to tell me what to do. The sun embraced me with its late day warmth. In the distance, I could see a speck of a man moving among his fields, placing hope in the ground. The same ground beyond the mountains that she walked on. I wouldn't be free until I left it.

There was simply no other way. I had to leave. Now sure of my break with the past, I penned one other letter, this to Leo thanking him for his help, wishing my good friend well, and telling him I was headed overseas, not likely to return to Hollywood or the film business ever again.

I placed the letters in envelopes and made ready to walk into town.

୧

In the weeks ahead, I was a child with a secret, smug and self-satisfied. At last I had the formula to rid myself of Eleanor forever — leave the continent upon which she walked. It seemed like the ultimate revenge, all the more gratifying because she would never know it had been visited upon her. It set up a satisfying possibility—that one day, years in the future when time had built a callus over both our hearts, I would be able to say, "Oh yes, I was in China during those years," and perhaps her jaw would drop as her illusions did as well, and any time spent pining for me would be doubly painful as she realized I'd not pined for her.

If my own plans were hidden, Ezekiel's were plain and on the move.

In what was a weekly ritual, Ezekiel handed the collection money over to his daughter after Sunday services. She was in charge of buying supplies, and she budgeted the money out with scrupulous care, telling him exactly what he could afford, and what had to wait.

After the crowd dispersed from their usual post-meeting social, Ezekiel solemnly handed her the collection basket, and she earnestly counted it, standing behind a table at the front of the room while we sat in two chairs watching her. Every week, she would announce the take with no emotion. Sometimes, it was hardly more than five dollars. Once, it was twenty. Another time, it was only a dollar-seventy-five.

Depending on the amount, Ezekiel would then express his desires.

"I need to get some wood for a fence," he said one Sunday. "The children should have a garden."

And then she handed over virtually all of the cash.

Some Sundays, when the take was low, he said nothing. Or he would mention an inconsequential item that would hardly cost more than a few pennies. Some thread to mend his jacket or the children's aprons. These were more reminders for Kate to do than to buy. She would be the one pulling the thread through the cloth when it was mending time.

On one of these Sunday afternoons in early May, when the collection had come to ten dollars and fifteen cents, Ezekiel slapped his knees in sheer joy and stood abruptly. "Then I can order those books!"

He wandered to one of the tall windows that let in the brilliant sun. It was the first sunny Sunday after many rainy ones and the meeting house had been full with people who'd stayed inside during bleaker weekends. Although still cool, the blue skies gave off a hopeful sheen. People felt warmth would be here to stay soon, even though I was told it could be the end of May before you could count on the heat. Ezekiel had preached well, too, inspired perhaps by the weather and the crowd.

He'd talked of new beginnings, of finding the extraordinary in the ordinary, of being content with the everyday.

"What books?" I asked.

He turned and grinned, glad for the question.

"Mandarin translations of the Bible."

"For father's missionary trip." Kate said it defensively, as if she wasn't yet convinced it was a good idea.

"It's a dangerous land," I offered. I didn't follow world events closely, but I knew enough from reading headlines at the general store and catching a bit or two on the radio the proprietor owned. China wasn't a place for the fainthearted.

"The Lord has promised good to me," Ezekiel quoted, smiling at his daughter. "But you're right, John. It is a dangerous place. Too dangerous for an old man to take his only daughter."

"Father!" Kate looked down, not at him.

"You'll not go," Ezekiel said forcefully. "Not unless we have more in our party."

"*You'll* be alone without me! Why is that different?"

"Far better for a man alone than a woman. If something should happen to me, and you were with me, I'd die a worried man. You don't want that for your father, now do you, Kate?"

"I don't want you to go alone."

"Someone needs to look after the mission here. Besides, I might not go alone."

"You can't possibly think Ida Perkins will go with you. She has arthritis in her knees! She caught pneumonia last year and still isn't recovered!"

"She's stronger than she looks." But Ezekiel said it with no conviction.

I'd noticed that Ida had not attended this Sunday, nor the last two.

"She's no such thing. It would be unfair to ask her to go. Far better for me to accompany you." Kate stomped her foot. "Me and John!"

"Who will look after the mission?" Ezekiel asked.

Me and John — she thought of us together.

"We'll have no problem handing the mission over. I can think of two families who'd eagerly take on the responsibilities," Kate said defiantly. Her eyes flashed with anger, and her toe tapped the floor.

Ezekiel snorted. "Huh! The Porters and the Andersons you're thinking of."

An angry nod from Kate.

"They'd want the job for the extra money. I don't see them taking the same care...."

"Father, don't judge them. They're good people." She folded her hands over her chest.

Today, she wore a white blouse that hugged her sturdy figure and accented its soft curves. Three rows of tight lace lined either side of the straight line of mother-of-pearl buttons. Her Sunday skirt was heavy black wool. It went nearly to her ankles where her feet were shod in winter boots. She was staring her father down. And she won.

His face softened. His smiled returned. "All right, Kate. You might be right about them. But I'm still not wanting to take you. I've got Ida."

"Huh!" Kate walked to the window, too angry to speak.

"When do you plan to go?" I asked.

"End of summer, if it can be arranged." Ezekiel started gathering the prayer books he distributed every Sunday.

Hearing her father cleaning up, Kate came back to the table and placed the money in a brown envelope and slipped it in a pocket inside her coat.

"What needs arranging?" I asked.

"Supplies ordered. Passage booked. And this taken care of..." He swept his arm around the church.

"And sponsors. Don't forget that. He needs to sign up sponsors to help foot the bill. The money from the mission won't be enough." Kate straightened chairs with sharp shoves along each row.

"The sponsors would come soon enough if I had more time to travel."

I knew what he meant. Once a week, Ezekiel set out for neighboring towns. I always figured he was going for supplies. But he must have been talking to other churches, trying to raise money. It was taking too long.

Looking at his tired face, I wondered why had I waited?

"You need a car," I said simply. "And I can drive you. That will be quicker."

"A car! John, where on earth will we get money for that!" Kate looked aghast.

"I have some money. It will be a gift to the mission. And I'll pay for passage for Kate and me," I announced. My grandfather's money, or at least the small part of it I now had, would at last go to the cousins he originally intended in his first will.

There, I'd said it. I wanted to go with them. With Kate, more specifically. She reddened, looked at me with gleaming eyes, and touched her hair. In the morning light, she looked lovely, a flower blooming in the spring, soon ready to be plucked.

Ezekiel's face broadened into a wide grin.

Chapter Twenty-Five

KATE HAD BEEN right about the Widow Perkins. Ezekiel asked her to marry him, and she turned him down. As much as she enjoyed his company, missionary work in China was a sacrifice she wasn't willing to make at that stage of her life. Persistent and stubborn, he tried again, and still she said "no." Kate was relieved.

I bought a fellow's old Ford in nearby Collingswood and fixed it up, using it to chauffeur Ezekiel from town to town so he could meet with fellow pastors about setting up sponsorship collections to fund his ongoing work once in China. I began to look forward to traveling to a foreign land, someplace where people looked and talked and acted differently.

Ezekiel gave in about turning the meeting house over to the Porters. After "praying on it," he decided it wasn't his place to decide who was worthy. If the Porters wanted it, he wouldn't stand in their way.

Driving around in the old Ford, smelling the just-turned earth and moisture-laden air, blossoms and pungent field odors—it made me optimistic about the future. I felt saved, as if I was on the right track for sure now, heading far enough from my troubles that they could not disturb me any longer, burying feelings that needed to die.

Time sped up as we made our final plans. Our tickets were purchased, sponsorships secured, supplies bought, connections made with a mission in southern China. All that remained was some last-minute shopping, and Ezekiel insisted that Kate and I do that in Billings where Kate could get the new clothes she had been hankering for.

But before that could happen, she was unexpectedly called to nursing duty. A young mother of three came down with scarlet fever. Kate offered to stay with her until the illness passed, taking care of her children while the husband was in the field from sunup until sundown.

Gone nearly two weeks with this corporal work of mercy, she returned to our house drained and exhausted. Ezekiel didn't like that look. He pressed some dollars into my hand before Kate and I took off for Billings.

"Take Kate out somewhere nice. She's tired and won't be seeing luxury for a long time."

In fact, she was so tired that she slept most of the trip into the city. But she happily shopped away the afternoon, buying at last the skirts and dresses she'd not had, and that few would appreciate in distant China.

After we'd piled the purchases in the trunk of the car, I sprang Ezekiel's surprise on her.

"We're not going home yet," I announced.

"What? It's late."

Lights in shops fought the shadows, but darkness was falling. Kate looked happy and confused, her head tilted a little to the right, strands of hair escaping from beneath her ruby-colored hat, a new purchase that made her look as sweet as a young girl on Easter morning.

"I'm going to take you out. Where do you want to go? To a restaurant?" I pointed down the street. "There's a steakhouse around the corner."

She smiled, and her face was so bright, I found myself wanting to kiss her.

"All right. Let's go."

I silently thanked Ezekiel for the money he'd pressed on me. Not because I needed it—I'd return it soon enough. But because it had planted the idea of taking Kate out to something nice. Maybe this was a good way to try to dredge from within my heart the feelings I knew she wanted. It would be like practice. Practice for the real moment of love.

We walked to the corner café arm in arm, like two old married folks out for an evening stroll.

A good start, I thought as I held out Kate's chair and then

took my own seat. The very act of sitting together in a restaurant with her was stirring some feelings in me already, a sense of anticipation, of wondering what was to come. It was all going so well, this little practice of mine.

She put down the menu and searched her pocket for a lacy handkerchief. She wiped the mist from her brow, smiled at me, and then replaced the handkerchief in her jacket. Smile turned to worried frown. Her hand lingered. She hesitated. And then, she pulled from the pocket a thin blue envelope.

"I forgot," she apologized. "I picked up the mail while I was in town."

My own smile froze. She handed me the envelope, and her eyes flit to its handwriting, then away again.

I took the envelope and stared at the California postmark, wanting to open it but not wanting to open it here. She saw my discomfort.

"Go on and read your mail, John. I'm still looking over this menu. So many things — I can't decide." She said it with false cheer.

When she picked up her menu, I let my smile fall. I slit the envelope with my thumbnail. I was angry, sad, frustrated — a parade of different feelings made their way through my pounding heart as I tore the note from its casing. Relief — it wasn't from Eleanor!

Dear Mr. Doyle:

I am Leo Bartenstein's son. I am sorry to tell you my father died a week ago. You might like to know he expired peacefully and in very little pain. I was with him at the end. He asked me to be sure to tell you that Mr. Walsh knows your name and you should mention my father to him when you apply for the position on his film. I am sorry for not being able to tell you more. I tried to remember it as best I could. I enclose a newspaper clipping about his death that I thought you might like to see. Yours sincerely, Benjamin Bartenstein.

Leo was gone. And up until his last moment, he'd been trying to help me get a foothold in new Hollywood. Had he done so because he liked me, or because he'd realized at last that sound was bringing with it good things, beautiful things? He couldn't be part of them, but he'd tried to make sure I would.

Dear Lord, don't let that be so. Let it be that he died thinking Hollywood's beautiful time was over, and he wouldn't be missing anything.

I remembered the last time I'd written—the note telling him I was going overseas. Had he read it? Or maybe his son had moved him to San Francisco to take care of him, and my note hadn't arrived. I should have gone to see him one last time. Poor Leo.

I swallowed and bit my lip.

"Anything the matter?" Kate asked me.

"Someone I knew passed on," I said. "That's all."

Kate reached her hand out and covered mine. "Oh dear, John. I'm so sorry. Was it someone you knew well?"

"Sort of." I didn't want to talk about it. Crap—I felt like talking to Leo. I felt like telling him I was sorry. I looked down at the newspaper clipping.

Cinematographer Leo Bartenstein, it read. He would have been happy with that—cinematographer and not cameraman. It talked about how he'd been born in Germany, raised in Brooklyn, worked in the studios in New York before coming west. It listed the movies he'd worked on, some I hadn't even realized. He'd married once and divorced, survived by one son, Benjamin Bartenstein of San Francisco. Passed away right after filming "Mexican Holiday." At least he was out of the coffin of the camera boxes....

But now he was in a real coffin.

My eyes clouded as I read. Kate said nothing, even shooed away our waiter so I could finish. I rubbed my eyes and removed my spectacles, then replaced them again.

Now my gaze caught sight of another story in the clipping, just the beginning of it. A snippet about an actress with a new "bundle of joy." Pauline Sloane, it read, was taking on the role of mother, bringing into her home the orphaned infant daughter of a distant cousin who had met with a tragic accident ...

I sat bolt upright. My face warmed. El had had the baby. Whose baby?

"We don't need to stay," Kate said. "You've had a shock."

I looked up at her, coming back to reality, angry to have El tear me away, angry at myself, too. "No, I'm all right. Just a little spooked, that's all. I'll be fine." I said it so fiercely that Kate was the one looking spooked now, but she went back to the menu and in a few minutes we ordered.

That's when that dinner ended for me, when I stopped remembering what I ordered — fish or fowl, steak or soup, I don't recall a bite — or even what I said. I know I talked with her, talked with some aching grin holding my face up, trying not to look in her eyes too much or she'd see — Kate was a smart one — she'd see that the note now in my pocket was sending out shoots to strangle my heart. She must have thought me crazed, hearing news of a friend's death and acting like I hadn't a care. But I could only pull off one act, and this was it — pretending not to be moved.

I must have rushed us through dinner because when we were done, Kate suggested we walk a spell. I know she said she wished we could stay longer. I know because she had to say it twice before it registered with me. I was still thinking of that clipping. Leo dead. El with the baby. *She'd had the baby.* Where was she now? What did the baby look like?

We ended up near the Bijou where a crowd was gathering for the evening show.

Kate pulled me there. Some movie whose name I didn't recognize. I found the money for the tickets, like a machine, not thinking, glad we would be headed in some place dark where I wouldn't have to keep pretending to be enjoying myself. My face hurt from the strain.

We hurried inside just as the screen crackled to life, and the lone piano player pounded out an overture of sorts.

"Come on. Hurry up," Kate whispered, rushing to find two aisle seats.

We sank into shadows. Thank god. Now I could think. Now I could rest.

Talkies were everywhere but in backwaters like this one. Here the silent movie still reigned, with some studios cranking out silents just for these old-fashioned theaters not yet wired for sound. A fitting way to celebrate my dead friend, by seeing a silent picture.

But no, this was not a good way to think of Leo. This was a mistake.

I sucked in breath. There she was. Larger than life. Staring out at me. Just me.

Her mouth opened, and her eyes lit up as she laughed. No sound came out, but I heard the laugh, the same one that had seduced me. It tripped down my spine and perfumed my nerves. These poor sods reading the intertitles didn't know what they were missing. She had a voice for film, a glorious voice, low and throaty.

I was the only living soul in that theater who knew what she sounded like.

Dressed in a shimmering satin gown, she glided across a ballroom with a short, balding man, gently making fun of him in a way that made the audience love her, not hate her. Her arms were bare, surely covered by makeup. The director caught her brilliance, following her around the room, filling the screen with her sad-happy smile. I thought of Leo, and it was as if he were behind that camera, pointing it toward her best side, capturing all her grace, forcing me to look at her ... to love her....

I closed my eyes but could not shut her out. I was alone in the theater with Eleanor. Nothing else existed but this torture. When I heard the audience react, I opened my eyes again.

She threw back her head and laughed again—*I swear I heard it! Little bells of laughter!* I didn't need the titles to hear her.

A dashing leading man with meticulously combed wavy

hair cut in, taking her hand and leading her around the floor in ways I never could.

Yet she had loved to dance with me. She had loved *me* to hold her.

She pouted and spoke, and the man mouthed his reply. Their dialog flashed before us:

—"Seems to me you should have asked me if I wanted to dance before you asked him!"

— "Why would I want to dance with *him*?"

The audience laughed, including Kate, whose deep, soft chuckle was as straightforward as Eleanor's was intricate.

She broke away and strode toward a nearby balcony, the phony lights of a cardboard city blinking below. He caught up with her.

—"Look here, Sally, I didn't travel halfway round the world just to have you treat me like a poor relation."

— "Don't flatter yourself, Mac. I treat poor relations *better* than I treat you."

Another laugh from the audience.

He swung around and took a step, then obviously thought better of it, the emotion cartoonishly playing out on his perfect features. Turning back, he pulled her to him in a Hollywood embrace. Her arms were limp at her sides at first, then moved up his while he kissed her.

What it must have been like to be on that set, to be a Leo behind the camera, following her, caressing her, embracing her with the lens! Sound everywhere—the director coaching her, musicians playing, construction of new sets nearby. What fun it must have been! I suddenly knew why Leo had mourned its passing so long and hard. It was a child's Eden, all joy and wonder.

And so it continued, image after image, her lithe figure glimmering in the dark, her face silent as stone but her voice speaking in my heart as I remembered.

I remembered her lips. They were soft and sweet. She smelled like oranges and rosemary. She needed to be loved. Just as much as I had needed her love. She and I were alike, damaged goods. No, prisoners. Hadn't she begged me to tell her how to escape? And I'd left. But I couldn't forgive …

The camera moved in for a close-up of Eleanor's face. Her large innocent eyes stared into the camera, her lips parted, her soul on display. Was that how she'd been as a child — wanting the world to love her and not understanding how cruel life could be? And the voice I heard, that no one else could hear, that velvety-tone, both sweet and seductive, forcing you to listen — *John, I love you. I need you now.*

I couldn't breathe. The theater was musty, filled with the dank odor of wet coats and smoke and perfume.

"Kate, excuse me." I made my way past her. Had to get out.

"You all right?" she whispered.

"Fine. Be right back."

I rushed up the aisle as the piano player began a tremolo. At the back of the theater, I made my way through the glass-paned doors to the cool, dark street. A light rain misted the night.

I sucked in the damp air, hoping to revive my parched spirit. Grief and regret overwhelmed me. I should have seen Leo before he died. And why hadn't I? Because it would have meant being tempted to see her too!

Why couldn't she leave me alone?

I stared into the night sky, cursing my past, cursing my decision to go to California, cursing my decision to leave it.

The cusp of spring with cold night air cruelly stealing the warmth of day. The night my mother died. Rain wiping away sunny happiness. Clouds and thunder, like the thunder in my heart when I'd run away. I'd told myself I wasn't going to take any more waiting and wondering when Earl would strike next. I'd set out down the road …

My eyes closed tight, and I held my breath.

Just a boy, and I'd felt a hundred. It hadn't been Earl I'd run from. It had been her. Leave, I'd told her. Let's go to Boston, where you're from. I have enough money for train fare, Mother. I've been saving. And she'd laughed and said, "You're so sweet, Johnny. What would I do without you?" But she'd refused to go with me!

The heavens felt closed to me. No prayers of mine had ever been answered in the past. Where were you, I wanted to cry at the unseen God, when my mother screamed out? Where were you when I sobbed silently into my pillow at night? Where were you when Pete was hurt and bleeding? Where were you when I was falling under Eleanor's spell?

Silence.

As a last gesture of defiance, I'd scooped some of Earl's change from his dresser top and added the coins to my meager pile. After tying my belongings in a sheet at the end of a pole, I tiptoed past my sleeping mother and left. When I got to the train station, I discovered I barely had enough money for my own fare, let alone hers too. It was nearly evening. Thunder rustled the skies. I could sleep in the train station and take off in the morning ...

A clap of thunder so loud I'd jumped. A ticket taker had laughed at me. Just some rain coming, son, he'd said. Nothing to get excited about. But it shook me so bad I couldn't stay there. It defeated me. And as I walked home, I had a bad feeling that I had to hurry before something happened, before the rain came, and before something, something evi l...

The rain had started just as I turned the corner to my house. It was a hard, noisy rain, so noisy that I didn't hear my mother until I was inside our little home. "I don't know where he went, Earl. I don't know, I don't know! For God's sake, Earl, let me out of here! Please, Earl, please!" Sobs, thunder banging, followed by her scream, Earl looking at me, picking up the shovel... You fucking bastard, let her out of there ...

If I hadn't left, if I'd stayed. If my mother had been a better woman. If she'd been strong and not weak. If life was fair. If I'd not been filled with so much anger. If I had been a better person myself, the sweet, different boy she'd thought I was. If I'd been there as I'd always been. If I hadn't left.

I don't know how long I paced, but it was long enough for Kate to come looking for me. With a troubled stare, she came out of the theater and put my coat around my shoulders.

"You'll catch your death," she said tentatively.

She could sense something was different, something had changed, and she didn't want it to hit her too quickly. That kind of feeling was an old friend to me by now.

"I'm sorry," I said, sliding my arms into the sleeves. "I needed some fresh air."

"You're upset about your friend... who died."

"Yeah. I guess so." I threw my head back and stared at the sky, vast and inviting. "C'mon. Let's walk awhile." I held out my elbow for her to grasp.

Smiling, she linked her hand through it. Her hand was warm on my arm, and I remembered how good her own lips tasted, how good it was to hold a woman.

We walked in silence past the bright lights of the Bijou, and as we walked my anger grew — at Leo for dying, at Eleanor ... for keeping me from him. At myself. Kate snuggled close to me, her shoulders rubbing mine. I put my arm around her.

Why shouldn't I have what Kate wanted to give? We were going to China together. We would probably marry there. It was only a matter of time before we were joined in both body and soul. Ezekiel expected it, as did Kate.

The rain increased in strength, moving from light drizzle to sudden downpour. I pulled her under the eaves of a nearby building and pressed her to the wall in a tight embrace. I kissed her as I'd never kissed her before, a deep kiss that left no doubt as to what I wanted.

My hands moved up her side and around to her linen blouse where I fumbled with the pearl buttons. She did not stop me. She responded by thrusting her bosom to me, by whispering my name. If I asked her, she would let me take her.

And I deserved her. I deserved to have a pure woman to make up for Eleanor. To make up for being used. Being good amounted to nothing.

"We can stay in Billings," I mumbled between wet kisses. "For the night."

Her grip tightened on my waist. "Yes."

We continued to kiss, desire growing with each press of

her lips against mine, her hands against my body. When I heard voices walking our way, I pulled back.

"Wait here." I squeezed her hand and rushed around the corner as passers-by talked about farm prices and taxes.

While she straightened her clothes, I went into the bright lobby of the Imperial Hotel. Out of a sense of perverse vengeance, I gave my grandfather's name and registered as Mr. and Mrs. Samuel Doyle. When the clerk asked me about luggage, I told him we were only going to be there the one night, and I'd fetch the bags from the car myself. I returned to Kate with cold determination in my heart.

Together, we walked back to the hotel in silence. This was doing the trick. I wasn't thinking about Leo or Eleanor. This was right. For me. For her.

Kate looked down at the worn red and gold carpet as we hurried through the lobby, not making eye contact with the clerk. She needn't have worried. The clerk might have been suspicious, but he looked away as we walked to the stairs, probably glad for the night's fee and not inclined to probe too deeply.

Upstairs, I unlocked our door and went inside first, throwing my coat on a chair by an oak veneer dresser. A metal-frame double bed was pushed against the wall to the right. The room was dark, only the wan illumination of a nearby street lamp casting a thin square of light through heavy curtains.

As soon as the door was closed, Kate left no doubt that she had made her decision to do this long ago and had only needed the invitation. She immediately took off her coat and started to disrobe with a naturalness that took my breath away.

While I sat on the side of the bed, she unbuttoned her shirt and skirt and let them fall away, revealing a soft, full body under a plain cotton slip. She stood before me like an offering. When I reached out to pull her to me, she began to unbutton my own shirt.

Desire coursed through my veins, my breath became

ragged. I embraced her on my lap and leaned her into the bed. Her eyes were open wide. She knew what she was doing and what she wanted.

Closing my eyes, I kissed her long and hard. God, it would feel good. How I had missed it. I deserved it.

"John," she murmured into my ear. "I love you so."

I love you so.

The rain beat a steady rhythm against the window, echoing her soft words. I love you so. The same words Robbie had spoken but that had been pulled from my gut. I love you so.

It is my baby, isn't it? It has to be. I love you so.

My eyes still closed, I held my breath. I saw Eleanor's face on the screen, her eyes staring at me, her heart accusing me. *Why did you abandon me, John? I love you so. Why did you run away – again?* Her voice seemed alive, in the room itself. For a moment, I thought it was Kate, her voice, the throaty sound of sensual pleasure mimicking Eleanor's own tones.

Why did you abandon me? I need you now. I love you so!

It was more insistent, more pleading. It would not be ignored.

It wasn't Kate. It was Eleanor.

My hands froze on Kate's shoulders.

"What's the matter?" she asked. Already, her voice trembled.

I sat up and ran my fingers through my hair, shivering in the cool room.

What the hell was I doing?

Kate sat up beside me and put her arm around me.

"Are you ill? You seemed sick in the theater." She stroked my back.

"No!" I shrugged her off and stood, buckling my belt.

Walking to the window, I stared out at the darkness as I leaned against the sill. Eleanor was there, somewhere. With the baby, maybe my baby. My heart was pounding so hard that I no longer heard the rain. I needed to leave. The anger was gone. I couldn't muster it. I wanted to. I wanted to be able to *not* forgive. I wanted to cherish the hurt, the injustice, so that I could make it right.

Make it right—how? By hurting Kate, innocent and loving Kate. That was no justice. That was more pain, and we'd all had enough. All of us. Me. Eleanor. Pete. Leo. My mother. And Kate... fresh Kate.

I wanted to run into the rain and let it wash me clean of everything. Clean of the hostility inside me and clean of the guilt I couldn't be rid of. Not the guilt for killing Earl. He'd deserved to die. The guilt for not being there at the one moment she'd needed me, the moment Leo needed me. I should have been there. If I had been there...

I should be there now. I had to go back. Leo had known it. He'd cleared the path for me. He might not have known about Eleanor, but he'd seen what I wanted. Maybe he had read my letter about going off to China after all, and decided that I wasn't meant for that life.

Without turning around, I whispered the words that I knew would knife Kate to the core.

"I can't go to China."

I heard her intake of breath, the bed squeak as she moved.

"Why not?" She came behind me and tentatively put her hand on my arm.

"There's something else I need to do."

There was no point in putting it off. A quick break was best. The truth was what counted, what always counted. I turned to her.

In the blue shadows of the room, her skin was milky white. Her eyes shone with unshed tears. She was beautiful, a goddess of strength and force and all that was good. And yet I'd been about to deliberately deceive her into thinking that I loved her so that I could make love to her. I'd wanted to hurt her. Pure Kate would have suffered just because my own soul had been crushed tenfold by people she didn't know. What had I become?

Her eyes blinked fast. "You'll stay—in Devil's Rock?" She sniffled. "I could stay with..." Her voice petered out. She knew I didn't want her to stay with me even before I told her.

"I'm going back to California."

"For your friend who died?" she whispered.

I shook my head. "Something else." No, *someone* else.

"I see." She turned sharply and went back to the chair to retrieve her clothes.

With quick movements that did not hide her anger, she pulled them on. Not looking at me, she took a deep breath.

When she was finished, she did not wait for me. "I'll meet you at the car." She strode from the room, letting the door slam behind her. By the time I'd locked the door, she was already through the front lobby and out that door as well.

The clerk raised his eyebrows when I paid our bill so suddenly, but he said nothing. By now, I was filled with the remorse that should have stopped me from ever leading her on. I had no right to hurt another just because I'd been hurt. I had no right to use my past as an excuse for any bad behavior. It was as if I'd learned nothing from Canfield or Milqueton or my own cruel experiences, and I angrily shook my head while I rushed to the car. I wouldn't let my past be wasted.

Milqueton had been wrong. I did need to dwell in the past. I needed to relive the awful moments so that I'd forever be reminded not to inflict them on another human being. Ezekiel had been wrong as well. Forgetting wasn't the key. Remembering was.

At last, I came to the car. She was already sitting in the passenger seat, staring stonily ahead. Her hair was plastered to her cheeks and forehead where the rain had drenched it. When I sat behind the wheel, she spoke without looking at me.

"I wish I didn't have to see you again. Ever."

I started the engine and began pulling the car into the street. "I'm sorry, Kate. I had no right to give you the impression that I was falling in love with you."

She let out a burst of laugh. "Don't be silly, John. You never told me a lie." She said it cynically, knowing full well I *had* lied, if not in words, then in deeds.

We drove past the theater where the doors opened with a

rush, and the crowd began to exit, couples laughing and talking, as in love as we were not. As if fearing that strangers would be able to see what she struggled to hide from me, Kate looked out the side window, away from the theater-goers.

"Father will worry," she said, and I stepped on the gas to go faster.

When we stopped at an intersection on the edge of town, I looked over at her. Tears shone on her cheeks. Her shoulders shook silently. I reached for her hand.

"Don't." She shrank from me and blew her nose into her handkerchief. "What makes you think..." She shook her head then let out a growl of anger. "I wish you could go away right now."

"I'm so sorry, Kate. You deserve someone —"

"Stop it!" She straightened her shoulders and stared ahead of her through the windshield. "Don't flatter yourself. I'm disappointed not to be able to go to China, that's all. I'd been counting on it. Father won't let me go now if you don't go."

She was lying, but the least I could do was let her keep her lie and her anger.

Billings receded behind us as I drove out to the dark roads that would lead us home. The night air smelled fresh and earthy and full of promise. Since it was late, no other cars were out beyond the city limits. The headlights cut the blackness, catching the trunks of trees in their glare, the lonely ribbon of road ahead.

After we drove in silence for a few minutes, I cleared my throat.

"I'll talk to your father about letting you go to China with him."

She laughed bitterly. "Do you think he'll listen to you now?"

For an hour, we rode in silence, lost in our own thoughts. Kate might as well have not been in the car with me — so far away was my mind. I plotted out how I'd get back to Eleanor, and every second that I wasn't headed in her direction made me sick with worry. I had to get back.

As we rounded the last curve toward Devil's Rock, I stole a glance at Kate. She sat with her hands in her lap, staring out the side window away from me. She was near the edge of her seat, as far from me as she could get. I couldn't blame her. I thought of things to say to offer comfort, but quickly discarded them. She was too stubborn and good to be insulted with false condolences.

At the cabin, Kate went to bed without a word. Ezekiel awakened and came out to greet us. When he saw Kate close her door, his sharp eyes looked at me full of accusations. I saw no point in delaying the blow.

"I told Kate tonight that I couldn't go with her to China."

A muscle in his jaw tightened then released. "Damn you, boy."

"But you have to take her with you. It's not fair — "

"Don't tell me what's fair."

For a moment I wondered if he'd ask me to go outside for the thrashing I surely deserved. But he wrestled for control, closing his eyes and, for the briefest time, holding his breath.

When he opened his eyes again, he let out a long sigh. "The Lord's work is more important than you or me," he said.

"I can help you get ready, take you to California to board the ship."

He glanced at Kate's closed door. "I don't think that would be wise."

We stood, facing off, neither of us knowing what to say to make things right or settle the score.

When Ezekiel looked as if he'd head to bed, I tried again. "I know it's not my place to tell you, but Kate would be a great help to you in your mission. I think you'd regret leaving her here."

"I think you'll be the one regretting that, son." He held his head high and walked to his room.

Ⴉ

For an awkward day, I was forced to linger. The Ford needed new brakes, and it took me all morning just to find a shop that could replace them. And I finally got around to having a new lens ground for my spectacles. By the time I got home that night, I wondered if the St. Claires would even take me in again. I half expected to see my belongings sitting outside the door.

Kate was too proud for that. Her pride was no sin. It was a virtue. She aggressively ignored me, turning away when I came in the door, talking loudly to her father as if I weren't in the room. They didn't ask when I'd leave. They didn't ask me *to* leave.

I curled up on my cot while they sat in front of the fire and had their silent revenge. I'd be gone soon enough.

Before I drifted off to sleep, I heard Ezekiel talking to Kate about the China trip. It was clear she was going. Perhaps he'd decided the moment I broke my bad news to him but wouldn't give me the satisfaction of knowing.

Kate's mute scorn was a gift. Had she moped and wept, I'd have been burdened with even more guilt for wounding her. Her loathing set me free. There's an honesty in hatred.

In the morning, I offered to help her bring in wood, but she brusquely refused by shaking her head. Without a word, she fed the fire, lit the stove, and made coffee. She did not set out a mug for me. When her father came to the table, she talked of how she'd fix a broken tiller that day, and then they'd both walk to the Church of the Nazarene five miles south of Devil's Rock in order to line up some last-minute sponsorships.

They were back to where they'd been before I arrived on the scene—tightly wound around their routine and their mission. I was now a stranger there.

I tied my things into a jacket and tossed them in the Ford.

I stepped back over the threshold. Kate and Ezekiel sat across from each other sipping hot coffee, the muted morning light pouring through the southern window, touching Kate's hair so that it shone like spun sugar. Her jaw was tightly set, her eyes bright, her shoulders square.

Kate would never really be any man's wife. She'd always

be her own woman, staring clear-eyed into the future, weathering storms, moving forward with a kind of rugged stubbornness regardless what lay ahead. Now that she had learned the fickleness of love, she'd not be tempted by it again. Kate was meant to be no one's partner but her father's. And when he left this earth, she'd forge on without him.

"I'm leaving," I said. Still they did not turn to me. "Thank you for all your help. Good luck."

Nothing. I turned to go.

Then, to my back, Kate spoke. "Farewell, John."

Neither came outside to watch me drive away.

Chapter Twenty-Six

I WAS ON THE ROAD for a week. The Ford broke down just over the Idaho state line and once again when I entered California. Sometimes, gasoline stations were so far apart that I'd run out of fuel on an empty road and have to walk to fill the tank enough in order to lumber forward. Sometimes, there were no roads at all, just rutted paths through fields. Impatient, I cursed each delay, kicking up dry dust when I had to wait for a lift into a town, or to a repair shop. I even considered abandoning the car and hopping a train, my trusty method of the past.

I tried phoning along the way, too. But the few times I was able to try, no one answered at Sloane Hall.

At last, I came upon the familiar roads, the known landscape. The chaparral-covered mountains. The flat valleys. Life and death crammed up against the ocean, cast in shadows, lit in blazing sun. I was home. I felt it in my bones. Leo had been right to beckon me back. I didn't know if I'd find work on the Walsh film, but somebody would surely have me if I mentioned Leo's name. Hollywood was filled with newcomers with less skill than I had. And they'd not remember any mistakes I'd made in the past.

Thanks, old friend, I murmured into the breeze.

ରଃ

The sun shone brilliantly as I drove up the winding road to the estate. With every turn in the road, my pulse quickened.

As I neared the top, I tried to tame my anticipation by reminding myself the house would be quiet. Marta herself would probably be in the kitchen, and Eleanor might be resting. If they weren't there, I'd find out from those who occupied the estate where they'd gone.

Around the last bend, a sharp elbow turn, and then I'd

see it, the large awkward "hacienda" with its red roof and stucco walls.

Craning my head to see, I caught a glimpse of wall.

But not much else.

Sloane Hall was a shell. The house was reduced to a burnt-out corpse of its former self.

Half the roof was missing, and what used to be Eleanor's room was completely gutted. The windows were all broken and the outer walls tarnished by huge smears of soot.

My hands gripped the wheel as I stopped the car and just stared.

The veranda roof had collapsed onto the porch itself, barring entry. Through the gaping windows, only black and ash were visible. The smell of smoke still singed the throat.

Quickly, I got out and turned to look at the garage. It, too, was gone, in far worse shape than the house itself. Only a few timbers marked its outline, and the blackened shapes of vehicles were ghosts in the open bays. The Duesenberg was still there but only in outline, its long, graceful nose a charred frieze that looked as if it would disintegrate with the barest breath of air.

In a daze, I wandered toward the house, now as unsure as I'd been confident during my drive up the road. Where my heart raced in anticipation before, now it pounded in fear. Perhaps I'd waited too long.

My god.

Because I could not enter the house, I walked around its southern rim toward the kitchen. Oddly, those rooms in the back were the least effected by the blaze. The kitchen was covered in ash, and its walls darkened, but the table still stood in the middle of the room as if Marta and Julia would lay out our dinner there at any moment. Marta. Julia. Were they gone? Had they been lost, too?

"Marta?" I called, as if she would come from some hidden place to explain it all.

Around to the back of the house, the sun room and great room were nearly roofless, light streaming into dusty space, making the charred interiors gray and iridescent. I entered the house through an open door on the sun room and walked the eerie hallways. The foyer and curved staircase were coal-black, the steps collapsed in the center. What fire had not destroyed, water had taken.

In the great room, Eleanor's mother's portrait was almost completely gone, darkened beyond recognition, all except her eyes which stared out upon the destruction now with what seemed like a horror-stricken gaze. Looking outside, I noticed the pool was empty except for some green brackish water at the very bottom.

A frantic scene played out before my eyes, the house on fire, pumping trucks arriving, using the pool water to contain the blaze until there was no more water and no more hope.

My breath came fast. Had they made it out alive? Was it my destiny to always be too late?

Christ, what an ass I'd been—listening for "voices." I couldn't swallow. I couldn't breathe. I couldn't think.

From my vantage point, I could see across the southern end of land where the vineyard began. Although the vines nearest the house looked trampled and dark from ash, healthier growth extended into the distance. Just visible beyond these was the red roof of the field house.

The field house. It was still intact.

I rushed out back and began walking through the rows of vines, then running, in such a hurry that I didn't care, I didn't feel, if vines ripped my sleeves or scratched my face.

Breathing hard, sweating, unable to feel anything but reckless hope, I made my way through the warm field. Sun beat down on my head and back, the dirt was hard and starved for water, the air smelled of sulfur. I was dimly aware of crickets chirping and a mourning dove cooing in the distance.

My lungs burning as I came upon the house, I dropped my hands to my knees and bent over to catch my breath. Perspiration clouded my vision and rolled off my nose. And then, I heard it. A woman's voice.

"Who's there?" she called in a low, throaty question.

I bolted upright. It wasn't Marta's voice. My eyes stung from the ash, the effort, that voice. Her voice.

Barely in view, she sat on a stone bench in back of the house, her back to me. Her hair was no longer blonde but chestnut brown, even shorter than before, almost boyish, in graceful waves near her neck and ears. Her dress was simple—short-sleeved, white. She wore a satin ribbon in her hair.

In that moment, I finally felt the touch of God's hand on my shoulder. No longer did hate and resentment simmer below the surface in my soul. No longer did I feel the need to set things right, to wrap myself in justice and exult upon some supernatural stage. There was no good and evil before me from which to choose. There was only truth and untruth. And the truth was that I still loved her.

Seeing Eleanor alive—it poured through me, golden and thick and light as honey. *You're free.* The wind whispered through the trees. *You're free.*

And so was she. Needle marks no longer scarred her arms. Instead, raw orange patches licked the skin up to the elbow. Her fingers looked stiff and knobby as she manipulated two knitting needles covered in gauzy pink yarn. She'd suffered. Real suffering. Not self-indulgent days of pitiful longing for her comfortable girlhood.

This alone caused a stab of pain, that she'd had to suffer, and I asked, too late, that the cup of bitterness pass over her. Too late. She'd suffered. That was done now.

She must have heard me breathe and twisted my way. Her neck was burnt as well, but her face, angelic and innocent, a smile teasing at her lips, was untouched. Her blue eyes stared straight at me.

And did not see.

"Marta?" she asked softly in my direction.

Breathing halted. Time stopped. So much risked on this next moment, so much at stake...

"El," I breathed.

Her smile froze. She stood, dropping the knitting to the ground. Shaking, confused, her mouth opened, her hands groped air, and she took a step forward, nearly stumbling on her knitting.

I am here. El. I am here.

I ran to her.

She felt my face, a gurgle of child-like laughter pouring from her throat as her worn fingers passed over my forehead, nose, eyes, mouth, shoulders. She breathed in.

She laughed out loud, laughter mixed with tears streaming from dulled eyes.

My own eyes clouded, and words caught in my throat. I kissed her fingers as they flitted by my lips again. I laughed too, and cried, and held her fast.

Oh Eleanor. How I missed you. How you hurt me, how you cut me to the core. Even the remembrance of pain was sweet in that moment of reunion.

Her head rested on my shoulder. Her calm tears gave way to sobs as she gripped my arms. "You shouldn't have left me," she cried. "You shouldn't have left."

I rocked her, my eyes closed. And it felt... it felt like dancing with her in the moonlight that first time, the night I'd said I loved her, when I hadn't known what love was, what it required of you.

"I know, I know," I murmured. I led her back to the bench where I sat beside her, my arm around her shoulder while she leaned into my chest. I kissed the top of her head.

"The house is gone," she said at last.

"I saw it. You were hurt in the fire."

Her hands flew up to her eyes, and she touched the closed lids. "The doctor says these could heal. I see shapes. I could see more with time."

"Is Julia gone?" I wanted to ask about the baby but couldn't bring myself to touch that pain.

She nodded. "I don't know where she is. I don't want to know."

"Robbie?" I had to ask. I had to know.

"Robbie is dead." She spoke flatly. "He … he started the fire."

"*He* did it!"

Her body shook with silent weeping, remembering something too painful to articulate.

"*Señor* Doyle! I thought I heard you. I could not believe." Marta's strong voice cracked as she came out of the house. "Thank God you are back."

I looked at Marta, her hands clasped in front of her dark dress, her eyes pleading with me.

From inside the house, I heard a baby cry. Thank God. Until that moment, I'd not realized how much I wanted that baby.

"You must see her," Eleanor said, grabbing a nearby cane, walking steadily away before I could object. I started to follow her, but Marta shook her head.

"Can she…?" I looked at Marta.

Marta nodded. "She can do many things now that she could not do before."

"Tell me what happened."

Marta's face crumpled, the memory terrible for her as well. When she spoke, her words came in a rush:

"We went away after you left, so that he would not find us. But we came back, after the baby was born. Only for a short time, we came back. Just a short time!" She shook her head, as if this should have afforded them protection.

"We came back to make the arrangements to sell Sloane Hall. She had the baby, and we were going to move someplace quiet. She had a little money, and she said she would find something to do. I told her I would find something to do. She said, yes, I would watch the baby while she worked.

"*Señor* Morgan, he had not found us, and we thought he was gone for good. Julia, she said he had not been around. But he did come around. He wanted to see the baby."

"Julia told him you were back?"

Marta shook her head again. "I do not think so. I think she was done with him. Ha! —she thought she'd become a star, but she has the accent, like me. Not the good voice. She was too late for the film work now that it has sound. She was afraid, like us, no work, little money..."

"And Morgan?" I prompted her.

"*Señor* Morgan came back." She shivered. "But the *Señorita*, she would not let him near her. Would not see him... ." She drew in her lips, fighting for control. "She locked the doors and the windows. Oh *Señor* Doyle, he banged on them so hard, I thought he'd bring the house down. He was so angry. Fierce and filled with hate." She wiped a tear from her eye. "But he went away, and we thought, this is good, he is gone. But he was not gone....

"She had to go to San Francisco, to meet with the lawyers she'd trusted with her mother's estate, to have them take care of this house, too. Oh, she was so fresh and wanting to do things. She changed, you see, after you left. Your leaving, it was so much pain for her, *Señor*. She thought you would stay, and she would talk to you, and it would be all right after a little while...."

Which was precisely why I had left that night. I knew she'd tempt me to stay.

"After she cried and cried, she thought you would come back some day. So she decided to be the woman you had loved, whether you came back or not. I know that is what she wanted for herself. And she did it at last. No drinking. No more of any of that. A quiet life. And she'd had a good birth for the baby, not too much pain, not too long. Like a gift from God for her hard work. She was so happy to be getting started again. She told me, 'I don't need very much at all' like it was a surprise to her to live so small....

"After the trip to San Francisco, she came back late at night, and I picked her up at the station, and she was very happy because she thought we would get a good price for the home, and the lawyers had been very kind to her, happy to help because they knew her family, but ... *Madre de Dios*! Even before we reached the top of the hill, we could smell it. Burnt wood. It choked us. We could see clouds. But they were not

clouds. It was smoke. The house was on fire. He was there —
holding a torch and laughing as the flames leaped into the air!

"When he saw her, he stopped. He was drunk. Or worse,
I do not know. All I know is he decided he wanted her after
all. He threw down the torch and ran to her, trying to hold
her...." She shuddered. "And Julia came running from the
house, just in time, before the fire went to her room...."

Marta closed her eyes for a second.

"*Señorita* looked at her and cried, 'Where is the baby?'
Julia said nothing, just looked back at the house, and we knew.
The baby was still in there!

"*Señorita* pulled herself away, knocking *Señor* Morgan
down, and she shook Julia. 'Where did you leave her? Where
is she?' she cried, over and over.

"Julia said, 'in her room,' and she was crying, too, the first
time I've seen that whore cry over anything but herself!"

Marta took a deep breath. "I thought all was lost then. I
thought we were all dead — that *Señorita* Sloane would kill
Julia and not live herself. She slapped her, and Julia fell to the
ground weeping, saying, 'I'm sorry.'

"But then *Señorita* Sloane, she looked up at the house,
those flames everywhere, from the windows, the door, the
roof, the smoke so thick it shut out the moon and stars, the
sound of timbers breaking, the house becoming ash before us.
She stared at it, the heat almost too much to bear even there on
the piazza. She put her hands to her head, wild with grief.

"And then, something changed. She stood straight, as if
touched by lightning. She stopped wailing. She... listened. She
grabbed a shawl from the car and dipped it in the fountain
She wrapped it around herself, and I... I..." She said something
in Spanish, as if she were still there on that horrible night.

"I cried out to her that all was lost. But she would not
listen. And then, oh it was horrible, *Señor* Doyle, it was
something I never wanted to see — she ran to the door, the very
door of hell itself, away from us, away from me. She would
not live without the baby."

So that was how her injuries happened. As she'd raced to

save the child.

"*Señor* Morgan, he cried like an animal when she got away. Oh, now he wanted her alive! The bastard! He'd tried to kill her, and now he wanted her alive." She spat. "So he stood and ran after her.

"It was a miracle she saved the baby. She told me later that the baby's room, on the back of the house, was not ablaze, that it didn't even have so much smoke. So she wrapped that precious babe in the wet shawl, and the angels, they led her from the house, because by then..."

She wept openly now. "By then, the fire had seared her eyes and burnt her legs and arms. She came out from the smoke and flame, like a corpse covered in ash, and for one moment I thought she would crumble to dust before my very eyes. She fell, coughing and hurt, and I took the baby.... I shouted at Julia to run for help."

"Robbie?"

"I saw him in the window of her bedroom, screaming as the fires consumed him. And I was glad to hear him scream. He deserved that punishment. *El Diablo.* He jumped to his death."

Marta's face smoothed suddenly. I looked up. Eleanor was returning, walking slowly, cooing to a red-haired infant in her arms. Red hair, like my mother's. Marta rushed to help guide them to me.

I kissed the child's head. I touched El's arm, still scarred. I touched *her*, not the dream of her. It shook me.

I looked at Eleanor, beaten, new. A phrase from scripture returned to me, the one Milqueton had been fond of quoting. *Whom shall I send*, the Lord asked in Isaiah. *Here am I, Lord. Send me.*

Is that what she'd thought before dashing into the flames? *Here am I. Send me.*

And here was I.

All the times I'd felt sent into battle, raging against injustice — no one had called me to that service except my own bruised heart. When she'd been called, it had been for real sacrifice.

In that moment, this was the truth I saw: I loved her. That love could be a firestorm. Or it could be, like the child's room on that terrible night, a sanctuary.

She'd rescued herself, as well as her child, and was clean now, but there would come a day when peace might no longer satisfy her, when ever my love would no longer satisfy her. She would want more, and the struggle would begin again. I knew this in my bones. I knew it as sure as I knew that child was my own.

I saw years of wondering and worrying, years of hopes dashed and revitalized, sleepless nights and struggles to find reasons to stay. I had, after all, lived with an alcoholic, and even in the euphoria of being reunited with my own drug — Ellie's love — I knew that changing this woman's ways and needs would always ultimately be beyond my power. It would always be up to her.

The baby gurgled. My heart filled.

Here was my destiny. To pay, at last, for the crime of indecision, of holding back when I should have stepped forward, of acting when it was too late to make a difference.

All those years at Canfield had not been enough. I'd pay now. And God, I wanted to pay. I wanted to lay my life down on that altar and give myself up to that sacrifice, not knowing if the sword would be stayed or if it would pierce my heart. There was a peace in this.

Here am I. Send me.

And so, reader, I married her.

About the author

Libby Sternberg writes literary fiction, women's fiction, romantic comedy and teen mystery.

The first of her teen mysteries, *Uncovering Sadie's Secrets*, was an Edgar finalist and a Young Adult Top 40 Fiction Pick by the Pennsylvania School Librarians Association. Her teen mysteries have been called "taut, vivid and stirring" (Library Journal), "simply a delight to read" (Romantic Times Book Club), "lively and captivating" (VOYA) and "an entertaining original" (Romance Reviews Today).

Her humorous women's fiction books, written under the name Libby Malin, have been called "hilarious," "inspired," and "laugh-out-loud funny" by book blog reviewers. One has been optioned for film by a major studio.

A native of Baltimore, Maryland, she now lives in Pennsylvania. She is married and has three children. Her website is at LibbySternberg.com.

Why and How I wrote Sloane Hall:
Don't read unless you've finished the novel; spoilers lie ahead!

I think any time you write a book like this, which clearly references a well-loved, well-read original, you struggle to keep it feeling new, as if it had never been told or written before.

When I decided to retell the story of *Jane Eyre*, inverting the genders of the main characters, I knew that some readers might have a problem with that. But, I wanted the story to be fresh.

I'm a huge *Jane Eyre* fan. I've reread the book countless times. I've watched numerous film versions of it. It's the emotional journey of the book that has stayed with me more than the actual details. I wanted to recreate that journey. I didn't think changing the time period or setting was enough to accomplish that.

I chose Hollywood in the 1920s because film stars make up a kind of American "gentry." And I chose the year film was making the shift from silent to sound to create a background tension that makes Eleanor's circumstances precarious. She's about to make her first talking picture, a very stressful time for silent stars of that period, many of whose careers didn't survive the change. That background tension helps create the sense of something ominous, something foreboding, about to happen that I remember feeling as I read the original. But, of course, there is no lunatic spouse in the attic, only poor Eleanor's inner demons.

In many ways, in fact, Eleanor is both Bertha Mason and Edward Rochester melded together. She's the mercurial head of the manor and the tormented alter-ego she hides from the world.

This was one of the most challenging aspects of writing the novel, coming up with the awful secret, the climactic moment to parallel when Rochester reveals he's married to insane Bertha. I kept asking myself: how did 19th century readers feel when reading that scene? Would their sensibilities about mental illness be the same as ours today? I think not. I believe today's readers probably feel most sympathetic to Jane in that scene and are, perhaps, troubled by Rochester's deception and the handling of his mentally-ill wife, even if they can spare a measure of sympathy for him, too.

I wondered if the original readers, however, had much more sympathy for Rochester in that scene, and experienced, perhaps, an "eww" moment when contemplating his wife's state. I wanted to recreate the feelings that 19th century readers might have had – equal measures of sympathy and disgust. I hope I succeeded.

While that scene was a challenge, the one where Jane hears Rochester calling to her across the countryside was easier to replicate. Since we're dealing with film in my book, I had several possibilities. At first, I wrote the scene as a "talkie," where John would really hear Eleanor's voice coming from the screen. But then, I thought, no, only *he* should hear it.

No one else. Since many movie theaters in the countryside hadn't yet been wired for sound, it made perfect sense that John would be going to a silent flick. And when he sees Eleanor on the screen—that's the moment he hears her, beckoning to him, and only him. It was an *aha* moment for me to realize the film should be a silent one in that scene.

There are other plot differences between the original and my tale, but a deeper divergence involves John struggling with the idea of forgiveness far more than Jane did. John has a much, much harder time letting go of his resentments of those who had wronged him in the past. This resentment and simmering anger gets him into trouble and ultimately drives his transformation. He has to learn to conquer it before he can ultimately accept Eleanor into his heart. And, of course, she has to conquer many inner demons, as well. I think her struggles are a bit more "on stage" than Rochester's were.

But, on the similarities list, John, like Jane, is a contrarian and a realist, especially about himself. He's a gentle soul wanting to be loved and to return that love in full measure to someone worthy of it. He is also a deeply spiritual man, although not in any denominational sense. He's an "outsider," a loner, someone who grew to expect little from life except what he could bring to it. And, like Jane, he considers himself plain, certainly unable to compete with the dashing stars surrounding Pauline Sloane.

I hope *Sloane Hall* allows those who love the original *Jane Eyre* to experience it afresh, perhaps going back to it with new eyes. And for those who've never read it, I hope they find *Sloane Hall* a satisfying tale that can stand on its own.

Libby Sternberg
Summer 2013

Reviews

The following review of the hardcover edition is reprinted with permission from the Bronte blog, October 4, 2010. www.Bronteblog.blogspot.com

Sloane Hall by Libby Sternberg can be categorised under different labels: a historical romance, women's fiction or a reworking of *Jane Eyre*, which is the reason why it is featured on BrontëBlog. *Sloane Hall* is all that and more than that, a clear example of a novel where the overall result is more than the sum of its parts.

The author has described elsewhere how her first intention (i.e. mirroring the *Jane Eyre* plot in a different setting, time and with an inversion of the sexes of the main characters) changed after the different manuscripts and revisions passed by the hands of several editors and publishing houses. We have to agree with the author when she says that the final result is much more interesting than her initial plan. Now, the original Charlotte Brontë novel still transpires through its pages but Sternberg has also built a personal universe where some of the characters have equivalents in the original *Jane Eyre* novel but don't behave as automatons remote-controlled by Charlotte Brontë's narrative. Their development and psychological characteristics are their own (Libby Sternberg's own) and the turns of the story are consistent with them.

The main elements of Jane Eyre are there. We have a main character, young and naïf John Doyle, who arrives in L.A hoping to enter Hollywood as a cinematographer, with a turbulent childhood (which includes a Lowood/Brocklehurst equivalent: Canfield), a fascinating woman with more life experience and dark, buried secrets who lives in a big house with strange sounds in the night, Eleanor Brickman[1], the great diva Pauline Sloane in the pictures. We have some distant cousins, the Saint Claires who live very far from Hollywood and whose dream it is to be missionaries in China. But even more important than the more or less obvious similarities are the more subtle elements which create a feedback between the two novels and provide a common intertext: a dog named Pilot, a young friend who dies because of the mistreatments in Canfield, Pauline saying to John that he dances 'a little', someone who gets hurt in a mysterious way, a fire...[2]

The main success of the novel as a *Jane Eyre* reinterpretation is that the way in which these connections are made doesn't steal *Sloane Hall's* inner autonomous narrative. Things don't turn out as you imagine[3], the common elements don't necessarily work as in the original novel and the decisions of the characters follow an internal logic not always equivalent to *Jane Eyre*. Small fluctuations in the text give way to unexpected outcomes. This causes an extraordinary situation in a novel like this for a reader who knows by heart Charlotte Brontë's novel. Even recognising the elements, you don't know what is going to happen. And this was one of Libby Sternberg's goals as she confessed previously:

"I began to wonder how it would feel to experience *Jane Eyre* as I had the first time I'd read it, to feel all those delicious emotions--Jane's joy at discovering Rochester did love her, her subsequent heartbreak and then the glorious soothing of her sorrow — in the same way I had on my initial journey into Brontë's story."

It is to Libby Sternberg's credit that this particular element works so well.

The time setting of *Sloane Hall* is also fundamental in this story. A bigger-than-life and at the same time tremendously fragile character, Pauline Sloane/Eleanor Brickman cannot exist but in the silent era of movies. The silent divas are evoked both explicitly (Greta Garbo, Clara Bow, Vilma Banky...) or implicitly through some elements of the plot which recall names like Barbara LaMarr or Lupe Velez[4] but we are not in the domains of Billy Wilder's Norma Desmond and our John is no Joe Gillis, the field play is the one that *Singing in the Rain* portrayed so well, the end of the silent era.

The particular moment chosen, 1929, marks both the

difficult and painful transition to the talkies (which put an end not only to the career of many actresses and technicians, but also axed the evolution of a language which suffered a severe leapback with the introduction of sound) and, of course, the October Wall Street Crash which similarly to the movies, ended the Golden Twenties for good. Although the Crash is only used in the novel in a tangential way, the coming of the Great Depression is crucial in the perception of the novel by the reader. It's like an unavoidable omen which flies over the story and adds to the feeling that something is going to happen: in *Sloane Hall*, in Hollywood, in the world.

One has to admit that the atmosphere of the end of an era and the *Jane Eyre* intertext are elements that greatly improve and inject life to a story that, in essence, orbits around the 'naïf boy meets interesting girl with a past and in need to be rescued' scenario. Without the different layers which Libby Sternberg builds around the core story the novel could easily have dropped in the domains of the romantic (no capital R) serialised fiction. Although some repetitions and descriptions border dangerously in those territories, Libby Sternberg's intelligent and intriguing *Jane Eyre* reimagining has achieved two of the most difficult goals in a novel: being a page turner and paying a worthy tribute to Charlotte Brontë's immortal story (which we can imagine being shot by some Douglas Sirk in glorious Technicolor... but probably with some *minor* script modifications).

Notes:
(1) Which is an obvious nod to Bertha Mason (as recognized by the author in a blog interview).
(2) Particularly nice is the transposition of the *Jane, Jane, Jane!* moment which in this novel becomes a completely different situation which works brilliantly.
(3) And even the author, through John, seems to laugh at these 'literal' mirrorings when the big secret of Pauline and Sloane Hall is revealed.
(4) The good movie aficionado will enjoy discovering through

the pages references to Gary Cooper's Duesenbergs, Raoul Walsh's eye patch, John Wayne when he was still Marion, Murnau's *Sunrise*, Louella Parsons, Lillian Gish, etc ...

❧

The following review of the hardcover edition is reprinted with permission from the journal Brontë Studies, Vol. 36 No. 3, September 2011, 306

Sloane Hall: a Novel. By Libby Sternberg.
Writer of mysteries for young adults, Libby Sternberg's latest offering, *Sloane Hall: a Novel*, is billed as inspired by *Jane Eyre*, 'an inverted re-telling of the classic Jane Eyre story'. Though not modern by any stretch, set in 1929, it is still modern compared to Charlotte Brontë's original tale and a more contemporary notion of female power. With the Silver Screen era as a backdrop, we are carried off into Sternberg's interpretation of a novel that has shaped the literary appreciation of many a reader.

John Doyle, the Jane Eyre character, is trying to make his way in the film world as an assistant cameraman to friend and mentor Leo Bartenstein. Caught in the moment of transition between the 'silents' and the 'talkies', Doyle is struggling to make his mark despite his youth and a rather sordid past. As a young boy, he was convicted of manslaughter and sentenced to eleven years in a boys' detention centre. Doyle had killed his abusive stepfather in an inconsolable fit of rage after he had unleashed his final wave of violence on Doyle's fragile alcoholic mother. Indeed, it was a final unleashing, not only because he died before he could inflict another, but also because Doyle's mother's state of fear led to a heart attack that robbed her of her own life. (Oddly, these tragic circumstances somehow recall Heathcliff in *Wuthering Heights* more than Jane.)

Canfield Home for Wayward Boys — Jane's Lowood School — was where Doyle served his sentence. It was here that for many years he manoeuvred to survive the abuses of his own Reverend Robert Brocklehurst, Brice Clement. In time, the scandalous behaviour of Clement came to light, and he was replaced by the Reverend Mr Milqueton, Jane's St John Rivers.

Milqueton reforms Doyle, makes a man and a gentleman of him, so that when he leaves, he is equipped to make his way in the world. He hooks up with Leo to pursue his dream in the movie industry; it was for this world that he developed a passion after finding solace from abuse in movies when he was a young boy.

A moment of inattention at Leo's side — film inserted into the camera the wrong way — leads to Doyle's demise in Hollywood. He is unceremoniously fired by the film director and, thanks to Leo, lands a job as the chauffeur/mechanic/all-around-fix-it-fellow at the estate of film star Pauline Sloane, *née* Eleanor Brickman. It is with this that Sternberg sets up the final elements for her retelling of *Jane Eyre*. With tension mounting between Pauline and Doyle, a love affair blossoms, and the knowledge of a terrible secret comes to light.

Though Sternberg does rely on the framework of Charlotte Brontë's tale for *Sloane Hall*, it is nevertheless an original story with complex character development. While Doyle's circumstances resemble Jane's in a superficial way, his character is entirely his own with original roots, ideas and personality. His past is developed to the extent that one cannot accuse Sternberg of having borrowed shamelessly; she knows how to develop and tell a story and she does it well. Pauline/Eleanor is an equally well-developed character who relies little on Rochester for her traits and quirks. She shares his penchant for sarcasm and momentary cruelty but is otherwise independent of him. And as for the secret that may destroy them, this reviewer will not reveal it. Bertha Mason's trope is a treasure all your own for the hunting.

Sternberg's novel is a refreshing tale, one that borrows bits and parts from *Jane Eyre*, but that stands squarely on its own.

Deputy Editor/Reviews Editor Carolyne Van Der Meer

ISTORIA BOOKS
Good stories, well told

Istoria Books is a boutique publisher of fiction in print and
digital formats.
Visit our website to see our quality inventory of good
stories, well told.
www.IstoraBooks.com

*Short story collections, young adult, mystery, literary,
romance, women's fiction, historicals*